BEAUTIFUL

LIE

THE

DEAD

Barbara
FRADKIN

RendezVous
Crime

Cover design by Emma Dolan

Le Conseil des Arts | The Canada Council
du Canada | for the Arts

We acknowledge the support of the Canada Council for the Arts for our publishing program. We acknowledge the financial support of the Government of Canada through the Canada Book Fund for our publishing activities.

RendezVous Crime
an imprint of Napoleon & Company
Toronto, Ontario, Canada
www.napoleonandcompany.com

Printed in Canada

14 13 12 11 10   5 4 3 2 1

Library and Archives Canada Cataloguing in Publication

Fradkin, Barbara Fraser, date-
        Beautiful lie the dead / Barbara Fradkin.

(An Inspector Green mystery)
ISBN 978-1-926607-08-5

I.   Title. II. Series: Fradkin, Barbara Fraser, 1947- . An Inspector Green mystery

PS8561.R233B42 2010   C813'.6   C2010-904966-7

The Inspector Green Series

ONE

To Hannah Green, the Number 2 bus was the lifeblood of the city, belching oily fumes as it rumbled along the narrow streets of the inner city. On Ottawa's transit planning chart, it was supposed to provide a link between two major shopping malls, the Rideau Centre at the heart of downtown and Bayshore Shopping Centre in the west. But it was the whacky journey in between that Hannah loved, first passing the gingerbread Victorian renos of Centretown, then the spice-laden clamour of Chinatown and the thrift shops of Hintonburg before it skulked like a smelly, overweight bag lady into the trendy kitsch of Westboro.

On Monday night the weather was working itself up into one mother of a snowstorm, adding to the fun. Hannah loved watching the people as they clambered aboard in a swirl of snow, juggling Christmas shopping bags and yanking their mittens off with their teeth so they could fish into their pockets for change or a bus pass. She loved reading the clues they gave away, a weird habit she'd probably gotten from her father, the bigshot detective. The student with the three-hundred dollar Gore-tex jacket and the swagger in his step would probably get off in Westboro, or worse in her own neighbourhood of Highland Park just to the west of it. The old Chinese lady wearing a long woollen coat, a thousand mismatched scarves and a huge brown vinyl sac was going shopping at the Asian grocery store, and the teenage mother with the neon green ski jacket would wrestle her second-hand stroller and her sleeping baby down the steps into a snowbank outside the St. Vincent de Paul thrift store.

Sometimes the people surprised her. Sometimes the tall, classy African family would not get off at the Ethiopian restaurant but at the library nearby. Sometimes the boozy trio of loudmouths whom she had pegged for the Royal Oak would head off instead to the stone church that hogged an entire block among the funky old stores of Hintonburg.

And sometimes, like the young woman who flopped down in the seat across from her, they confounded her. The woman had boarded the bus at the corner of Bank and Laurier Streets, in the middle of the business district. She looked like a fashion natural. Long tumbling hair a shade of burnt red that you couldn't buy in a bottle, perfect nails buffed to a natural shine. No make-up, but with cheekbones like that, who needed it?

Hannah would have guessed high-end civil servant, except that it was eight thirty in the evening, too late for even the keenest government workers, and the woman was dressed in skinny jeans, high boots and a red suede jacket with awesome beadwork around the hood and hem. She was put together like a woman who knew what she was doing and had the money to do it.

But her expression suggested a different story. She leaped aboard, wide-eyed and jumpy like someone high on coke. Her fingers didn't work; she couldn't open her purse, couldn't pick up change. Hannah had been there enough times to recognize the signs. Even when the woman yanked her leather gloves off with her teeth, she took forever to snag the toonie at the bottom of her purse. And then it flew from her fingers and skittered across the floor.

"Oh fuckety fuck shit!" she wailed, shocking even Hannah,

who said much worse herself before she even got out of bed in the morning. The suede jacket and the high boots went better with a ladylike "oh pooh!"

A dozen fingers groped on the floor to retrieve the coin for her, but among them Hannah noticed only the woman's. There was a rock the size of Gibraltar on her fourth finger that caught every ray of feeble lighting inside the bus. She looked at the woman again. As rich as she might be, she had obviously snagged someone way richer.

So why did she look like she'd just witnessed the end of the world?

Having finally plunked the money in the slot and picked up her transfer, the woman stumbled over a stroller, two backpacks and a walker in the aisle, not seeming to see them as she headed for the one empty seat on the bus, across from Hannah. She flounced down, flipped back her snowy hood, and shook her hair loose. Long auburn curls flew past Hannah's face. She seemed to be trying to get herself together. Took a deep breath, shut her eyes and pressed her fingers to her temples.

The drama over, Hannah turned her attention to the next challenge. Where would the woman get off? Not too far west, or she would have taken a transitway bus. If you wanted to get anywhere in this weather and you didn't want the grime and dejection of the masses sticking to your soul, you took the rapid transitway. Hannah was betting on one of the trendy high-rise condos in Centretown, but when the bus trundled west past Bronson Avenue, she switched her bets to the Civic Hospital area. It was full of upscale homes where lawyers and bureaucrats paid for the privilege of being in town. But the bus inched past Holland Avenue and elegant Island Park Drive without a flicker of interest on the woman's part.

A cellphone trilled. After much rummaging in her humungous bag, she pulled out a Blackberry. She stared at the Call Display and seemed to hesitate, but when it rang again, the passengers around her scowled and she punched a button impatiently.

"I don't want to talk to you," she hissed. She gave the person two seconds to respond before whipping her head back and forth. "I don't care, I don't care!"

Trouble in fiancéland, Hannah thought, vaguely disappointed. There was no life-shattering crisis, no grand tragedy, just pre-wedding hysterics. Maybe Mr. Rock-of-Gibraltar had hired a photographer without consulting her.

"It's not true! You just want to ruin everything!"

Not the photographer, then, Hannah decided, intrigued by this new mystery. What besides sex could ruin everything?

"How could you do this to me? Oh my God, why?" The woman pressed her hand to her mouth, crying softly. Hannah felt a twinge of pity. Definitely sex. "It makes me sick to... No! Don't! Fuck!" The woman glanced out the window. The bus was just leaving the shopping bustle of Westboro and entering the residential neighbourhood where Hannah lived. Abruptly the woman shoved her Blackberry into her purse, leaped up and dashed to the rear exit. Hannah had one last glimpse of her standing on the street corner, juggling gloves, hat and purse. She was peering through the blowing snow, looking bewildered and lost.

As if she had no idea where she was, or where she was going.

* * *

By four a.m. Tuesday, Frankie Robitaille had been on the job for nearly twelve hours and he was dead tired. His arms throbbed from the constant shifting of levers and gears and from the

4

bone-rattling vibrations of the snowplow on the icy streets. He longed for a hot cup of soup and a warm bed, but that was still a long way off. Still, the overtime was amazing. As an independent operator, he only got paid when it snowed. This blizzard was going to pay for his kids' Christmas presents, and if the forecast was right, maybe even for the trip to Disney World too.

He could always sleep once the snowfall was over and all the streets were cleared in his quadrant. The main arteries had been done, as had the bus routes. He was doing the side streets now, and his big yellow snowplow was the only machine in the quiet residential grid he'd been assigned. Up one street, around the corner and down the next, his massive curved plow spewing the snow up into a neat bank along the side of the road. The monotony was broken only by the occasional car parked by the curb.

It was his favourite time to plow, because no one was out. The quiet was unreal. The wind had eased up and the snow was falling softly through the dim yellow halos of the street lamps, cloaking the ground in a white glitter that was almost magical. Christmas lights lit up the front yards, smudges of red and blue in the soft white snow. The roads dipped and twisted, full of surprise sights. Frankie smiled as he steered the big rig around a corner. His mind drifted.

The curve was sharper than he expected and he had to fight to get the plow around the corner. The bump barely registered. A mere nudge of his steering wheel and a tremor through his floor. He'd hit something buried under the snow, possibly a garbage bin or a kid's sled forgotten outside. He peered in his rear view mirror and at first could distinguish nothing in the unbroken berm of white snow he had banked along the curb. Maybe a flash of something in the feeble street light. Orange or red, like a kid's plastic toy.

He shrugged and carried on. Not his problem. He had miles

of road left to plow before the rush hour began, and his hot soup beckoned.

*   *   *

Ottawa Police Inspector Michael Green fought to stay awake but couldn't help himself. The heat in the deputy chief's conference room was cranked up to keep the frigid wind at bay, and the lights were dimmed to improve the visibility of the PowerPoint presentation. A director from Strategic Support droned on as she read, almost word for word, the contents of each slide.

"These are the tenure targets for 2011 in each division..."

Green's eyes drifted shut. A foot kicked him under the table, and he jerked awake to see Superintendent Barbara Devine glaring at him across the expanse of blue folders, coffee cups and empty sandwich wrappers littering the table. He blinked and rolled his shoulders surreptitiously. Every muscle ached from shovelling a foot of snow from his driveway that morning, in the pitch dark of the winter solstice. He had begged, bribed and threatened but utterly failed to persuade his two children to join the fun. Five-year-old Tony was glued to his favourite cartoon and eighteen-year-old Hannah could not be coaxed out from under the covers. "Wake me when it's spring," she'd said.

His gaze drifted to the window, through which he could see an endless string of red brake lights snaking along the Queensway. Barely two p.m. and the afternoon traffic jam had already started. More accurately, the morning one had never ended.

The door opened, wafting cooler air into the room. Superintendent Adam Jules knifed his gaunt form through the narrow crack and all too soon closed the door in his wake. The surprise woke Green up completely. His former boss, now

Superintendent of East Division, was always precise and punctual, his charcoal suit pressed to a razor's edge and his silver hair perfectly in place. Today Jules was an hour late and dressed in clothes he appeared to have slept in. His tie was crooked and his hair had seen nothing but a passing swipe of his palm. His cheeks were tinged a self-conscious pink, and he avoided the questioning gazes around the table as he slid into a vacant chair.

At his best, Jules was a man of few words, but today he didn't utter a single word throughout the entire meeting. But more than once Green felt his eyes upon him. Mercifully the meeting ended at three thirty and the various inspectors and superintendents began to file out of the room. Jules hung back, seemingly engrossed in a study of the file before him. Green felt the man's gaze tracking him, however, and as if by serendipity, the two men found themselves face to face as they edged out the door.

Jules bent his head close. "Michael, a word."

Green stepped into the hallway. In the distance he saw Devine gesturing him towards her office, but he pretended not to notice. Devine, ever mindful of career advancement, would want to be the first senior brass to get on top of the tenure issue, even if it meant trading away some of Criminal Investigations' most experienced officers. Having no such professional ambitions, Green sidled down the hall towards the elevator. Jules appeared at his elbow as silently as a cat, his gaze scanning the hall behind him.

"My office, sir?"

"No. Outside. Let's walk."

Green hid his surprise. There was still a foot of snow on the sidewalks, and the blizzard continued unabated. Even Jules realized his mistake when he opened the lobby doors to a blast of sleet. Instead, he nodded towards a small conference room off the lobby. Once inside, he steepled his fingers and pressed them to his lips as if in supplication. Green kept his silence with an effort. No one rushed Adam Jules.

"Michael," he began eventually, "this is off the record. A personal inquiry. Is that acceptable to you?"

Green stared at him. Never had he seen the man so discomfited. In all his twenty years under Jules's tutelage, he'd never caught a glimpse of the private man behind the pressed suits and impeccable manner. There were lines that before now had never been crossed between them.

"Of course," he said, not daring to venture further.

Jules flushed and ran his manicured hand through his hair. "In the past twenty-four hours, have there been any missing persons reports? Anyone unaccounted for?"

Green frowned at him, puzzled. Before his present post, Jules had been Superintendent of Criminal Investigations for over ten years, overseeing Green's Major Case Investigations as well as other criminal code cases. Surely he knew Missing Persons didn't fall under his command any more. Green had received the usual morning briefings from his own NCOs but nothing unusual had been reported, and there were no rumours of people lost in the storm. It was a cold day to go missing.

"Not that I know of," he said. "But I don't get those reports."

"I know, but I wondered...sometimes you hear..."

"I can check with MisPers."

Jules bobbed his head. He straightened his crooked tie and seemed to notice his rumpled suit for the first time. He smoothed the creases in vain. "Thank you. Any accidents? Hospitals reporting unknown victims?"

"Not that I heard. But I can put out an alert—"

"No!" Jules stopped himself. "No, that's not necessary. I was just wondering..."

"What's this about, Adam? Someone missing? Someone hurt?"

"No. It's simply an inquiry. For a friend. It's not important." He lifted his head as if relieved and for the first time met Green's questioning gaze. "I trust your discretion in this matter, Michael. If something should arise... If you learn something..."

Green saw the steel grey of authority return to the older man's eyes. Jules had drawn the curtains back down on his private world. Green found himself nodding, but before he even knew what exactly he was agreeing to, Jules had slipped out of the room.

* * *

Constable Whelan had just come on duty when the missing person's call came in. Despite it being the holiday season, he had expected the graveyard shift to be dead because a blizzard was howling outside. He'd barely made it into work with his four-wheel drive. Temperatures were frigid, the winds were brutal, and the snow was slanting in sideways sheets. Snowdrifts made the side roads impassable. No one, not even the most drunk and determined reveller, would be out tonight. For the second night in a row, school pageants and Christmas concerts had been cancelled, neighbourhood potlucks rescheduled and holiday shopping put off for another day.

Most of his fellow shift workers would be busy on the streets, handling fender benders and rounding up the homeless into shelters while he sat with his feet up on the tiny corner desk on the second floor dedicated to missing persons, reviewing, updating and cross-checking the active files against information from across the country. The two aboriginal girls were still missing, and so were the twins who were last seen going through airport security with their Iranian father.

The call surprised him. He logged it in automatically as he picked up the line. 12:32 a.m. It was a young man's voice, brusque as if he were trying to conceal his fear.

"I want to report a woman missing."

"Name, sir?"

"Meredith Kennedy."

"I mean your name."

"Dr. Brandon Longstreet."

"Address?"

Longstreet supplied an address on one of the classy avenues in Rockcliffe. Already the case was unusual, Whelan thought, pulling up the MisPers form on his computer. "The missing person is Meredith Kennedy, you say? Age and address?"

The young man's voice cracked slightly as he supplied her age, thirty-two, and an address in McKellar Heights. Not on a par with Rockcliffe, but a respectable middle-class neighbourhood nonetheless. The mystery deepened.

"And how long has Meredith been missing?"

"I'm not sure of the exact time. Possibly since Monday evening."

Whelan did a quick calculation. "That's less than forty-eight hours, sir. What's your relationship to her?"

"But it's not like her. She's not home, and her parents haven't seen her since Monday morning."

"She lives with her parents?"

"Temporarily, yes, but we're in touch every day. Often more than once." Longstreet broke off, and Whelan could imagine him trying to muster his argument. "She wouldn't be out tonight. Not in this."

"Normally it would be her parents filing the report, sir—"

"I said I'd do it. They're as worried as I am, I assure you."

"And what's your relationship to her?"

"She's my fiancée. We're getting married in less than three weeks."

Whelan's fingers paused over the keys. This wouldn't be the first bride to get cold feet.

Longstreet was ahead of him. "She's very happy about it."

"No pre-wedding jitters?"

"None."

"Anything on her mind? Any disagreements with family—hers or yours?" Whelan's daughter had been married the previous summer, and both she and his wife had been in a constant flap for a month beforehand. Caterers had quit over budget disputes, the bridesmaids hated their dresses, the hall had jacked up its rates. "These arrangements take their toll."

There was a slight pause. "The wedding isn't the issue. It's exactly what she and I want—a small crowd, just close family and friends, held at my mother's home, buffet dinner reception afterwards. Non-denominational with a lay clergy, and even her parents are okay with that even though they're Catholic. Meredith isn't, at least not any more."

It was a lot of information for the question he had asked, which Whelan found odd. He couldn't resist a smile as he pictured all the trouble brewing beneath the surface of this perfect wedding. The groom's mother masterminding the whole thing on her own turf, the Catholic parents pretending not to care. A Kennedy marrying a Longstreet. It was enough to make his West Quebec Irish grandparents roll over in their graves.

And worst of all, a poor dumb groom oblivious to it all.

He leaned back in his chair. "Have you tried her friends and family?"

A long silence hung in the air. When Longstreet spoke again, his tone was deeper. Angrier. "Look, I'm not a complete fool. I know this woman. She's a strong, capable, responsible adult. If she wanted to call off the wedding, she'd tell me to my face. Of course I've tried her family and friends, and none of them has heard from her since Monday at six. Her father and I have checked her computer, and she hasn't emailed or texted or posted on Facebook either. She hasn't been near her home, and it's after midnight in a fucking blizzard! So please take the damn report!"

Whelan could hear the gravel in the young man's voice. He knew all about fear and loss; he'd recently watched his wife lose a brutal fight with breast cancer. He relished the night shift so he wouldn't have to spend hours alone in the dark. Now he felt a twinge of shame for his own lack of compassion. He worked his way through the rest of the questions and asked Longstreet to email a photo before he signed off with a promise to be in touch.

As the photo downloaded, Whelan watched the screen with a sinking heart. The girl looked far younger than her thirty-two years, with red curls tumbling around her face, big blue eyes and a classic Irish turned up nose that gave her an impish charm. She was wearing an over-sized UNICEF t-shirt and grinning into the camera with a big thumbs-up.

This was far too pretty a girl to be wandering the streets alone at night, in any weather.

TWO

The sound of doors slamming and voices in the street penetrated Brandon's sleep. He bolted awake, disoriented and full of hope. Stumbling to the window, he peered down to see a CTV media van parked in the street and two crew members lugging a shoulder camera through the snow to the front door. The blizzard had spent itself, leaving sculpted swirls of snow across the front yard. Winter dawn washed the snow in a rosy glitter. For once, he was unmoved. Awash in fatigue and despair, he peered at his bedside clock.

Seven fucking o'clock, and the vultures were already out.

He'd managed two hours' sleep after spending most of the night on the internet and on the phone, pacing the kitchen and speaking in low, urgent tones to avoid waking his mother. They had barely talked when he'd returned from his evening shift, but he'd felt her gaze upon him. There was doubt in it, but also pity. He kept his distance, not trusting himself to be civil should she reach out. Not trusting himself not to blurt out: "She didn't leave me! You never did like her, and you know it. You made her feel common, unworthy, tolerated only because I insisted."

Part of him knew that was immature and unfair, a deflection of blame to avoid looking at his own failings. At his own small niggle of doubt, which didn't bear thinking about.

His mother was up now, and he heard her hurrying towards

the front door to intercept the crew before they rang the bell. Reluctantly he headed down the hall. On two hours sleep, he didn't feel up to facing the media, so he hung back in the stairwell as his mother opened the front door. A microphone was thrust in her face. If anyone understood the media, it was his mother. She understood the drama—had used it often enough herself—but how would she choose to play this scene? On Meredith's side, or against her?

With the camera rolling, the media were the essence of respect. The young female reporter whom Brandon recognized from the local news introduced herself as Natasha, confirmed his mother's identity and asked if they could do an interview inside. Their breath billowed white around them, and his mother hugged her velvet robe tightly around her.

"Certainly," she said but without moving. "As long as I will do. My son has only just gone to bed after working and staying up all night tracking down leads—" ·

"That's fine," Natasha interrupted hastily.

His mother led them inside and left them to set up while she disappeared. In her absence, the cameraman positioned his tripod in the bay window and trained his lens on the loveseat opposite. Brandon knew his mother would be pleased with the choice. It captured the gentility of the room—carved mahogany frame, rose floral brocade, delicate antique lace pillows—and it went well with her royal blue dressing gown.

When she re-entered the room carrying a tea tray, Brandon felt a flash of frustration. Tea before Meredith—how like Elena Longstreet. To her credit, Natasha ignored the tea and ploughed straight into the questions with no chit-chat or preamble.

"I understand your son and Meredith Kennedy are engaged. When is the wedding?"

"New Year's Eve. A choice they may later consider unwise, but at the time it seemed romantic."

"When was the last time you or your son had contact with Meredith?"

"I haven't seen her in nearly a month, although she's due to come to my annual eggnog party on Christmas Eve. She's been extraordinarily busy—"

"But your son?"

"He had dinner with her Sunday evening, I believe."

"How did she seem?"

"As far as I know, she was fine. She's a bride, so she has a lot on her mind. She may have been a little anxious recently, but certainly nothing to worry about."

"Any particular things she was anxious about?"

"Oh, the usual. One of her bridesmaids has withdrawn, and her family wants some young cousin to be a ring bearer, but he's only two and naturally there are concerns—"

"Any disagreements with your son?"

Brandon saw his mother lift her chin to face the interviewer squarely. He knew the fluff she'd supplied so far would not survive the cutting room, but this question was the heart of the interview. The clip that would be replayed throughout the day and possibly across the country. The clip that would be dissected by the police. He found himself holding his breath.

"They are blissfully happy. They have both waited a long time to find each other, and I truly believe that their love is far more important to them than any disputes over menu or wedding procession. They always find a middle ground."

"What do you think has happened to her?"

Elena hesitated, and Brandon wondered how she would answer. This too might play across the nation. To his relief, she settled on a message of hope. "I hope she simply wanted a day or two of solitude to regroup. We invest so much emotion in our wedding, as a highlight of our lives and expression of our hope for a perfect future. Yet the reality of planning it—balancing out the guest list, finding the right shoes for the dress, choosing between pecan-crusted salmon and Cornish game hen—robs the event of its romantic sheen. Brides in particular struggle with that. She did seem distracted of late, as if her mind were elsewhere."

"Distracted by what?"

"Possibly the move. They were going to Ethiopia after the honeymoon for a two-year posting with Doctors Without Borders. Meredith worked in Haiti for a brief stint, but neither of them have ever been to Africa. Perhaps she was apprehensive. Natural enough."

"Are she and her family close?"

Brandon moved down the stairs. So far, his mother had said all the right things, but he knew she was playing to the jury. He wasn't sure he trusted her to keep her views of Meredith's family quite so benign.

She must have heard his footsteps, for she raised her voice. Warning him, he wondered? "Very. She comes from a lovely family." She rose to her feet. "Now if you'll excuse me, I hear—"

"There is no trouble," Brandon said, striding into the room. He knew he was a sight, still dressed in yesterday's rumpled hospital garb and sporting a day's growth. His blue eyes were probably bloodshot and his thick hair plastered in unruly spikes. When the camera swung to him, he faced it square on. A spectacle for sure, but also raw truth.

"You need to get that message across," he said. "Meredith was not an overwrought bride who got cold feet. She was excited about the wedding and looking forward to working overseas.

She has not run off. Something has happened to her. An accident, a slip on the ice that knocked her out. She could be out there somewhere. Buried. In this weather, hypothermia could set in in minutes..." He broke off, quivering.

Elena moved to his side, deftly shielding him from the camera.

"The police are taking this very seriously," she said. "I believe they have patrol cars on the look-out and are going to search her home for clues." She glanced outside and allowed herself a small shiver. "We ask for everyone's help. Check your driveways and the walks in front of your houses. If anyone saw her or has a clue where she might have gone, please call the police. The more eyes we have looking, the sooner we'll find her."

*　　*　　*

Once again, Green glanced at his phone. Almost eleven a.m. and Sergeant Li from Missing Persons still had not returned his call. He didn't want to phone again, concerned that his impatience might arouse suspicions. A routine inquiry, that's all it was supposed to be.

Green loved being interrupted by a real life enigma. By Wednesday, the desk in his little office was awash in memos, updates, reports, and his computer inbox was stuffed with more of the same. As the city dug out from its first major snowstorm of the season, the second floor of Elgin Street Headquarters was eerily calm. Criminals too had been deterred by the weather. It was tricky robbing a bank when the getaway car might get stuck in a snowbank, and sexual assault was much more of a challenge in bone-chilling cold and knee-deep drifts. Only the serious and the desperate were out on the street looking for trouble on days like this.

In the Major Crimes Unit, detectives were using the lull to catch up on paperwork or follow up on existing cases. They hunched over computers or talked on the phone, jotting notes. Green could see Detectives Bob Gibbs and Sue Peters at their adjacent desks, unconsciously leaning towards each other as they worked.

On his desk in front of him, Green had assembled the stack of performance appraisals prepared by his NCOs, and he was trying to make decisions he hated. Who to transfer out, who to keep. Organizational policy required police officers to move at least every five years. He knew all the bureaucratic reasons. In theory, it was to ensure a well-rounded, experienced police service, to allow for fresh perspectives and enthusiasm, and to avoid burn-out in the high stress jobs. In practice, it usually meant that just as an officer became really good at the job and developed a network on the street, he or she was moved out, leaving the supervisors with a continual pool of inexperienced, uncertain staff.

Bob Gibbs was one of the officers he'd been trying to shelter for months. The young detective had always been the most valuable geek in the unit, roaming the vast world of cyberspace with ease to track down bad guys and ferret out information. Now, however, he was finally beginning to gain some confidence and skill as an interviewer. He was a far better detective than he would ever be a front line officer, a paradox Green could relate to. If he himself hadn't had Jules to rescue him from the uniform division, he likely would have been turfed out of the force within a year. Or quit in a fit of righteous pique.

Yet Superintendent Devine, herself the master of job hopping her way up the ladder without staying long enough in any job to get really good at it, had issued Green an ultimatum after yesterday's meeting. She had her quota of underlings to move as well and had hinted that Green's own name could be on the list if he didn't play the game. He knew that he was well past due for a transfer and stayed at the helm of Major Case Investigations only because she'd decided no newbie inspector would make her look as good. It was a dubious vote of confidence that could be rescinded on a whim. Barbara Devine was famous for whims.

Devine argued that more experience in other areas, particularly in Patrol, was just what Gibbs needed to put the necessary swagger in his step and teach him to make decisions in the span of two seconds. "Not just high-pressure decisions, Mike, *any* decisions," she'd said. Green wasn't so sure. It might make him, but it might also break him.

Mercifully, the phone rang before he had to decide. He pounced on the distraction, expecting the MisPers sergeant, only to hear a slight pause followed by a breathy, little-girl voice from long ago.

"I want her home for Christmas, Mike."

He felt his jaw clench. How his first wife still had the power to do that was a mystery. She'd walked out on him eighteen years ago, putting a bitter, moribund marriage out of its misery. His second wife, Sharon, had brought him infinitely more joy in the years since then, along with a son who had the dark, curly hair and laughing brown eyes of his mother, but whose stubbornness and intensity was all Green.

Green glanced at his watch. Barely eleven o'clock in the morning, eight o'clock in Vancouver. The crack of dawn for Ashley. She must have been stewing all night.

"Good morning to you too, Ashley."

"It's time this nonsense ended. I want to see her. It's the least you can do, Mike. You don't even celebrate Christmas!"

"She's eighteen. I'm not stopping her. She makes her own decisions."

19

"She's done that since she was two years old," Ashley retorted. "But you could encourage her. Tell her it's time to mend fences. You have Tony too, but Hannah's all I've got."

Green heard the catch of well-rehearsed tears in her voice. He could have argued the point. Children were not interchangeable or replaceable, and Ashley had had Hannah all to herself for the first fifteen years of her life. But he knew she was right. For her own sake, Hannah needed to reconnect with her mother. She was no longer the defiant, resentful teenager who had landed on his doorstep nearly three years earlier. She was on track to graduate from high school with full honours this spring, an edgy, thoughtful young woman who could run rings around her empty-headed mother.

In the silence, as Green struggled with his own reluctance, Ashley pressed her case. "I'm not going to force her, Mike. Fred and I have done a lot of talking, and I know that doesn't work. But she'll listen to you. She's just like you. Tell her I'll promise not to fight with her."

A promise that will last precisely half an hour, Green thought. In a tight spot, fighting was still Hannah's preferred mode of expression. It was all she'd known when she'd arrived in Green's life. Fortunately, however, conflict resolution between mother and daughter was not his responsibility. He only had to get Hannah on the plane, and the rest was up to Ashley and Fred. Disguising a tightness in his chest, he agreed to try.

No sooner had he hung up than there was a soft knock at his door, and the Missing Persons sergeant poked his head in. A twenty-four year veteran of Patrol, Li had been on modified duties for nearly a year while he awaited hip surgery. Most of the time, Missing Persons was a clerical job of filling in forms, making internet and phone inquiries, and liaising with other units and agencies. Every few months a genuine mystery came along that the missing persons team could sink its investigative teeth into. Li looked as if he was long overdue.

Green beckoned him in and watched as Li eased himself into the plastic guest chair wedged in the narrow space between the desk and the door. He had packed an extra fifty pounds onto his mid-size frame since being parked behind a desk, and his bad hip obviously complained at each new move.

"I'm guessing this is about the missing girl," Li said before Green could even form his question.

Green masked his surprise. "What's the story?"

"So far, it's not clear. Her name's Meredith Kennedy, thirty-two years old, good family, no known criminal ties. Fiancé called it in last night."

Green's thoughts were already racing ahead, wondering about Jules's connection to a thirty-two-year-old from a "good family". Jules was a lifelong bachelor at least twenty-five years her senior. "Any leads yet?"

"Dead ends. We did the usual checks—hospitals, ambulance, accident reports—with no results. By all accounts the young woman has fallen off the face of the earth. Family hasn't heard from her for two days. She was set to get married soon, and her fiancé and friends say she was looking forward to the big day."

"Banking and cellphone enquiries in the works?"

Li nodded. "We should have that info by tomorrow."

"What's the last known contact?"

Li flipped through the file. "That's the really interesting part. Jessica Ward, a close friend, spoke to her at 5:45 Monday evening. Our girl sounded upset, said she really had to talk to her, and could they meet somewhere for coffee. Jessica couldn't because she was working an evening shift, so they arranged to get together the next day after Meredith's work."

21

"That would be Tuesday? Yesterday?"

"Yes. She never showed up, never phoned to cancel, didn't show up for work either."

"Any prior history of similar behaviour? Or mental health issues?"

Li shook his head. "Everyone says she's pretty solid."

"What's Jessica's theory on the disappearance?"

"She's scared. Thinks something has happened to her."

"What kind of work does the missing girl do?"

"Contract work for the government. Citizenship and Immigration."

"Immigration?" Green let his imagination roam. "Could there be anything there? Sensitive file?"

Li chuckled. "No. She was in Haiti last winter after the earthquake, helping to sort through immigration red tape, but back in Ottawa she mostly drafts policy positions for someone else's signature. I talked to her boss, who said she does a good job but really wants to get back overseas. That's their plan after the wedding. He was going to work for Doctors Without Borders in Ethiopia and she was going to teach school."

Green was still searching for a connection to Jules. "What's the fiancé's name?"

"Dr. Brandon Longstreet."

Green's interest spiked again. "Related to Elena Longstreet?"

Li looked alarmed. "Who's Elena Longstreet?"

"Big name attorney in town. Years ago she used to do criminal cases, but now it's mostly complex appeals. Charter challenges are her big thing. She also teaches criminal law at the University of Ottawa." Green searched his memory for long-forgotten details. Only two stood out. Elena Longstreet was as much a master of courtroom drama as of the law. Her regal elegance and sleek black hair captured centre stage whenever she was in the room. As well, she'd been a ferocious critic of the police for lazy and incompetent case preparation. If the police had fouled up a single step of an investigation, Elena would find it and demolish the case. Even experienced officers had been known to quail under her cross-examination.

Being her daughter-in-law would be no walk in the park. But surely not enough to drop out of sight.

Green pondered the other revelations in the case. "So we have a bright, optimistic young woman on the brink of an exciting new adventure, who becomes upset about something she doesn't tell her fiancé and then disappears in the middle of a Canadian winter."

Li grimaced. "Gives me a bad feeling."

Privately Green agreed with him. Teenagers went missing on a whim, but seemingly happy, well-adjusted women did not. He couldn't ignore the darker side of love, which slipped so easily into the toxic swamp of obsession, betrayal and murder. Dr. Brandon Longstreet would have to be investigated.

"Expedite those enquiries," he said. "And take a close look at the fiancé. Anger issues, jealousy, previous girlfriends. Also previous men in *her* life. Have you asked Inspector Hopewell for extra manpower?" Green had learned the hard way not to step on other people's turf. Luckily Li had not asked him the reason for his sudden interest in the case.

Li nodded. "She asked if you could give us someone to search Meredith Kennedy's living quarters. She's living with her parents at the moment."

That in itself sets the girl apart, Green thought. He was mentally running through the list of general assignment detectives when a raucous laugh burst out. It sounded familiar, but it was a long time since he'd heard it. He rose and peered through the door into the Major Crimes room. Detectives were unhurried, coasting towards the holiday season when loneliness, alcohol and too much family togetherness would give them plenty of work.

A familiar fuchsia jacket caught his eye. It was a long time since he'd seen that either. Sue Peters was sprawled in her chair like old times, legs outstretched and head tossed back. Bob Gibbs had evidently told a good joke, for she was still laughing. The affection between them was palpable.

A plan began to take shape. Green turned it over in his mind, weighing its wisdom. Missing Persons did not fall under his command and rarely would a Major Crimes detective be tied up in a MisPers investigation unless something sinister was suspected. But all was quiet on the second floor, and this case felt wrong. Staff Sergeant Brian Sullivan, head of Major Crimes, was out on indefinite sick leave and his acting replacement, seconded from Patrol, was over his head trying to keep track of the dozens of active cases currently on the books, let alone managing to give the detectives any useful advice.

Detective Sue Peters was currently relegated to entering data in online tracking forms, a mandatory but tedious clerical job that would not provide her with the confidence and skill to return to full duties. She had come a long way physically in her recovery from a near-fatal beating two years earlier, but the fuchsia jacket and the hearty laugh were the first signs that her spirit was returning as well. She was not yet well enough to pass her Use of Force test that would allow her back on full active duty, but a simple, behind-the-scenes assignment supporting Bob Gibbs might be the perfect nudge.

He called them both into his office, watching her try to

conceal her stiffness as she hovered in the doorway. Li struggled to rise and offer her the only chair, but she dismissed the offer and stood warily just inside the door. Green had not missed the spasm of alarm that crossed Gibbs's face as well, and realized its source. Everyone was afraid of being transferred out.

He held up a reassuring hand and explained the case. "Bob, I'd like you to search the missing woman's room for clues to her whereabouts and explanations for her disappearance. While you're there, re-interview her parents. Sue can follow up the leads you uncover."

Peters flashed a grin, lopsided now due to her injuries. "I get to go out on the call, sir?" she asked as if not quite believing her luck.

He looked at her in silence and saw her smile slowly fade. To his surprise, she didn't argue. "There will be plenty of leads to follow up on the phone," he said. "Interviews with friends, old boyfriends…"

Despite her obvious disappointment, Green knew even this was a huge step for her. He was aware of the anxiety she was trying to hide. Peters had been alone when she was attacked, making inquiries in a rough bar while her partner was elsewhere on the strip. To ask her to make cold calls to potentially violent men was a risk, but he knew the challenge was crucial for her. The old Sue Peters would have bulldozed forward without a backward glance.

"Sergeant Li is running the case," he added. "He'll fill you two in on everything you need to know."

"She was about to get married, wasn't she, sir?" Peters asked.

Green and Li nodded in unison. "Reason enough to disappear," she said with another hearty laugh. This time Green sensed it was forced, and she cast a small, uncertain glance in Gibbs's direction as she did so.

THREE

Sue Peters kept quiet as Bob steered the unmarked Impala cautiously through the narrow residential streets, dodging the piles of snow pushed aside by hasty plows. She was marshalling her arguments for the next battle. Once they'd left Green's office, she'd managed to persuade Bob to let her ride along in the car.

"I have to get away from these four walls, Bob," she'd said. "I've been staring at computers for so long, I've forgotten what a field call feels like. How am I supposed to get back on my feet if I don't start somewhere?"

She could see him wavering, so she pushed. "I can just sit in the car and observe the neighbourhood, make calls while I wait for you. It will hardly be different from the station but it will *feel* different."

It wasn't really a fair fight, for Bob Gibbs never could say no to her. Not when she faced him square on and looked up into his brown puppy-dog eyes. She said nothing more while they were driving out to the Kennedy house. She knew he was taking inventory of the neighbourhood and mentally preparing himself for the encounter with the distraught parents. The initial police notes had described them as a "good family". From a police officer's perspective that usually meant nothing more than gainful employment and a lack of criminal connections. It said nothing about whether the father drank or the wife beat the kids, as long as nothing had landed on their police database.

The neighbourhood wasn't rich but had a certain charm if you liked the post-war *Leave it to Beaver* look—little houses peeking out beneath massive old trees, one-car driveways neatly carved by snowblowers, and handmade Christmas wreaths on the door. Despite being built in the 1950s, the homes were being snapped up by young couples eager to avoid cookie-cutter plastic houses and hour-long commutes from suburbia. Sue wouldn't be caught dead living here. She wanted acres of land somewhere in the rugged Canadian shield west of the city. Hardwood forests, granite bluffs, a meadow for a horse, and lots of trails for the dogs to roam off-leash. She grinned at the image of shy, self-conscious Gibbsie and her lying in the meadow with the sun beating down on their naked bodies and not a prying eye for miles.

Would she ever be whole enough?

The Kennedy house came upon them unexpectedly, breaking into her daydreams. It was a red and white dollhouse sitting on a corner lot, surrounded by a trim cedar hedge. Cars crammed the single driveway and crowded the street against the snowbanks, making it difficult for Bob to squeeze by. Only once he'd parked up the block and had one foot out the door did she stop him.

"Bob, I can observe much better if I'm in there with you."

"Impossible." He didn't look at her. "The inspector would have my head."

"Only if you tell him."

"Or the family does."

"Why should they? They won't think anything of it. Two detectives look better than one anyway. One to interview and one to take notes. Looks like we're taking it seriously."

"Sue, you know—"

"I'll be as quiet as a mouse. You know how hard it is to deal with upset families, plan questions *and* take notes."

She'd thought that would be incentive enough, but still he shook his head. She changed tactics. "Darling, I need to do this. I need to feel normal again, start thinking like a police officer again. How am I ever going to recover...?" She grabbed his chin and turned his face to hers. "How am I ever going to be a hundred percent?"

That simple phrase proved the key. She suppressed a small smile of triumph as she followed him up the icy street, trying to disguise the slight drag of her left foot. The family would not want a cripple assigned to their daughter's search.

The snow on the front walk had been trampled by dozens of boots and as soon as Bob rang the doorbell, the door was flung open. A look of expectation followed by surprise raced across the face of the man who opened it. The loud buzz of voices could be heard inside.

"Mr. Kennedy? I'm Detective Gibbs of the Ottawa Police."

The man didn't answer. His jaw dropped and he stepped back to yell into the house. "Reg, it's the cops!"

A roly-poly sparkplug of a man rushed up. He had a crooked nose, curly silver hair and that Irish leprechaun face Sue had seen in dozens of small Ottawa Valley towns. Minus the jaunty grin and the twinkle in the eye. This man's eyes were bloodshot, and his skin was bruised grey with fatigue and fear. Behind him came a dumpling of a woman with mousey hair all askew and the same hollow panic in her eyes. Others anxiously crowded into the tiny hall.

"There's nothing new," Bob said quickly, and their faces sagged. He lowered his voice. "Just a few questions. Is there somewhere we can speak privately?"

The Kennedys led them through the crowd to the tiny kitchen in the back, which was probably outfitted before Sue was born.

Only the massive gas stove looked modern. Sue remembered from the file that Norah Kennedy was a housewife and Reginald was a chef by trade, although he was now a bartender at a pub on Merivale Road. It obviously didn't pay well enough for them to replace the painted white cabinets and arborite counter.

Two women were hunched over the small counter, making sandwiches. Reg Kennedy asked the women to leave then invited the officers to sit in the homemade bench built under the window overlooking the backyard. The father squeezed in opposite them, but the wife seemed too jumpy. She fussed around, wiping sandwich crumbs from the counter. Reg tilted his head towards the crowd in the living room.

"We got a search on, everyone wants to help. We've lived here almost thirty years, and they all watched Meredith grow up. We've checked all her friends and the places she usually goes. Right now we're checking along the route she would have walked from the bus to home. She could have slipped on the ice, and with the snow the last couple of days..." He broke off as if he couldn't say it aloud.

Taking out her notebook, Sue waited dutifully while Bob took up the interview. He looked efficient and in control. No hint of the stutter that sandbagged him when he was nervous. "Any leads from her friends on the places she went? We need to track her latest movements. We know she called her friend Monday evening. Anyone see her yesterday?"

The father shook his head. "She didn't go to work, didn't call in sick. She never answered the emails and texts people sent her asking where she was. Jessica, her maid of honour, left her three messages on her cell and two texts saying 'call me.' No answer."

"Was the maid of honour concerned about something?"

"Not at first. Meredith had called her, upset, and they were supposed to meet. It wasn't like Meredith not to show up."

"Why was she upset? Did Jessica know?"

"It was probably about the bridesmaid who quit."

"What happened?"

Reg grimaced. "My nephew's wife. She's always taking offence, and I think Meredith said something to upset her."

"They don't get along?"

"Caryn doesn't really get along with anyone—"

Mrs. Kennedy looked up from her cleaning irritably. "Well, she's going through a hard time, losing the baby, Reggie."

Sue eyed the exchange, noting the spark in the wife's eye and the guilt in Reg's. Crises always brought out the cracks in even the best marriage. Bob ploughed ahead. "So Meredith was c-concerned this might interfere with the wedding?"

Reg glanced at his wife. "She did seem annoyed—"

Norah sighed. "She was fine. Caryn would have come around. She just needed a few days to calm down."

"Did she have any disagreements with anyone else?"

Both parents shook their heads simultaneously.

"Any former boyfriends who might cause trouble?"

At this, Reg and Norah exchanged uncertain glances before Norah answered. "She was engaged a few years ago, but they never saw eye to eye on things. Fought all the time. Meredith does have a temper. I think they were both glad to be out of it."

Bob paused like he was looking for another thread to pick up.

"Any trouble with the current fiancé?" Sue blurted out impatiently. Beside her, Bob tensed, but he was too smart to say anything. "Were they fighting too?"

"Nothing the two of them couldn't handle," Reg said. "They really adored each other. You could see it in their eyes whenever they were together." A look almost like longing crossed his face.

"Like they were made for each other. If ever two souls fit together perfectly..."

Norah grunted. "Perfect, right. Except for that holy terror of a mother."

Sue raised an eyebrow. "Trouble with the in-laws?"

Reg flinched but said nothing. Doesn't want to put his foot wrong again, Sue thought. Norah replied for him. "Mother-in-law. Meredith's got her work cut out for her there, but if anyone's a match for that woman, it's Merry."

Bob finally found his tongue. "The mother-in-law doesn't approve?"

"Of Meredith?" Norah flushed. "That woman wouldn't approve of anyone, but certainly not us."

Nose up her ass? Sue wanted to say, but she'd already stuck her neck out far enough. The preliminary notes from MisPers said that Mrs. Longstreet was a well-connected lawyer. Bartenders who looked like they'd gone nine rounds with Joe Frazier wouldn't fit around her formal dining table.

Bob was more diplomatic. "Different backgrounds?"

Reg bobbed his head knowingly. "It's good the kids are going halfway around the world. Gives them a chance to find their own way."

"What about the father-in-law?"

"Dead," Reg said. "Years ago."

"Violently," Norah added. Sue thought she heard triumph in her voice. "That's a deep, dark secret she never mentions."

Sue perked up. There had been no mention of criminal links from the past. She jumped back in. "What happened?"

"No one knows, it was all hushed up." Norah's triumph was obvious now. Something to hold over the too-good-for-us Elena Longstreet. "It was back in Montreal. Harvey Longstreet was a law professor at McGill. *Her* law professor in fact before they got married. That's all we know."

"Probably murdered by a client who didn't like the verdict," Reg interjected.

"Or his legal bill. Brandon was only a baby at the time and grew up listening to what a great lawyer his father had been. But Meredith says his mother never told him a thing about how he died."

*   *   *

Meredith's room had the dishevelled, disorganized look of a temporary lodging. She had moved back there only a month earlier when her apartment lease had expired, and suitcases and boxes cluttered the floor. Decorated in frilly blues and yellows, the room had retained its little girl feel, but the stuffed animals on the shelf over the bed looked like they hadn't been moved in years. The flowery duvet was flung back in a heap, and the sheets were rumpled as if the woman had leaped out of bed at seven a.m. and never given them a second thought. Jeans, a sweater and a bra were slung over the back of the desk chair, and socks and underwear spilled out of a suitcase on the floor. The desk was piled high with papers, and an unopened laptop perched precariously on top.

Six books teetered on the bedside table, splayed open half-read. This woman had six books on the go, Sue thought in awe as she wandered over for a peek. Multi-tasking or easily bored? Two were travel books on Ethiopia, another on family law, but one was a Mary Jane Maffini mystery. Sue warmed to the woman. Maffini's light-hearted mysteries had lifted her own spirits many times during those awful months at the Rehab hospital, when doctors said she'd never walk again, let alone return to police work. When she was relearning to guide a spoon to her mouth.

One book, almost hidden at the bottom of the pile, piqued her curiosity. *The Quiet Revolution and Beyond: Quebec in the 1970's.* A weird selection for a woman preparing for a teaching job in Africa. She picked it up and noted that it was splayed open to a chapter on McGill and the erosion of English higher education.

She turned to Norah and Reg, who were hovering in the doorway. "Any idea why she was reading about Quebec history?"

They shrugged like matching marionettes. "Maybe because of her immigration work with Haitians last year? She was helping families sponsor their relatives to come here after the quake. Lots of Haitians families settled in Montreal." Reg paused, and a hint of a scowl crossed his face. "French connection, you know."

"But Meredith reads everything," Norah added. "Ever since she was a little girl. Always had one book or another with her, read on buses, walking down the street, even at the dinner table." She waved her hand towards the IKEA bookshelf under the window, from which books stuck out every which way. No Nancy Drews, but Sue recognized two entire shelves of Hardy Boys. "I don't even know where she got them half the time. The shelves kept filling up faster than I could give them to the rummage sale."

"Our girl's got a quick mind. You gotta keep it fed," Reg countered. "She was always asking questions, and when she wanted an answer, she'd turn to a book." He glanced at the laptop with a frown. "Or nowadays, a computer. Whenever she was home, she spent hours up here on that thing."

"Too many hours," Norah muttered her usual two cents.

Sue joined Bob, who had walked over to study the computer. Her gaze drifted over the desk, which was an innocent-looking clutter of travel print-outs, receipts, drafts of wedding invitations, seating plans, to-do lists. She scanned one of these for clues but nothing seemed unusual. *Order corsages, speak to E about dessert? nut allergies, dye shoes.* A bride trying to keep track of the massive details of a wedding. Sue shuddered at the thought. Not hers. Barefoot on a beach somewhere.

Bob opened the laptop, and they all watched as the screen lit up with icons. Dozens of them. Meredith's laptop was as cluttered as her desk and bedside table. Despite her months being chained to the computer at work, Sue didn't like the things. She still blundered around causing crashes and error messages.

"I'd like our computer experts to take a look at this," Bob said. "Is that all right?"

Reg nodded. "Brandon and I have looked at it, hoping maybe there would be clues, you know? She's got thousands of emails—saves every one, I think— but we couldn't see anything strange. Except all the people emailing 'where are you?'"

"Anyone you didn't recognize?"

Reg hesitated. "Kids these days have so many friends, her mother and I can't keep up. She's got one of those Facebook accounts too, but it has a password. We tried every one we could think of, but no luck."

Bob tucked the laptop under his arm. "No problem. I'll get it back to you as soon as possible."

*   *   *

Despite her obvious effort to hide it, Sue Peters' limp was visible from across the squad room as she and Gibbs made their way towards Green's office. She was perspiring as if fighting pain. *She's still not ready for full-time hours,* Green thought with a twinge of guilt. He'd seen her head out with Gibbs earlier but was of two minds whether to intervene. He'd subscribed to the "don't ask, don't tell" school of boss management often enough himself in the past.

The grin on her flushed face soon dispelled his doubts. Whatever role she'd played, the field excursion had galvanized her. She let Gibbs give the official report of his interview, but she couldn't resist jumping in at the end.

"From what Bob told me, it sounds like Mom wears the pants in that family, and Dad's a lovable lump who takes his cue from her if he knows what's good for him. They've still got her room decked out in frills and girly colours from her childhood, and she's filled it with jeans, Hardy Boys, books on hiking in the third world and law. Books everywhere, but hardly a make-up kit or lacy thong in sight. She mystifies them, and although Dad loves her to pieces in spite of that, I got the feeling—I mean, Bob got the feeling Mom is less forgiving. She thinks her daughter should be more loyal, and don't get her started on the future mother-in-law."

Green sat back, impressed by the glimpse of the old Sue, but wondering if she and Bob had a shred of tangible evidence to back up their gut. "Any conflicts that may be relevant to the investigation? Any sign she may have got cold feet?"

"Just one small hint." Sue laughed. "One of the millions of pieces of paper on her desk? 'Elena's fucking to-do list.' But I think the worst Meredith might do is drag Brandon off to get married on a beach in Majorca." Her grin faded. "But I'd like to keep working on the follow-up tomorrow, sir. On the phone, I mean. I think there's more there."

A smile twitched at the corners of his mouth. "Like what?"

"Like her computer. Apparently she spends hours on it. We should see what she's up to."

Green nodded. "Okay, but keep Sergeant Li informed."

"And..."

Green raised a questioning eyebrow.

"She was reading a book about McGill."

"How's that relevant? I thought the parents said she reads everything."

"It may not be relevant, but both Brandon's parents went to McGill. Don't you always say, in a murder investigation you have to shine a spotlight into the darkest corners that no one wants you to find?" She flushed. "I mean, I know this is not a murder inquiry, but..."

Green smiled at her. He loved the light in her eyes, the unorthodox insatiability of her mind. He loved especially that she had been listening to him. "Shine away, detective. We don't know what this is yet."

She left his office with a new bounce in her step, giving her dreary computer the finger as she yanked her coat off the rack and headed home for some much-needed rest. Green's final words seemed to reverberate forever in his tiny office. *We don't know what this is yet.* True, but the alarm bells were getting louder. Tips and reports of sightings had been pouring in all day but all had proved useless.

So far, Li's cautious probing into Brandon Longstreet's background had turned up no dark side. Despite his silver spoon birth and Ashbury private school education, the young man seemed to take his commitment to the common good seriously. As the end of his family medicine residency drew near, he had rejected more lucrative private practice offers across Canada in order to join an international aid team. He was a card-carrying member of the Green Party and had never received so much as a speeding ticket. Even his ex-girlfriends thought he was a gem. No temper, no wild side.

Perfection made Green nervous. It was time to find out what

Adam Jules knew about the mystery.

He had phoned Jules's East Division office that morning when Sergeant Li first told him about the missing woman. To his surprise, Jules had not yet called him back. Green had also sent an email update to which Jules had not replied, although his clerk assured Green that he was at the station. Green suppressed his annoyance. First the man had waylaid him with a cryptic request about hit and runs and people unaccounted for, and now he was ignoring all Green's attempts to contact him.

But if Jules knew something, the investigation had to be informed.

Opening his address book, Green looked up Jules's private cell phone number and picked up his phone. The cell phone went to voice mail after two rings, leaving Green nearly speechless. Jules was screening his calls! Not only ignoring him, but actively avoiding him.

Whatever the hell this was about, Green could keep the investigation low-key no longer. A young woman was missing, and the early darkness of another frigid night was closing in.

Something more had to be done, he thought, picking up his phone again to call the duty inspector.

FOUR

Within an hour, a full-scale ground search was underway, and although the duty inspector pulled out all the stops, he was not optimistic.

"The goddamn city is more than 4500 square kilometres, Green, and that's assuming she even stayed in the city and isn't sunning herself on a beach in Cuba."

"At least we know that's unlikely," Green replied. "There's no record of her leaving the country."

"But in case it escaped your notice, we got forty centimetres of snow since she disappeared and more coming down as we speak. We could be standing on top of her and not know it. Plus the rivers aren't frozen yet, and if she thought she could take a short cut across the Rideau River, she could be on the bottom somewhere."

Green was silent. Inspector Doyle was just sounding off. The two of them were in the communication centre, and Doyle was merely saying in private what he would never say on the record. Somewhere in this dark, frigid city, a young woman was lost and no one had a clue where to look. Officers were still piecing together her final day, which according to her parents had started normally enough. She had taken Monday off work to run errands for the wedding, and after her usual breakfast of yogurt and granola, she had set off on the bus for downtown. She'd been a bit vague about the errands, and her mother had not pressed her.

Meredith had always liked her independence, she'd said, and she was getting a little tense as the date drew near.

The bus driver remembered her getting off at the Westboro transit station, but from there she was swallowed up in the crowds of commuters and Christmas shoppers heading downtown.

Using "Elena's fucking to-do list" which Gibbs had taken from the house, officers were tracking down each of the businesses involved, from florist to travel medicine clinic, but by eight o'clock that evening there had not been a single confirmed sighting. Whatever Meredith had done that day, she had not made a dent in the fucking to-do list.

She had phoned her friend Jessica at 5:45, but from her cellphone, so she could have been anywhere. Jessica remembered chatter and Christmas music in the background, so volunteers had been dispatched with her photo to all the malls between downtown and Bayshore.

"But it's a goddamn needle in a haystack," Doyle said. "Every two-bit corner store plays Christmas music. So does the radio. I heard 'Sleigh Bells' a hundred times today alone!"

Meredith's description was on every radio station, her photo on every television channel and in every patrol car. Taxi drivers had been alerted. "Something will break," Green said. "Now that it's caught the public eye, someone will remember seeing her."

Doyle eyed him grimly. Both men knew there would be a thousand sightings, and nine hundred and ninety-nine would be false.

By the time Green finally left the station at nine p.m., however, that one useful lead had not materialized. Snow was falling thickly again, blanketing sound and snarling pre-Christmas traffic on the slippery roads. Red tail lights stretched solid along the Queensway in both directions as cars crawled out towards the suburbs. Turning his back gratefully on the gridlock, Green steered his Subaru along Catherine Street towards his Highland Park home. On his quiet residential backstreet, Christmas lights caught the snowflakes and glistened like rubies and emeralds on the freshly fallen snow. For a moment he forgot how much he hated winter.

He was reminded again when he reached his house to find ten centimetres of fresh snow waiting for him on the driveway. The double furrow of tire tracks from Sharon's car was fading under new snow. His wife had long since gone to work, leaving Hannah in charge of Tony and dinner.

The television was blasting "So You Think You Can Dance" in the living room and the teenager and the five-year-old were sprawled on the floor eating chips and laughing. The only one to notice his arrival was Modo, who padded into the hall wagging her tail shyly. Modo was a humane society acquisition who even after two years in their home still acted as if she feared she was unwelcome. He ruffled her ears as he glanced at the mail Sharon had left on the hall table. Nothing but Christmas flyers.

A commercial came on, and Tony leaped to his feet and came running into the hall. He laughed when Green swooped him up into the air. "What are you still doing up, buddy!"

"Hannah said I could watch instead of a story."

Green glanced at Hannah, whose expression said "I've fed him and entertained him. You want to make something of it?" Not tonight, sweetheart, he thought. Not when we have other things to talk about. At least Tony was in his pyjamas. With a final hug, Green set him down. "As soon as that's over, then. You've got school tomorrow."

He went into the living room to drop a kiss on his daughter's head before heading into the kitchen to see what he could scrounge. The remains of pizza sat congealing in the fridge. Pizza had been ordered in for the teams in the central command post at the station, and he had snagged two slices while he and the duty inspector reviewed reports. Now he bypassed the pizza in favour of chocolate cake. No sooner had he taken his first bite and found the Sudoku in the morning paper when Tony came flying into the kitchen, ricocheting off walls as he imitated the latest contestant. Hip hop. Green shuddered.

"You want *Tom Sawyer*, or are you going to read your own book?"

"I want to stay down here with you and eat cake!"

Green eyed his son's broad, infectious smile. Sharon's smile, dazzling in its warmth. He'd hardly seen the little guy today. Conceding defeat, he cut another slice and listened while Tony chattered on about the show. Through the chatter he heard Hannah switch off the television. She came to stand in the kitchen doorway a minute, watching them, then turned to head upstairs. She looked unusually worried. He wondered if her mother had already been working on her.

It was almost an hour before he gave Tony his final goodnight kiss and shut his bedroom door. Barely five years old, the little boy seemed to need less sleep than most grown men and had devised a remarkable repertoire of stall tactics. Half an hour of bedtime story was essential, despite the fact that Tony was beginning to read for himself. Then came a dozen questions about the chapter they had read and what was going to happen to Tom Sawyer next.

Hannah's door was closed by the time Green finished, and he went down to pour himself a glass of wine before facing her, fortifying himself not for his daughter but for the tricky foray into the mother-daughter minefield.

To his surprise, she was standing in the kitchen doorway when he turned around. The worried look was back. "That missing woman. That's where you were tonight?"

He nodded.

"Any luck finding her?"

"Not yet. But she may just have taken off." Green didn't like bringing his work home. He needed some walls, not only to shield his family but himself. There had to be a place in his life where evil was barred at the door. He took a deep breath, preparing to change the subject. "Want some wine?"

Hannah's smile grew wary. "Uh-oh."

He grinned, hoping to ease the path. He had no worries about the example he was setting. In her wild eighteen years, Hannah had done far worse. "Your mother called."

"I figured something like that."

"She wants you home for the holidays."

"I am home."

It was three simple words, but it packed a punch. For a moment he couldn't speak. As if she feared she'd strayed too far into mushy land, she shrugged. "Christmas in Lotusland isn't the same. It rains, everyone gets hammered and Mom gets the whole thing catered with the weirdest food. Peking duck, Pad Thai, seaweed soufflé. She and Fred get in a fight, he goes off to see his kids and I have to listen to Mom say I'm all she's got."

Green smiled at her sadly. It sounded so like Ashley; she'd always had the brains and maturity of a two-year-old. "Maybe things are different now."

"Yeah, maybe she'll have had so much botox and nip and tuck that I won't recognize her. Maybe she'll have dyed her hair black."

"She misses you, honey."

"She doesn't even know who I am!" Hannah shot back. She had

joined him at the kitchen table, and he noted that she'd already drained her wine glass. He didn't offer another, suspecting that even the first had been a mistake.

"Honestly, all those years I lived with her, I never felt like I belonged. I kept thinking there was something wrong with me, because I'd look at Mom with her bleached blonde hair and her pretty dresses and her little girl oohs and ahhs, and I'd feel like a big, ugly lump!"

Green suppressed his astonishment. Hannah was barely five-foot two, as petite and delicate as a pixie. "You're gorgeous!" he said, feeling like all fathers the inadequacy of the praise. As he expected, she snorted in dismissal.

"Why couldn't I love her, why couldn't I be what she wanted? I thought she must have messed with some alien from outer space. Until I met you." She looked across at him and reached for the wine bottle, daring him to disapprove.

He held his tongue. "The alien from outer space?"

She grinned. "Yeah, I know. It took me a long time to realize I was staring in the mirror. But I feel more like me here, with you and the Ritalin kid and Zaydie than I ever did in fifteen years with her." She took a hefty slug. "And in case you start getting ideas, that just means you're as edgy and crazy and angry as me. You don't look at the world through this lacy film of superficiality. Mom doesn't live, she floats. She's got no anchor, and the minute she bumps up against something ugly, she bounces off into sparkly waters again. I couldn't stand going back with her, Mike. Not after—"

"But she's your mother."

"Is she?"

Startled, Green laughed. "Of course! Of that I'm sure. I wasn't sure of much else back in those days, but I remember your birth.

43

Your mother was as far from pretty dresses and perfect hair as you can imagine. She sweated and cursed and howled in pain to have you, and when you finally decided to come out—ass first, I might add—she loved you from the first second she held you in her arms. We both did."

Hannah stared into her wine glass. She was still, as if the air was too thick to breathe. Green waited, understanding her well enough now to know she was hard at work behind the stillness.

"Fuck," she muttered eventually.

"It doesn't have to be for long," he said. "A week, maybe?"

"I don't want to miss Hanukkah," she said, still not looking at him. "Who knows how long Zaydie..."

There was no need to finish the thought. It was one he himself thought almost every day. His father was eighty-eight, with a feeble heart and failing lungs, facing each cold winter even frailer than the last.

"Well," he said cheerfully, "that's the great thing about Hanukkah. It's eight days long."

FIVE

Only the faintest blush of pink smudged the horizon up ahead as Green drove eastward along the Queensway towards East Division Station. Traffic was light, but he winced at the long line of headlights inching into town in the opposite direction. He would be coming back that way in less than an hour.

He held a coffee in his right hand and balanced a bagel against the steering wheel with his left, trying to avoid smearing cream cheese or spilling black coffee onto his pants. He'd left home at this ungodly hour because he was determined to catch Adam Jules before he got busy with his day. Before his old mentor could dodge him one more time. He knew Jules lived alone in a high-rise condo downtown, but in all the twenty-five years he'd known the man, Green had never been privy to his home address or phone number. As far as Green knew, no one in the police department knew, except the senior brass.

Green had had a restless night interrupted by dreams of his ex-wife spiriting Hannah away from him just as she had eighteen years earlier, smashing the fragile affection that had been building between them. Adam Jules was in the dream too, much younger and new to the department, still possessed of his slight French Canadian accent. He had been chastising Green for neglecting his baby daughter and lecturing him that a police officer who was not grounded in family love would ultimately crash and burn on the punishing front lines of Major Crimes.

This was a peculiar sentiment coming from Jules. Even more peculiar, Jules was animated, even passionate.

Green awoke from the dream unsettled and confused. After a quarter century picking up the detritus of mankind's more brutal clashes, he'd grown used to bizarre dreams. His subconscious at work, cleansing his soul. Vicious criminals resurfaced in his dreams along with poignant victims and unlikely heroes, all intermingled during sleep in startling new ways. He'd learned to accept the wild rides through his subconscious without questioning. Actors in his dream dramas were seldom who they seemed.

In all those years, though, Jules had never been anything but quiet and still, a ghost-like constant in the emotional chaos around him. In reality, Jules had never admonished him for neglecting Hannah. They had barely known each other back then, Jules a new sergeant in Major Crimes and Green an undisciplined young uniform grappling with his first undeserving death, a naked toddler drowned in the family pool. Green had been the one with the passion. Outrage that the parents were passed out on the couch after a night of partying. Horror that they blamed the child, who'd unlatched their makeshift lid on his crib and clambered free.

Jules had encouraged Green to look beyond the surface, to probe the parents' backgrounds and to interview more than a hundred people in pursuit of the truth. All the while he'd never once raised his voice or clenched his fist, even at the end when the Crown declined to prosecute, having decided that the parents had done all they could to protect a very difficult, ingenious child.

Yet last night Jules had appeared to him in his dream vibrant with passion. What was his subconscious trying to tell him? What had it detected in Jules's mysterious request about the missing woman?

46

The morning shift was just gearing up when Green arrived at the spectacular new station known as the Colonies. He signed in, traded greetings with the officers on the front desk and took the stairs two at a time to the top floor. Jules's clerk wasn't at her desk but his door was ajar, so Green strode in without knocking. Jules was at his closet, unwinding a long scarf from his neck.

"I was hoping I'd catch you."

Jules pivoted, his hands smoothing his collar. A spasm of concern crossed his face, quickly erased. "Michael," was all he said.

"You're a hard man to reach."

Jules didn't reply. Never explain, never make excuses, had always been his mantra. He closed his office door and gestured to a seat opposite his massive desk, which sat against the window. "I'm afraid I can't offer coffee just yet."

Green sat down. Orleans was a huge suburb which spilled over every inch of farmland and hillside for miles. The Colonies were tucked into the countryside part way up the Orleans escarpment, and Jules had a sweeping view of the Queensway, the lowland swamp and the Ottawa River beyond. He stood now with his back to Green as if fascinated by the view.

"Like a luxury hotel, isn't it?"

"Adam, what's your connection to Meredith Kennedy?"

Jules didn't move. Green could read nothing in his rigid back. "None."

"Give me some credit. The woman is missing and an entire city is looking for her. And you know something—"

"I know nothing."

"Then why did you ask me about a missing person even before she was reported missing?"

Finally Jules turned around. He was faintly pink but otherwise unmoved. "I can assure you I know nothing useful to the investigation. If I learn anything, I will tell you."

"But how did you know she was missing?"

Jules grew pinker. Green realized he was angry, although his only gesture was to draw back his white shirt cuff and check his watch. "None of that is relevant. You have my word, and that should be enough." His nostrils flared as he calmed himself with an effort. "A concern was raised to me privately, but now that there is an official investigation and every effort is being made to find the woman, I have nothing useful to add. Now if you'll excuse me—"

He crossed the room to open the door. Green stood up and approached him. "What did you think had happened to her? Did you have some knowledge that she'd been in an accident?"

"Michael, it was a general inquiry. I knew no details, about an accident or anything else."

Green left the Colonies profoundly dissatisfied. He'd never known Adam Jules to lie or to obstruct a police investigation— the man was obsessively honest—yet this time he had come perilously close to both. He knew something, but no amount of badgering was going to pry it from him. Jules was an honourable man, and it was obvious that he'd given someone his word not to divulge what he knew. After twenty-five years of working together, he did not trust Green enough to confide in him. Was this distrust just an expression of Jules's secretive nature, or was there a more sinister reason for his stonewalling? Green hoped it was the former, but his instincts prickled.

He had a search to conduct, yet he felt as if there were a door behind which he was not allowed to look.

The pathetic winter sun had barely crawled over the windowsill into her third floor apartment when Detective Sue Peters sat down at her computer. She had already showered, dressed and brewed herself a full pot of kick-ass coffee. She wanted to get a head start before Gibbsie the computer whiz showed up. He was a sweetheart, but she really didn't need him holding her hand all day, and if she blundered around in cyberspace for hours instead of skipping nimbly to the websites she needed, who the hell cared? It wasn't like the inspector was holding his breath for information. She hadn't even told him the whole story in case it turned out to be a dumb idea.

Her computer was an aging clunker that hated all the fancy new graphics and regularly crashed when she asked too much of it. The trick was to be patient, not ask it to do two things at once, let it go at its own speed, and it would get the job done. She could relate to that. She and her computer were best buds, and she resisted all Gibbsie's threats to throw it in the dump. Even the idea felt like a personal affront.

She already had a plan. She'd been awake half the night, too excited to sleep, and as she lay in the dark knowing that at least her body had to rest, she'd let her mind run loose. It still tripped up, forgot where it had been and where it was going, forgot why too sometimes. But much less now than a year ago or even a month ago. That in itself was as exciting as any case she might work on. Harvey Longstreet was going to get the full brunt of what her healing mind could do.

After coaxing her computer to load Google, she typed in his name and hit "search". That yielded a huge bunch of garbage about a circus performer in Australia. What a dumb name for a

49

circus performer—whatever happened to Flying Ace? She added Montreal to the search. The circus had been to Montreal, but in between the mush, she found a single link to a lawyer at McGill.

It was a posting about a student who had won the Longstreet Prize for Criminal Law. A single footnote indicated that the prize had been established in memory of Harvey Longstreet, a popular professor of Criminal Law who had died in 1978. Sue tried a few other search terms to dig up more information but to no avail. Nineteen seventy-eight was just too long ago to have much presence on the web. After surfing pointlessly for an hour, rebooting four times and drinking all three cups of coffee, even she was ready to toss the old pile of crap into the garbage. Time for Plan B. At least she had a date of death to work from.

She had recently had her driver's licence reinstated, so she headed down to the parking lot, where she stood looking in dismay at the mound of snow in her spot. Somewhere under there was her Toyota Echo. The roads were still an unpredictable mess of ice and slush. The sun was trying hard but at these temperatures, nothing was going to melt in a hurry. No point in wearing herself out shovelling before she was halfway through her day, so she left her car for Gibbsie to dig out and called a cab.

The Ottawa Public Library was only a short hop from her Centretown apartment and the cabbie wasn't pleased, but that was his problem. The library was in a contest with the police station for the ugliest building in the city. She'd heard the architectural style of both was called Brutalism, as if that was something to be proud of. Brutal it surely was, an ugly chunk of rough brown concrete squatting on the corner like a toad at a garden party. Inside, she made her way straight upstairs to the newspapers and periodicals section and approached a bored-looking library assistant picking his teeth and staring into space behind his computer.

Judging by how long the *CSI*s and *Law and Order*s had been around, everyone loved a good old-fashioned crime investigation, so Sue produced her badge and asked for his help tracking down an old lead. The toothpick was whipped out and the guy was all ears. The *Montreal Gazette* was on microfilm and he could get it in a jiff, but 1978 was a lot of papers. Any idea when in 1978?

"Bring them all. You'll have to show me how to use the machine," she said, giving him a wink.

He sat her in the corner at one of the viewers and loaded the first tape for her. January 1978 appeared on the screen, blurry and harsh black against white. This is going to give me one mother of a headache, she thought as she turned the dial and the pages whirred past. She'd barely been a twinkle in her mother's eye back then and had no memory of life before computers. This is goddamn prehistoric. How the hell did cops do research back then?

In 1978 the economy was in shambles—what a surprise—and the politicians in the minority government were bickering— another surprise. Quebeckers were on strike, and businesses were crashing all over Montreal. The *Gazette*, which she knew was Quebec's main Anglo voice, was full of screaming headlines about the Quebec government's new language law and the repression of English rights.

Quebec sure was a lively place, she thought as she scrolled through the months. Being a small-town Ontario girl, the only politics she'd grown up with was whether the town council had been paid off when developers won their bid to pave over some prime farm land.

She was skimming so fast through the blurry print that she nearly missed the first article entirely. It was tucked into the bottom of the second page of the July 13 issue, a mere mention of an unidentified male found dead in an apartment on McTavish

Street near McGill University. McGill was the word that caught her eye. There were few other details, other than to say the body had been found by the landlord after a family member expressed concern. The city was engulfed in a heat wave. The landlord was quoted as saying the man was hanging from a hook in the closet, but police refused to confirm any details.

She spun the dial forward to the next day's paper, but despite a careful search, there was no mention of the man. The following day had a small sidebar that the man had been dead for several days but that his identity was being withheld pending notification of family members. It was not until the weekend that a half-page spread on the front page of the Local News section identified the dead man. "Popular law professor's life ends in tragedy", the headline said. There was a large photo of him in full court gown, looking into the camera like he was about to address a jury. But even the silly outfit and the prissy expression could not hide the guy's good looks. Dark curly hair, wide eyes, cheekbones and nose like a perfectly carved Greek god. He looked no more comfortable in that pointy, strangling collar than she would. He belonged at the helm of a yacht in the Caribbean. Below the photo was the caption "Maître Harvey Longstreet divided his time between McGill Law School and a select law practice involving criminal code appeals, but still found time to author several books on appellant law."

Sue combed through the article carefully. It read like a press release from the family. Although Longstreet had apparently taken his own life in the apartment he maintained downtown close to the university, the word suicide wasn't even mentioned. According to his Uncle Cyril, Longstreet used the apartment as a retreat for rest and work during his hectic, sometimes eighteen-hour days. There was a bunch of quotes from students who adored him, from colleagues who hailed him as the next Clarence Darrow—Sue wasn't sure who that was but had a vague recollection of a famous American human rights trial lawyer—and even from an old schoolmate at Lower Canada College. She assumed Lower Canada College was like its Upper Canada equivalent, an incubator for future captains of the country.

Everyone regretted the loss of a man taken at the pinnacle of his powers, who'd left a legacy of cases untried and a young wife and infant son to mourn his loss. In all this gushing, there was precious little about the death itself. No autopsy results, no mention of nooses or closets. Montreal police were briefly quoted as saying foul play was not suspected, and the landlord who'd blabbed about the body hanging in the closet now had no comment.

Things sure were different in those days, she thought. Today the landlord would have cashed in big time, selling his story to some trashy rag that didn't give a damn about facts, integrity or family sensitivities. It was interesting to see that in 1978, Harvey Longstreet's family had enough money, or clout, to muzzle a story that might have blown the guy's perfect image to smithereens in their faces. Had the police investigated at all, or had the family's embarrassment shut them down too?

There were many questions that remained unanswered, many secrets that the family and Elena had kept to themselves. But the story seemed deader than a doornail, and Sue couldn't imagine how an old suicide, no matter how tragic, had anything to do with anything.

* * *

At ten a.m. Thursday morning, sixty-four hours and three

53

brutal winter nights after Meredith Kennedy had last been heard from, Constable Whelan of Missing Persons finally managed to persuade his contacts at Meredith's bank to give him a peek at her records. Officially banks and phone companies required search warrants to permit police access to a citizen's records, but a warrant required proof of a crime. Being missing was not a crime, no matter what the private fears of the police were. Like all businesses, however, banks didn't want to appear uncooperative when a young woman's life might be at stake. After ten years in Missing Persons, Whelan had enough inside contacts to persuade someone to open the books.

By Thursday, things were not looking good. The city had been turned upside down by a burgeoning army of friends, family, women's groups and other concerned volunteers, and the media was dogging their every move. Medical and weather experts had been thrust on the air, counting down her diminishing chances for survival if she lay injured somewhere. The mood in the incident room had turned sombre, and the search coordinator was already talking in terms of recovery more often than rescue.

Constable Whelan refused to give up. He had been there from the first call, heard the anguish in Brandon Longstreet's voice, and seen the hopeful laughing face of the girl in the photo he'd sent. When he finally got the official okay on Thursday morning at the end of his graveyard shift, he headed directly over to the TD Canada Trust branch Meredith used. Everyone at the branch had heard of the disappearance, and everyone knew the woman well. She'd been a customer since she was six years old, when her father had brought her to open her very own account, and she still came in regularly to do business.

Recently she'd been in to discuss a small loan to cover some of the travel expenses to Ethiopia. She had a smile and a friendly hello for everyone, they said, and she was so excited about this trip. So thrilled about the wedding. She'd been engaged once before, she'd told the branch manager, but they were too incompatible. This time it had felt perfect.

The branch manager ushered Whelan directly into her office and typed some commands into her computer. "This will show a record of all her transactions in all her accounts, no matter where they occur. She can take money out of an ATM in Vancouver and it will show up here instantly." She paused as the screen flickered and loaded a long list of entries. Her brow furrowed in concentration as she studied the list. "She has a modest RRSP but that hasn't seen any activity since last February. Tax time. Besides that, there's the unsecured line of credit and one personal bank account, a full-service chequing account that typically sees several transactions a day. She uses web banking to pay her bills. Right now this is the balance on that account."

She paused to write the figure down for him. $11,328.32. His eyebrows shot up in surprise. So much for the global economic recession.

"The five thousand dollar loan came through," the manager explained. "It was deposited three days ago, and it's reflected in her line-of-credit figure."

"Can I have a printout of that entire banking summary, and also of the recent transactions in her chequing account?"

"Of course. How far back do you want?"

"The last two weeks." He hesitated. You never knew what would be important. "Make that the last two months."

She clicked some buttons and the printer beside her began to hum. While they waited, she studied the screen, then glanced at her calendar with a frown. "That's funny."

"What?"

"Her last two transactions were December 14. That was Tuesday."

The day after she disappeared, he realized, just as the manager must have. "Is there a delay in registering it in the system?"

She shook her head. "Not with debits. On weekends or after business hours, yes, but only to the next business day. Not a whole twenty-four hours later." She plucked the printed sheets from the machine and handed them to him.

He glanced at the latest two entries. One was an ATM withdrawal for $300 and the other a payment of $176.25 at The Bay department store. Neither one would have been a pre-authorized automatic withdrawal.

"Can you tell where these transactions occurred?" he asked.

"I can tell you the ATM right away." Her fingers flew over the keyboard. "The TD bank on Pretoria Avenue in the Glebe."

Whelan frowned. The Glebe was an old residential neighbourhood south of Centretown and Pretoria was a short street running along its northern edge. However, neither Pretoria nor the Glebe was anywhere near Meredith's work, her home or her fiancé's home.

"For The Bay, you will have to find out their store code through them." The manager smiled. "But I'm sure with a little detective work you can find out not only what store she shopped at but what she bought there. It's all on computers now."

Whelan nodded absently as he folded the printout into his growing file. His mind was already racing ahead to a better idea—the security camera at the ATM in the Glebe. As he rose to leave, she looked up at him, startled.

"Don't you want to know credit card activity too?"

He sat down with a thud, cursing his stupidity. Getting old and soft behind a desk.

She clicked more links. "Now, there is a time lag with credit cards, because businesses have to submit the charge to VISA, which has to approve it. It can take a couple of days, so to get the most up-to-date charges, we will have to contact the VISA office itself. However, this list is worth a look." She printed off the past two months, and Whelan studied them. At first glance there was nothing suspicious. The card had a modest balance of $2110.36 owing, and the latest charge had been posted on the Monday of Meredith's disappearance—a charge of twenty-five dollars at D'Arcy McGee's, a trendy downtown pub, the previous Saturday. Other charges over recent weeks were for shoes, liquor, gas, adventure gear, pharmacy supplies and odds and ends. As he scanned the list, he was aware of the bank manager on the phone with the credit card company. She was jotting notes as she listened and a flicker of curiosity crossed her face. When she hung up, she glanced again at her calendar.

"Any activity after Monday?" he prompted.

"No, but on Monday she did make another charge, which is just going through now. To the bus company for sixty-eight dollars."

Whelan blinked. Bus company! "What did she buy?"

"You'll have to ask the bus company. Our records just show the transaction."

He was already on his feet again, ignoring the creaking in his knees as he stuffed the papers into his file. His heart was racing with excitement. If the purchase was for a bus ticket out of town, the woman might still be alive!

*   *   *

In his excitement, Whelan revved his unmarked car so fast that the tires spun on the ice coming out of the parking lot. Sunlight glared off the snow and snowbanks canyoned the streets, further reducing visibility. Cars raced by, splattering salty slush on his windshield as he tried to merge onto Carling Avenue. He steered carefully towards downtown, his thoughts running ahead. First the bus station and the ATM. Should he call this in? At least ask for some help with the security tapes? He was an old desk jockey working a double shift and in the field again for the first time in three years.

He slipped onto the Queensway for the latter half of the trip and took the exit for the bus terminal. First things first. Find out where the woman had gone, and when.

Just before Christmas, the inter-city station was full of travellers, many of them students laden down with backpacks and shopping bags of presents. Long lines had already formed at the platforms for the Montreal and Toronto Express buses. A chatter of voices reverberated around the huge room. The station manager looked harried from his efforts to handle the overflow, but he barely glanced at Whelan's badge in his eagerness to cooperate. The plight of Meredith Kennedy had captured the city, and any assistance that the bus company could provide in finding her would be not only a goodwill gesture but a PR coup as well. It took the manager less than two minutes on his computer to locate the purchase involved.

"It was a return ticket to Montreal purchased at 9:27 a.m. on December 13. Departing at 10:00 a.m. and returning at 6:00 p.m."

"What day?"

"The same day. Monday. She bought the ticket and left right away."

"Do you have confirmation she was on the bus?"

The manager's face fell. "Not in the system. But why would she buy a ticket? She bought it right here." He gestured out his office window to the large open area where customers snaked behind guide ropes up to the wickets.

"Then one of the ticket agents would remember her?"

"Possibly, although with these crowds...and of course, she could have used one of the machines."

"You mean you don't keep a record of who actually gets on the bus?" Whelan allowed some cop disapproval to resonate in his voice. He knew that the bus company had been under fire for their poor security controls, knew also that there was little money or political will to invest in changes. The bus system ferried Canada's poor and working class from one little town to another across the country. Those with money and influence generally preferred planes, or at least VIA rail.

The manager glanced anxiously at the crowds milling in the room outside his office. Ticket sellers were overworked and frazzled, and carriers scrambled to add extra buses to handle the long lines. He started to shake his head then spoke reluctantly. "Well, we could check the ticket stubs. The bus drivers hand them in at the end of their shift. Do you want me to have someone go through those?"

Whelan arched his eyebrows. "Yes, please. And could I have the names and contact information of the bus drivers on those two runs?" Hauling himself to his feet, he stifled a grunt. Each hour his joints stiffened more. He handed the man his card and was pleased to see that before he was even out the door, the manager was already on the phone, eager for his own small moment of playing hero.

Outside the bus station, Whelan had to lean on his car roof to steady himself. Black spots floated before his eyes and a wave of fatigue crashed over him. The ATM had better be the last stop for today, he decided, before he became more a liability than an asset to the case.

SIX

He moved between sleep and wakefulness, drifting up and down as if billowing on a soft, fluffy cloud. He felt no pain or anguish, drugged by the Valium he'd taken at two in the morning. After two sleepless nights, he'd finally acknowledged he needed chemical help. He could barely think straight. On his latest shift, he had misread a consultant's order and forgotten to sign a patient's chart, and yet he'd lain awake at the end of it, exhausted but staring at the ceiling, unable to escape his thoughts. Meredith needed him. What help would he be to her, what guidance could he offer the police if he collapsed? If he could just get some rest, maybe everything would be clearer and calmer when he woke up.

But the Valium didn't quite pull him under. He could still hear voices. The radio news droning on, the commercials blaring. Time stretched. Slipped away. More voices, different now. His mother on the phone. Endless people calling. How many friends did she have? He knew some of the calls were probably for him. Friends and colleagues wanting to help, the Addis Ababa people wanting to know if he was still a go. Curiosity seekers, psychics and other disaster junkies salivating for their next fix.

Meredith, what have you done? The cry welled from deep within him, jerking him above the surface. He wondered if he had spoken it aloud, and he clamped his hand over his mouth. He'd better be more vigilant. Valium was dangerous stuff, lowering his guard and loosening his tongue when he could least afford it. His mother had already warned him about that.

"Of course you're angry!" she'd said at two in the morning when she found him pacing the kitchen. "No matter what happened, no matter who's to blame, she's gone. But you mustn't show it. Anger loses public sympathy, no matter how justified it is. People don't like anger; it scares them, offends them and raises their suspicions. You're the victim here, Brandon. Fear and grief are acceptable; they arouse sympathy and understanding. The police expect you to be panic-stricken and distraught."

"Mom, I don't give a fuck what the police think!"

"But you must," she'd countered. "They are studying every inch of your life and your demeanour, looking for cracks, inconsistencies, and yes, emotions that don't ring true."

He'd fought his outrage. He was not some damn client of hers being prepped for the witness stand, undoubtedly guilty but trying every legal manoeuvre to stay out of jail. She might mean well and she certainly knew far more about the police than he did, but what the hell was she saying? That he had something to hide?

"You talk as if I'm guilty!"

She barely batted an eyelash. The queen of the courtroom stage, trained to make every muscle obey her purpose. "Of course not, honey. But to take liberties with the old legal adage, one must not only be innocent but appear to be innocent as well."

He'd hoped the Valium would give his battered mind the strength to protect itself, but as he lay on his bed with the duvet pulled up to his chin and the curtains drawn against the pallid winter sun, he felt his mind teeter instead on the brink of disintegration. Despite the prescriptions he routinely wrote for others, he almost never put drugs into his own system.

Even during the exhausting years of med school, he'd avoided the uppers and downers that others used to cope. He'd hoped a small dose of Valium would do no harm, but obviously even that was too strong for his unaccustomed brain.

Now he gripped his head in his hands, hoping the sheer physical force would stifle the scream welling inside him and still the urge to run blindly from the house.

How could he control how he acted, let alone what he said, in this disintegrating world?

"He mustn't know!" His mother's voice shafted through the fog of his mind. "I don't care what you do, he mustn't find out."

He bolted up in bed, his ears straining. Her voice dropped to an indecipherable murmur. The room spun as he struggled to regain his equilibrium. Scraps floated up from downstairs. Was she on the phone in the kitchen?

"Hundred thousand dollars," she said. Then "Never...that woman...not that way...search warrants... I'll meet you." Silence, followed by a muffled voice he didn't recognize. Not a phone call then, but a visitor. His mother moved towards the front hall and opened the front door. She sounded calmer as she said goodbye, as if she had resolved something, but before he could mobilize himself to demand an explanation, he heard the distant rumble of her car as she accelerated down the drive.

He could hardly breathe. Who was she talking to and what the hell did all that mean? Who mustn't find out? Who was "that woman"? What was his mother trying to hide, and the most dreaded question of all, what did it have to do with Meredith's disappearance?

His head pounded with the effort needed to focus. His mother was a highly respected lawyer with a string of high profile wins and an unassailable reputation. She held herself and all around her to a high ethical standard. She had always taught him that right must prevail and that the moral high ground would be rewarded in the end. It seemed impossible that he was harbouring the fears he was, impossible that she could have strayed so far off course.

*　　*　　*

Green had called a briefing for noon that Thursday, anxious to follow up on leads and put the pieces together as quickly as possible. In the crowded incident room, the smell of stale coffee and the sound of murmuring voices and rustling papers filled the air. As police officers filtered in from the field, they draped their bulky parkas over their chair backs and rubbed their chilled hands to restore circulation. Once Gibbs had activated the smart board and pulled up the list of assignments, the search coordinator summarized the progress of the ground search.

It was a brief report. Zero. The neighbourhood around her house had been gridded and searched, as had the blocks on either side of the bus routes she typically used. Meredith was nowhere around her usual haunts.

Green turned to the computer specialist, who had just started on Meredith's laptop and was working on accessing Facebook. He launched into an explanation of passwords and security settings, and Green's mind was just beginning to glaze when Whelan came limping into the room. He was red-faced and breathless. Frost still clung to the scarf around his neck.

"Sorry I'm late, sir," he began, looking more triumphant than sorry as he slapped a file down on the conference table. "We're on the wrong track."

All heads turned, and Green abandoned the password conundrum in a flash. "Something to report, Whelan?"

"I've been checking bank records. On Monday, our subject bought a return bus ticket to Montreal, leaving on the 10 a.m. bus and returning at 8:00 p.m."

All murmuring stopped. "She's been confirmed on the bus?" Green asked.

"Not yet. The bus company has to check the ticket stubs with the drivers of those buses. One is due in from Montreal at noon and the other at two."

Green riffled through his memory of the case but could turn up no connection to Montreal. "Anyone know any reason why our subject would make a day trip to Montreal?"

"Fashion centre of Canada?" the computer tech said with a grin. "The girl was getting married."

Green poked the idea for holes. "Possibly, but why wouldn't the family or friends mention it to us?"

"It could be a surprise. A special wedding dress or a gift for her bridesmaids."

"Good point." He signalled to Gibbs. "Follow up with the family, see if she hinted at anything like that."

Out of the corner of his eye, he saw a flash of checkered fuchsia as Sue Peters leaned forward in her chair. He felt a surge of delight at the garish outfit. Bit by bit, the old Sue was coming back to them. In her eyes too was a glint of the old excitement.

"I don't know if this is important, sir," she said, "but there is a bit of a mystery about the death of Brandon Longstreet's father. He was a prominent lawyer and he was found hanging in his Montreal apartment, supposedly a suicide—"

Green perked up. "When was this?"

"Thirty years ago, but the whole thing was hushed up. It looks like the investigation was just stopped."

"Thirty years is a long time ago," Green said doubtfully.

"Suicide was much more of a stigma in those days."

"I know," Peters said, undeterred. "But maybe Meredith wanted to know more about him and the family secret before she got more involved with them. A day trip suggests she wasn't going to visit family or go out for an evening on the town with a friend. She just zipped in and out for a few hours, long enough to check something out."

"Or to pick up a wedding dress," the computer tech said.

Green saw a scowl gathering on Peters' face. "First things first. Whelan, confirm that she took the trip and came back. It may in fact be irrelevant, but if she went to Montreal, that's the last thing she did before she disappeared. People do not disappear over a wedding dress, even the worst tailoring job in the world. But a discovery about the family might make her drop out of sight, at least for a day or two, to think things through." This trip to Montreal was a ray of hope in an investigation that turned gloomier with the passing of each frigid day. The longer they could all hang on to hope, the better.

Whelan leaned on the table, propping his head in his hands, but at Green's last words, he lifted his head and blinked in surprise. "There's more, sir. It looks like she may have been alive on Tuesday morning." As he explained about the ATM withdrawal, everyone held their breath and even Bob Gibbs stopped typing.

"Someone could have been using her card," Peters said.

Whelan reached into his pocket and pulled out a computer memory stick. "That's why I brought the video from the ATM camera for that day."

"Have you looked at it?"

"No sir, I only just pried it loose from the bank."

Jesus! Green looked at the man in astonishment. For ten

minutes he had sat there listening to them discussing wedding dresses and family secrets, while all the time he was sitting on a piece of evidence that could potentially throw the whole basis of the investigation out the window. Whelan's eyes drooped and his fingers fumbled as he groped through his file. He would probably fall asleep within two minutes of starting to watch.

Green instructed Gibbs to load the stick into the computer, and the entire table watched in silence as the distorted, fish-eye view of the small ATM booth came up on the screen. In the bottom right corner, the seconds ticked by on the date recorder.

"Do we have the time of this transaction?" Green asked, trying not to sound impatient. Whelan consulted the accounts print-out. 10:38 a.m. Gibbs flashed ahead to 10:35. A hazy figure was standing at the machine, back to the camera. Gibbs backed it up a couple of minutes and caught the figure pulling open the glass door and entering the booth. It looked like a woman, but she was wearing not only a scarf wrapped around her neck and chin but a coat with a fur-trimmed hood pulled up over her head. Large sunglasses completed the camouflage.

"Jesus, that could be anybody," Peters muttered.

Gibbs zoomed in on key parts of the figure, trying to pick out distinguishing features. The person wore gloves throughout the transaction, so that it was impossible to identify rings. She worked quickly without consulting any notes, more like someone familiar with the PIN number and the transaction process than someone trying to remember, read or guess an unfamiliar PIN or trying to choose between unfamiliar accounts. She kept her head bowed as she punched the keys, never giving the camera a chance to capture her full face.

"Our subject does have a winter coat with a hood," Whelan said, still awake. "The family could probably tell if this was it.

Also the purse. Women's purses are pretty individual."

Green's thoughts were way ahead. He was beginning to get a queasy feeling about this whole business. The person at the ATM had been very clever, using posture and clothing that seemed very normal and yet completely concealed their identity. If Meredith had come to deliberate harm, the person responsible would have easy access to the clothes and purse needed to impersonate her at the bank machine. And to throw the investigation completely off track.

But Whelan was right. Follow-up with the family was the next logical step, but Whelan would probably wrap his car around a lamp post before he got there. Green sent the exhausted man home and had Gibbs print out stills from the video. He checked his watch.

"Bob, get over to the bus station and grab those drivers before they go off again. After that you can follow up with the families."

Sue Peters was hovering behind Gibbs's shoulder, and finally she broke in. "Sir, can I help Bob with the follow-up? Maybe check out the Harvey Longstreet suicide angle?"

Green eyed her carefully. She looked wide-eyed and bursting to go, almost her old self. He suspected the true intent behind her carefully vague request. The old Sue Peters let loose on Elena Longstreet was not a pretty sight, but on the other hand, she now knew the case as well as anybody.

"Let's get confirmation that she went to Montreal first, before we do any kind of follow-up. Once Gibbs has that, we can discuss it."

Peters grinned widely but Green thought he detected a flicker of alarm on Gibbs's face. This office romance could get tricky, he thought.

Barely thirty minutes passed before Gibbs phoned in his report. The bus driver doing the morning route to Montreal last

Monday remembered the missing woman well, and he'd been wondering whether to call the police. She hadn't done anything wrong, in fact she had not been acting strangely at all, but he had later wondered whether the police were looking in all the wrong places. Maybe she'd dropped out of sight in Montreal, he said to Gibbs. She didn't look like a bride excited about her wedding. She looked worried, as if she had something big on her mind, and she'd sat curled up in her seat by the window, staring out and ignoring the young guy who tried to pick her up.

Did she speak to anyone, Gibbs wanted to know. Or speak on her phone? Text or email?

She was writing notes, the driver said, and she checked her cellphone often as if she was expecting something. But then kids these days checked their cell phones sometimes fifty times an hour.

Did she have any luggage, Gibbs asked. Nothing big, maybe a daypack, the driver said, scrunching up his face as he tried to remember. An experienced guy, Gibbs said to Green. Fluent in both languages and been doing the routes around Quebec and Ontario for ten years. If Meredith hadn't looked worried, he would barely have noticed her. He'd pegged her for a student going home for the holidays, maybe worried about the exams or term papers she still had to face.

The bus driver doing the afternoon route back to Ottawa had had little time to think of anything but the road. The bus was packed with students travelling home to Ottawa or to the small towns in the Ottawa Valley. At six o'clock it was already dark, and the snow had begun blowing in thick, horizontal gusts that formed icy sheets on the road and swirled into drifts at each curve. The four-lane divided highway between Montreal and Ottawa was bleak at the best of times, passing through acres of desolate bush and farmland. In a blizzard, it could be lethal. The bus driver counted himself lucky to have stayed on the road while smaller cars and less experienced drivers spun out into the ditches.

All the passengers on the bus seemed to sense the danger, he said, because there was none of the laughter and rowdiness of most holiday season buses. They had stayed pretty quiet as if afraid to distract him, but no one had slept. Everyone watched the road and the pinpricks of red light from the cars up ahead.

The driver stared at Meredith's picture for a long time as though he were trying to place her in the bus. "She was in a window seat about halfway back," he said finally. "I remember because she was upset about something. She had this clipboard and she was always scribbling on it and flipping through pages to look at things. I caught a quick look at them while she was looking for her ticket, and it looked like pages of death announcements, like from the paper? I thought maybe someone had died in her family."

"Did she use her cellphone?"

The driver looked blank. "Like I said, once we were rolling, I hardly took my eyes off the road."

"Did she talk to anyone on the bus?"

"Not that I saw, but I couldn't see much." he shrugged, his long, jowly face sad. He looked like a man who was ready to retire, weary of the long hours on the road and longing for more time in his armchair with his favourite sports show.

"Well done," Green said once Gibbs concluded his report. He felt his excitement mount. "This puts a whole new spin on things. We need to find out why she went to Montreal and what she was so upset about."

"I thought of that, s-sir," Gibbs said with a hint of pride in his voice. "I got the passenger manifest and put out a media call asking anyone who spoke to Meredith on either leg of her trip to phone us. Maybe she told someone where she was going. Or maybe her seatmate was able to see more of what was on her clipboard."

"Good thinking. Bring the manifest to the station for Sue to work on while you follow up with the families." Green glanced into the main room, where Peters had been working at her computer. Her desk was vacant and her winter jacket gone from its peg. He felt a flash of consternation. Had she grown fed up with playing back-up and gone off herself, ready to confront the family with only half the facts?

Good God, was the old Sue Peters truly back?

SEVEN

When Frankie Robitaille finally had a chance to sleep, he didn't wake for thirteen hours. During the two-day storm, which saw wave after wave of snow and sleet blanket the capital, he had put in eighteen-hour days behind the wheel of his plow, keeping himself awake with Tim Hortons coffee and endless country and western songs on his iPod. For over two days, he managed no more than the occasional break to grab some food and a catnap on the couch before heading out again.

By Wednesday evening, the snow was under control and his shift supervisor had sent him home before he became a serious hazard on the road. Dinner, a quick stop to give his kids a goodnight kiss and a promise of Disney World at March break, and he fell into bed. He slept through the alarm the next morning and the kids' preparations for school, not waking until the dog shoved her cold, impatient nose into his face. Frankie stared at the clock in disbelief. It was almost noon.

He turned on the television as he stumbled around the kitchen brewing coffee and fixing himself a heaping plate of bacon, eggs and toast. Every muscle of his body ached. He allowed the local news show to drone on in the background with a mixture of patter, features and brief news bytes. Gradually he became aware of a story about a missing woman. The camera panned the scene of volunteers trudging through snowy streets, probing snowbanks with ski poles.

He picked up his plate and carried it to sit down in front of the TV. A police spokeswoman was asking all residents throughout the city to check their own properties for any sign of the woman, who was believed to be wearing a hooded red jacket. She had last been heard from on Monday evening, and if she had been injured, she might be lying beneath forty centimetres of snow. So far the official search had concentrated on the residential areas between downtown and Carlingwood, but the woman could have gone anywhere.

More than two days beneath the snow, Frankie thought. She's dead, no doubt about it. He got to thinking about all the miles he'd covered in those days, all the acres of pure white snow. The garbage bins, snow shovels and kid's sleds he'd tossed up from under that pristine cover. A memory rose up, of a slight bump, a flash of red on the snow behind him. Slowly he set his fork down. A strange sensation churned in his gut. Was it possible? What day had that been? Where had he been? On a residential street somewhere, in the dead of night. Wednesday. No, Tuesday.

He felt sick. Tuesday morning, more than fifty-four hours ago.

He grabbed a city map and began to retrace his routes, trying to remember where he had been plowing early Tuesday morning. Somewhere in the east end not far from downtown, but nowhere near where the police thought she might be. But what if they were wrong? After five minutes he threw the map aside in frustration. He had to see the streets for himself and replay the night in his mind's eye.

He revved his pick-up out of the drive and headed into town. The roads were clear now and a brittle sun glared on the fresh snow. Salt crews had covered the main roads, polishing them a glossy black. Frankie lived in Cumberland at the far eastern extremity of the city, but at midday it took him less than half an hour to reach the fashionable old neighbourhood nestled in the crook where the Rideau River joined the Ottawa. He had covered Vanier to Manor Park that night, but as near as he could remember, he had been around Lindenlea and New Edinburgh when he'd bumped something. Both neighbourhoods bordered the more exclusive enclave of Rockcliffe Park, home to ambassadors and wealthy CEOs, and Frankie was never sure where one area ended and the other began. Rockcliffe had no sidewalks and had an English village feel, despite the multi-million dollar homes set back on huge properties. Lindenlea was quaint and smaller in scale, but still way beyond his bank balance even if he had wanted to rub shoulders with associate deputy ministers and university profs. His black pick-up with the roof rack and the trailer hitch would look like a bouncer at a tea party among the Audis and Volvos in the drives.

Beechwood Avenue bisected the area, dividing the haves from the have-nots in neighbouring Vanier. Once he'd turned onto the narrow streets of Lindenlea, he eased off the gas and tried to visualize that night. It had been dark and dead quiet, poorly lit by streetlights. He'd been driving around a sharp curve and was just picking up a bit of speed when he'd felt the jolt. Now he drove slowly through the looping streets, searching for the right layout. Nothing. The neighbourhood was full of short, curvy streets clogged with snowbanks. He widened his net, venturing into the nearby fringes of Rockcliffe, where unassuming bungalows worth close to a million peeked from behind snowladen cedar hedges. Turning off Juliana Road onto Maple Lane, he had a memory flash. The stretch had looked like this. He had turned left just like this and had been accelerating towards a wide-open stretch when the bump occurred.

73

He inched down the street peering closely at the snowbanks made by plows over the past days. No hint of red. No telltale lump in the snow. He parked his truck and began to walk. There was almost no one out on the street. No volunteers probing the snowbanks or checking under the boughs of huge spruces that drooped to the ground under the weight of snow. Only a solitary woman walking her Labrador retriever off leash. The dog looked at him suspiciously and barked, like a stranger was a weird sight in the area.

The woman took in his salt-splattered pick-up, his well-worn bomber jacket and his three-inch growth—he'd left without shaving that morning—and her eyebrows shot up. "Can I help you?"

He started to shake his head then stopped himself. "I'm a snowplow operator, and I think I hit something with my plow a couple of days ago. I'm just checking around."

Her eyebrows drew together now, like a teacher who'd heard that line before. "What did you hit?"

"I don't know. A sled, maybe? Red shovel? Do you live around here? Did anyone find anything like that?" He wasn't sure why he didn't tell her the real reason. Maybe just because she looked like she could get him in a whole lot of trouble if he even mentioned he might have hit someone.

She was backing away now, her dog tightly leashed at her side. "I think you're wasting your time. Wait till the snow melts in the spring."

He watched her stride off up the street and knew she didn't believe him for a minute. He took a deep breath. Now what? He hadn't brought a ski pole, and although he had a shovel in the back on the truck, it was a hell of a big snowbank to be digging up.

Nonetheless he took out his snow shovel and tested the mound of snow left by his plow. It was granular now and hard to penetrate. New snow had been blown on top of it by the homeowners clearing their own driveways. It seemed an impossible task. He needed help, but if the dog lady was any indication, the neighbours on this street wouldn't lend a hand. On the other hand, it was too early to call the police.

Up ahead the dog was barking again, and when Frankie looked up, he saw the animal circling a pile of snow by a driveway halfway up the block. The dog was pawing excitedly.

Jesus, Frankie thought. Grabbing his shovel, he headed up the block. The woman glanced towards him, her jaw dropping. She yanked at her dog, dragged it away from the snowbank and set off almost at a run.

I bet she calls the police, Frankie thought. Well, at this point, maybe that's not a bad idea.

*   *   *

Brandon entered his mother's home office, which was located on the second storey at the back of the house. Her desk was positioned in the bow window and flooded with sunlight. In the summer, the yard would be a paisley print of perennial beds but a blanket of pristine snow hid them all, and even the snow-laden Colorado blue spruce at the rear of the yard could not improve his mood. The Valium was wearing off, leaving him a brain of cotton wool through which thought moved sluggishly.

He knew his mother would be out most of the day. The Superior Court calendar had been booked months in advance and nothing, not even the disappearance of her future daughter-in-law, would keep her from the arcane motion being heard today. She hadn't even tried to send her junior. It was as if she knew there was no great crisis and Meredith was off somewhere for her own selfish reasons, as if the police were poking snowbanks in vain and there would be no gruesome discovery to disrupt her in the middle of her argument.

What the hell did she know?

When the desk itself yielded no answers, he spent an hour meticulously going through the papers in her filing cabinet. Like her life, they were carefully compartmentalized. Her university lectures, course notes and student assignments were all in her faculty office, and her case files, court transcripts and legal research were in her law office downtown. Only her personal papers, and perhaps the occasional work in progress, were kept at home, but even so, thirty years of personal papers presented a daunting challenge. Bank and investment statements, household bills and receipts, tax records, minutes of her charitable and committee work. He was astonished to discover an entire file drawer devoted to him. Not just every report card he'd ever received, but every letter he'd sent from camp, every crayoned art offering and handmade Mother's Day card he'd ever drawn. He knew that as an only child he was important to her, but he'd always thought she had a busy, fulfilling life beyond the home. He remembered her being constantly on the phone, delayed at meetings, and listening with half an ear to his childish chatter while she scanned the latest judge's decision. He remembered a childhood of cleaning ladies, babysitters and even catered meals when she was in the middle of a case.

She'd always seemed slightly aloof, avoiding the mushy cuddling that Meredith's family bestowed at the smallest excuse. He couldn't recall her ever saying "I love you" except in jest, and the unfamiliar words had not come easily to his own lips when Meredith had first demanded them. His reticence had almost cost him the warmest, most exciting woman who had ever come into his life.

He sat cross-legged on the floor in front of the open file cabinet, his child's drawings crackling with age as they filtered through his hands. She had cherished every single artefact of his past, squirrelled it silently away in her own private drawer, never told him how much she loved them or how proud she was of him. In rare moments, uttered only the words "Your father would be so proud." He had no memory of his father, who had died when he was two months old, but his mother had painted an idealized image. Even as a child he'd suspected no one could be as loving a husband, as devoted a father, as brilliant a lawyer nor as beloved a professor as the Harvey Kent Longstreet of her descriptions. He'd been her professor, thirteen years her senior and light years ahead of all her other suitors in maturity, wisdom and allure. Brandon had once overheard her saying to a friend that, despite plenty of offers, she'd never remarried because a love like Harvey Longstreet came along only once in a lifetime. At the time, he'd been startled, even discomfited, by the tremor of passion in her impeccably modulated voice.

Now she surprised him again with the strength of her devotion to him. He remembered the urgency in that fragment he'd overheard that morning. *"He mustn't know!"* took on a less sinister, more protective meaning. Was she just trying to shield him from something? What? The answer was not on her desk, which was filled with mundane household matters, nor among the drawings and letters of his childhood. He shut the file cabinet and pulled open another one, chock full of carefully labelled file folders. Taxes, telephone, travel, wedding, will... Neither the wedding folder nor the will held anything unusual.

On a whim, he pulled open an upper drawer for the H's. Nothing under husband, but thumbing through files in search of Harvey, he came across a file labelled "Hatfield". Not recognizing the name, he almost skipped by, but its thick, unruly contents gave him pause. He pulled it out, and a jumble of yellowed newspaper clippings from the *Montreal Star* fell out. He caught the reporter's name—Cam Hatfield—and a couple of headlines. *Tributes pour in for dead professor. The private anguish of a public man. A new brand of teacher.*

His scalp prickled. He picked up one article, unfolded it along its brittle seam, and began to read:

Confusion continues to surround the death of one of McGill's most popular professors, who was found dead in his McTavish Street apartment on Monday morning. Harvey Longstreet was a member of the prominent Montreal family that founded the Anglo-Canadian Transportation Company, now known as CanTransco, in 1855. The professor's young widow and two-month old son are in seclusion at his uncle's Westmount home and the family is requesting privacy to deal with the tragedy. Colleagues willing to speak to the newspaper expressed shock and disbelief, stating that Longstreet had shown no signs of depression or stress—

The doorbell rang distantly. Brandon looked up, confusion giving way to fear. Meredith! Quickly he stuffed the articles back into the filing cabinet and kicked the drawer shut as he headed out the door.

A young woman stood on the doorstep, bundled against the cold in a blue parka, a red tuque with a red and white pompom and matching mittens. Was there a hint of excitement in those blue eyes, he wondered? His hopes stirred.

Then she held up her badge. "Detective Peters, Ottawa Police," she said, enunciating carefully as if the label were unfamiliar to her. "Are you Brandon Longstreet?"

He nodded. "Any news?"

"We haven't found her, no sir, but we're making progress on

her movements. May I come in?"

He invited her in and suppressed his impatience as she removed her boots and coat. She took so long, he wondered whether she was stalling. Settled on the floral living room couch, Peters eyed him gravely. "Did Meredith tell you her plans to go to Montreal?"

"Montreal?" He was equally incredulous and startled. When Peters said nothing, he shook his head. "Why would she go to Montreal?"

"That's what I'm asking you."

He felt a flare of annoyance. "We have a wedding in two weeks, she has a million things on her to-do list. Why would she go there!"

"What's in Montreal? A dressmaker? A friend?"

"Nobody," he said, fighting off the absurdity of the idea. Belatedly, reason penetrated the cotton wool in his brain. "You have evidence she went to Montreal?"

The detective nodded. "She took a bus there Monday morning and returned here Monday evening."

He stared at her. That made no sense! He'd last seen Meredith on Sunday evening. They'd had dinner together and tried to finalize the table seating for the dinner. She hadn't mentioned a thing about Montreal. Brandon closed his eyes, recalling the unpleasant memory for the hundredth time. She'd been furious with him, frustrated at all the Longstreet guests who needed places of importance, resentful that their parents would share the head table with them instead of their friends. In fact, she hadn't wanted a head table. She'd wanted a series of round tables that made everyone feel equal and included.

It was such a modern, Meredith idea, and he loved her for it. But his mother was paying for the dinner, and she naturally expected a clear gesture of respect in return.

Meredith had stormed off in a huff. He hadn't told the police about it because he wanted them to take her disappearance seriously. He'd seen their cynical, world-weary attitude towards victims too often in the emergency room waiting rooms, and he didn't want them to think that Meredith was just another immature, spiteful girlfriend looking for payback. She was a fiery, impassioned woman, but she would never go to this extreme. Surely, no matter how angry or doubtful she became, she would never put him and her family through this anguish.

Yet now, in the cold light of reflection, how well did he actually know her? The sense of connection had been instantaneous, the romance and passion breathtaking, but his long hours at the hospital kept them from actually spending as much time together as they wished. He still didn't know much of her past, nor of her friendships beyond their shared circle.

But Montreal? What did Montreal have to do with anything? What was so urgent in Montreal that she would drop her entire to-do list and travel four hours through a snowstorm on a cramped, noisy bus to deal with it?

"I don't know," he said, trying to control the alarm in his voice. "She has some family there, and friends from her Haiti posting."

"Anyone she might visit? Anyone she stayed close to?"

"Just a few work colleagues and some obscure cousins."

"Can I have names and contact numbers?"

"We've called them all. No one's seen or heard from her."

"All the same, we have to follow up. They may know things."

"I only have a few names, from the wedding guest list." He rose to fetch the list from the kitchen and waited in silence as she laboriously copied the names down. She seemed to do everything in slow motion. He toyed briefly with a diagnosis of

80

MS before noticing the fine scars at her hairline and another just above her brow, camouflaged by hair. The woman was fighting back from a catastrophic head trauma. He felt a wave of respect and sympathy. It was on the tip of his tongue to comment when she raised her head.

"No one else?" she demanded, as if daring him to say a word.

He shook his head. "Her parents would know more of the relatives down there."

"What about grandparents? Any in Montreal?"

"Her grandmother's alive, but she's in a nursing home. Advanced Alzheimer's. In the past couple of years she's barely recognized Meredith. Meredith used to visit often but recently she's found it hard."

The detective stopped taking notes and leaned forward, her eyes drilling his. "But she could have gone to see her. With her wedding coming up, maybe she felt sentimental. Did the grandmother come up in conversation recently?"

Brandon shook his head. He felt the detective pressing against the secret fault lines of their relationship and felt himself resisting. But the grandmother hadn't come up. Not really. "We discussed whether she should come to the wedding or not, and everyone else—especially Meredith's mother—thought it would be a bad idea. She can't really travel. She gets confused and agitated, she wouldn't know what's going on."

"Maybe Meredith got to feeling guilty?"

Brandon tried to fit that idea with Meredith's mood on Sunday night. She *had* struggled, but maybe more with regret than guilt. Was it possible she went to Montreal to visit Nan? Nan had been a force when Meredith was growing up, always ready with a big hug, a plate of oat cakes, and a listening ear. He knew it hurt Meredith to see the old lady so diminished.

He felt uneasy. Maybe he'd been wrong. Maybe he'd misread the depths of her distress. Maybe she was feeling the absence of her grandmother at her wedding and the overwhelming force of two dozen Longstreet guests while a key person from her side was missing. Maybe that, along with his stupid blunder about the head table, had made her second-guess her desire to join her life to his.

The detective was waiting for an answer, with that challenging look in her eyes again. He forced a shrug. "It's possible. But you said she came back to Ottawa afterwards, so I don't see what difference it makes?"

"Because she disappeared almost immediately afterwards, as if something happened on that trip to make her take off. That's more than some simple family visit."

He turned the idea over slowly. None of this made any sense. It didn't fit with the Meredith he knew. She loved him, she wanted to change her whole life course to go with him to Ethiopia. She could have—no, *would have*—just said, "The hell with it all, let's elope."

* * *

When Sue Peters came out the front door of the Longstreet house, Detective Bob Gibbs was leaning against her car with his arms folded. She could tell he was trying to look fierce, but he couldn't hide the delight in his eyes. He had pulled his hat down low and turned the collar of his parka up over his ears, but even so he looked frozen. Adorably so.

That was the trouble with Bob. She wanted to be mad at him for checking up on her and not believing she could do anything by herself. For hovering like a mom on the first day of kindergarten.

She'd even gone so far as to wonder, during their pricklier moments, if he really wanted her to get well. But then she'd see his goofy face at moments like this one, and she knew he just plain loved her and was terrified to let her out of his sight. Terrified she'd discover a life without him, or terrified someone would jump out of a dark alley and beat her up again, this time for good.

She knew he was watching her as she negotiated the slippery path to the road. Watching for a limp or a slight stumble that would betray her fatigue. She drew herself rigidly upright and summoned every ounce of will to force her muscles to obey. The truth was, she was dead on her feet. She'd felt it during the interview, when she could barely persuade her fingers to write and her brain to form words. She'd been at work more than seven hours now, much of it in the field. She'd forgotten lunch and had had no time for a ten-minute power nap to refresh her.

She smiled up at him as he welcomed her into his arms. "You weren't supposed to do this," he said.

Ignoring his attempt to look fierce, she punched him playfully. "We have a lead."

He kissed her. She loved his kisses. They weren't very smooth, but they were all quivery with passion he didn't know what to do with. Who needed slick when you had real?

"You're bad," he whispered when they came up for air. He headed towards his own car, an identical beige Impala parked behind hers. "You can tell me all about it while I drive you home."

"No, you don't. What about my car?" She wasn't sure she even had the strength to turn the key, but he wasn't to know that. "What about the Kennedys? We have to ask them about Montreal. And about the ATM."

He opened his passenger door. "Someone can pick up your car. And I'll handle the Kennedys."

She sank into the seat, finally letting her muscles go and feeling the last vestige of energy drain from them. She opened one eye. "Only if you let me come with you, so I can tell you what questions to ask."

"But Inspector Green—"

"Inspector Green knows. And he didn't exactly say no, did he."

He sighed as he navigated the snowy street, and after a while he glanced over at her. "You learned something useful?"

She smiled inwardly. She felt too tired to make sense of the nagging suspicion in her brain, but there *was* something... If the person I loved went missing, she thought, I'd be excited to learn about the trip to Montreal. It signalled hope, a possibility that the person had gone off on some secret quest. Why had Brandon seemed determined to downplay the importance of the whole thing?

The Kennedys displayed no such ambivalence. Norah Kennedy came alive as soon as the Montreal trip was mentioned. For the first time, Sue Peters saw a hint of warmth in the woman's haggard face.

"That means she's alive!" she exclaimed. "Maybe she realized it would never work if she married into that family. Brandon's a lovely boy, I'm not saying he's not, but she'd be taking on that mother too. He's all she's got and don't think she wants to share him, no matter what she says. I bet she said something to Meredith to scare her off."

"Like what?" Sue leaned forward. She'd promised Gibbsie he could do the interview while she kept quiet and observed reactions. It had been either that or he'd take her home, and she'd been too wiped out to argue. But a short snooze in the car on the way over had revived her, and she couldn't restrain herself.

Norah's gaze flicked from Gibbs to Sue, probably trying to figure out who was running the show. She shrugged. "Maybe she sent Meredith to talk to that great-uncle. Lives all alone in a big house on the Circle with a creepy servant with a black belt in karate. He's sitting on the Longstreet family fortune, and he's scared off more than a few kids who wanted to marry into it."

Gibbs scribbled in his notebook at top speed so he could get back in the conversation. "Has anyone contacted him about your daughter's disappearance?"

"That would be up to Elena. Not too many people are on speaking terms with the old goat."

"Meredith's not going to be scared off by a crazy old man," the father said. He'd been fidgeting, building up a head of steam. "No matter how nasty he is. Brandon's the one she's marrying."

His wife swung on him. "Well then, maybe the old man threatened to disinherit Brandon and the boy got cold feet. That would be like our Meredith, to go charging in to set the old man right."

"Norah, Brandon would never do that. These are modern kids out to save the world, for Pete's sake."

Believing love conquers all, Sue thought, suddenly aware of the nagging twinge in her shoulder that was held together by pins. "What about her grandmother?" she asked.

Norah's eyes widened. She shot her husband a look of alarm. "What about her?"

"Could Meredith have gone to see her?"

"Unlikely. My mother's in a home. Most of the time she doesn't even recognize Meredith. Even me she confuses with her sister, who's been dead twenty years."

"But she might still have gone to see her. Maybe she felt a duty. Were they close while she was growing up?"

"I've told Meredith not to go. Mom gets agitated and upset at the sight of her because she thinks she's a stranger out to trick her with lies. It's not worth it to get the poor old lady upset."

That didn't mean anything, Sue decided. Meredith might have paid a secret visit despite her mother's wishes. Weddings could make people act all mushy inside. If the visit had gone badly, it would explain Meredith's mood on her return. "Maybe we should call the nursing home, just to doublecheck."

"I did," the father said. Seeing the flicker of surprise on Norah's face, he mustered a sheepish smile. "I was trying to spare you, dear. They didn't think anyone's been to see her in a month."

"We'd like to follow up anyway," Sue said.

Norah flushed. "I don't want my mother upset."

"How will speaking to the nurses upset your mother?"

"Because the nurses will ask her, remind her, maybe even tell her that Meredith is missing!"

Sue felt Gibbs's hand on her arm. He leaned forward, an envelope in his hand. "Can you describe M-Meredith's winter clothing? Her coat, gloves, hat?"

Norah blinked, the flush slowly receding from her face. "Why? We've already told you people that. Over and over."

"All the same. To s-save me having to search all the notes."

Norah described the red suede jacket and leather boots. "I don't know what kind of hat she might be wearing. She doesn't like hats." Hope crept into her face. "Has someone seen her?"

"Does her coat have a hood?"

The hope grew. "Yes. Why?"

Gibbs withdrew two photos from the envelope. Sue guessed they were probably the best images he was able to glean from the shadowy ATM video. "Do you recognize this person?"

The photos trembled slightly at the edges in Reg's hand as he and Norah bent over them. The silence was broken only by their breathing. Slowly Sue saw their hope fade, until finally Norah shook her head. She looked questioningly at her husband. "Do you think it's her?"

"Do y-you recognize any of the clothing?" Gibbs pressed when Reg shrugged.

"No. She doesn't have a parka like that. But—" Norah raised her head. "She could have bought one, right? I mean, if she is trying to hide? She'd know everyone would be on the lookout for a red suede jacket. It's pretty distinctive. Whereas this parka—it could be anybody in there! Where was it taken? When!"

Gibbs slipped the photos back into the envelope. He didn't answer for a moment, and Sue knew he was trying to decide how much to reveal. The first rule in crime detection was always to look first at those nearest and dearest. Were these just desperate parents entitled to the latest information on their missing daughter's investigation, or were they two more on the growing list of suspects in her disappearance?

"Just following up every lead, Mrs. Kennedy," he said, unfolding his tall, lanky body from the chair. "We'll keep you posted if anything comes of it."

EIGHT

Frankie Robitaille leaned on his shovel and wiped sweat from his face. He was starving and remembered that he'd left his plate of bacon and eggs barely touched on the coffee table in his TV room. He had dug half the length of the snowbank where the dog had been pawing but still hadn't turned up anything. He was surprised the police hadn't shown up yet. Maybe they were too busy with the search to respond to a suspicious lady complaining about a stranger on her fancy street.

After catching his breath, he plunged his shovel into the next chunk of snow, dreading every new move. Dreading the idea of a young woman freezing to death on a dark, cold night, dreading the idea that he might have hit her, knocked her out and left her to die. Dreading the trouble he'd be in. Nightmare scenarios flashed through his mind. Charges of speeding and reckless endangerment, leaving the scene of an accident, vehicular manslaughter, what the hell else? His livelihood, his licence, his kids and mortgage...all gone.

Just when he was beginning to hope there was nothing, he hit something soft and solid. He yanked his shovel away, his heart rate spiking. Cautiously he began to explore the area with the tip of the shovel, scraping away the snow from the object that emerged. Something red. Leather. He swallowed and fell to his knees, pawing with his gloved hands to uncover the object. Not a body, not an arm. He worked it free and pulled out a frozen, misshapen lump that he finally identified as a woman's purse. The zipper was half open and the contents scattered in the snow. He tugged at the frozen zipper to open it the rest of the way and looked inside. It was nearly empty. No wallet, no cards, nothing to show who it belonged to.

He gathered up the keys, scraps of paper, lipstick and breath mints and stuffed them back into the purse. He was almost afraid to dig further. Maybe this flash of red was all he'd seen. Maybe it was a discarded purse that had nothing to do with the missing woman.

But he remembered the jolt to his steering wheel and the dog pawing excitedly. This red purse, big as it was, would not have caused that. Reluctantly he picked up his shovel and began another careful probe. Ten feet farther on, he encountered more resistance. This time, as he cleared away the snow, a hand appeared.

Bare, waxy white, and frozen stiff.

He sank down in the snow, sick at heart. Pulled out his cell phone and with tremulous fingers, punched 911. He had just pressed the final digit when he snapped the cell phone shut and dropped it from his nerveless fingers into the snow. He clutched his head in his hands, hyperventilating. Glanced up and down the street. No sign of the cops, nor the dog lady.

He snatched up his phone and shovel and raced back to his truck, his large work boots scrabbling on the ice. He had to get out of here. To use his own cell phone and make himself known to the police was to invite the ruin of his life. He could just as easily call from a pay phone and leave an anonymous tip.

He flung himself into the cab of the truck, revved it to life and spun its wheels in a U-turn back towards Beechwood Avenue. But just around the corner, he stomped on the brake. He had probably left a dozen footprints and tire tracks the cops could trace, and who knows how many eyes had been watching him through the fancy curtains of those houses? Watched him pick the spot and start to shovel. If the cops ID'ed him, it would look even worse for him if he fled the scene a second time. If the dog lady had called the cops, he might even meet them on the road out, giving them a perfect make on his truck.

He started the truck again and headed deeper into Rockcliffe Park. He would take a roundabout route out so that he'd be less likely to meet the cops, and if anyone noticed a black pick-up leaving the area, it would be from a different direction altogether than the suspicious black truck noticed at the scene. He drove through the maze of streets, trying to act slow and calm like a workman going to a routine job site.

By the time he reached Beechwood, he had a plan. He parked the truck in the middle of the grocery superstore parking lot and headed in through the automatic doors. Inside, he wandered up and down one aisle, grabbed a bag of chips and a chocolate bar and went through the cash before exiting the store farther down and walking away from his truck. He tucked the grocery bag in his pocket and kept a sharp eye open for surveillance cameras, but he spotted none. He only had to walk to the corner to find a pay phone outside a gas station. No cameras there either. Maybe they were hidden or miniature, but he could only hope.

Holding the phone with one leather glove, he took the other off and wrapped it around the mouthpiece. Using his scarf over his fingertip, he punched in 911. When the operator came on, he spilled out the first line of his carefully rehearsed speech without even having to fake the tremor in his voice.

"There's a body! I think I found a body!"

"What's your name, sir?"

"In Rockcliffe, on Maple Lane. Hurry!"

He heard some clicking and then, "Can you tell me exactly what you found, sir?"

"In the snow! Oh God, I'm going to be sick!" he gasped and slammed down the phone. He almost was, had to swallow back bile as he shoved his hands into his pockets and strode purposefully away from the phone. He knew 911 would already have located the pay phone and dispatched a cruiser. He needed to be nowhere in sight when it arrived, but he couldn't afford to draw attention to himself by running.

He ducked back behind the gas station to the far edge of the grocery parking lot. Heading back into the store, he retraced his steps and re-emerged near his truck with his grocery bag back in plain view. He was into his truck and already sitting at the light two blocks up by the time the first cruiser came screaming down the Vanier Parkway with its blue and red lights flashing.

He drove on. Figured if they did manage to connect him to the scene, he could say he'd gone to the nearest pay phone to report it because his cell phone was dead, and he'd been too shaken up to stick around.

*   *   *

The call came in to the Incident Command Centre at 3:54 p.m., fifteen minutes after Frankie Robitaille's initial 911 call. The first responders had confirmed the sighting of a frozen human hand in a snowbank, which at first glance appeared to be female, but since the body had been only partially excavated, they were requesting direction.

Green's heart sank. Not matter how much you steeled yourself for such an outcome, you always hoped. He forced himself to think through his sorrow. Partially excavated, he wondered. By whom, and why?

Still on the phone, he headed down the hall towards his office. "Are there footprints in the vicinity?"

"Yes, sir," said the patrolman, whose voice had cracked slightly. He sounded young. Probably his first body. "I didn't disturb them."

"Good work," Green said. "Secure the whole area, protect the footprints, and look for more arriving and leaving the scene. Teams are on their way."

"Should—should I contact the coroner, sir?"

Green had already reached his office and was pulling on his jacket, wedging the phone against his shoulder. At this point there was no indication the death was suspicious—indeed, hypothermia was the most likely cause—but the fact that someone had deliberately dug it up, on an obscure side street nowhere near Meredith's usual locations, raised a red flag. He wanted the expertise of a forensic pathologist rather than the routine coroner.

"I'll call Dr. MacPhail and Ident," he told the patrolman. "Your main concern is to secure that scene."

He rode with the duty inspector, and on the drive over, they listened to the 911 tape. Dispatch had identified the origin as a pay phone on Beechwood Avenue, the nearest main street to the scene and likely the nearest pay phone. It was a male caller who spoke English with no discernible accent, and to Green's practised ear, he sounded shaken up. But the muffled tone suggested he was also trying to disguise his voice. Another red flag. From the passenger seat of the inspector's cruiser, Green radioed the dispatcher again.

"Send a unit to secure that pay phone until an Ident team can check it out." Half an hour had passed since the call, but with any luck there might still be fingerprints. Not too many people used pay phones any more.

By the time they arrived at Maple Lane, a crowd of about twenty had gathered around an area halfway up the block. Two police cruisers were parked diagonally to block access to the spot, and yellow tape had been strung in a large semi-circle in the road. Onlookers craned their necks and several people were taking pictures with their cell phones, dragging voyeurism down to new depths in Green's opinion. No sign yet of the media, but they'd soon join the voyeurs.

He left the duty inspector to manage the crowd and ignored the barrage of questions as he pushed through. The hand looked unreal, reaching up through the snow like a prop in a bad Halloween horror flick. It was a left hand, small and delicate with its nails painted a metallic turquoise that looked garish against the waxy white skin. He felt a twinge of intrigue. Meredith Kennedy was reportedly wearing a large diamond engagement ring. This hand had no rings, nor any circular marks on the skin to suggest where a ring used to be.

He stayed well back, respecting the integrity of the crime scene while he studied the snow. It bore the deep, straight cuts of a shovel in a line all the way along the bank, as if someone had been systematically searching. Numerous overlapping boot prints were visible in the snow, large and deeply treaded like a man's work boot. Each was marked with an Ident number.

"There's a purse too, sir," said the young patrolman, pointing to a red object about ten feet away. He sounded in control now, excited by his role in the drama.

"Did you search it?"

"Yes, sir, there was no ID." The patrolman looked alarmed, as if realizing he'd overstepped. "But I put it back where it was."

The purse lay on top of the snowbank. The snow beneath it was undisturbed, but beside it was a large hole scored with glove marks as if someone had been digging through the snow.

The duty inspector joined him. "What do you think?"

"I think our mystery man found the purse first, checked it, tossed it aside and then began to search the snowbank for the body. Maybe he spotted the purse half buried and thought he'd check it out."

"While he was walking down the street?"

Green raised his head to scan the neighbouring houses. By Rockcliffe standards, they were modest, but security would still be paramount. "Get someone to check for surveillance cameras and photograph this crowd—"

"He wasn't walking," came a voice at his elbow. He turned in surprise to see a petite woman in a ski jacket and jeans. Her face was a web of wrinkles, her blue eyes grim. "He drove a black pick-up truck."

"Licence plate?"

She shook her head. "He parked it near the corner. I knew he was up to no good, walking along the snowbank as if he were searching for something. He told me he thought he'd hit a sled or a garbage bin during the storm a few nights ago. I almost called the police." Her lips tightened. "I wish I had."

"Would you describe the man for us?"

The woman gave a surprisingly vivid description of a workman in his mid-forties, tall and fit with leathery skin that suggested a lifetime in the sun. But he had three days' growth and baggy eyes which hinted at recent stress. "A working man, uneducated and probably of French origin."

Green smiled. The perfect witness. Before he could ask how

she could be so certain, she smiled grimly. "I'm an artist. It's my job to see behind the face. I can draw him if you like."

Green took her name and address before sending her off to do just that. He beckoned to a patrol officer who had just arrived. By now, two more cruisers had shown up, along with the Ident van, and Green could see Dr. Alexander MacPhail's black van rounding the corner. He hastily sent the young patrol down to the corner to look for truck tire tracks before anyone flattened them.

MacPhail arrived with his usual drama—booming voice, large boots, white bunny suit and kit of macabre tools for taking temperatures and samples. Ident produced supplies for gridding, excavating and sifting the snow, then erected a tent over the snowbank, mercifully shielding the scene from view. By now the audience had swelled to several dozen, and the media cameras were snapping. Green cursed to himself. In these days of instant communication, the discovery of the body would be up on Twitter and on the twenty-four hour news channels within minutes. The Kennedys and the Longstreets had to be warned.

Doyle seemed to read his mind. "I'll get a unit over to the Kennedys right away."

"I'll send my man Gibbs over with a photo of the purse. As for Brandon Longstreet—"

"That's easy. He lives near here." He consulted his phone, which showed a GPS on its screen. "Just a couple of blocks farther up."

Green's head shot up. If this DOA was Meredith, maybe that's why she was here on this street. She didn't have a car, so she might have got off the bus on Beechwood and cut through here. Had she been on her way to her fiancé's house, or had she just left?

And what did a man in a black pick-up truck who claimed he'd hit a kid's sled have to do with it?

It would be at least an hour before MacPhail and his crew would have news for him. Meanwhile, he'd never met the formidable Elena Longstreet. Now might be the time.

As a poor kid growing up across the Rideau River in Lowertown, Green had concluded long ago that the Village of Rockcliffe Park had been designed to keep the riff raff out. Or at least to get them so thoroughly lost in the higgle piggle of streets that they escaped at the first exit they came across. There was not a vinyl-sided cube to be seen. Massive gabled mansions of stone or brick confronted him at every turn, some behind wrought-iron gates and others at the end of circular drives. Expecting to get lost at least twice en route, he was surprised to find the house exactly where Doyle said it was. One block up and one over—an easy walk up from Beechwood along the road where the victim had been found.

Elena Longstreet's house looked like a dwarf among Goliaths, a one-and-a-half storey brown brick home that had once probably been the gatehouse for a lumber baron's estate. Someone had done a good job of gentrifying it, adding leaded pane windows, intricate black trim and a front door of polished honey oak. Curtains were drawn tightly over the windows to keep prying eyes from seeing inside. A black ornamental fence high enough to discourage intruders surrounded the property, and a two-car garage was partially hidden behind the house. The one jarring note in the tightly sealed façade was the garage door, which gaped open to reveal an empty interior.

Green rang the doorbell and listened to the elegant chimes echo through the house. Nothing. He peered through the small diamond-shaped lead window in the door. The inside vestibule door was wide open, offering him a glimpse of glass-fronted bookcases and terra cotta tiles in the main hall. He rang again. Still no answer, but this time he spotted something familiar hanging from the old-fashioned coat tree standing in the corner of the vestibule. It was a long woollen scarf in an exquisite and distinctive grey cashmere. As he rifled through the images in his memory, his heart began to pound. He had seen that scarf before.

Around the neck of Superintendent Adam Jules.

NINE

When Detective Peters had dropped her bombshell about Meredith's visit to Montreal, Brandon Longstreet's mind had nearly reeled out of control. He had maintained his composure only long enough to see the detective out of the house before he raced upstairs to access his computer.

In passing, he thought of phoning Reg and Norah but dismissed the idea. If hugs and kisses were any indication, Meredith loved her family to pieces, but she didn't confide in them. She hadn't since she was a little girl, because their comfortable, traditional outlook on the world did not welcome her questions or her doubts. Norah still baked pies for the St. Basil parish Christmas bake sale, for God's sake. They didn't disapprove of her wanderlust, exactly, just didn't understand it.

Meredith felt the same estrangement from her cousin Wayne, especially since he married and moved to a four thousand square-foot McMansion in Kanata. Meredith felt an obligation—no, a passion—to save the poor and dispossessed, whereas Wayne played golf with his corporate clients and dropped four thousand dollars on season tickets to the Ottawa Senators. Despite all his business savvy, he didn't have a tenth of Meredith's vision.

Tears blurred Brandon's eyes briefly as he thought of her. A pearl among stones, a woman with a love that encompassed not just him but all humanity and the planet itself. What had she been doing in Montreal? Why had she kept it secret, and what had she discovered there that so altered her course?

Once on the computer, he went straight to Meredith's Facebook page and scoured her recent entries, as well as the comments of others, for details that she might have revealed of her trip. There was not a single mention. Meredith hadn't posted much in recent weeks, and then mostly thank-yous for the good wishes posted by her friends. She had over nine hundred friends. Brandon did a quick search of their locations and found dozens from Montreal. He recognized a couple of distant cousins but most friends were probably Haitians she'd met last year. The limited profiles he could access gave him no further clues. But Facebook friends could have only the most tenuous connections, from a mutual interest in a political cause to shared work ties. None of her Montreal friends had posted on her page in recent weeks.

Brandon sat back in frustration. The trail was cold. What had she been up to, and of all her friends and family, who was the most likely to know?

Reluctantly, unwillingly, his mind kept coming back to his own mother and to the conversation he had overheard earlier that day. What did she know, and what was she determined to keep from him? Did it have something to do with Meredith?

He was no stranger to relationships, but he had never before sensed reluctance on his mother's part. He'd assumed it was because the relationship had moved so fast, from their first meeting eight months ago to the engagement six months later and a quick wedding planned over Christmas. A wedding with none of the extravagant planning and traditional trappings that the mother of an only child might want.

He'd also wondered whether she blamed Meredith for his sudden passion for overseas work. Until last February, he had

99

been pursuing family medicine at the hospital with no thoughts beyond finding a good practice once he'd qualified, but then he'd attended an information session at the Ottawa Hospital about relief work in Haiti. Speakers from the International Red Cross, CARE Canada, the Ministry of Immigration, and Doctors Without Borders had shared stories of tragedy, inspiration and need. There had been hundreds in the audience and at least a dozen speakers, but it was Meredith's passion that caught his eye. She had been sent to Haiti by Immigration to help reunite Haitian Canadians with orphaned island relatives who had lost everything, including identity papers, beneath the rubble. She was supposed to stay a week but had stayed six.

"We live a life of comfort and security most of the world cannot even dream of," she'd said. "I can't sit at Starbucks sipping my low-fat, double shot latte and texting my friends while in Haiti children sit all day waiting for a single drink of water. If I have to carry that water myself, I will. I am going back."

Normally he was partial to tall women with long, dark hair and sexy brown eyes. Meredith was a petite woman with an impish face and red hair. She wrinkled up her nose when she was confused, and her blue eyes crinkled shut when she laughed. But that evening, watching her on stage, passionate, angry, even tearful as she talked about her moment of revelation, he'd found her irresistible.

Intrigued, he'd looked her up on Facebook and found out to his astonishment that not only did they share an idealism and commitment to humanity, but their favourite music was Beethoven's Ninth, and their favourite book was *Crime and Punishment*. It felt like destiny. They corresponded sporadically through Facebook while she was back in Haiti and he was completing his residency, and the sense of destiny grew. She laughed at his jokes and finished thoughts he didn't even know he had.

Three months later, when she bounced into the coffee shop for their first real meeting, late as always, he felt he'd known her forever.

They had talked without stopping for four hours, going through three cups of coffee and half a dozen scones. Eager to share their thoughts and explore their common ground, they had jumped from topic to topic, sampling their lives. Movies, university courses, politics, music, favourite foods, childhood fears and dreams. The thrill of discovery grew. By the end, when he took her small hand in his, he knew he'd found his kindred soul.

Somehow his mother had been peculiar about this relationship almost from the first time she'd met Meredith. Initially she'd seemed to admire Meredith's idealism as much as he did, but something had caused her to withdraw. Was it the whirlwind wedding or their plan to work overseas?

Or did it have to do with Montreal?

On impulse, Brandon shut off his computer and hurried downstairs to snatch his jacket off the coat tree. Juggling gloves and scarf, he locked the house and followed the well-shovelled path to the garage. The door glided silently open to reveal a large concrete room lined with neat rows of shelving and hooks. Skis and hockey sticks were propped against the walls, and bicycles, kayaks and a canoe hung from the rafters. His Toyota Prius sat in its usual spot.

Normally he cycled or took the bus to the hospital. Even if parking and traffic congestion hadn't been appalling, he would have made the greener choice out of principle. This time, however, he revved the car out of the garage without a qualm.

* * *

"Mom!" he whispered, leaning in close. "We need to talk."

His mother barely reacted, telling in itself, he thought. He'd gone downtown only to learn that she was still in court, and had charged straight up the broad stone steps of the Ottawa courthouse and into the courtroom without a moment's hesitation.

The lawyer for the Crown was on his feet, surrounded by a stack of banker's boxes and thick sheaves of notes. He sifted through these as he droned on at the judge, who looked half asleep. Not so Elena Longstreet. She sat ramrod straight, her sleek silver hair glinting in the harsh court light and her expression one of a cat watching a songbird. When Brandon slipped into the chair behind her and whispered in her ear, she didn't move. A faint furrow between her eyes was the only hint of consternation. Or disapproval.

"Brandon, we recess in fifteen minutes," she whispered back, her lips barely moving.

"What do you know about Meredith's disappearance?" He was aware of the judge waking up and blinking at them in confusion. Heads turned at the Crown counsel table, and even his mother stiffened.

"Fifteen minutes!"

"Is there a problem, Mrs. Longstreet?" the judge asked, almost hopefully.

His mother rose, radiating dignity and respect. Only Brandon would have known that she was furious. "Begging your lordship's indulgence, if the court would grant me a five-minute recess—"

"Granted." The judge was already on his feet, his black robe flapping behind him as he charged towards his chambers. The half-dozen observers, most of whom appeared to be lawyers, descended into chatter. Elena swung on Brandon.

"I realize the stress you've been under, but surely this can wait—"

Irrational anger swept through him at her patronizing tone, as if she knew so much more about life than he did. She was always protecting him when he least wanted or needed it. *"He mustn't know!"* As if he were a fragile shell.

"Mother, what are you hiding from me? About Meredith and Montreal!"

For the briefest instant, she recoiled as if slapped. No amount of self-discipline could prevent the shock that raced across her face. But she recovered well, restoring a perfect mask of puzzlement and curiosity to her fine features.

"Montreal? Who said anything about Montreal?"

"Did you know Meredith went to Montreal?"

Elena looked mystified. "Why would she go to Montreal?"

"That's what I'm asking you. I overheard you talking to someone this morning, downstairs."

She sat very still. Too still. Her eyes searched his. She's trying to remember what she said, he realized with a jolt. To remember how much she gave away. He remained quiet, hoping she'd assume too much. However, she must have read the bluff in his eyes, for she shrugged.

"Nothing relevant, I assure you. I'm trying to take some of the burden of this off you, so I've been making some inquiries through my own contacts. So far they've proved fruitless."

"But you found out something! You said 'He mustn't know!' What—"

His mother started and reached beneath her court gown into her jacket pocket. She extracted her Blackberry, which hummed in her hand, and glanced at the screen. For an instant her features froze, and Brandon thought she even paled.

"I should take this," she said, rising and turning away from him.

Fear surged through him again as he watched her face. Her lips tightened and she spoke just three words, "No...thank you," before clicking the phone off. She turned back to the table and leaned on it as if she were drawing strength.

"This may mean nothing," she began slowly.

He didn't breathe.

"They've discovered a woman's body."

"Where?"

"Two blocks from our house. But they don't yet know..."

He heard no more, because he was out the door.

*   *   *

Dusk was descending as Green headed back out to the far east end for the second time that day. Jules was not answering his calls, and this time the gloves were off. Jules was an officer sworn to uphold the law, and he damn well would. At the very least, the cashmere scarf cried out for explanation.

Mercifully the Queensway was dry, but the afternoon rush hour clogged all the lanes as far as he could see. Green flicked on the emergency flashers of his staff car and enjoyed the rush of adrenaline as he streaked along the bus lane past the endless stream of brake lights disappearing into the twilight.

He had stopped briefly at the excavation site to check for updates, but progress had been slow. MacPhail, apparently suspicious of the body's appearance, was determined that not a molecule of trace evidence would be lost in the excavation process and that the body's position would not be altered. The whole scene was shrouded in a white tent through which spotlights glowed eerily. No one else, including Green, was allowed inside in order to avoid inadvertent contamination, but

Lyle Cunningham, the Identification officer, showed him some preliminary photos of the woman's bare hands and stocking feet protruding upwards from deep inside the snowbank.

"What do you think, Lyle?" Green had asked as they hunched over the laptop screen in the Ident van. "Looks like she was buried that way by a snowplow."

Cunningham pursed his lips in disapproval. Conjecture was not in his repertoire of tricks. He preferred to gather facts, present them coherently and let them speak for themselves. In the witness box, it was a laudable stance, but in the early stages of an investigation, it was a pain in the ass. Thorough crime scene analysis could take weeks, during which potential witnesses and criminals slipped through their fingers.

"Give us three or four hours, and maybe we can confirm that," Cunningham said.

Green did a quick calculation. "How about two." As he spoke he was aware of the media pressing forward and of Inspector Doyle handing them empty platitudes to fill their sound bites on the six o'clock news. Media conjecture would be way ahead of Cunningham on this one.

Two hours should take him to and from the Colonies with time to spare, but even with the emergency lights, it was past four p.m. when he arrived at the east end station. Jules's office door was closed, and he caught Jules's clerk just pulling on her coat to head home. She flinched at the sight of him. Mrs. Capstick was a middle-aged woman who'd worked for the police service for twenty years. In that time she had juggled marriage to a tactical unit sergeant and two daughters who played competitive ringuette, so she did not disturb easily. Perhaps she knows I'm angry, Green thought, and with reason.

"He's not in," she pre-empted before he could speak.

"Where is he?"

"I don't know." She frowned. "He went out this morning shortly after you left, and he hasn't been back."

"What did he say when he left?"

"That he had a meeting in town." She hesitated, and Green sensed she wanted to say more but had been well trained to respect her boss's obsession with privacy. Jules would be a fair and kind employer but uncompromising in his expectations.

"What was the meeting?"

"He hadn't marked it down. I didn't ask." She locked her drawer.

"I'm worried," Green said, hoping to draw out her own worry. "Something seems to be wrong."

She said nothing but buttoned her coat as if to signal the conversation was over.

He drew closer. "Judy, did he phone you at all today?"

She blinked her eyes rapidly. Plunked her purse down as if making a decision. "Yes, just to tell me to cancel his appointments until further notice, without a word of explanation. Two meetings here today and a speech at the local high school. More tomorrow if he doesn't show up."

"That's not like him."

"No, it's not. But this week..." She paused, fighting her loyalty. "He has really not been himself. Perhaps he talked to the deputy chief and asked for some time off. In the five years I've worked for him, Superintendent Jules has never asked for personal time. But we never know, do we, what's really going on with him."

Green murmured agreement, wondering whether to ask the deputy chief what he knew. But he suspected he'd meet the stone wall of confidentiality, and rightly so. He waited until Mrs. Capstick had gone into the elevator then tried Jules's office door.

It was locked. Of course it was locked. He tried the clerk's desk drawers, hoping to find keys, but they too were locked.

A metaphor for Jules himself.

En route back to the accident scene, Green phoned the Major Crimes Unit and snagged Gibbs just returning from the Kennedy home.

"How did the parents take the news?" Green asked.

"Upset." Green could hear the distress in Gibbs's voice. Delivering bad news to family members was never a cop's favourite job. "But they don't really believe it's M-Meredith. Especially Mrs. Kennedy. She didn't recognize the photo of the purse."

"MacPhail should have more details for us in a couple of hours. Formal ID probably tomorrow morning at the morgue."

"You want me to take them there, s-sir?" The distress was stronger now.

"If it comes to that, yes, Bob. But meanwhile I've got another assignment for you." Green explained about the black pick-up truck and the stranger searching in the snow. "It's a hunch. Find out the names of the snowplow operators assigned to that area in the past three days. Find out the exact times they plowed that street and what vehicles are registered to their names."

There was silence on the line, then, "Tonight, sir?"

Green suppressed his impatience. As an investigator, he'd put in twenty-four hour days as long as there were leads to follow, and it had cost him in relationships and in subordinates. His best friend, Brian Sullivan, was on indefinite sick leave because he'd pushed him to do one last thing before he booked off for the day. Green hated having to slow down to allow for the demands of other people's lives, but since Sullivan's health crisis, Green had been trying to turn over a new leaf. He knew Bob Gibbs was anxious to get home to Sue's waiting arms.

"Whenever you can get to it is fine, Bob."

He disconnected as he was rounding the corner onto Maple Lane. The tent glowed in the deepening darkness, and the street was still jammed with media and police vehicles. Knots of police officers stood around on guard, but most of the curiosity seekers had drifted away. The temperature had dipped several degrees since sundown, and frosty breath danced in the lights that blazed on the scene.

Green spotted two civilians standing in the middle of the road arguing with Inspector Doyle. He didn't recognize the tall, slim young man dressed in a battered bomber jacket, but the woman's silver hair and regal bearing stirred a long-forgotten memory. Elena Longstreet.

He pulled the staff car to a hasty stop behind a cruiser and jumped out. As he approached, Elena turned on him. She was as striking as ever, but pale in the garish light. Her eyes glittered.

"Are you in charge here?"

"I'm Inspector Michael Green, Mrs. Longstreet." He extended his hand. "I was looking for you earlier."

She blinked, and her rage evaporated like a dramatic prop. She frowned at him shrewdly. "Well, Inspector Green, I would like some information on—"

"Is it Meredith?" the young man burst in. He looked even ghostlier than his mother.

"I don't know yet," Green said. "Are you her fiancé, Dr. Long-street?"

He didn't seem to hear. "How can you not know? Just look at her!"

Green eyed him thoughtfully. The man was gaunt and desperate, and his whole body shook with fear and cold. Green suspected he hadn't eaten or slept in days. He turned to Doyle.

"Why don't they warm up in your car while—"

"I don't want to warm up in the car! I want to see her!"

Green nodded. "Let me see what I can find out. Meanwhile, you could both use warmth and a cup of hot tea."

"Don't patronize me!"

Elena placed a slim gloved hand on her son's arm. "Brandon, the officer is right. Let's see what he can find out."

With a nod towards Doyle, Green turned to head towards the tent. At the edge of the cordon he spoke to the log officer. "Can you get Cunningham out here?"

"Want a peek, Mike?" came Cunningham's shout from inside the tent. "Just watch your feet."

After signing in, Green ducked under the yellow tape and stepped carefully on the white paper squares laid down to make a path. Inside the tent, two Ident officers were bent over the snow, digging with trowels. On the ground beside them sat an evidence bin containing a purse, a boot, and a red woollen beret, each in its own plastic bag. Other bags contained assorted small items. Green distinguished a lipstick, keys, scraps of paper, a map, a pack of Dentine and two ballpoint pens, probably all from the purse.

Beside the bin, a grotesque shape was beginning to emerge from the snow. The woman was lying on her back with her arms and legs flung up in the air and her neck twisted to one side. One arm was bent in the middle as if broken, and her coat was torn. Her hair, matted dark red with blood, was splayed out over her face, obscuring her features. MacPhail was easing the hair away from the wound at her temple, uncovering eyes opaque with horror.

Green backed away from the sight. He had always hated that first instant when he stared down death. Felt the ugliness and horror of that last moment of life. He turned instead and gestured to the bin.

"Can I show the purse and hat to the family?"

MacPhail didn't even look up. "Be my guest."

Green lifted both evidence bags gingerly and retraced his steps. As he ducked back under the tape, Brandon Longstreet flung open Doyle's car door and came across the street. He took one look at the bags.

"That's not her purse. Nor her hat. I've never seen either before."

"Could she have changed—"

"No, it's not even her style!" He shoved Green aside and rushed forward, ducking under the tape before anyone could stop him. He froze at the entrance to the tent, staring.

"That's not her! It's not her!" He teetered, turned bloodless, and began to laugh.

TEN

Green arrived home at seven thirty to find Hannah's backpack on the floor by the front door, stuffed to overflowing. The house was warm, humid and redolent of garlic and basil. He followed the sound of laughter into the kitchen, where a pot of pasta bubbled on the stove. The two women in his life were sharing a bottle of Chianti while they chopped peppers and tomatoes into a salad bowl. From their flushed cheeks, he judged they were well ahead of him, so he kissed them both and poured himself a glass.

"What's the occasion?"

"My last night before the descent into hell," his daughter said.

He paused to consider the evidence. Hannah's favourite meal and her backpack by the door. "You've booked a ticket to Vancouver."

"The great detective scores again," Hannah said. "So don't get too cosy with that wine. My flight's at ten p.m."

Sharon had been eyeing him with concern. As she handed him a green pepper slice, she touched his arm. "You look tired."

"It's been quite a day." He didn't want to talk about Jules's vanishing act or the ongoing mystery of the poor dead Jane Doe. He wanted to retreat to the sanctity of his cave, draw his family close and revel in their company for the short time until Hannah left. But at that moment Tony came bounding in with his usual shriek.

111

"Daddy!" His eyes were shining. "You were on TV! Where they found that body! Is that Meredith Kennedy, Daddy? Did they find her?"

Green hugged him, but a little pain crept into the warmth that he always felt when he held his son. Even here, in his kitchen with the pesto pasta cooking and the Chianti flowing, he could not escape. The fate of Meredith Kennedy was on everyone's mind, even his five-year-old son's.

"It doesn't look like it, buddy," he replied.

"It's not?" It was Hannah who spoke, half rising from her chair in surprise.

He shook his head. "This woman is older. We're working on identifying her, but it looks unrelated."

"But where's Meredith?" Tony persisted.

"I don't know, son. It's still a mystery. We'll just have to keep looking for her. Now..." He set down his wine glass. "I'm going upstairs to wash up and then you and I are going to set the table!"

In his bedroom, he stripped off his work clothes and turned on the shower as hot as he could bear, trying to scrub the encounter with death from his mind. He knew he wouldn't succeed but as always, he had to try. When he emerged from the bathroom, he pulled on a clean sweatshirt and jeans, and was just combing his damp hair when he heard a soft tap at the bedroom door. He opened it to find Hannah leaning on the doorframe. She averted her gaze.

"You got a minute? I mean, before the Energizer bunny blows in here?"

Green didn't laugh, although the image was apt. There was very little private talk when Tony was awake. He stepped aside to let her pass. She perched on the edge of the bed and plucked dog hairs from the duvet.

"I should have told you about this ages ago."

His heart spiked as his fears ran wild. She was never coming back, she'd applied to the University of British Columbia... He held his tongue with an effort.

"I kept thinking, well, I don't really know anything, it's not like I saw where she was going. You must have found out more details since—"

"What are you talking about, sweetheart?"

"I think I saw Meredith Kennedy. No, I know I—"

"When?"

He must have snapped, because she shot him a sharp look. "Monday night. I mean, it was before she was really missing—"

"When Monday night?"

"Must have been about eight thirty? I was coming home on the Number 2, and—"

"What were you doing on the Number 2?"

"I like it, okay?" Her voice took on an edge. "I was at the Rideau Centre, just hanging out with some friends, shopping and stuff. It was in that snowstorm, so all the transitway buses were taking forever anyway. She sat right across from me."

"Why are you sure it was Meredith?"

"She had red hair and a red coat exactly like the one on the news."

His interest stirred. "Where did she get on?"

"I'm pretty sure it was Bank Street. I've been trying to recreate it, but the bus was crowded. The thing is, Mike, she was upset. That's why I paid attention. She seemed stressed and then she got this phone call that really freaked her out. I figured she was talking to her fiancé."

He tried to recall what they had learned about Meredith's last movements. She'd arrived on the bus from Montreal shortly after eight p.m., so it appeared that she had travelled up Bank Street and caught the Number 2 west, towards her home. She had phoned her friend Jessica at 5:45, presumably just before getting on the bus in Montreal, but there had been no known word or phone contact after that. Certainly Brandon Longstreet had mentioned no call at 8:30. Green reminded himself to check the status of the phone records in the morning.

"What makes you think it was her fiancé? Did you hear a name?"

Hannah shook her head. "Whoever it was, they phoned *her*, and she said she didn't want to talk to them. She said they just wanted to ruin everything and how could they do this to her?"

Green felt a rush of excitement at this new twist. *Ruin everything.* A pretty strong sentiment, strong enough perhaps for her to drop her wedding plans and disappear for awhile to think things out? Was the perfect Brandon Longstreet up to something after all?

"Did you see where she got off?"

"Just before my stop. Roosevelt, maybe?"

Green pictured the intersection. There were no major bus transfers at that corner, nor was it anywhere near Meredith's home, which was about two kilometres farther west. "Do you recall what direction she walked?"

"She was just standing there looking up and down, like she had no idea where she got off. Just that she had to get off."

Green frowned. "Why?"

Hannah shrugged. "She just said 'No, don't!' and she got off the bus." She looked puzzled and worried as she studied his face. "This is important, isn't it. Fuck. I should have told you earlier. It's just I didn't really know what it meant, and I was thinking about Mom..."

He took her hands in his. "It could be important, yes. It could mean she had reason to drop out of sight." He kissed the top of her head. "Thank you, sweetheart. This could be the best news we've had in days."

* * *

Work had always been therapeutic for Green, and nothing gave him a greater adrenaline shot than a good mystery. When he woke up the next morning, he barely had time to dwell on Hannah's absence, because he intended to get an early start on his long to-do list for the day.

First on his list when he arrived at the office was to check for updates on the dead woman. Ident had little to report except that there had been nothing in the contents of her purse to hint at her identity. Suspicious in itself, Green thought, although the wallet and the IDs could have been stolen by a later passerby. To rule that out, Green really had to talk to the man who'd discovered the body. Neither Bob Gibbs nor Sue Peters were at their desks yet, however, so Green moved on to his next task—assigning a lead investigator to the Jane Doe case.

A week before Christmas, the major crimes unit was short-staffed and in considerable disarray. The head of the unit, Staff Sergeant Brian Sullivan, was still on sick leave and refusing to clarify whether he intended to return to his post, accept a less stressful assignment, or take early retirement. Despite Superintendent Devine's badgering, Green did not intend to pressure him. He wanted his best friend back on the job he did so well, and he suspected that beneath the bitterness and the self-doubt, Sullivan missed the action. But he'd had the scare of his life, as had his wife. Mary was dead set against his return, and she was a force. If Brian wanted his marriage to survive, he might have to make a choice.

The staff sergeant who was attempting to fill Sullivan's shoes was a thoroughly modern bureaucrat who watched the clock, followed procedure to the letter, and took all the vacation and sick leave he was entitled to. This year it meant a two-week holiday to Disney World with his family over the Christmas break. He had flown out the day after Meredith Kennedy was reported missing.

On paper, the sergeant on duty took over his essential responsibilities, but in practice Green had merely stepped in to fill the gaps. That morning as he consulted the staff roster, he saw that his newest, greenest sergeant was on duty, Sergeant Marie Claire Levesque.

Levesque was not only green but she was cocky, stubborn and disinclined to appreciate Green's meddling. With this case, Green intended to meddle. So far there was nothing tangible to tie Meredith Kennedy to the dead Jane Doe except the location of her body less than two blocks from the Longstreet home. Both Elena and Brandon Longstreet swore they didn't recognize the woman, but with Adam Jules linked to Meredith's disappearance in some mysterious way, Green intended to keep a close eye on both cases.

Green had passed Levesque at her desk when he came in and knew she was just gearing up for the morning's briefings. When he summoned her to his office, he saw a flicker of annoyance cross her brow. She left her computer with reluctance, picked up her notebook and strolled through the unit room. As always, she moved with the fluid grace of a panther, her long blonde ponytail swishing down her back. All eyes, male and female alike, followed her across the room. She leaned against his doorframe and cocked her eyebrow, sending a jolt of electricity through him. Studiously ignoring his body, he invited her to sit.

"The Jane Doe in Rockcliffe—" he began.

She perked up, her pout vanishing. "You want me to work it?"

"If it comes to that, yes. The post is being done this morning at ten a.m. and I'd like you to attend. Ident will be there too, of course, and if Dr. MacPhail rules it suspicious, you'll be lead."

She did nothing to hide her delight as she flipped open her notebook. "What do we have so far?"

He filled her in on the few known details. "Detective Gibbs and Peters are following up on the snowplow operator. They should be coming in shortly."

She looked up. "They'll be reporting to me, sir?"

He hesitated. "You'll be at the autopsy. I'll keep you informed." Seeing an incipient frown again, he held up his hand. "There are coordination issues here, Marie Claire, between this case and the Meredith Kennedy case, and between us and MisPers."

Fortunately wisdom won out over petulance, and she rose without complaint, slipping her notebook into her pocket. "We'll all keep each other informed."

Progress, he thought after she'd gone. Next on his to-do list, Sergeant Li. He reached the MisPers sergeant at his desk. "Any word from Bell Canada on Meredith Kennedy's phone records?"

"Oh!" Li sounded flustered. "They were supposed to fax them. I'll check."

"If they've arrived, bring them over to my office. There's an interesting call I want to check. Anything else new?"

"Oh!" said Li again. Green wondered if the man had been asleep. "That reminds me! Whelan tracked down that Bay purchase which was charged to Meredith's debit card the day after she disappeared. It was made at the Bay in the St. Laurent Shopping Centre."

Green considered the location. It was in Ottawa's near east end, far from any of her work or home haunts, but not too far from Rockcliffe. "What did she buy?"

"A parka and a big bag. Whelan is thinking—and I'm beginning to agree—that maybe this woman really did want to disappear, and her red suede jacket was too easily recognized."

*   *   *

In the past eighteen hours, Frankie Robitaille had barely eaten or slept. The night before, he had held himself together long enough to get dinner, supervise the girls' homework, and tuck them into bed, but then he had sat glued to the news network, unable to stop crying. He had killed a woman. Not even aware she was there, marking her death with a mere bump of his snowplow. That poor girl! Her whole life ahead of her, about to be married, and in an instant it was snuffed out.

How could he not have seen her, he kept asking himself. Sure, it was snowing. Sure, the street lighting was poor on the back roads of Rockcliffe. Sure, he was tired and maybe a bit zoned out. But he'd never hit anything before. The lights on his plow were strong and flooded the street for half a block ahead of him.

It had been a tight curve, he remembered that, and it had taken him by surprise. Corners were always tricky and the visibility poor. The cab sat so high and the blade so far in front that it was impossible to see the road right ahead. The year before, a plow operator in Montreal had crushed an elderly couple to death as he turned a corner. A nightmare Frankie knew the poor man would never overcome.

Even so, Frankie blamed himself. A woman walking down that quiet street at four a.m. should have caught his attention, especially with that shiny red hand bag. Everything else around was so white, so still.

In the morning, he waved his girls off on the school bus and went back into the house. He forced himself to shower, shave and brew a cup of coffee, tuning in to the local TV's morning show in the background. There was nothing new to report. The dead woman had not yet been identified but did not appear to be Meredith Kennedy. That's no help, he thought, cradling his coffee in both hands and fighting fresh tears. Some other woman was dead, crushed in a few terrifying, excruciating moments by a ton of sharp, unforgiving steel.

The doorbell rang and Frankie started, spilling coffee all over the sofa and carpet. He trembled, debated not answering, and sat cowering waiting for them to go away. The bell rang again, longer this time. He set down his coffee, wiped his eyes and headed for the door. Through the small window in the door he could see two strangers, one a tall, lanky young man and the other a short woman with frizzy brown hair. Both were wearing identical black parkas. Cops.

As he opened the door, he pasted a mask on his face that he hoped looked calm but curious. Right off the bat, the man showed his badge.

"Are you François Robitaille?"

Frankie nodded but couldn't find his voice. The cop introduced himself and his partner, but their names flew right over his head. "We have a few questions, Mr. Robitaille. May we come inside?"

He stepped back to let them in. No point in pretending to know nothing. If they had found him, they already had him. His mind raced ahead frantically to figure out how much he should tell.

"Can I..." He cleared his throat. "Can I get you some coffee?"

They shook their heads in unison and sat down at opposite ends of the living room, trapping him in the middle so that he couldn't watch both at once. The woman took out her notebook while the man leaned forward.

"At 3:16 yesterday afternoon, did you place a 911 call from a payphone at the corner of Beechwood and Charlevoix Avenues?"

He swallowed. He thought of his two girls, expecting to come home this afternoon to his bad jokes and even worse cookies, expecting him to be there forever like he'd promised when their mother took off to Calgary and left them all high and dry. He didn't dare answer. Let's see what they've got, he thought. Don't admit to a thing.

The cop waited a moment, then consulted his notes. "Do you drive a black 1999 Silverado, Ontario license plate KKLT 809?"

The cops would know that from Motor Vehicles records. No point denying that, so he nodded.

"Was it parked in the vicinity of Maple Lane in Rockcliffe on or about three p.m. yesterday?"

He thought of the dog walker. Had she reported the license plate, or were the cops fishing? He said nothing.

"Was it, Mr. Robitaille?"

"Why are you asking? Is that a no-parking area?"

"What were you doing there?"

"I didn't say I was there." Frankie knew he came across as stupid and risked pissing off the police, but he felt like he was standing in the middle of a mine field. One wrong step...

The woman laid down her notebook and flexed her wrist

irritably. She had a lopsided face and spoke with care. "You can make it easier on yourself if you just tell us what happened, Mr. Robitaille. We have a witness who saw you digging in the snow in the vicinity where the body of a woman was later found buried in the snowbank. We know that street was plowed only once during the snowstorm. According to the city's public works manifest, it was plowed between three and five a.m. on Tuesday of this week. We also know you were the driver of that plow. Tell us what happened."

Frankie sat a long time in silence. He didn't want his voice to shake. "I don't know."

"You don't remember hitting her?"

"No. I don't know if I hit her."

"According to the pathologist, she's got broken bones and gashes all over her body, consistent with blows by a large, heavy, sharp-edged instrument like the blade of a plow. The actual post mortem examination will establish that more conclusively, as well as match the shape of the blade to the shape of the wounds."

Frankie winced. He felt his stomach rebel, and he wanted to bolt to the washroom, but he forced himself to stay still. Barely breathed. "There was a snowstorm that night. Everything was white, and it was hard to even make out where the road was. And there was a curve."

"You're saying you didn't see her."

He nodded, trembling.

"You didn't see her at all?" Like she didn't believe him.

"Do you think I'd have left her there if I saw her?" Frankie began to cry. "I'm a family man, just trying to earn a decent wage for my kids. I've never done anything wrong in my whole life."

The first cop broke in. "We know that. You're not in trouble here, Mr. Robitaille. You're right, it was snowing hard, visibility was very poor and the roads in Rockcliffe are very narrow. We just need to know what happened. We need to know whether she was walking, what direction she was going in and how she was acting. Not too many people would choose to be out at night in the middle of that storm."

Frankie dragged his sleeve across his eyes. "I didn't see her, I swear. I came around the corner and all I saw was white."

"If you didn't see anything," the woman interrupted, "then why were you back there yesterday, digging in the snowbank?"

"I–I felt something." He explained about the bump and about not thinking anything of it until a few day later. "But I swear to God I never saw her. She must have come out of nowhere, because there was nothing, nada, on the road!"

He hoped it sounded convincing. He believed it. Goddamn it, yes, the more he thought about it, he thought—I wasn't *that* asleep. Where the hell did she come from?

ELEVEN

Inspector Green was in the midst of an argument with Media Relations over the release of information about the dead woman when Gibbs phoned in their report on Frankie Robitaille. Green was grateful for the distraction. Two mystery women within a four-day span barely a week before Christmas had the public hungry for details. However somewhere, someone was frantically worried about a missing middle-aged woman with dark hair and, judging from the red purse and the turquoise nails, a flair for drama. She was someone's wife or mother or daughter, and Green didn't want them learning her gruesome fate in a sound bite on the News at Noon.

He listened to Gibbs's report carefully. "He seemed genuinely shaken up, sir," Gibbs concluded. "Sue is gung ho to charge him with leaving the scene or criminal negligence, but he claims he never even knew he hit her. Didn't see her at all."

Green massaged his temple. The old Sue was coming back with a vengeance. "Sounds sensible to me, Bob. At least for now we don't have reason to believe there was a crime involved. Let's wait for the PM."

"Do you want me to go to that, sir?"

"Sergeant Levesque is there now. She's handling the Jane Doe, you and Sue stay on the Kennedy case with Li."

"Oh."

Hearing the disappointment in the young detective's voice, Green was about to fill him in on the latest developments in the Kennedy case—the cellphone call from the unknown caller and the purchase of winter clothes at The Bay. At that moment, however, he glanced up to see Sergeant Li himself at the door, waving some papers. Hastily Green told Gibbs to come back in to the station for details then signed off.

Li set the top paper down on Green's desk. "Kennedy's cellphone. Lots of calls from the Ottawa area, usually short. Our girl doesn't seem to be the chatty type. I'll track them all down of course, but there's one number that jumped out at me. It's not local and there's no record of it before ten days ago. Then six calls, both incoming and outgoing. The most recent one was at 8:32 Monday evening. Duration ninety seconds. That's the last call ever made on Kennedy's line."

That doesn't bode well, Green thought. He studied the number, which had a 514 area code. Montreal. "Who is it?"

"It's registered to a Lise Gravelle. I called the number but got no answer."

Green frowned. Lise Gravelle rang absolutely no bells. Her name had not come up in the investigation at all, yet judging from the snippet Hannah had overheard, Lise wanted to ruin everything. A secret lover of Brandon's trying to sabotage the wedding, perhaps?

"I could get the Montreal police to interview her," Li was saying. "She lives in an apartment in the Côte Des Neiges area."

Green tried to recall his paltry knowledge of Montreal. Côte des Neiges was a major shopping street that sliced through the mountainside deep in the heart of English Montreal.

"Let's hold off on that until Gibbs and Peters can do some background inquiries. We need to know how this woman fits in before we start asking her questions. Judging from what we do know, she and Meredith Kennedy were not on good terms."

Li shrugged. "Kennedy's not such a priority any more, now that it looks like she disappeared on purpose—"

"There are still some serious question marks," Green interrupted. "Like the death of this Jane Doe so close to the Longstreet home. It could be a coincidence, but I'm not a fan of coincidence. Until we know the circumstances of her death, we keep Kennedy active."

"I've been making some inquiries on Jane Doe." Li had another file in his hand, and now he held it out. "There's no active MisPers case in our own system that fits her description, so I checked everything within a hundred kilometres. The OPP, Gatineau, Sûreté du Québec, Kingston, Brockville... No women aged 30 to 50, 190 cm., 60 kilos have been reported missing in the past month whose whereabouts are still unknown."

"She could be a visitor. It is the holiday season." Even as Green suggested the idea, he thought it unlikely. Visitors and tourists stayed in the major downtown areas. Wellington Street past Parliament Hill, fashionable Elgin Street or the Byward Market. No visitor would be walking along the back roads of Rockcliffe at four in the morning. In a blizzard.

"There may be more information once MacPhail finishes the PM," Green said. Apart from the obvious clues like tattoos and birthmarks, a post mortem could tell them whether she'd had surgery or broken bones, whether she'd had children, when and what she'd last eaten, whether she used drugs, and sometimes even where her dental work had been done. All details that would help narrow the search for her identity. "My sergeant is attending, and I'll let you know what she reports."

"Okay," Li said, hauling himself stiffly to his feet, "I'll keep tracking down these other phone numbers to see who else Kennedy spoke to in the hours before she disappeared."

After Li left, Green turned his attention to his own private Missing Persons case. Superintendent Adam Jules. Jules's cell phone now went directly to voicemail as though it were turned off or out of battery power. He was not answering his office phone either, and according to his clerk, he hadn't called in that day. She had been busy on the phone all morning cancelling his appointments with feeble excuses and lying outrageously to his colleagues. She was frazzled, annoyed and worried.

So was Green. But Jules was a very private man. He might have a perfectly valid reason for his absence, and if Green launched a full-scale manhunt to find him, Jules would be outraged. Green didn't even dare call the deputy chief to obtain Jules's personal contact information. Instead he used his back door contact at Bell Canada to find out Jules's unlisted home address and number. When the home phone also went to voice mail, Green hung up in disgust, threw on his coat and boots, and headed out the door.

Jules lived in an old limestone school board building that had been converted to tasteful condo apartments. Living at the heart of Centretown only a short walk from police headquarters and from the pubs and restaurants of Elgin Street, he led the perfect bachelor's life. When he was in charge of Criminal Investigations at headquarters, he had walked to work daily.

Briefly Green debated walking to the condo himself, aware that it might take more time to find a parking space than to walk. However in the end, thinking he might uncover clues in that apartment that would lead him elsewhere, he took his Subaru.

There was no answer when he rang at Jules's apartment. Rousing the building property manager, he used his badge and some outrageous threats to bully his way inside the apartment.

The property manager left him just inside the door, no doubt unwilling to incur the wrath of the austere, fanatically private Superintendent of Police.

Green stood in the entranceway, astonished. The open-concept room before him was stunning. Huge, vibrant landscape paintings hung on the walls, each spotlighted by track lighting on the ceiling. The walls were painted the creamy yellow of a winter sunrise and the floor was a dark polished oak. The twin leather couches glowed like rich Merlot and the end tables were uniquely sculpted pieces of wood. Each lamp was an elegant, minimalist work of art.

Opposite him was a wall of floor to ceiling windows with built-in, barely detectible Venetian blinds. They were closed against the western sky but Green could imagine the afternoon sunlight bathing the room in colour. Another wall was entirely covered with bookcases. More books were splayed open on the coffee table. General Rick Hillier's memoirs of his time in Afghanistan, Senator Romeo Dallaire's *Shake Hands with the Devil*, and the recent biography of Pierre Elliott Trudeau, *Just Watch Me*. Stories of great men who had been given the reins of power and guided Canada through turbulent, controversial times.

Jules also had a Bose sound system and a huge collection of CDs which ran from the classics to some startling surprises. Félix Leclerc and Claude Léveillée, classic voices of Quebec, but also Bob Dylan, Ian and Sylvia, and other folk voices of the Sixties. Green tried to imagine Jules as a child of the Sixties, singing protest songs and throwing himself into the peace, drugs and free love culture. He could not.

Art and culture aside, the living room yielded few clues as to the whereabouts or recent activities of its owner. There were no dirty dishes or take-out containers, no daily newspapers spread out on the coffee table. The air held a trace of Jules's expensive French cologne but otherwise gave no hint of recent habitation.

Green moved on to the kitchen, which was small but exquisitely designed. Here he found an immaculate granite counter, stainless steel appliances, and half a pot of cold coffee in the coffee maker. A single empty cup sat in the sink, sporting the dregs of café au lait. The thick skin on the top suggested it hadn't been touched for at least a day. Had Jules been in a hurry yesterday morning and rushed off without his second cup and without cleaning up his first?

There was more artwork in the kitchen along with a wall calendar of smiling third-world children put out by the Plan. A neat stack of mail sat on the corner of the counter, mostly bills and Christmas flyers, but there was no sign of a daily newspaper to give him a clue what day Jules had mostly recently been there.

Feeling like a voyeur, Green hovered in the doorway to the bedroom, reluctant to invade his mentor's ultimate privacy. The bedroom was small, and in contrast to the sleek living room and kitchen, it felt homey. A snowy winter landscape of trees and tobogganing children hung over the double bed, which was covered in cream satin sheets and an old-fashioned country quilt. An antique country pine dresser, armoire and rocking chair completed the impression of a French Canadian farm house.

The surfaces were pristine, the clothes neatly folded in the drawers and the many Harry Rosen and Boss suits arranged by season in the closet. A single book sat on the country pine night table. Margaret Atwood's latest release, *The Year of the Flood.* Hardly Green's idea of bedtime reading. Beside it, however, stood a small photo album propped open as if he looked at it often. Curious, Green picked it up. There were photos of children smiling, blowing out birthday candles and posing proudly on shiny new bikes. Sometimes the same child growing older from page to page. There seemed to be at least a dozen children. His nieces and nephews, perhaps? Green pulled one photo from its plastic sleeve and turned it over.

Alain, 12 ans. Merci, mon oncle!

A nephew, then. Too bad there was no address. He slid out another, this one a young girl with big pink bows in her blond hair. On the back, in what was probably a parent's writing: *Heather at 9. A thousand thank yous.* On the dresser was a single eight by ten picture in a silver frame of a young black man looking very serious in wire-frame glasses and a graduation gown.

Green turned slowly, taking in the country feel. Here was a whole other side to Adam Jules. Not the austere, solitary, obsessively private man he knew, but a man who surrounded himself with children, enjoying not only their smiles but their milestones and triumphs. None of them his own.

Green left the apartment more puzzled than ever. Jules had a private world that embraced children, art and Sixties folk music, all of which gave Green some bittersweet insight into the man, but none of it gave him the slightest clue where he had gone. Nor what he was up to.

*   *   *

At a loss, Green returned to the station. If this were a standard investigation, he would be working his sources to check bank and phone records, but he had no basis for doing that. Jules himself had asked his clerk to cancel his work commitments and no one had reported him missing, although to Green's knowledge he had no close friends or family in the city who would notice his absence. There was nothing to suggest that he had come to grief.

Nothing but the unease in the pit of Green's stomach. By the time he arrived back at his office, he had resolved to have a confidential word with the deputy chief. Charles Poulin was an outsider from the Peel Police, and he had won the job over the head of Adam Jules, who'd been considered next in line. Poulin was as outgoing as Jules was taciturn, as folksy as Jules was austere, a family man who had quickly become engaged in a number of community agencies and charities. In a job that required both PR and people management skills, Green could easily see why he had come out on top. But it had been a crushing blow to Jules, who had borne his hurt and disappointment as stoically as always. Few other than Green noticed that his shoulders stooped a little more and his gaze was often distant, like a man who was detaching himself.

To discuss Jules's disappearance with Poulin would add a further layer of humiliation, but Green feared he had no choice.

Back at the office, however, he found Marie Claire Levesque at her desk, busy on the phone. When she hung up, she caught sight of Green and snatched up her notebook with a flourish. Green was impressed. Despite all his years of attending autopsies, he'd always arrived back at the station looking and feeling noticeably green. Levesque was a healthy shade of pink, and her blue eyes sparkled.

She followed him into his office and settled in the guest chair before he even had his coat off. Makes herself right at home, he reflected, feeling an unexpected pang. The only other person who made himself at home was Brian Sullivan, who'd spent hours in the little office with his huge feet up on Green's desk. God, he missed the man!

"How did it go?" Green asked.

She spoke entirely from memory. "The victim was a mature female approximately fifty to sixty years old, 60 kilos, 194 cm.

That's five foot five, a hundred and thirty pounds," she added, her tone suggesting Green was a dinosaur still stuck in the imperial system. He let it slide. "Natural grey hair, dyed brown, blue eyes, fair skin. She was healthy and physically fit, a non-smoker, non-drug user, moderate alcohol user. She'd had a hysterectomy long ago, and X-rays showed several poorly set old fractures, probably from childhood."

Green considered that. Poorly set implied that the child had been either poor or abused. A clue to her past, perhaps, but not her death. "Anything on time or cause of death?"

Levesque smiled. She likes to control, Green thought, irrationally annoyed. "The body was completely frozen with a core temperature of minus seven degrees, equal to the snow she was buried in, so time of death is difficult to estimate. No decomposition, no insect activity, obviously. Using a formula of 1.3 degree loss in body temperature per hour, *and* assuming she'd been in the snow since death, MacPhail calculated she'd probably been dead a minimum of about thirty hours. Of course we know it was much longer, since she was hit at approximately four a.m. Tuesday morning. However, MacPhail's not sure she was in the snow since death, at least in that position."

"Oh?"

"There were some signs of lividity suggesting she was lying face down for several hours after death before being moved. Again because of the cold, hard to say for how long."

Levesque's eyes shone, prompting Green to revise his earlier impression. This wasn't about control; it was the science that intrigued her. The piecing together of the puzzle. His own curiosity stirred. "What did he find as cause of death?"

"Well, sir, she had a broken arm, broken shoulder, broken neck—"

"That would do it."

She smiled again. "No, sir, all those fractures were post mortem. There were also lacerations and gouges to the skin on her hips, legs and arms, but no bleeding or bruising, suggesting those were also post mortem."

Green tried to visualize the scenario. "So major damage was done to her body after she was dead. How long after?"

"The doctor took tissue samples to examine microscopically, which will give him a more accurate picture, but judging from the lividity, at least several hours."

Green's interest rose as he grasped the implications. No wonder Levesque had been excited. "So what you're saying is that she'd been dead for several hours before the snowplow came along and hit her at four a.m."

Her grin was now ear to ear. "That's the hypothesis, sir." The grin faded. "I mean, not that I'm happy about that, sir. The woman is dead. But it means the snowplow operator is not a suspect and we need to modify our investigation."

"But I do remember a lot of blood. If all these injuries occurred post mortem, where did that come from and how did she die?"

"The head had a compressed fracture at the back of the skull which produced extensive bleeding, both internally and externally, especially around the brain stem. MacPhail estimates it likely would have rendered her unconscious instantly and killed her within minutes."

Green pictured the dark snowy strip of road. "What caused the fracture? Could a car or another snowplow have caused it?"

"He wants to examine the tissue and the lacerations on the skull more closely before he draws a conclusion."

"But surely he can give us a tentative opinion, something to go forward with."

She shrugged. "Too complex, sir." Here she did consult her notebook. "With the disturbance and damage caused by the snowplow and with the freezing temperatures affecting bleeding, body cooling and oxygen use, he is not prepared to say."

Green snorted. MacPhail had seen hundreds of bodies in his career, and Green had never known him to be shy about his opinions. Perhaps he was trying to enhance the mystique of his powers for the benefit of the attractive new sergeant. Green snatched up his phone and dialled the man's cell phone.

Just as he feared it would go to voicemail, MacPhail's thick brogue growled over the phone. The flamboyant Scot's voice grew more gravelly every year, the victim of Scotch and Cuban cigars.

"Don't rush me, laddie!"

"MacPhail, come on. When have you not known as soon as you got the body on the table?"

"When the poor woman's been knocked from pillar to post."

"But I saw the head wound. Lots of blood."

"They always have."

"I know, but give us a guess. Do you think someone hit her or—"

"A fist couldn't cause that damage. Not unless it was wearing iron knuckles."

"Okay, so something harder than a fist."

"That much I can say. Something hard but not sharp. The skull showed a diffuse radiating fracture pattern, more crushed than penetrated."

"So we're talking the proverbial blow by a blunt object, delivered with enough force to crush the skull?"

"Lad, you put words in my mouth. I'm a long way from that conclusion. She could have been shoved or tripped backing up, and hit her head on something hard like the curb."

"Is that likely?"

"As likely as not. All I can give you is that her head met up with a hard, blunt object, and it didn't end well for her."

Green thought the scenarios over. By late Monday evening, when this Jane Doe would have been walking down Maple Lane, at least six inches of snow had already fallen, blanketing the road and the surrounding ground. Even if she was shoved or running when she hit the ground, the snow would have cushioned her fall. Not to mention covered up any hard blunt object that might have done her harm.

"Either way," he said, "she didn't incur this fatal blow taking a leisurely stroll through Rockcliffe."

"That much I concur. I've ruled the death suspicious."

When Green hung up, he grinned at Levesque, who was trying to hide her eagerness beneath a bland look. "Okay. We open a major case file. And we get you a team."

TWELVE

Major Crimes was abuzz. Levesque's excitement was contagious, and the tedious paperwork of the past few days was dropped in a flash. This was unlike most homicides they investigated. Not a routine domestic, nor a barroom brawl or settling of accounts in a drug war. This was a mystery. A well-dressed, middle-aged woman had met a bizarre death in the middle of a snowstorm in the exclusive enclave of Rockcliffe. Many of the detectives had never been to Rockcliffe, let alone had the chance to gain access to the elegant homes to interview potential witnesses. The possibility of diplomatic immunity and jurisdictional squabbles with the RCMP responsible for diplomats' security only added to the spice.

Who was the woman? Whom was she visiting? And who had left her for dead? Speculation and rumour galvanized the whole force, and the brass crowded in for updates. Even the Chief dropped in to the newly set-up incident room to address the troops and to caution them to be on their best behaviour. "These people have lawyers" was the gist of his message. "Hell, these people *are* lawyers."

Within an hour, Levesque had the bones of an investigation drafted and detectives assigned to canvass the neighbourhood, re-interview the plow operator, and check with taxi and bus drivers on duty in the vicinity that night. Ident had worked up a decent photo of the dead woman, to be shown to all potential witnesses. Others were expanding the missing persons search across the country.

Because it was home to numerous embassies and high-ranking members of the judiciary and government, the Village of Rockcliffe Park was reputed to have more surveillance cameras per square foot than any other municipality in Canada. Cameras were not just trained on the entranceways but also on the streets and backyards nearby. Some were on embassy grounds and were operated by the foreign governments themselves, presenting a nearly insurmountable barrier to access by the Ottawa Police, but many were operated by the RCMP. In this age of paranoia and national security, Green expected resistance to his request to view the RCMP footage, and he was happy to hand over that delicate jurisdictional dance to the Chief himself. Green suspected lawyers on both sides would get dragged in, and in these days just before the holidays, he doubted he'd see results for at least a month.

Into the midst of all this discussion came Sue Peters and Bob Gibbs, looking as if they'd struck gold. Heads turned in the incident room as the door burst open and Sue Peters thunked in, leaning hard on her cane but eyes blazing. Gibbs trailed her, quieter and more apologetic but with a small smile trembling at the corners of his mouth.

"They're connected!" Peters announced.

Levesque, who'd been marking assignments on the smart board, scowled.

"Well," Gibbs amended, "we think they are."

"What's connected?" Green asked. He'd been conferring quietly with the Chief at the back, trying to let Levesque run the show.

"Meredith Kennedy and this Jane Doe."

Green snapped alert. "Explain!"

"That cell phone number you gave us—the person who called Meredith at eight thirty Monday night?"

"Lise Gravelle? Yes?"

"We called Montreal and spoke with the Montreal cops. Turns out Lise Gravelle was reported missing by her neighbour Wednesday."

"They're sure it's the same Lise Gravelle?"

"Well, not absolutely," Gibbs said, cutting Peters off. "It's a different street address than the cell phone company gave us, but it's in the same neighbourhood, and the neighbour said she'd only lived there a short while."

"How did this neighbour know she was missing?"

"Her dog was barking non-stop," Peters said. "The neighbour had to go in to try to shut it up, and she said the poor dog hadn't gone out in over a day. There was poop all over the place and the dog was starving." Peters swung around to Green. "I grew up with dogs, sir. No dog owner would leave a dog like that without phoning someone or making arrangements, unless something bad had happened to them."

"What investigation have the Montreal Police done?"

"Just the usual hospital, ambulance, accident reports," Peters said. "They probably don't think a nosy neighbour and a barking dog are enough to put manpower on."

In a busy metropolis like Montreal, with its chronic staffing shortages, bankrupt coffers, systemic corruption and organized crime wars, that was probably true, but Green kept his thoughts to himself.

"But they did open a file, and we have a photo." Peters whipped an eight by ten glossy from the papers in her hand. "I have a jpeg of this for us to distribute, but I think she looks damn familiar. I'd say Lise Gravelle and this mysterious Rockcliffe Jane Doe are one and the same!"

Green took the photo and studied the face. Hazel eyes, brown hair, the beginnings of crows' feet and the suggestion of a hard, bitter life in the set of her mouth and chin. Sue was right.

* * *

"Sir, Gibbs and I want to go to Montreal."

Sue Peters had followed Green back to his office from the incident room at the end of the briefing. She was now crowding into the tiny room and leaning over his desk. Peters wasn't big, but she took up a lot of space. Behind her, Gibbs stood uncertainly in the doorway, peeking over the top of her head.

Green glanced from one officer to the other. What a pair. Combined, they almost made one good detective. "It's Sergeant Levesque's case," he said.

"But it's ours too. We're the ones who tracked down the snowplow operator, the cell phone number and the dead woman's identity."

"You're not even cleared, Sue."

"Then send Bob! This death is obviously connected to Kennedy's disappearance. *Our* case."

Peters had raised her voice. Flushing, Gibbs squeezed inside and closed the door behind him.

"I haven't said anyone is going to Montreal," Green countered, keeping his voice even. "The follow-up at that end can be done by the Montreal Police. They can track her known associates, interview friends and neighbours, and trace her movements there. Our job will be to find out when and why she came to Ottawa."

"That obviously means finding out what was going on in Montreal," Peters shot back. She was still leaning in over his desk.

Laying a hand on her arm, Gibbs murmured, "Sue, sit down."

She looked ready to take his head off but thought better of it. She sat down with a thud and took a deep breath. "Meredith went to Montreal on Monday. Before she was even back home, she got a phone call from this Gravelle woman, and by the end of the night, Gravelle was dead. What was their connection? What was it that freaked out Kennedy and left Gravelle dead? We can't leave all that to the Montreal cops! They don't have the background."

Gibbs was visibly cringing, but insubordination aside, she had a point. He had been wrestling with the same dilemma. The Montreal connection seemed to be at the core of the case. It made no sense to farm that part of the investigation out to the Montreal force. Peters was also right that she and Gibbs had done the lion's share of the detective work on the case and knew much more about Kennedy's background and activities than did Levesque. On the other hand, Levesque was higher ranking, Francophone and—he had to admit—more skilled at handling the intricacies of inter-agency cooperation. With one swish of her ponytail, she would dazzle.

The truth was, he wanted to send none of them. Levesque was needed here to coordinate the Lise Gravelle homicide investigation as a whole, which was still in its early stages. Peters was still medically unfit, and Gibbs would be hopeless let loose in the ranks of Montreal's tough, overworked police force.

Further complicating things, it was now two p.m. on Friday, barely a week before Christmas. The Montreal cops would be thrilled at the added workload. After a moment's deliberation, he rose, opened his door, and signalled for Marie Claire Levesque to join them. Once all three detectives were squeezed in a line opposite him in the tiny room, he addressed them all.

"The Kennedy missing persons case and the Gravelle homicide are clearly linked. As the last person to talk to Gravelle, we need to find Meredith now more than ever. Sergeant Levesque, I'm assigning Detectives Gibbs and Peters to your team, where they will continue to pursue the Kennedy angle under your direction."

Sue Peters scowled, but Gibbs nudged her before she could open her mouth.

"Follow-up is clearly needed in Montreal to share information with the Montreal Police and to obtain their assistance in tracing both Kennedy's and Gravelle's activities. All of you are needed here in Ottawa to follow up on leads. In the staff sergeant's absence, I will go to Montreal."

All three jaws dropped. Before Peters could say anything to get herself into trouble, Green stood up. "It should only take a day or two. I'll be accessible by cell phone at all times. Marie Claire, you'll be in charge of the unit while I'm gone."

*   *   *

Brandon Longstreet drove quickly, both hands gripping the wheel of his Prius in case he encountered an unexpected icy patch. The road surface was dry and bleached white by salt, but the Ottawa-Montreal highway was notorious for white-outs and drifting snow.

It had taken him almost a day to cancel or rearrange his shifts, take care of emergencies and cajole colleagues into handling everything else. By the time he had freed up a couple of days to make the trip, he was feeling the pressure of lost time. The car's acceleration was effortless, and in his excitement he didn't notice how fast he was going until he spotted an OPP cruiser up ahead. He forced himself to slow down. He had so many questions to ask and so many leads to follow up that he'd better arrive in one piece.

Having recovered from the shock of the discovery of the body, he was now absolutely convinced that Meredith was alive. She had uncovered something upsetting that had taken her on a mysterious trip to Montreal then prompted her to drop out of sight, for reasons as yet unknown. She was running from something, or hiding from someone, or desperately on the hunt for someone. He didn't understand why she hadn't confided in him, but Meredith was a stubborn, independent woman, and recently he had not shown her the loyalty she deserved.

He blamed himself. Replaying their last fight endlessly in his head, he knew he'd screwed up by taking his mother's side. Years of living with such a forceful, confident personality had taught him to take the easy route, to give in on the little battles. Over time, everything looked small compared to the colossal thrust of his mother's will.

But at least he understood that now. He only had to find Meredith, take her in his arms, and promise her that no matter how awful the obstacle, she could conquer it with him at her side. Deep down, he had a nagging suspicion that his mother was at the centre of Meredith's discovery. Disjointed fragments seemed to hint at that: his mother's secrecy, her cryptic *"He mustn't know!"*, the lies about his father's death, Meredith's refusal to confide in him...

Anger rolled over him. Enough! What was he? A fool and a child? There were too many secrets, and he was damned if he was going to be shielded any more. Meredith's search had brought her to Montreal. He was flying blind with no idea whom she'd met or where she'd gone, but he figured he'd start with the family and see how many secrets he could pry loose himself.

In his pocket he also had the newspaper clippings about his father's death. As the highway curved left onto Montreal's crumbling expressway, boulevard Métropolitaine, he wondered where to begin. In Westmount, he decided, steering for the Decarie exit ramp and following the sign to Centre Ville.

* * *

Sid Green's face sagged as he watched his grandson light the Hanukkah menorah. It was the first year the five-year-old had been trusted with the honour, and it should have been a celebration. Yet even Tony looked as if he'd lost his best friend.

It was the first night of the eight-day Festival of Lights, and the single candle looked lonely all by itself on the candelabra. Green felt the ache of its symbolism. Hannah hadn't bought a return ticket, claiming she'd play it by ear depending on the reception she received. She'd said she wanted the freedom to come back after two days if things went badly, but Green feared the opposite. That she would never return.

Judging from the wistful faces around the festive table, the rest of the family harboured the same fear. Sharon had dressed the table in white and sparkling silver to honour both Friday night Shabbat and the first night of Hanukkah. A platter of golden latkes filled the air with the scent of onions and oil, but the beauty only sharpened the sense of loss. Hannah's place was set, as a symbol of her inclusion, but the empty chair spoke volumes.

"Mike's going to Montreal tomorrow," Sharon said to Sid brightly. "I've given him a Hanukkah shopping list."

Sid raised a desultory eyebrow. "Montreal? What's in Montreal?"

"A couple of witnesses," Green said. "And I have to talk to the Montreal Police. I won't be there long. A day, maybe two."

"You bring back Lester's smoked meat?"

Green laughed. "It's at the top of Sharon's list. How much you want? Ten pounds?"

"Ach." Sid waved a dismissive hand. Green's father was nearing ninety and seemed to be shrivelling before their eyes. Now, hunched over and turned in on himself, he looked barely a hundred pounds. Green's heart constricted as he watched him push his single latke around on his plate, uneaten.

"I'll miss a couple of Hanukkah nights, but we'll have a big celebration the last night," Green said, matching Sharon's gaiety. "Hannah should be back by then, and we'll make a big spread of smoked meat and kosher dills."

Sharon rubbed her hands with glee. "With presents from the Sherbrooke Street boutiques for Hannah and me!"

Green smiled. They both knew that trusting him with the selection of designer accessories, even if they could afford them, was an invitation to catastrophe. His taste ran more to discount department stores than Yves St. Laurent.

Sid glanced at Green. "You're looking for this missing *madeleh*?"

Green was surprised, for his father rarely paid attention to the news. He left the television blaring all day in his minuscule senior's apartment, but it was tuned to talk shows and old friends like *Wheel of Fortune*. They provided a background of silly patter that gave no reminder of the darker side of life. Sid Green needed no reminder.

Green weighed his answer carefully. While it was true he would be investigating Meredith Kennedy's movements in Montreal, his main focus was Lise Gravelle. He had spent the rest of the afternoon getting the necessary travel permissions and making arrangements with the Montreal Police. They had made no progress yet in tracking Lise's next of kin, but Green suspected up till now they hadn't tried very hard. To them she was a throwaway, an anonymous citizen of the city with no one to mourn her loss or push the police for answers. She'd had an erratic history of low-paying jobs and welfare, broken relationships and frequent moves, most recently to a small apartment in one of the dozens of cheap low rises in the Van Horne area. The Montreal Police made the obligatory grumbling noises about the upcoming weekend but agreed to get a search warrant for the place.

"We're hopeful Meredith Kennedy is alive," was all he said now. "She has some friends and family in Montreal."

Tony had been listening with rapt attention. "She's going to be in big trouble when you find her, right, Daddy?"

Green chuckled. "I think everyone will just be happy to have her home again, buddy."

Sid had retreated into one of his faraway places. Back in the Warsaw ghetto with his little children, perhaps. Children who had been lost to him forever. An all too familiar sight to Green.

"So!" he announced, reaching down and putting a shiny silver gift bag on the table. "Tonight's presents are from Hannah, who wanted to make sure we wouldn't forget her." He distributed the small wrapped parcels around the table. Tony pounced on his and gleefully unwrapped *The Adventures of Huckleberry Finn*.

Green was afraid he'd be disappointed it wasn't a Nintendo Wii game he'd been angling for, but he brandished it with delight. "Cool! We're almost finished *Tom Sawyer*."

Green opened his own present, a CD from some indie rock band he'd never heard of. Bit by bit, his daughter was dragging his musical taste out of the eighties into the modern age.

Sid was looking at his own present, his chin quivering. It was a framed photo of Hannah with her soft orange curls and her sparkling hazel eyes. She'd come a long way from the blue Mohawk and corpse-white make-up of three years ago. She had taken the studs out of her eyebrow and lower lip, and she looked angelic. Across the bottom she had written in a beautiful, elegant script, "To my all-time favourite zaydie, Love Hannah."

She sure knows how to tug the heartstrings, Green thought. She better be coming back to us.

THIRTEEN

It was just past eight o'clock Saturday morning when Green headed east on the highway towards Montreal. Luckily, a crisp northwest wind had blown away all danger of snow, and the morning sky was already a rich blue. The rising sun seared his eyes.

The four-lane highway was nearly deserted. Setting cruise control, he slipped his new CD into the player and settled in to enjoy his morning coffee and bagel. He had intended to use the two-hour drive to sort out his thoughts on the case and to plan his day, but the indie band was so good that he found himself listening to it over and over, fascinated by the guitar riffs and flourishes hidden in the harmony. Fascinated too by how similar Hannah's and his tastes were. Before he knew it, the warehouses and big box stores of the West Island were whizzing by and up ahead rose the majestic twin humps of Mount Royal, topped by the rounded dome of St. Joseph's Oratory on the right and by the white tower of the Université de Montréal on the left.

Compared to Ottawa, which was confounded by three rivers, a canal, two lakes and a severe shortage of bridges, Montreal did not pose much of a directional challenge. It did, however, present other hazards. The expressways were old, impossibly crowded, and made even narrower by three-foot snowbanks on either side. The road surface was riddled with patches and potholes. In response,

Montreal drivers drove as if rules such as speed limits, lane markings and signal lights were just further inconveniences to be ignored. Boulevard Métropolitaine was transformed into a Grand Prix racing circuit, and Green needed every trick he'd ever learned in his defensive driving and emergency manoeuvres courses in order to navigate the trip across the city to the east end.

Unlike Ottawa, which until a hundred and fifty years ago had been nothing but a rough timber town, Montreal was the birthplace of Canadian commerce. Ornate brick and limestone heritage buildings stood alongside sleek glass towers in the colourful and lively downtown core. Green was disappointed to learn, however, that instead of being housed in the new Montreal Police headquarters on legendary St. Urbain Street, Major Crimes was located in what looked like a glorified shopping mall way out on Sherbrooke Street East. At the height of Saturday morning, cars fought for space as Christmas shoppers tried to get at the shops along the commercial strip, and Green nearly missed the unprepossessing building amid the crush of chain stores and discount hotels. The only advantage to its location, he admitted grudgingly, was quick access to the expressways that crisscrossed the city.

He was relieved to find state-of-the-art security inside the building with full-body turnstiles controlled by a coded keypad, and a front desk enclosed behind glass that Green assumed was bullet-proof. The ongoing war with Montreal's biker gangs had been ugly.

Green stopped at the desk to introduce himself. The head of Specialized Investigations had promised to obtain the necessary search warrants and to assign one of the weekend investigators to assist Green in the Lise Gravelle case. The man had sounded brusque and impatient on the phone, however, even when Green had dusted off his best French, so he was not holding out much hope. He was pleasantly surprised when a huge black man came off the elevator and bulldozed through the turnstile. He would have looked more at home on a football field than he did in his polyester suit, but his broad smile was dazzling against his ebony skin.

"Inspector Green! Detective Sergeant Magloire. Jean Pierre to my friends." He engulfed Green's hand in a crushing handshake. Magloire had a deep gravelly voice and a slight accent that sounded like African tinged with French Canadian. Green guessed it was Haitian.

"Mike," he managed through rattling teeth.

"You must be tired. Hungry. The warrant's not quite ready. You want to see our offices? No, I bet you want to eat."

Since Green's bagel was now a distant memory, he nodded. "Food would be nice, if there's some place close by."

"I know exactly the place. It's a bit of a drive, but on our way out to the victim's home."

"But the warrants—"

"Don't worry about them." Magloire tossed on his coat as he strode down the front stairs, leaving Green hustling to keep up. He realized he'd been managed. With fluent ease, Magloire had steered him out of the police station and away from the tardy paperwork. Magloire selected an unmarked Impala from the lot and squealed its tires as he accelerated into the line of traffic headed west along Sherbrooke. He drove the staff car one-handed, weaving in and out of the traffic at a speed that left Green clinging to the shoulder strap.

Magloire grinned. "Montreal is a living thing, full of fight," he said. "She does her best to turn you upside down. You have to push back."

They zipped past thickly treed parks and the shiny silver

dome of the Olympic stadium before heading deeper into the older French parts of Montreal. The cityscape changed gradually from modest residential duplexes to an ad hoc mix of hospitals, agencies and older tenements, their weathered brick and limestone façades pressing close to the street. At boulevard St-Laurent, he turned right into the bumper to bumper traffic inching up the historic street. Magloire began a running patter about the gentrification of the Main, pointing out the strip clubs and drug dealers side by side with fashionable boutiques. All the while he was smiling as if hugely pleased with himself.

When he slipped the car into a no-parking spot in front of a nondescript storefront, Green looked up at the sign, *Chez Schwartz, Charcuterie Hebraïque de Montréal,* and realized how thoroughly he had been managed. Schwartz's Main Hebrew Deli was known around the world for its exquisite smoked meat and its dubious ambiance. Briskets and gallon jars of peppers were piled high in the front window. Green eyed Magloire with a new respect.

Even in the winter, the line-up of customers straggled down the block. Ignoring the glares of those in line, Magloire pushed inside, where the harried waiter immediately caught his eye. The tiny place was packed with customers crammed into banquette-style tables along the wall. Miraculously two vacant chairs opened up in a spacious corner and the waiter gestured to them to sit down. This gives community policing a whole new meaning, Green thought, reminded that in Montreal, alliances and understanding were everything. From the lowliest sex trade worker on the street corner to the CEO of the largest construction firm, everyone knew someone to watch their back.

The menu was printed on the placemat, but Magloire ordered for both of them before Green could even decipher it. Smoked meat sandwiches with fries.

"And a side of peppers," Green shouted at the waiter's disappearing back.

The waiter turned, his grease-stained apron flapping. "Hot?"

"As hot as you got."

The waiter scurried off, and Magloire gave Green his trademark huge grin. "You been here before."

"Not here, but it's a legend." He leaned forward to reassert control. "Jean Pierre, I'm on a tight timeline here. When will the warrant be ready?"

"By the time we finish lunch. I told them to bring it here."

"Good. Meanwhile, what have you guys uncovered about Lise Gravelle?"

"Apart from getting the warrant, not much. We're trying to find next of kin but she appears to be alone. Parents dead, one sibling—a sister—estranged. No children or husbands. There may be nobody to claim her or bury her."

"Not even cousins? Nieces or Nephews?"

"We're still doing inquiries. The sister hasn't lived in the province since 1982, so the trail is stone cold." Magloire recited all this from memory, reminding Green again that beneath the easy cheer and big smile, the man was no fool. But so far there was no apparent connection to Meredith Kennedy or the Longstreets.

"Where did she work?" Green asked.

"Here and there. Semi-skilled, for the most part, like secretarial work, sales. We're still checking background. The local PDQ—sorry, that's Poste de Quartier, neighbourhood police station—did some inquiries when her neighbour reported her missing, but to be honest, it wasn't a high priority for them."

"Is her neighbourhood a high-crime area?"

"No, no. But with the snowstorm, and the Christmas preparations..." Magloire shrugged as if no further explanation were needed. "I grew up in Côte des Neiges. It's mostly low-income, immigrants, students, families struggling to pay the bills. Lise Gravelle would be just one of thousands who live alone in a cheap apartment."

"Well, maybe there will be some clues there to tell us where she worked, or why she went to Ottawa." Or why she died, he was thinking, but then two enormous smoked meat sandwiches arrived, and their fragrant succulence drove all other thoughts from his mind.

*   *   *

Brandon sat in his car staring at the huge stone mansion on the hill. He'd never been inside. His mother, only connected to the Longstreets by marriage, didn't merit an invitation, although to hear her talk about his Great Uncle Cyril, it was just as well. Cyril did not entertain, he summoned, and family members didn't receive a summons unless they were being given instructions on how to run their life or a reprimand on how they had failed to.

Cyril was a bachelor, now well into his eighties, and he lived in the house on Summit Circle that he'd inherited from his parents. The very air smelled of money and privilege. Here, on the western summit of Mount Royal, the denizens of the graceful old limestone homes and modern, multi-million dollar mansions controlled the fate and pulse of the city below them.

Brandon recalled vague speculation from other relatives that Cyril had been normal enough until he'd spent three years in a German POW camp and the woman he'd planned to marry had eloped with his best friend. Brandon suspected there was more to the story, but among the Longstreet clan, communication through innuendo and understatement had been honed to a fine art. No one liked Uncle Cyril, and in fact those who'd felt the lashing of his tongue despised him, but no one dared reject him outright. Spending beyond their trust funds was another skill the younger generations of Longstreets had honed to a fine art. Uncle Cyril was sitting on millions, and some day he was going to die.

Brandon's mother had never cared about the millions, and neither did Brandon. She had built her own legend, and he had his own dreams. He and Meredith.

It was the thought of Meredith that forced him out of the car. He would face anything, slay any monster, to find her again. He had not called ahead, preferring to catch the old man off guard and give him less chance to refuse. Or to sharpen his knives. He'd stayed Friday night with his aunt, his father's sister, and when he'd told her his plans, she'd been appalled.

"You don't sneak up on Cyril, Brandon. You don't try to outfox him because you will lose. He aims for the jugular, and he'll tell you things that will cut you to the bone. Believe me. He hates the fact that both his brothers avoided the war and had wives, children, and now grandchildren. He hates the fact that they both had the decency to die at the height of their powers. He hates being old and shrivelled and feeble. You don't want to surprise him."

Brandon had told her that he had no time for subtleties. He needed answers; Meredith's life might depend on it. So far none of the younger Longstreets, including his aunt, had been able to supply them. Meredith had not contacted any of them on her mysterious trip to Montreal, nor had they known anything was amiss until they heard about the missing persons search.

"What makes you think it's even about us?" Aunt Bea asked. "Maybe she was visiting her own side of the family."

"And I will visit them too, but she doesn't have much family left in Montreal. Most of her cousins have moved to Toronto, Ottawa, or Vancouver, part of the great Anglo-Quebec Diaspora." He balled his fists in concentration. "I think she discovered something, or someone told her something, that freaked her out. Maybe that's because I learned something awful too. My father hanged himself." He gauged her reaction. "The trouble is there were absolutely no details as to why."

Aunt Bea sucked in her breath, blinking rapidly. For a moment she said nothing, as if choosing a course. "That's as much as I know, Brandon. I was away at Cambridge when my brother died, and I got this cryptic phone call from mother. Not hysterical. Longstreets don't do hysterical. Your father was the golden boy of the family, the one to carry the Longstreet banner forward into the next generation. I know that sounds ridiculous in today's world, but remember this was nearly half a century ago and the air up on the west mountain was pretty rarefied. Harvey was supposed to use law as a springboard to go into politics. There had been a Longstreet in the Senate and a few at the helm of Crown Corporations, but none of them had ever been an MP. There was talk of a cabinet position, Liberal, of course. Maybe even the successor to Pierre Elliott Trudeau. He had the same élan, the same silver tongue. But my brother wouldn't play the game. Blew off the Liberal fundraisers in favour of student protest rallies and wrote scathing articles for the *Montreal Star* on the corruption of the elite. I loved him for it, but Uncle Cyril was not amused."

Brandon digested the news with surprise. His father had been an activist. Maybe the two of them were not so different after all. Why had his mother never told him this?

Aunt Bea sighed, her eyes shining at the memory. "But in the end, it was his tawdry side that caught up with him. Another

Longstreet fine art—dalliances with common girls that have to be hushed up at all costs, while the Longstreet wives keep up the brave front."

Brandon struggled to hide his surprise, but his aunt was too quick. She squinted at him. "Ah. You didn't know. I'm sorry, I thought you did."

"Another detail my mother failed to mention."

"What does it matter, Brandon? It's all a long time ago. He was a handsome, charismatic teacher surrounding by nubile, adoring co-eds. The oldest cliché in the book. It doesn't have anything to do with you, or your mother, both of whom he adored. It doesn't diminish his legacy as an idealist or a human rights lawyer, either."

"Did my mother know about the affair?"

"Affairs." She scrutinized him. "She did. Not the specifics of any one, probably, but the concept, yes. She'd been one of those nubile, adoring students herself. She knew his weakness."

Brandon pushed the revelation around in his mind. His mother had known this seamy side but had continued to paint him as a saint in his son's eyes. Well, what would he have done in her place, he wondered. *Son, your father was a great mind, but as a man, he was a cheating little shit.*

"Did the whole family know this?"

"I'm sure, and if they didn't, the circumstances of his death would have given them a clue. Harvey always had way too much fun with life."

Brandon studied her discomfort and finally the light dawned. "You mean it wasn't suicide at all."

"Harvey was about as depressed and suicidal as a new winner of Lotto 649. But..." She broke off, looking embarrassed. Aunt Bea was his favourite aunt. Among the earnest Ladies Auxiliary types who peopled the older branches of his family tree, she was the one with the heart of a rebel. She used her money and influence to campaign for wildlife conservation and waved her Green Party membership card triumphantly at family functions. Brandon knew she was trying to spare him.

But he'd seen far more bizarre sexual experiments during his years in ER. "Extreme sexual sport was right up his alley?" he said gently.

She flushed. "Obviously it was never proven. But that's the real reason the whole thing was hushed up. The official coroner's verdict was suicide, but really neither he nor the police did a lick of investigation." She leaned forward to grasp both his hands. "I'm sorry, Brandon. I promised my mother, and yours, that I would never, ever tell you. But honestly, if you're going to see Uncle Cyril, you need to know."

"Why?"

"Because, of all the Longstreet men, Cyril was the only one who disapproved. He was outraged by your father's behaviour, I think deep down because he himself had been betrayed by infidelity. It made him very unforgiving, another reason why the circumstances of Harvey's death were suppressed. A lot was riding on that lie. Harvey's legacy as a professor and lawyer, his reputation as a father and husband, and of course, a family fortune."

Brandon frowned. "My mother's never cared about that, never taken a penny she didn't earn."

Bea's hands tightened spasmodically around his, and for a moment she looked about to speak. Then she released his hands and shook her head as if to dispel the thought. "Of course not. But his reputation and his legacy, she guarded that. She was fiercely loyal."

That she was, he thought now, as he steeled himself to meet

the legendary patriarch who'd spurned her all these years. He was beyond caring whether his father's name was attacked by a bitter, judgmental old man. If she had visited him, Brandon only wanted to know what the old man might have told the woman he loved. Meredith was a thoroughly modern woman who would have been unfazed by this ancient tale of infidelity and sexual misadventure. What else might she have learned?

Given Aunt Bea's description, he expected Cyril's doorbell to be answered by a butler who would usher him into a stifling hot parlour full of antiques and old books. He was surprised when instead, after an interminable wait, the heavy black door swung open to reveal a shrivelled old man. His face was oddly mask-like, and Brandon recognized the telltale rigidity of Parkinson's. As if by force of will, he leaned on a polished wood cane and peered up at Brandon over gold framed glasses perched on his nose.

"You're Brandon," he said. "Come in, I've been expecting you."

Brandon's carefully rehearsed introduction flew out the window. First point to Cyril. Had Bea contacted him?

Cyril gave a cold, triumphant little smile. "Even if I didn't have a copy of your graduation photo on my piano, you're the image of your father."

Brandon struggled to recover from this second surprise as he stepped into the foyer and bent to remove his boots. Who would have sent Cyril a photo? His mother, still trying to curry favour after all? Cyril had turned and headed across the hall without a backwards glance, leaving Brandon to hang up his own coat. The cavernous foyer was spotless, but its decor was yet another surprise. The honey oak floors shone with a simple, timeless elegance, but the walls were hung with vivid abstract expressionist art. Not a sombre ancestral portrait among the lot. Brandon recognized a Jean Paul Riopelle and a Jackson Pollock, both of which would likely command seven figures at Sotheby's.

"Pick one," Cyril said as he turned to see Brandon staring. "I'll put it in my will for you. A wedding present...or a consolation prize." He uttered a little snort at his own wit and shuffled through an archway into a sitting room, where the decor was more predictable. A large Victorian fireplace, wing chairs, ornate bookcases and a Persian carpet in jewel hues. The walls were hung with still lifes, with not a human figure among them. However, the baby grand piano sitting in the window bay was covered with family photographs, among them Brandon himself and several cousins.

Cyril was lowering himself carefully into a wing chair by the fire. He waved a gnarled, tremulous hand at the piano. "Might as well put it to some use now that I don't play any more. No point in playing if you can't do it well. Insult to the instrument. Sit. I'll get Armand to bring us something. Sherry? Scotch?"

Brandon's stomach lurched. He'd barely been able to get through Aunt Bea's greasy plate of sausages and eggs an hour earlier. He wondered what response Cyril wanted from him—to accept a drink he didn't want in order to avoid offence, or to stand up for himself.

"I'll have a coffee instead, if it's on offer," he said.

Cyril's blue eyes flickered. He sat back in his wing chair and clasped his hands together to control their shaking. "So your bride has flown the coop."

"I don't know, sir. Has she contacted you?"

"Why would she? Checking out the family moneybags, to see if the marriage is worth her while?"

Brandon held his gaze with an effort, hoping his anger didn't show. "I think more likely to check out the family background."

"Whatever for? Aren't you enough for her? I hear you're a

doctor. Plenty of prestige and income potential in that."

"I don't believe it's about me, sir. I think she may have learned something disturbing about my background." He hesitated. Steeled himself. "About my father."

"Afraid depression and suicide might run in the family?"

"I understand there's some doubt it was suicide."

"Any fool who puts a noose around his neck mustn't hold his life in very high esteem, don't you think?"

A whispering footfall on the Persian carpet startled Brandon. He turned to see a diminutive middle-aged man in a crisp white shirt and perfectly pressed trousers balancing a tray of coffee cups and shortbread biscuits in one hand. Cyril nodded his approval as Armand set the tray with catlike precision on the coffee table between them.

"People give me these biscuits every Christmas, and I never know what to do with the damn things."

Brandon resisted the distraction. "Wasn't the suicide theory just to protect the family?"

"Protect the family? You think it's better to have a defeatist coward in your midst than a man who pushed the boundaries of sexual experience?"

"Well, to protect my mother, then. It would be a sufficient blow to have lost him—"

With a snort, Cyril snapped a biscuit in two. "Your mother was just as happy to be rid of him. She'd moved on before the grass was even laid on his grave."

Brandon tightened his grip on his coffee cup to control his outrage. "My mother loved him. She's never even remarried."

"Didn't want all the trouble that came with it, and no doubt she thought it would jeopardize your inheritance. She always was a schemer. Part Gypsy, I've always suspected. Harvey suited her very well dead. Gave her a respectable name—not Kerestsy or Kasanova or some damn thing, but Longstreet. She's done well with that name, without the bother of a reckless, sexually deranged husband."

Almost too late, Brandon reminded himself of his aunt's warning that Cyril would try to cut him to the bone. To what purpose, he wondered, other than to relieve his own pent-up venom? He wondered if this was why the man had so readily invited him in. For sport rather than for the pleasure of human interaction.

He took a deep, determined breath. "Do you have any information you can give me that might shed light on my fiancée's disappearance?"

Cyril picked up his coffee cup in both hands, took a long, careful sip, and then used a linen napkin to wipe his mouth. Brandon resisted the urge to throttle him.

"Son, I have no intention of encouraging your ill-advised obsession with this search. However, I suggest you ask yourself why, if only you mattered to her, she would be digging around in your background in the first place."

FOURTEEN

Midway through the smoked meat sandwiches, Magloire got a phone call. He talked for a few minutes in flawless French Canadian marked only by the musical cadence and slightly rounded vowels of his Haitian heritage. Then he snapped the phone shut.

"The warrants are ready. A uniform is bringing them over, so we can go straight to the victim's apartment." He cocked his head. "Is that okay? I am at your disposal for the day."

Green glanced at his watch and weighed his options. The day shift hours were flying by. "I prefer to start with the MisPers file and the investigating officer first." He didn't ask if that could be arranged. He suspected Chief Inspector Fournier had given orders to assist him in any way. Why else the lunch at Schwartz's, the car, the expedited search warrants, and the detective sergeant at his beck and call?

Magloire had just paid the bill when an unmarked but unmistakable Impala pulled up outside. Despite the wind whipping down boulevard St-Laurent and the salty slush splashing up from passing cars, the line-up to get into the iconic deli still stretched down the street. On Saturday just before Christmas, tourists jostled with ex-pat Montrealers and local shoppers for a place at the tables.

Magloire retrieved the warrants and headed around to his

car. Once again they accelerated out into the traffic with mere millimetres to spare. Lanes were narrowed by the snowbanks, and illegally parked cars cluttered the street still further. He stomped alternatively on the brakes and the gas as he fought his way up town.

"We're going to PDQ 26 on Decarie," he said. "That's in the old northwest part of the city, where there are more languages and cultures packed into one area than anywhere else in the city. The place is full of duplexes and cheap apartments, with good buses and the Metro, and nearby is Côte des Neiges, the major road that takes you over the mountain into downtown."

In preparation for the trip, Green had studied the map of Montreal and Googled the area where Gravelle lived. It was indeed a United Nations, where new immigrants mingled with students at the nearby University of Montreal in what had decades earlier been the heart of the Anglo-Jewish community. As they'd become more established and prosperous, that community had moved further west, or even out of the province, leaving the low-rent housing for newer groups.

Green caught a glimpse of the wide open slopes of Mount Royal as Magloire accelerated up the hill and entered a residential district of dignified old brick homes. Outremont, Green surmised, home of old French money, Jesuit seminaries and the university. Soon they were crossing raucous, colourful Côte des Neiges, teeming with shops, restaurants and shoppers. Magloire jogged north and continued west along Van Horne Avenue past Chinese take-outs, Korean markets and a Jewish religious school. Beneath tuques and scarves, black, south Asian and oriental faces dominated among the shoppers scurrying along the sidewalks, but every now and then Green spotted an ultra-Orthodox Chassidic family walking home from synagogue.

"I wonder why the victim lived out here," he mused. "I assume from her name that she's Francophone."

"We just learned she had a clerk's job at St. Mary's Hospital, which is just up there." Magloire nodded south towards the mountain.

After a few minutes he reached Decarie Boulevard, turned with a flourish and shot backwards up the one-way street. He screeched to a stop in front of a glass and concrete box that Green had taken for a bank until he saw the police logo and the big blue sign indicating Poste de Quartier 26 Ouest.

Magloire waved and was buzzed through the glass door into the brightly lit interior painted a cheery blue and yellow. A uniformed officer rose behind the counter. He was obviously expecting them, for he smiled in welcome. "Sergeant? Inspector?"

Magloire flashed his dazzling smile. "Guilty," he said in English. "Are you the lucky officer assigned to review the file with us?"

"No," the man replied in near-perfect English. "The investigator from St. Laurent station is off-duty, but one of our patrol officers will assist you. She took the original MisPers call and has been active on follow-up."

Green wondered how high up the order to cooperate had originated, and why. On the other hand, perhaps the neighbourhood patrol constable was just eager to see a high-level homicide investigation in action. The latter, he decided when Agent Yvette Tessier came bouncing through a door at the back. She looked impossibly young and impossibly tall, matching Magloire inch for inch in height, although half his girth. Her short black hair was spiked, almost as if to add even more height, and her expression radiated focus. She pumped Green's hand with enthusiasm.

"Any assistance we can offer, Inspector, any witness you want to interview, Detective Sergeant Giotti has authorized me to provide."

"*Merci.*" Green rescued his hand. Tessier's English was heavily accented, but he decided it was better than his French. "I'd like to review what your missing persons investigation has uncovered so far."

"Certainly! I have all that prepared for you." Tessier led the way into a large, immaculate conference room. A file folder sat in the centre of the table and a coffee maker gurgled in the corner. The smell of over-brewed coffee overpowered all else. Tessier reached for the carafe. "Coffee?"

When both detectives demurred in hasty unison, Tessier's face fell. Recovering quickly, she flipped open the folder. "Lise Gravelle," she began, reading from the top page. "Fifty-four year old white single female, reported missing by her neighbour in the next apartment on December 15 at 16:30 hours. Mme Gravelle asked her to take care of her dog for Monday night, but when she not return by Tuesday, she get worried. After she keep the dog a day, she call us. The neighbour did not know the missing individual before she move there and did not know her family or associates. However, I interviewed the building property manager. He said that Mme Gravelle is living there since one year and work at St. Mary's Hospital as a clerk. He had no complaints about her, and she always pay her rent on time. No next of kin is listed on the rent form."

Tessier pulled out a sheaf of papers that looked like an action log. "We check hospitals, clinics, ambulance, other police, no reports. I interview her employer and colleagues at St. Mary's. She quit work—" She shook her head sharply. "*Non,* left work at noon last Monday, she said because of the storm, but a colleague say she seemed upset—"

"Upset in what way?" Green interjected.

"*Distraite* is what the colleague said. Like something was on her mind."

"You mean scared, worried, sad?"

Tessier paused a moment, frowning into space as if trying to replay the interview. "My English is not one hundred per cent, but I think maybe nervous."

Nervous, Green thought. Rather different from frightened or sad. "Did this colleague know why, or offer any theory?"

"No, sir." Tessier shifted uncomfortably. "Nobody seem to know Lise very well, not even her colleague and neighbours. After one year, normally people make some friends, but Lise didn't mix. Never go out with the girls after work, always say she has to go home because of her dog. I have the impression she's a solitary person."

"What about the neighbour who reported her missing? Had she any information on what happened or why Lise was upset?"

Tessier referred to the file. "The last time she talk to Lise, it was Monday when she ask her to care for her dog. Lise didn't appear upset at this moment, on the contrary she was happy. Said she was celebrating."

"Why?"

"That's all she said."

"What time was this?"

"Sixteen hours—four o'clock. Just after."

Interesting, Green thought. On Monday she left work early, looking nervous, but by four o'clock she was celebrating. A few hours later she phoned Meredith Kennedy, they argued, and a few hours later still, she was dead on a street in Ottawa, not five minutes from Meredith's fiancé's home.

He glanced at Magloire. "Let's take a look at her apartment, see what she was up to."

Tessier looked up from her file, a worried frown on her face. "I hope that it was permitted, sir. Yesterday when I learn she died, I take her photo and I ask on the streets close to her apartment, and the shop and restaurant. Many people recognize her, see her walk with her dog, but no one talk to her except for 'nice day'. She appeared very ordinary and was taking very good care of her dog."

"Good work. Anyone seem especially curious or worried about her?"

Tessier took out her notebook and busied herself flipping slowly through it, as if trying to recapture each encounter. Her excitement faded. "No, sir. But there was many neighbours absent, because of the work day. I can go back today if you like. Maybe I find more people at their home on Saturday."

Green glanced at Magloire again. "Do you have officers to assist in a street canvass?"

"I can get whatever you need," Magloire said.

"But I can do it," Tessier said. "I know the neighbourhood very well, and not everyone is trusting the police."

Her initiative and enthusiasm were palpable. "Okay," Green said and turned to Magloire. "If you can get two more officers assigned to help her, that should be enough."

Once Magloire had dealt with that, they secured some evidence bins and the three set off in convoy with Tessier leading the way. Lise Gravelle's apartment was on the third floor of a brown brick low-rise that probably dated from the period between the wars. Identical brick buildings lined either side of the street for the entire block. A lot of neighbours to canvass, Green thought, revising his estimate of the officers required. But an easy place to get lost in if one wanted to be anonymous.

They parked at the curb outside, and Green sent the eager, efficient Agent Tessier in search of the building super while he leaned against the Impala and surveyed the street. Cars were parked all along the curb, competing for road space with the snowbanks. Some cars were still covered in snow, indicating they hadn't been moved all week, whereas others were hemmed in by the latest snowplow pass. The cars were a motley collection of old American gas guzzlers, cheap Korean subcompacts, and aging Toyotas and Hondas that had probably been recycled through several owners.

Green scanned the windows of the apartment building directly across the street and caught the faint flicker of a curtain falling into place. Smiling, he counted windows to pinpoint the apartment. This was his favourite kind of neighbour, the nosy kind with too much time on their hands.

When Tessier returned with the key, he pointed out the window across the street and told her to interview all the second-floor residents on this side of the building first. Drawing her long, lean frame to attention, she set off across the street almost at a run.

Green and Magloire took the ancient elevator that rumbled slow motion through the floors until it jolted to a stop on the third. The two detectives stepped into a narrow, dimly lit hall carpeted in brown some time in the past century. The air was thick with the smell of damp wool, fried oil and diapers. On the positive side, Green noted the walls were clean and graffiti free, and all the hallway lights worked. The building was modest, but proud.

Apartment 307 had a peephole, an extra dead bolt, and a chain lock dangling on the inside. Both detectives snapped on latex gloves out of habit before stepping into the room. The stench of feces and urine hit them full force, reminding them the dog had been abandoned for some time.

"Shall I clean up?" Magloire asked, holding his nose. Green

nodded and the big detective headed into the kitchen. Left alone, Green stood just inside the door to gather his first impressions of the dead woman.

She was neat, but either poor or indifferent to material possessions. The living room was small, sparse, and furnished with a Seventies-style orange sofa that she had probably picked up at the Salvation Army. A small TV, teak coffee table and gold shag carpet completed the secondhand look. But a newer IKEA desk and filing cabinet sat in the corner by the archway to the kitchen. Amazingly, the desk was uncluttered, and not a single magazine or discarded newspaper marred the order of the room. Two teacups were knocked over on the coffee table, however, and a brown stain blotched the carpet below.

In contrast to the shabby furniture, the walls were covered with stunning photographs. Some were landscapes and cityscapes, but most were black and white portraits that played with light, shadow and mood. There was a whole wall dedicated to dogs and another to small children. Green was drawn to a black and white portrait of a girl, younger than his own son but with the same luminous eyes and impish smile. She was gazing, not at the camera, but at her hand, which was reaching up towards a much larger, adult hand. She seemed to be both touching and drawing away, a study in connection and resistance that Green found fascinating. Wistfulness, yearning and connection were themes of many of the photos. Even the landscapes were exquisite but lonely—snow on gravestones, moonlight on barren trees.

Green took the photo of the girl off the wall and turned it over. On the back, the title, photographer and date were inscribed in black calligraphy. "Summer on Mount Royal, Amélie series, Lise Gravelle, 1981". Another photo showed the same scene, but this time the little girl was looking up at a young man. The young man's profile was in partial shadow, suggesting an illusion almost out of reach.

Green turned over another photo, this one of a long-eared dog resting its muzzle on its paws mournfully. "Mon Ami, Lise Gravelle, 1989". He crossed the room and selected a colour photo of a stream in springtime, the water rushing around the shards of ice still clinging to the bank. "Espoir, Lise Gravelle, 2002".

Hope, he translated. A world still frozen but coming alive again. Did they mean anything—these portraits of hope and yearning and loneliness—or were they just interesting studies by a talented artist exploring human experience?

Magloire emerged from the bathroom grasping in his fingertips a smelly garbage bag, which he placed in the hall outside the door. "Where do we begin, Inspector?"

Green had no idea of the man's investigative skills, although his apparent lack of interest in the photographs on the wall was telling. He nodded towards the bedroom. "You start in there, and I'll check this desk. We're looking for..." He raised his hand to tick off his fingers. "A computer and cellphone, papers that identify friends and family, any family photos, an agenda book, address book, letters, postcards... Most importantly, any connection to Meredith Kennedy or Ottawa."

Once Magloire had disappeared into the small room off the living room, Green took out his digital camera and methodically took pictures of every photo on the walls. He wasn't sure what use they would serve, but in a murder investigation, irrelevance was always better than regret. He then photographed the whole room from different angles before beginning a methodical search. He looked under the sofas, lifted the cushions and the carpet, leafed through the photographic and home decorating magazines stacked on the end table and the small pile of mail on the kitchen counter. Bills, flyers, charity requests—nothing out of the ordinary. He unfolded the bank statement and the credit card bill. The woman had a modest bank balance of two hundred dollars and no large deposits or withdrawals to suggest unusual activity in the last month. The credit card bill showed a similar frugality. She had paid off the card in full at the last due date and made only three small charges in the past month, to a pharmacy, a restaurant and Sears. If this woman had anyone on her Christmas gift list, she had not made her purchases early.

Green put the mail into the evidence bin, jotted down the names of the charities and turned his attention to the desk. Here too, Lise Gravelle was orderly and minimalist. The desk contained nothing but stationery supplies, stapler, sketch pads and several rolls of film. Where were all the negatives and copies of the photos on the wall? In his experience, photographers had several cameras and took hundreds of photos to get one perfect one. If her career had spanned thirty years, as the dates on the photos suggested, she had very little to show for it.

In the bottom drawer of the filing cabinet, he found a modern SLR camera, a box of lenses and a whole stack of CDs. He turned the camera on and thumbed through the recent photos. Images of the snowstorm, Christmas lights and bundled up pedestrians slogging through the snow. Portraits of winter life in Montreal, providing no obvious clues to her murder. He placed the camera and CDs into the evidence bin to take back to Ottawa for closer study.

In the upper drawer, he found neat file folders labelled bills, job applications, finances, taxes. He sifted through all these carefully, seizing anything that looked promising. Lise had no major debts or unexpected sources of income. Last year's taxes showed no mention of earnings from photography, only her income from her clerical job at St. Mary's, a pittance that would have been difficult to live on. She was emerging as a solitary, cautious woman who lived a methodical life without much joy or adventure. Like her photos—a life lived on the outside.

From the back of the filing cabinet drawer, he pulled out a thick file folder with no label. Inside was a jumble of brittle, yellowed newspapers. Green glanced at the dates. 1980, 1978. He froze as a name leaped out at him from the newsprint.

Longstreet.

He sat down at the desk, his heart racing, and skimmed the newspaper articles. With one exception, they were all from 1978 and chronicled the life and death of Harvey Kent Longstreet. Obituaries, police press releases, and newspaper features in the *Montreal Star*. The one exception was an article published in the *Westmount Examiner* in 1980 announcing that Mrs. Elena Longstreet, widow of prominent McGill law professor Harvey Longstreet, had accepted a position with the prestigious Toronto law firm of McGrath, Wellington, and Associates. Mrs. Longstreet cited exciting job opportunities and a fresh start as reasons for her departure from Montreal.

Beneath the stack of newspaper articles were some much newer pages, computer print-outs from the web. There was no sign of computer equipment in the apartment, so she must have used a public computer, possibly at her place of work. Most of the print-outs contained stories about Elena Longstreet's professional successes, including reports on high-profile appeals she had won and charities she supported. It was the last page that nearly took his breath away. A brief announcement of Brandon's and Meredith's upcoming wedding at the Ottawa home of prominent attorney Elena Longstreet, complete with a photo of the happy couple.

All the pages had been printed out on the same date, barely three weeks ago.

Green took the entire folder over to the evidence bin. His pulse was racing and his hands shook with the familiar rush of adrenaline. Here was the connection he'd been seeking! For whatever reason, Lise Gravelle had been obsessed with Elena Longstreet, enough to track down and preserve every possible piece of news on the woman, including her son's marriage. The question was why?

He went into the bedroom where Magloire was sitting on the floor by the bed, sorting through a plastic bin that had obviously been pulled out from under the bed. Green could see camera equipment and packets of photographs.

"Jean Pierre," he said, "get on the phone to your office and ask them to pull the police file on Harvey Longstreet's death in July 1978."

"Nineteen seventy-eight?" Magloire looked dismayed. "Is it an open file?"

"Not likely. It was ruled a suicide."

"Then the original would be in a box in a warehouse somewhere, open week days only. It might also be on microfilm in the archives, but they wouldn't be open today either."

Green pulled a face at the prospect of microfilm. "Can you pull some strings? And if possible get the original file. Once we're done here I'd like to go back downtown and have a look at it."

FIFTEEN

Magloire spent the next ten minutes on the phone, arguing in a French too rapid and colloquial for Green's unpractised ear, although it was liberally peppered with "*Non*!" He seemed to be repeating his request over and over as he went up the chain of command, his tone changing from jovial to cajoling to impatient until he seemed satisfied that the request would be carried out. Once he hung up, he shrugged.

"Budget cuts. On the weekend there is no one in records administration to deal with such a request."

Green opened his mouth to protest, but Magloire held up his hand. "But I have my ways. The original file I can't promise, but with luck at least the microfilm should be sent to us."

"Thank you. Have you found anything useful in the bedroom?"

"Besides these expensive cameras and hundreds of negatives she had stored under the bed?" Magloire lifted his broad shoulders in another shrug, as if the whims of women were beyond him. "I can tell you, for a Montreal woman and a photographer, her fashion sense is terrible. Striped socks, flowered polyester, nothing elegant, nothing sexy. No sign in her bathroom that she has a boyfriend or a sex life. *La pauvre*. Just lots of vitamins, medicines and an empty prescription bottle for Paxil."

"An anti-depressant."

Magloire nodded. "Filled last year at St. Mary's hospital pharmacy."

A sharp knock at the front door caused them both to turn. Tessier was standing in the doorway to the apartment, gazing at the photos on the wall. "*Tabernac!*" she breathed. "She was good!"

Green nodded, pleased at the young officer's perceptiveness. "When you get back to your station, you can research whether she's ever had a show or worked as a professional. Anything from the street canvass?"

Tessier snapped to attention. "You were right about the apartment across the street, sir. He is an old gentleman with a walker who passes all the day to observe the street. He saw her get into a taxi at..." she consulted her notebook, "just after sixteen hours last Monday. He remarked the time because it was getting dark and the snow was beginning to fall. She was all dressed up—boots, hat, winter coat, large hand bag..."

Green calculated quickly. Lise could have been heading for the five o'clock bus to Ottawa, one hour earlier than Meredith, in which case she would have arrived at seven p.m. An hour and a half before she phoned Meredith. Why wait so long? Perhaps to find a hotel?

Or to track down Elena Longstreet's address?

There was another knock at the door, softer and more tentative than the previous, and a thin, tired-looking woman peered in, clutching her winter coat around her. Her eyes were huge as she stared at Tessier.

"Is it true? She's dead?" she asked in French. "The news trucks are outside."

Green stepped forward before Tessier could respond. "You're her neighbour?"

The woman nodded, switching to English. "I reported her

missing. Poor woman. What will happen to T'bou?"

"That's her dog," Tessier said. "This is Mme Lasalle from the next apartment."

Green showed the woman inside. Mme Lasalle perched on the edge of the sofa but kept her coat wrapped around her as if guarding herself against the chill of death. Green began the routine battery of questions. How long had she known her? One year. Did Lise have any family or close friends? No, she never talked about her family, said her parents died years ago. Did Lise have any enemies or disputes with anyone? No, she was quiet and kept to herself. Did Lise ever talk about Ottawa?

Here Mme Lasalle coloured and dropped her gaze. "She didn't have much use for the government. Not for the English either, in fact. All rich, all stuck up, she thought they controlled everything and got all the breaks. I don't think she ever wanted to visit there."

"Did she mention any rich English person in particular?"

The woman shook her head. "She only mentioned it a couple of times, when she was angry. Most of the time we avoided politics. I think she was just sounding off, you know? Because she had a lousy job in an English hospital."

"Did she ever mention the name Longstreet?"

She shook her head again.

"Meredith Kennedy?"

"We didn't socialize much. She was a bitter woman, not fun to be with." She shrugged in apology. "I should have been more sympathetic."

"I understand she asked you to take care of her dog last Monday evening."

"Yes, just that night. But he's still at my place."

"Did she say where she was going?"

"No, but I told the officer she seemed happier. Maybe..." Her eyes widened. "Wait a minute! There was someone coming out of her apartment earlier that afternoon. I was coming back from the store, and this woman nearly knocked me over as she got on the elevator. She was very upset, crying, and I think she didn't even see me. I never saw her before." She leaned forward, excited. "I can't be certain where she was coming from, naturally, but when I go down the hall, Lise is there in her doorway. She appeared... I can't even describe the expression on her face."

"Nervous?"

"Oh no! It seems strange, but almost...triumphant."

Green blinked. Triumphant was a hell of a strong word. It implied a battle. A conquest. A victor. "Can you describe this woman in the elevator?"

"Thirty years. Quite beautiful, red hair, beautiful red coat."

Bingo, Green thought.

* * *

Early winter darkness was already seeping into the streets as the two detectives emerged from the apartment building. A Radio Canada media van was parked at the curb, and they had to dodge the glare of camera lights and the press of microphones as they made their way to the Impala. Magloire stopped only long enough to flash his trademark smile at the camera and say that he could not release any details at this time. He herded Green into the car and accelerated away in a spray of ice.

While Magloire drove, Green sat in silent thought, trying to plan the next steps in the investigation. The Kennedys needed to be interviewed about whether they'd ever heard of Lise Gravelle, and Elena Longstreet needed to be questioned about what possible connection there could have been between Lise Gravelle and her husband's death. Knowing Elena, Green suspected it would be more a confrontation than an interview. No one up in Ottawa—not Sue Peters, Bob Gibbs nor Marie Claire Levesque—was ready to go up against her.

In fact, even Green hesitated to face her down until he had all the facts he could muster about that old case and about the intervening years. Had Lise Gravelle nurtured her obsession with Elena in private, or had she contacted the woman? If so, why? In the end, he phoned Gibbs. From the sound of rock music in the background, he suspected he'd caught the young detective off duty. At five p.m. on a Saturday, why not?

"When you're back on, Bob, I want you to do some deep background digging on Elena Longstreet. Perform your magic with the internet. Go back as far as you can, 1978 if possible, and find out if she ever had dealings with Lise Gravelle, if their paths ever crossed in any way. Do the same with the Kennedys, both Meredith and her parents."

"You want me to do this tomorrow, sir? S-Sunday?"

"No rush," Green said, knowing full well Gibbs would be on it the moment he got off the phone. "Get Sue to help you. I know it's a needle in a haystack, but whatever that connection is, I think it's the key to both cases."

Just as the two detectives were arriving back at major crimes, Green's cell phone rang. It was Chief Inspector Fournier with the news that the Longstreet file was not immediately accessible but should be delivered to headquarters first thing in the morning. The chief inspector apologized but jokingly suggested that Green might enjoy a night on the town in Montreal. The chief inspector would love to join him but unfortunately had family obligations. He could, however, recommend some excellent restaurants. Green thanked him and hung up, quelling his impatience. He didn't want a night on the town, he wanted the warmth and comfort of his own home.

The lights were dim and the sixth floor was almost completely deserted as the two detectives lugged the evidence bins upstairs. Presumably, the day shift had gone off and the evening shift was already out on the streets. Magloire showed no inclination to punch the clock, however, but instead immediately set Green up at a desk adjacent to his in the open office area. The floor was a maze of cubicles equipped with the latest in computer and telephone technology. Except for the bulletins and lists of assignments covering the walls, it looked more like a corporate high tech firm than the hub of police investigations.

Magloire checked his phone and email messages and muttered a few curses under his breath. "Nothing worse than a bottle of Christmas cheer and a guy with no reason to celebrate."

Chuckling, Green gestured to the computer in front of him. "If you'll get me into your system, I can entertain myself while you deal with the drunks and domestics."

Magloire pushed himself away from his computer screen. "The evening boys have all that under control. I'm assigned to you, so what's next, *patron?*"

Suppressing a smile, Green pulled out the file of newspaper clippings he'd found at the victim's apartment. He sifted through the faded papers. The eulogizing and the dead man's achievements filled pages, but details of the investigation were surprisingly thin. The same reporter, Cam Hatfield, had covered the story from the initial report to the final wrap-up, and Green could almost feel his skepticism. It was worth finding out what else he remembered. But a subtle, oblique approach would be best, without the intercession of the large, amiable but decidedly cop-like Magloire.

"We need to widen our net," he said instead. "Lise Gravelle has had no contacts with Montreal Police, but I want you to run checks on possible relatives—"

"Agent Tessier had no luck finding any so far."

"Then check all the Gravelles."

"That will be hundreds!" Magloire exclaimed. "Montreal has more than three million people. Here!" He swung back to his computer and Green could see him typing in a 411 search. His face fell. "Okay, maybe not that many."

"Good. See what you can learn about them, and their relationship to Lise. Run checks on the Longstreet name too, and the Kennedys. See if any family members have been in the system." Green affected a yawn that was not entirely fake. "The 411 stuff can wait till the morning. I'm going to check into a hotel, grab some dinner, and maybe follow up on a couple of these news stories. Once you've done the police checks, you should knock off for the night. It's Saturday night. You got a family? Girlfriend?"

"Can I say both?" Magloire laughed. "Just kidding. I've got a wife and a beautiful little girl who keep me too busy to get into trouble." He hesitated. "You want to come meet them? Come for dinner?"

Green heard the reluctance in his voice and shook his head. "Thanks for the offer, but you've gone above and beyond today. I'm going to make it an early night." He stood, stretched and nodded to the evidence bins. "I'll leave those for you to sign in, and I'll just use the photos I took with my own camera."

Stepping out the front door of the major crimes unit five minutes later, he took a deep breath of the bracing winter air and drew in the scent of crisp snow, salt, car fumes and the hint of grilled steak from a nearby restaurant. Cars streamed along Sherbrooke Street East in a blur of red and yellow lights, their engines revving and their tires hissing on the salt-slushed pavement.

He had already booked a room for the night in an inexpensive boutique hotel on Sherbrooke Street West near McGill University, and once he'd checked in, he connected his laptop to the internet. Thirty years was a long time in the life of a news reporter, and since the *Montreal Star* had been defunct for decades, Cam Hatfield might be anywhere in Canada, or even abroad. Green was delighted when a simple Google search turned him up as a freelancer writing the occasional political and current events piece for the CanWest chain. Even more delighted when a Canada 411 search found him living on Greene Avenue, less than five kilometres from Green's hotel.

* * *

The old women were lined up along the wall of the sunroom like gargoyles, mouths sagging, empty eyes staring at the TV across the room. Most were propped in wheelchairs, although a few clutched canes or walkers in palsied hands. The two closest to the door did not react when Brandon appeared in the doorway, but a woman with a walker in the middle of the room perked up. Eagerness replaced the boredom in her eyes.

"Well, hello, stranger," she said, struggling to turn her walker towards him. "Who let you in?"

Brandon smiled doubtfully. One of the nurses on duty had offered to introduce him to Meredith's grandmother, but she had looked overworked and harassed. Out of sympathy, he'd declined her offer but confronting this parade of blank faces, he regretted his decision.

"I'm here to see Mrs. Callaghan," he said.

"Oh, pooh. She's gaga. You won't get the time of day out of her." The woman inched towards him across the room, her wraith-like frame hunched over her walker. "You'll get a lot more out of me."

Brandon was acutely aware of the locked doors, the bars on the windows and the bright, washable decor. He tried to picture his mother reduced to this. Geriatrics had been his least favourite medical school rotation because it felt like looking into the abyss. Meredith's grandmother had once been the glue of her family. She'd left school after Grade Eight to work in a clothing factory to supplement the family income during the Depression, but she'd always had a strong sense of folk wisdom. Nan had an answer for every question and a salve for every hurt. Mostly it consisted of "God has his reasons," and if that didn't work, she fell back on "That's life, get on with it."

She had worked in the factory throughout the Second World War but married the first Irish lad to disembark from the troop ship in Montreal harbour afterwards. Her folk wisdom continued to dominate the family throughout the raising of her five children and nine grandchildren. Meredith's eyes always danced when she talked to Brandon about her Nan, even when the woman was at her most old-fashioned and infuriating. Nan believed in family, church and babies; to fail at those elements was to fail at life.

A shell was all that was left of the woman now, and the sight would be excruciating for all the children she had nurtured. Had Meredith come to visit her that mysterious Monday afternoon, Brandon wondered. And had something spooked her from taking the next step along her own life path, as if by not getting married, she could stop the clock and prevent her own bodily decay?

The nurses at the station had no record of such a visit, nor did they remember the young woman in the photo Brandon showed them. That would have been a different shift, the charge nurse said, although usually something as important as an out-of-town visit would be charted. Mrs. Callaghan didn't get too many visitors. Only one daughter still lived in Montreal and she came twice a week. But there hadn't been an out-of-town family member in at least two months, and they would have noted it because any unfamiliar person could be upsetting to the patient. Families meant well, but they stirred up feelings. Sometimes the patient didn't remember them or mistook them for someone else, and it triggered unpleasant memories.

Another nurse who was nearby had pitched in. "The last time Meredith's mother visited, it was like that. Mrs. Callaghan accused her of hiding things, keeping secrets and lying."

"Lying?" Brandon's interest was piqued. "About what?"

The nurse shook her head sympathetically. "It doesn't matter, it doesn't mean anything. When the mind gets confused and no longer remembers connections, it's easy to think people are lying and keeping secrets. It's a very scary place to be. Please remember that when you speak to Mrs. Callaghan. When she gets upset, it's hard to calm her down again."

Brandon was still holding Meredith's photo when he entered the sunroom. He was just debating how to proceed when the woman with the walker reached his side. Her whole frame shook with the effort, but her eyes were bright as she spied the photo.

"I remember that girl! She came to see the old bat. Not that it did her any good."

Brandon assessed the woman dubiously. She had two round circles of rouge on her cheeks and a matching bow of red lipstick. Pearls encircled her thin neck. She looked about four feet tall and a hundred years old, but she smiled like a young girl and her gaze was shrewd. His hopes lifted. "Do you remember when?"

"Of course I do. Nothing wrong with my mind. Or my eyes," she added with a slow smile. "Just last week."

He sucked in his breath. "Did you hear their conversation?"

She rolled her eyes. "You can't talk to her! Nothing but gibberish. She shooed the poor girl away. Said she wasn't part of the family and shouldn't try to trick her."

Poor Meredith, Brandon thought. To come all this way and be forgotten. "What did her granddaughter say?"

"She kept telling her to remember when she was little and such. The old bat just screamed at her to go away until the girl gave up."

"How was she? Upset?"

"Mad as hell." The woman mouthed a flirtatious "Oh" and pressed her fingertips to her lips. "Not supposed to say that. Perhaps you'll have more luck with the old bat than the girl did, although she's not having a very good day."

She edged her walker out of the way and gestured towards an elderly woman in the corner. Meredith's grandmother was slumped in her wheelchair with her large bony knees protruding from her nightgown and her hands hanging like claws over the arms of her chair. Her pure white hair clung to her pink scalp in strands like a thin cirrus cloud, and spittle collected at the corner of her mouth. Her pale blue eyes were fixed on the television.

Brandon slowed midway in his approach, struck by the futility of his quest. Struck too by the voices on the television. A woman reporter was standing in the snow outside an aging brick apartment building.

"The police are not yet releasing any details about the dead woman, pending notification of next of kin, but neighbours have confirmed that she is fifty-four-year-old Lise Gravelle, an employee of St. Mary's Hospital, who lived alone in this apartment building with her pet dog." Briefly the Missing Persons photo filled the screen. "This afternoon, detectives from both Montreal and Ottawa searched the apartment and removed two large boxes of evidence."

The camera panned through the dark and caught a brief glimpse of three people climbing into cars at the curb. Brandon squinted. Shock raced through him as he recognized Inspector Green. What was he doing in Montreal?

"Keep away from her!"

The screech jolted him back. He swung around just in time to see a cane flying through the air towards him. It clipped him on the shoulder before he could duck. The grandmother's eyes were bulging as she looked wildly at him.

"Stay away! You think I don't know who that is? Devil's child! Devil's child!" A slipper flew across the room.

The staff moved quickly to whisk her away to her room, leaving the rest of the patients muttering in annoyance. And leaving Brandon open-mouthed in the middle of the room, wondering what the hell all that was about.

"Well, you sure made an impression," said the little old lady, reappearing at his side.

SIXTEEN

Green stood outside the old Montreal Forum building, looking up at its modern metal cladding with dismay. A Futureshop and an AMC theatre now occupied most of the building, their gaudy red lettering replacing the sturdy brown brick of the original façade. He recalled the only other time he'd been inside. His father, the timid immigrant tailor from Poland, had never watched a hockey game in his life but had believed his twelve-year-old son should share the quintessentially Canadian father-son dream of watching the Montreal Canadiens during their legendary Stanley Cup run.

"*Meshugas,*" he had announced after three hours of plugging his ears and trying to watch the tiny black disc ping-pong around the rink. Craziness. Green had never been to a game since, although Tony was beginning to wheedle, and he knew he'd have to give in. History had a way of racing ahead, leaving nothing but regret in its wake. He pushed aside the twinge of nostalgia as he reached for the door of Guido and Angelino's.

Once a news hound, always a news hound, he thought as he walked into the bar and caught sight of the rumpled figure perched on a barstool at the very end of the bar. The man was facing the door, keeping an eye on the action as he nursed a drink. Not much got by him, Green suspected, meeting the man's gaze. Without a flicker of acknowledgment Cam Hatfield picked up his drink, slid off his barstool and moved to a table in the corner. He was a stubby man, and in his yellow parka, he reminded Green of a fire hydrant. His feet were encased in massive boots that clumped as he walked and he had to shove the table out nearly a foot further to accommodate his gut. Dirt and age had faded his clothing, and his greying hair stood in unkempt spikes. He looked as if he'd spent the previous night under a railway bridge, but his blue eyes, set deep in his leathery face, were keen.

He grinned as he appraised Green. "You don't look much like an inspector."

To avoid the intimidating inspector persona, Green had dressed in his favourite jeans and faded sweatshirt for his night on the town and had tossed on his battered suede jacket. He knew that with his slight build and boyish freckled face, he didn't look very inspectorish. The reporter was good.

He returned the man's grin. "But you knew it was me."

"Cops have an aura. The way you scan a room, always aware of your surroundings. We're not so unalike, you know."

"Thanks for meeting me."

"Yeah, well, don't go all Pollyanna. I'm intrigued. You know what that means."

Green nodded, suspecting the man needed a big story more than he let on. "I'll do what I can. For now, this is just background."

"To do with the Lise Gravelle murder, I assume?"

Green kept his face blank. Cam Hatfield was no fool. Why else would a high-ranking Ottawa police detective be in the city in the first place? "I'm exploring leads."

"Right," Hatfield said drily. He signalled the barman for a refill. "So what leads did you uncover in Lise Gravelle's apartment that bring you back to the thirty-year-old Longstreet case?"

"When I know, Cam, you'll be among the first to know." The barman approached and Green ordered a local St. Ambroise pale ale. Catching Hatfield's scowl of disgust, he held up a cautionary hand. "I know that sounds like bullshit, but the truth is, I'm flying blind right now, and I can't afford to jeopardize the investigation. I have a feeling you knew there was more to the Longstreet case than was reported. If you can help me get to the truth, you have my word you can be in on the Gravelle story when it's safe to break it."

Hatfield studied him in silence, twirling his Scotch glass on the beer coaster before him. Despite his rumpled, down-on-his-luck looks, his gaze was astute. Finally he picked up his glass and took an appreciative sip. "Well, my sources in Ottawa tell me I should stick to you like glue, so I'm in."

Green laughed. "Don't tell me. Corelli." He and the *Sun* reporter had a chequered history of cooperation.

Hatfield shrugged, giving nothing away. "So, for some reason that you will at some future date reveal to me, you want to know about the Longstreet clan and most specifically about the peculiar death of Harvey Longstreet thirty-two years ago."

"You remember it?"

"Oh, I remember it. I quit my job over it. Mind you, I knew the *Star* was about to fold, so it was no big loss." He chuckled. "I couldn't stand my new boss, or the direction the paper was taking under the new management, so it felt great to stand in the news editor's office and say 'That's it. This is my line in the sand, and I quit.' Of course, I had a lead on a much better job with Canadian Press wire service before I did my *grande geste*."

"I had a look at the press clippings from both the *Star* and the *Gazette*. It looks as if the story just died."

"Killed." Hatfield made a slicing motion through the air. "The word just came down from on high. 'There's nothing there but prurient curiosity that is damaging the reputation of an honourable man, so the *Star* is no longer participating.'"

"Who was putting on the pressure?"

"Oh, the Longstreet family, without a doubt, through one of their Westmount lawyers who played footsie with the *Star*'s owners over drinks at the St. James Club. Old English money in Montreal is completely incestuous. Everybody who's anybody is married to someone or related to someone who's somebody, and the Longstreets, from their castle on top of Westmount, are right in the thick of it. It's a dying class now, with most of the power brokers moved on to Toronto or Calgary, but thirty years ago they were still a force."

Hatfield took another sip of his Scotch, nursing it and relishing his soap box. Green was silent, happy to let him fill in the context. "You have to understand, thirty years ago the English were under siege. René Levesque and his Parti Québecois had won their first victory in 1976, businesses were deserting the province in droves, real estate values were in the tank. The separatist wolves were at the door, smelling blood. The Anglo elite was circling the wagons to protect its image and honour from the contempt of the Quebec intelligentsia and the resentment of the Quebec masses. During his life Harvey was one of the few to earn their respect, because he took on the English establishment. If the truth about his death came out, it would have been a humiliation, proof of the utterly corrupt and decadent depths to which the great Anglo industrial complex had fallen."

At this point Green rolled his eyes. "Back to earth, Cam. I get it; the bigwigs wanted the story suppressed. But who exactly were these bigwigs?"

Hatfield pouted. "But you have to understand the Anglo-Quebec dance. Nowhere was it more exquisitely executed than right here in this building in 1955. When it was still the Montreal Forum, thousands of Montreal Canadiens fans took to the streets in a riot because their beloved hockey icon, Rocket Richard, had been suspended by the English-speaking rulers of the NHL."

Green sighed. "I live in Ottawa. Trust me, I know the English-French dance. But behind the politics, there are always personalities pulling the strings. René Levesque, Pierre Trudeau, Lucien Bouchard... Who were the people pulling the strings in the Longstreet affair? Elena Longstreet? Her father-in-law?"

Hatfield grunted in dismissal. "Elena Longstreet was a nobody. The daughter of a Hungarian immigrant who'd fled the communists in 1956 claiming he was a count. Elena had looks, brains and charm, and luckily for her, an infant son with Longstreet blood in his veins. Without that, she'd have been back making goulash."

"She's not a nobody any longer."

Hatfield nodded. "So I hear. But in 1978 she was a bewildered, heartbroken young widow barely out of law school."

Green raised an eyebrow. "Heartbroken?"

"That may be an exaggeration. She certainly knew what she wanted—to preserve her husband's good name and of course by extension, her own."

"Was there money involved? Insurance?"

"A drop in the bucket compared to what Uncle Cyril controlled from his perch at the top of the Circle."

Green perked up. Here was a name. "Uncle Cyril?"

"The actual man at the helm of the Longstreet fortune. Others had shares and trusts, but these were set up so that Cyril maintained control. Cyril never married and he had no children, but after his brothers died, he decided who among all the nephews, nieces and grandwhatzits got any money."

"Is he still alive?"

"Oh, he'll never die. He's pretty much housebound now, but too stubborn to relinquish his iron grip on other people's lives."

Green sipped his beer thoughtfully. The picture was taking shape. Realizing he was starving, he signalled the waiter. "So Cyril quashed the story."

Hatfield said nothing until the waiter arrived with a menu. "Try the cannelloni, it's a safe bet if you're cheap like me."

With a grin, Green ordered the meat cannelloni while Hatfield ordered another Scotch. Single malt this time, Green noticed and realized that the Ottawa Police Services would be paying. Once the new Scotch was in front of him, Hatfield closed his eyes in bliss. "Yeah, I always assumed Cyril quashed the story. No big thing for him. He and his pals had been manipulating the news for years."

Determined to divert Hatfield from his favourite political soap box, Green plunged ahead. "Tell me what you do know about the Longstreet case."

"I know it wasn't suicide."

Green's eyebrows shot up. "What did the autopsy find?"

"Asphyxiation due to strangulation. That much was released before the hammer came down. But get this." Hatfield leaned in close, breathing Scotch. "He was naked as a jaybird."

The penny dropped. "Ah. And the cops knew this?"

"Of course they did! So did the coroner. But they killed it to avoid the scandal. It wasn't that common back then, or at least as openly talked about, but obviously sex was involved. But whether the guy was doing himself, or had an over-enthusiastic partner who miscalculated, the cops never said."

"But surely the cops would have at least investigated whether there was another person in the room. There was no DNA back then, but they would have looked for fingerprints, a second wine glass, hairs on the sheets..."

"Everything was wiped clean."

"Everything?" Green leaned forward. "You mean door knobs, toilet seats…?"

"And the dishes in the drainboard. All washed, all whistle clean, according to the investigating cop."

Green sat back in disbelief. "Didn't that strike anyone as suspicious? If you were about to engage in a little game of auto-erotic asphyxiation, you don't wipe all the dishes and surfaces clean. You don't expect to die!"

Hatfield laughed. "You'd think. I asked the cop that, in fact. Some fresh off the farm kid who'd just landed his first case. Not even a detective. The force hadn't even called in the big guns, and when the coroner ruled it suicide, they just left this kid with this stinking political mess in his lap."

Green sidestepped the political reference. He knew the force wouldn't have left the young officer to his own devices. Someone higher up had pulled the strings. "So what you're saying is there was no investigation. What about witnesses? The landlord, the neighbours?"

Hatfield shrugged. "Suddenly blind and deaf, even after I offered a substantial sum. Never heard a thing. Professor Longstreet was a quiet, considerate neighbour who wasn't there very often, and when he was, he was as helpful and hard-working as you could possibly want. Even offered to help one woman with her restraining order and another with some minor traffic charge. All-round saint."

Green's cannelloni arrived, smothered in thick sauce and

fragrant with basil and garlic. He sank his fork into the cheesy mixture and prepared to take a bite. "Okay, but you know something, I can tell. Something the *Star* wouldn't let you print."

Hatfield chuckled. "I *had* something, but it vanished between my fingers the minute Cyril Longstreet's minions paid a visit to the apartment building with a chequebook in hand. The tenant in the apartment underneath was a med student working eighteen hours a day at the Montreal General and off-hours as a bartender to pay for her studies. She was upset at all the noise— the parties, the singalongs, the gung-ho student meetings to plan their next protest that always ended with some bed-banging deep into the night. She told me Longstreet had sex every night he spent there, got so she hated to see him arrive because she needed her sleep."

Green's pulse quickened. "So there was almost certainly a lover present when he hanged himself. Any idea who?"

"Some pretty young thing. The med student, who was anything but, was not very specific."

"Always the same girl?"

"Well, there were lots to choose from back in those days before all the politically correct sexual harassment crap. And it would be in keeping with the type of sleaze who screws co-eds while his wife is home with a two month-old baby."

"Co-eds? It was one of his students?"

"That's just a guess, but it was his pattern. Elena herself had been his student, and thirteen years his junior."

"Did the Montreal Police know this?"

"I told that baby-faced cop, but I doubt he followed up. Too much work. He might even have to investigate. Nobody wanted this case to be anything. They all just wanted it to go away." Hatfield grinned and drained his glass, rolling the last of the

Scotch around on his tongue. "It's kind of poetic justice in a way, that now it's come back to bite everyone in the ass."

*   *   *

The aroma of coffee wafted into her dreams and wrapped itself languidly around her naked body. Tickled her nostrils, brushed lips across her forehead.

Lips?

Sue Peters opened her eyes to see the morning sun carving slats of shadow on the wall opposite. Above her, Gibbsie bent his sleep-tousled head, a smile on his face and a cup of coffee in his hand. His other hand roamed her belly, tentative and tender. What a hardship to wake up to on a Sunday morning. Fighting the stiffness of her damaged body, she pushed herself partially upright against the pillows and took the coffee. Strong, black, fabulous. He fetched his own coffee and slipped in beside her.

"I love waking up beside you in the morning," he said.

"Mmm..." she said, wary. "You make a mean coffee."

He reddened and his Adam's apple bobbed. A bad sign. "I've been thinking, we'd save money so much faster living together."

"Money maybe, but not sanity. I told you, I'd drive you nuts in less than a month."

He leaned over to kiss the little ridge of scar below her breast. Once she'd been ashamed to let him see her, let alone explore every inch of her.

"You could never drive me crazy, ever," he murmured. "Except by saying no. You know you're going to marry me someday."

She rolled her eyes. "And you know it's not going to happen until I can keep up my end one hundred per cent."

"You can! You said you'd marry me when you could walk

down the aisle without a cane, and you can!"

"Sometimes. But I'm just as likely to pitch sideways into the pews."

He didn't answer right away, and she figured he was thinking the same thing she was, that she might never be one hundred percent. After all, it was nearly three years since the assault. Then he touched her hand. "Don't you dream about it sometimes?"

She nodded, took a sip of coffee and silently swore at her shaking hand.

"Then let's do it! Just go for it. Grab it. Holy jumpin', Sue, you of all people understand that we never know what's around the corner. Look at poor Brandon Longstreet—one minute he thinks he's got his dream in the palm of his hand, and the next minute it's ripped from his hand."

"Meredith's choice, Gibbsie. Obviously not such a perfect dream after all."

"We don't know that. We only know this Lise Gravelle spooked her and made her take off."

"But not even telling Brandon where she is? You got to admit, Bob, that's a pretty good kick in the teeth."

"Oh, Sue, that's not the point!" He shoved himself up in bed. "The point is, b-bad stuff happens. We can't control that, but we can control what we do. I love you just the way you are. I don't want to wait months or years to be with you—"

He was winding himself up into a rant she'd heard before, but this time she was barely listening. An awful thought had occurred to her, and she wondered why they'd both missed what had been staring them in the face for days.

She clutched his arm. "Bob, why do you suppose she hasn't contacted Brandon?"

He sputtered mid-rant. "What?"

"Think about it. If they loved each other, if they trusted each other, why wouldn't she send him a sign?"

"Because...she's freaked out?"

She whipped her head back and forth. "That might work for a few hours, but not days. She's supposedly an intelligent, level-headed woman, not some hysterical bimbo."

"Then because she's mad at him? I don't know! Sue, it's Sunday morning. I haven't even finished my coffee yet, I'm in bed with the woman I love, talking about marriage—"

"This is important, Bob!"

"So's our marriage!"

"Oh, for Pete's sake, I never said I wouldn't marry you—"

"This spring?"

"What?"

He grinned. Still red but no longer sputtering. "This spring. When the tulips are in bloom and the fruit trees are budding."

"Can we discuss this case?"

"We can have an outdoor wedding, maybe in the arboretum, on the little footbridge."

She stared at him. He wasn't grinning any more. His cheeks were flushed and his dark eyes sparkled. He was serious.

"Yes or no," he said. "And I'm not taking no."

A strange heat raced through her whole body from her toes all the way to her scalp, setting her skin on fire. A laugh bubbled up in her. Relief. Joy. Who the hell knew?

"Is that a yes?"

"I guess it is."

He dived for her, spilling the dregs of her cold coffee over the blanket. "Finally!" he managed before burying himself in a kiss.

It was a full hour before he turned to her with a puzzled look. They were both showered and dressed, and the remains of eggs and toast sat on her tiny breakfast table.

"Were you saying something about Meredith Kennedy before I...?"

"Before you dragged me off topic?" She smiled. The brilliance of her insight had dimmed now, but it was still a damn good idea. "I was. I was saying there are only two reasons I can think of why she hasn't sent word to Brandon in all this time, especially if she knows how frantic everyone is."

"Well, obviously if she's dead..."

She nodded slowly. "That's one."

"I know you have your doubts about that, since her credit card was used and Lise Gravelle turned up dead, but it's hard to see why else—"

"The other reason is if she's the one who killed her."

SEVENTEEN

"Don't you think we should tell the sergeant?" Bob asked. He was driving the way he always did, eyes straight ahead, both hands on the wheel. The roads were dry as bleached bone now but still narrowed by icy snowbanks on either side. As the crow flies, it was a short hop from Sue's apartment to the station, but the one-way streets turned the trip into a labyrinth.

The sun, just days from its winter solstice, was barely making it over the rooftops and its pale glare was blinding. No warmth to it, though; the car thermometer read minus fifteen and the exhaust from cars and chimneys billowed white in the bitter air.

Sue suppressed a shiver as she figured out an answer. "We will," she said, "but Inspector Green assigned us some background checks, so I think we should do those before we tell anyone our theory." She could see the little smile on his lips, and she knew he didn't want to report in to Marie Claire Levesque any more than she did. This was their case and the inspector had made the requests to them personally, so she was damned if Levesque was going to get all the glory for their work.

Luckily, when they arrived at the station, the sergeant wasn't even there. Murder cases didn't take days off—how many times had Sue seen the inspector work all week without a break—but Levesque was probably off tobogganing with her daughter.

Let's not go there, she chided herself, pulling herself back to the task at hand. Marriage, kids, the impossible Mommy dance—that was getting ahead of herself. It was bad enough she was now staring at a spring wedding!

She stopped at her desk next to Bob's, and they hung up their coats and fired up their computers in perfect unison. He looked at her and laughed. On the way over, they had divided up the computer searches, with Bob ferreting out the links and her following along behind to jot down any relevant findings. No one navigated the web like Bob, and if there was information to be found linking Lise Gravelle to Elena Longstreet or the Kennedys, he would find it.

At the end of three hours, they'd found precious little, although Bob claimed that in itself was significant. From what he could find, Lise had never crossed paths with Elena, either as a client, witness or adversary. They did not belong to the same associations, support the same charities or frequent the same online sites. In fact, although Elena showed up on the web all over the place, Lise's cyber footprint was very small. Almost invisible. The woman barely existed. There were a couple of payments to the Parti Quebecois, some charitable donations to Médecins sans Frontières and Plan, nothing more.

By comparison, Elena was a cyber star, showing up on the boards of several charities and law associations, frequently featured in the social columns and lifestyle pages of both Toronto and Ottawa newspapers. Interviews with local radio and television stations were archived on sites. The woman was a passionate defender of the Charter of Rights, which may have been Prime Minister Trudeau's proudest achievement and a defence attorney's best friend, but an obstructive pain in the ass to law enforcement efforts across the country.

Still, as she listened to the videos and read the articles, Sue couldn't help admiring the woman. She'd fought for respect and equality among the white-haired, middle-aged men who controlled positions of power in the legal profession. She'd quit a prominent law firm in Toronto when she found herself bashing her head against its glass ceiling, and she'd come to Ottawa to establish her own firm. Hired her own juniors, taken on the white-haired bastards in court, and won more times than not.

All the time raising a kid entirely on her own.

In all this blitz of media coverage, however, there wasn't a single connection to the poor little invisible woman who worked as a hospital clerk in Montreal. Bob had even less luck with the Kennedys. Norah had virtually no presence on the web, only cropping up as the secretary of her local church women's group and a few years ago on an amateur curling team. Reg had written some letters to the *Citizen* editor complaining about high city taxes, police inaction on low-level crimes such as vandalism, and the decline in parental supervision due to single-parent families. But besides being a complainer and a hard-nosed, law-and-order type, Reg Kennedy kept out of the spotlight. He was in their police system as witness to a few disturbances and impaired driving cases, but being a bartender, that was to be expected.

In his perusal of public records, however, Bob did discover one interesting fact. Both Reg and Norah had grown up in Montreal and had moved to Ottawa only after their marriage.

"Plus Elena Longstreet left Montreal in 1981. That's all pre-internet, so if the connection between them all dates back to Montreal, it will be on paper records only," he added in frustration. "We need to find out what part of Montreal they grew up in, what schools they attended, what children's camps, college activities..."

Sue raised her eyebrow skeptically. "You think the Kennedys

went to college?"

He shook his head. "Probably not, but the Quebec CEGEPs are like junior colleges, and I'll bet back then there weren't very many of them, so English kids from all over Montreal might have been thrown together. You have to go to CEGEP for two years before university, so even Elena would have attended. One way to find out. They'll have records." He reached for the phone.

"But Lise Gravelle is French."

He hesitated in mid-dial before shaking his head. "Still worth a shot. We're going to have to use the phone to get at this earlier background anyway."

He looked adorable, bent over his computer clicking through links as he dialled with his other hand. She pulled herself to her feet stiffly and went over to drape her arms around his neck. She nibbled his ear. "It's Sunday, Gibbsie. Nobody's going to be there."

He flushed deep red, jotted down a number and hung up. "Damn."

"We could just ask them, you know. Drive over to the Kennedys and ask them where they lived in Montreal, where they went to school, if they ever met Lise Gravelle."

He turned into her arms. "The inspector just asked us to do background. Maybe he doesn't want to tip them off just yet."

"Tip them off about what?"

"About Lise Gravelle. That we suspect a connection."

She stood up and snatched her jacket off her chair back. "For Pete's sake, Gibbsie, we won't give away any state secrets! It's a routine inquiry, all part of trying to track down where their daughter might have gone."

She knew he'd cave. He could never say no to her. As he drove them to the Kennedy home, she leafed through her notes and papers in Meredith's case, trying to see if they'd overlooked some small detail she could use as a wedge. Her pulse jumped when she found one.

Norah and Reg Kennedy had just come home from church and were still in their finery—Reg looking like an undertaker in a navy wool pullover and white dress shirt, and Norah in a black knit dress that stuck to her in all the wrong places. The week of worrying had worn them out. Their skin was grey and their eyes had sunk into their skulls as if in retreat from the world. They flinched at the sight of the two detectives. The house smelled of a thousand foods—chocolate, basil, cabbage and vinegar. Sue suspected the parade of friends and helpers had continued all week, but the living room was so clean you could eat off the floor. Funny how some people cope.

Figuring to put their fears to rest, Sue spoke as soon as she sat down. "No news, I'm afraid. We're just doing some routine follow-up to see if there's anything we missed."

Without her having to ask, Gibbs took out his notebook and let her lead. "Have you thought any more about who Meredith might have visited in Montreal?"

Norah shook her head. "She knows people there through her work, so maybe it was one of them."

"You're both from Montreal, right?"

A flicker crossed Norah's face. The briefest hesitation. "Yes, but we moved here years ago."

"Where did you live there?"

"Beaconsfield. It's..." Norah gestured in vague dismissal. "It's a suburb on the lakeshore. West Island."

"Do you remember the address?"

Norah frowned. "I can't see why..."

Sue improvised. "In case Meredith felt like tracing her roots. Feeling sentimental..."

"There's nothing sentimental about Montreal—"

Reg interrupted to supply an address, earning a scowl from Norah. "Anything that helps, Norah," he said.

Norah watched Gibbs record the address. "I doubt anyone will remember us there now. Pretty well all our neighbours were leaving too. Probably all French now."

Sue tried to sound casual and sympathetic. This Norah was proving a tough nut. "Is Beaconsfield where you two grew up as well?"

Norah snorted. "I wish! Neither one of our families could afford to own a home. We both grew up in a tougher neighbourhood near downtown."

"You know Montreal?" Reg asked.

Sue shrugged, trying to sound believable. "I have relatives there."

"Park Extension, in the top floors of duplexes." he said. "Hot, airless and cramped. The Irish, the Jews and then the Greeks moved through there, kids grew up tough. Not mean—they had good, hard-working parents—but they learned the value of a dollar early."

Sue shifted her stiff body so she could aim her next question at Reg. "Were there English schools around? Could you at least get a good education?"

"Oh yeah, we both finished high school no problem. There was no money for college, but that never held me back."

"College? You mean CEGEP?"

"Oh, we went to CEGEP. Had to travel halfway across the city to get to the English one back then—"

"Dawson College?" Sue plucked the only name she knew.

"Yeah, it was free, and both Norah and me got our start that way—me in small business and her in typing and book-keeping—"

"Reggie!" Norah snapped. "I don't see how the detectives could be interested in our life story."

He was undaunted. "Norah even got her first job working for the police—"

"Reggie!"

"Wow," Sue said. "Right in the mean streets of Montreal?"

Norah bolted to her feet, tugging to get her dress in line. "Where are my manners? How about some tea?" She was halfway through to the kitchen when she paused to glance back at her husband. Doubt was written all over her face. She doesn't want to leave me alone with Mr. Chatterbox, Sue thought.

Sure enough, she returned and sank back on the sofa with an exaggerated sigh. "Reggie, why don't you get us tea? I'm dead on my feet."

Once he was gone, Sue turned to tackle Norah. "Did you ever meet a woman named Lise Gravelle during your Montreal days?"

"It was so long ago. I don't recognize the name."

"She's the woman found frozen in the snowbank in Rockcliffe last week."

"Oh! I never heard her name. Poor woman. She was from Montreal?" When Sue nodded, she shrugged. "Montreal's a big place."

"She never phoned here?"

"Here?" Norah's tired eyes widened in shock. "Why should she?"

"To speak to Meredith. She phoned Meredith six times on her cell phone in the week before her death."

Norah suppressed a gasp and stared at Sue in bewilderment. In the stillness, the only sound was Reg moving around the kitchen, running water and clattering cups. Norah swallowed. "I have no idea why. Maybe Meredith knew her from work?"

"Meredith never mentioned her? Never asked about her?"

"No."

Sue reached into her folder and drew out a single photocopied page containing the phone records to the Kennedy's home line obtained through unofficial channels by Sergeant Li. She pretended to study it. "This is a record of Lise Gravelle's phone calls."

Norah recoiled. "What?"

"The records from her cell phone."

"What—what…?" Norah reached for the paper, which Sue deftly moved from view. Luckily Bob didn't utter a peep, just sat as transfixed as Norah.

"Sorry, this is confidential information. Part of a murder inquiry."

Norah was silent, staring at Sue's file. For added drama, Sue drew her finger down a column of numbers. "The records show she placed six calls to Meredith's cell in the past two weeks. However, your home phone number also shows up on her list of calls."

Still Norah said nothing. Sue could feel the faint quaking of her body on the sofa beside her. She softened her voice. "Lise Gravelle phoned this house last Monday evening."

"I don't understand. Maybe she was looking for Meredith?"

"Meredith wasn't home. She never came home, remember?"

"But perhaps this woman called looking for her."

"This call to your house was placed at 8:54 p.m. Just after she'd spoken to Meredith on her cell."

"There was no call. I don't remember a call."

A footfall sounded in the hall and Reg appeared. "There was a wrong number, you remember, honey? While we were watching *Little Mosque*."

Norah swung around to stare at him. She looked the colour of death. "What are you talking about?"

"I answered it, remember? A woman mumbled something and hung up."

"Oh!" Colour rushed back into Norah's face. She made a funny hiccupping sound. "Of course. So much has happened that I never gave it a moment's thought. We get telemarketers all the time."

"And you spoke to her for how long?"

"Oh..." Reg blew out a breath. "Seconds."

Norah was still the colour of a corpse. Sue leaned towards her. "The records show the call lasted four minutes."

"Nonsense." Norah hiccupped again.

Again Reg stepped in. "I must have forgot to press the 'off' button. I do that all the time."

*   *   *

Brandon trudged through the snow, trying to match his aunt's description to the blurry white landscape that lay all around him. Gravestones were strewn across the gentle slopes of the mountainside as far as the eye could see. Bea had mentioned a big pine tree, but the cemetery seemed to be full of trees as old and majestic as Mount Royal itself. Thick oaks, pale, arching poplars, maples that spread their lacy crowns wide over the tombstones below. Brittle morning sunshine bleached the snow, and wind tugged at his dishevelled hair. He hunched his shoulders and turned up the collar of his jacket.

Brandon had always thought Ottawa's Beechwood Cemetery was a stunning resting place, with its dappled shade, terraced gardens and meandering paths. But it could not rival the location of the hundred-and-sixty-year-old Mount Royal Cemetery nestled on the northern slope of the mountain. The spectacular domes of the university and St. Joseph's Oratory peeked over the distant trees, and the northern cityscape faded into the pale horizon beyond. Here the snow seemed whiter and the air crisper. Against the grandeur of the natural setting, even the mausoleums and obelisks of the wealthy old Montreal families looked humble.

His aunt had told him the section of the cemetery where generations of Longstreets had been laid to rest, and he trekked in the snow from grave to grave, studying the names with detached bemusement. These were his relatives. Why had he never heard of them, met them, or heard the stories of their lives? His mother had never even brought him to visit his father's grave. When he'd thought about it, which was rare, he'd assumed she was trying to spare him the stark reminder of his father's absence. Or trying to spare herself. Now he wondered just how false her devotion and grief had been. Had she instead been trying to blot the man out of her mind and erase all reminders of his betrayal?

Brandon found himself on unfamiliar, shifting ground, the illusions of his childhood destroyed amid questions about who his mother and father really were. After leaving Meredith's grandmother the day before, he'd spent the day poring over the old newspaper files he'd taken from his mother's office and surfing the internet in vain for further details. Bea had been no help, suddenly changing her tune after his visit to Cyril and suggesting that he should let the past rest.

"Your father was fundamentally a good man, with more ideals and ethics than the rest of the Longstreet men put together, and your mother was right to preserve that in your mind. Not his one weakness. Sexual appetite can bring down great men, but it shouldn't be the only yardstick by which they are judged."

She must have seen the dismissal on his face, for she pressed further. "You were the centre of your mother's world after he died. Everything she said, every choice she made, including leaving Montreal, was for your wellbeing. I don't think it hurt you to have an idealized father to live up to."

She made him feel childish and petty, like a small boy who'd believed in Superman and now pouted at the truth as if he'd been personally betrayed. He wanted to tell her this was not about his father's sexual appetite nor even his mother's lies, but about the corrosive effect of those secrets thirty years later. A woman was dead, and Meredith had disappeared.

But the truth was, Bea was partly right. Tramping through the graveyard in search of his father's tomb, he did feel like a small child, not sure why he'd come and perilously close to weeping at the potent symbolism of the act.

He pulled himself back to reason with a sharp shake of his head. The grave must be farther over, set apart from the older Longstreets who had lived out the full measure of their lives. There was a tall pine just up the slope, its boughs bent almost to the ground with the weight of snow. The vague indentations of a path wove towards it through the sparkling white quilt crisscrossed with the prints of rabbits and squirrels foraging for food.

He veered towards the pine, braced against the wind that whistled up the mountain. The cold snow seeped into his thin leather boots. He had less than an hour before his meeting with the reporter, whom he'd managed to track down on the internet the night before. Cameron Hatfield had revealed little over the phone and had grilled him with numerous questions about who he was and what exactly he wanted to know, but he'd finally agreed to meet with Brandon. Noon for brunch—on Brandon's tab—was the earliest he was willing to face the world. Hatfield warned him it would be a waste of his time. He recalled the case only in the vaguest detail, because there hadn't been much to it.

As Brandon trudged closer, he could make out a black shape through the thick branches. Closer, a curious splash of colour. Red. He quickened his pace as the black shape became a tombstone nestled in the hollow beneath the tree. Protected from the snowfall, its polished granite was almost completely bare. He ducked under the pine bough and stepped close enough to read the inscription.

Harvey Kent Longstreet

1938-1978

A beautiful soul, taken before his time

His brief moment of triumph faded as the scene registered. Propped against the tombstone and partially covered by a light mantle of snow, was a bouquet of red roses. Fresh and crisp, as if they'd been placed only yesterday. Brandon frowned and glanced at the ground at the base of the grave, noting for the first time the delicate footprints half-filled with snow. Footprints came in under the bough, trampled around and then faded out again into the deeper snow of the open field. He bent closer to brush the snow from the petals, looking in vain for a card. Who still cared enough about his father to bring flowers thirty years after his death? Bea had not mentioned it. His mother? She hadn't left Ottawa all week.

For one crazy, hopeful moment, he thought of Meredith.

EIGHTEEN

Green awoke late Sunday morning, the result of one too many St. Ambroise with Cam Hatfield. Lying in the unfamiliar bed, he felt a wash of loneliness. He phoned Sharon and could hear the staccato chatter of his son in the background. She sounded mellow, and he pictured her at the kitchen table, reading the paper and sipping her mug of french roast. Envy seeped into his loneliness.

"Miss you," she said with a playful hint in her voice.

"Miss you too. Did Hannah call?"

"No, but it was Saturday night and this is Hannah we're talking about."

"I hope she's not having too much fun. I want her to come home."

"She will, because she has the rest of Grade Twelve to finish. After that..."

She didn't have to complete the thought. Hannah had spent the past month researching and applying to university programs for next year, and on her short list along with McGill and Ottawa's Carleton University was the University of British Columbia. The very possibility was unthinkable.

"They do grow up, Mike," said Sharon gently.

He sidestepped the comment, which was laden with too much innuendo for this hour on a Sunday morning. He missed his daughter, he missed his wife and son, he even missed his dog, and in a moment of weakness, he might agree to her wish.

"I hope to be home tonight," he said, sitting up on the edge of the bed. "Maybe we'll call her then."

She backed off, as she always did. But for how long, he thought? To be fair to her, he had to face the issue of another child head on sometime. She would be forty next month, and her chance was ebbing away.

Determinedly, he refocused his thoughts on the day ahead. Interviews with Cyril Longstreet, other relatives, and the old super at Longstreet's apartment if he was still alive. But before he could do any of that, he had to see what was in the Longstreet police file.

When he finally arrived at the police station, however, he was greeted by an irritated, apologetic Jean Pierre Magloire. Neither the microfilm nor the original Longstreet file had arrived. He'd been on the phone harassing everyone he could think of, but the only response he'd received was, "We're trying to locate it."

Settling into his temporary work station next to Magloire, Green roused Inspector Fournier at home. This time the chief inspector was far less cordial.

"The request has been made, Inspector. It's a very old file and since it's a closed case, the original may be in one of several warehouses. In order not to inconvenience you further, may I suggest you return to Ottawa and I will send you the microfilm once we locate it."

Green had no intention of letting up the pressure. He needed to check the witness statements, the officer's notes, and other details that had not found their way into the official police press releases. He needed most of all to know what everyone was hiding.

"Thank you for the offer," he replied in his best French. "I

209

have several leads to follow up here today, and the file is essential to my investigation, so I will wait for it. Please continue to do all you can."

When he hung up, he saw Magloire's dark, watchful eyes upon him. The detective was smiling, but he looked thoughtful. "Why is that file so important?"

Green wasn't about to admit he had no idea. Call it a hunch, or maybe his obsessive drive to uncover everything about the cases he investigated. Or just maybe because the Montreal Police seemed reluctant to show it to him. He was saved from providing any answer by the ringing of his cell phone.

It was Bob Gibbs, sounding excited and out of breath. "I-I hope I'm not disturbing you too early, sir."

Green glanced at his watch, which read eleven thirty a.m. Hardly early. He asked what was up.

"Reporting on the results of our searches, sir. Not much luck on the internet, because the Longstreets and the Kennedys left Montreal too many years ago. Nothing really connected them. But..." Gibbs broke off and Green sensed his hesitancy. He could almost see his flushed face and bobbing Adam's apple.

"What, Bob?"

"Well, maybe we shouldn't have. I mean, I-I know you didn't tell us to—"

"Bob!"

"Sue thought maybe we should just ask them. I mean, where they lived in Montreal, what schools they went to..."

Green sucked in his breath. "You talked to Elena Longstreet??"

"Oh no, sir! N-not her! Just the Kennedys."

Green's pulse settled. "That's okay. What did you learn?"

As Gibbs began to summarize the interview, Green grabbed his notebook to jot down the details of the Kennedy's past. He hadn't realized they too were from Montreal. In fact, no deep background had been done on them at all, because it hadn't seemed relevant. Something else to follow up on. "This raises a new—"

He heard Gibbs suck in his breath. "There's something else, sir. Lise Gravelle placed a four-minute phone call to the Kennedy's house at 8:54 the night she died."

Green bolted up in his seat. "After her call to Meredith's cell?"

"Yessir. It's the only call she made to that line. The thing is, I think the Kennedys are hiding something. They pretended it didn't happen, then they said it was a telemarketer. The husband seemed to be coaching the wife."

Green leaned forward. "What's your take on it?"

"Well, Sue thinks—and it makes sense—that they didn't take that call at all. That Meredith did."

"But she wasn't home."

"She could have got home. We know she hung up on Lise twenty minutes earlier, so maybe this time Lise called her on the home line."

Green weighed the new possibility. "But the Kennedys said she never came home. You're saying she came home and went out again without them knowing?"

"Yes, sir, that's possible. Maybe the TV was loud or they weren't even home. But Sue has another theory."

He could hear Sue's voice in the background, arguing. "Bob?" he said. "What?"

"Um, she thinks they know Meredith took the call but they're lying about it because...well, because..."

It hit Green like a flash of light. So simple, so clear. "Because they're afraid Meredith killed her."

211

*   *   *

Green scribbled furiously in his notebook, drawing connecting lines between facts as he tried to make sense of this latest twist. Emotions had run high between the two women when they'd met Monday afternoon at Lise's Montreal apartment. Meredith had been devastated, Lise triumphant. Was it triumph or determination that had made her follow Meredith to Ottawa and phone her twice in the span of half an hour? Six hours later, en route to the Longstreet house, Lise was dead and Meredith had dropped out of sight. Had they connected during that second phone call? Had Lise told her where she was going? Had Meredith chased her down, desperate to stop her from contacting Elena? Or Brandon.

Why?

He shook his head in frustration. Certainly the timeline was plausible, but there was still a huge hole in the theory. Motive. He studied the photo of Meredith from the missing person file. What would make this intelligent, attractive, seemingly well-adjusted young woman desperate enough to kill? It had to be an act of desperation or panic. He did not see flash rage or opportunistic cunning being part of her make-up.

Still, it added even more urgency to their efforts to find her.

"Jean Pierre," he said, breaking the silence that had enveloped the room. Magloire thrust his swivel chair back and spun it around. His smile lit the gloomy room.

"Yes, boss!"

Green laughed. "We need to check out the past connections between Lise Gravelle, the Longstreets and the Kennedys here in Montreal. As far back as their childhoods if we need to. I've got a team working on it in Ottawa, but this is where the

212

connection probably is. You may have to wait until offices open tomorrow—"

Magloire's smile faded. "Schools and many offices are already closed for the Christmas break."

"I know, but harass a few administrators if you have to. I don't want to wait two weeks while a young woman is missing and the temperatures are in the minus teens at night."

Magloire's smile returned, gleeful this time. "Harassing bureaucrats is my specialty!" He spun his chair back to his desk just as Green's cell phone rang again. Another cheerful voice sang through the air.

"Hey, Inspector! How's it going?"

Green peered at the call display. A blocked number. "Who's this?"

"Hatfield. You got anything for me?"

"It's been barely twelve hours, Cam."

"Twelve hours is a lifetime to a news hound nowadays. I've been busy. You interested?"

Green could hear the barely controlled excitement in the man's voice. Was the guy going to be useful or a pain in the neck, pretending to have tips so he could pump Green for information?

"Always. With the same caveat, Cam. Silence for now."

"I know," Hatfield said, his cheer unabated. "But this is fun! I haven't been on a good crime story in a long time, and man, this is going to be good! Such sweet revenge!"

Green winced as he imagined the story Cam Hatfield would ultimately spin, full of class struggle and political hyperbole. "What have you got?"

"Guess who I just had brunch with?"

"Cyril Longstreet?"

"Hah! Like that's ever going to happen." Hatfield chuckled. "Another Longstreet. Brandon."

It was Green's turn for surprise. "Where are you?"

"Here. In my home."

"Brandon Longstreet is in Montreal?"

"Yup. On the trail of the disappearing fiancée. Spitting image of his old man. If he has his old man's sexual—ah, proclivities, it's no wonder the fiancée split."

Green absorbed the news along with Cam Hatfield's observation. He himself had only had one brief meeting with Brandon, but in that time he'd seemed distraught and desperately in love. "Did you get the impression he'd cheated on her?"

"No, but as a reporter, it never pays to trust too much in man's better nature."

Nor as a police officer, Green thought wryly, making a mental note to check on Brandon's love life more thoroughly. "What did he want?"

"Same as you, he'd read my stuff on his father's death—his mother kept the clippings—and he wanted the rest of the story."

"What did you tell him?"

"Don't worry, not much. He has no clue who Lise Gravelle is, not even that Meredith had met her here, and I didn't enlighten him. He knew his father liked it varied and kinky, but he didn't know specifics. He'd asked all his relatives including scary old Uncle Cyril, but no one budged. No one admitted to seeing Meredith either. However, he did uncover one really interesting fact that I thought you should know."

"Uhuh," Green said drily. Waiting. Once a storyteller, always a storyteller.

"He went to visit his father's grave this morning, and someone had put fresh red roses on the grave."

"How fresh?"

"Well, he said hardly any snow had fallen on the flowers and on the footprints around the gravestone, and the flowers still looked fresh, so they were probably put there in the past few days."

The snow had started Monday, Green thought. The day Lise Gravelle died, and Meredith disappeared. "Meredith?"

"That's what the kid thinks, although I'm not so sure. Why would Meredith go there, to put flowers on the grave of a man who died years ago? No matter how much she loved the son."

*   *   *

Green drove through the stone archway into the cemetery and eyed the rows of tombstones stretching out over the snow-covered slopes, bleak markers of death in this strangely idyllic scene. Armed with the section number Hatfield had given him, he studied the map displayed just inside the gate. Longstreet's section was off to the right. He found the grave without trouble by following the trail of footprints leading up the slope. More than one fresh set of boots had tromped through the deep snow on the same path, Green observed. Clutching his camera, he bent to peer under the overhanging pine bough, careful not to disturb what was left of the footprints. Ahead of him, a simple granite tomb was cradled in the hollow of snow. Green read the inscription.

Gotcha.

Trying to see past the fresh boot prints, Green took in the scene. The older trampling of the snow had been made by delicate, high-heeled boots. The rose petals were still plump and red, and the leaves glistened a bright green, but a frosting

215

of fresh, fluffy snow covered everything despite the thick shelter of the tree.

He stepped further inside to check the depth of the fresh snow. Everywhere beneath the tree, it was only an inch deep. Brandon was wrong. These flowers had been placed before last week's snow, but they were high quality silk that looked as lush as the real thing. He snapped half a dozen photos of the footprints and the grave before reaching forward to brush the snow away from the base, revealing something Brandon, in his haste to capture hope, had not seen—a shiny red satin heart pinned to the stem of the bouquet. No card, no insignia. A simple heart.

This bouquet had been left not by Meredith on her journey to discover Brandon's father, but by a woman who, after thirty years, still loved him.

He took more photos before retracing his steps through the snow as quickly as the uneven path allowed. Finally he was on the hunt! Here was physical evidence to confirm his speculation. This mystery stemmed from the past, with the man in that grave at the centre of it.

Back in his car, Green booted up his laptop and searched for Cyril Longstreet's address. Green suspected the old man knew exactly what had happened thirty years ago and who all the players were. At the time, he'd had the power to have the whole investigation stopped, but Green was counting on old age and frailty to have mellowed his defiance and perhaps piqued his conscience as well.

As he followed the narrow, twisting road up the mountain towards Summit Circle, Green could see glimpses of the city far below; silver steeples, glass towers, and the St. Lawrence River glittering blue in the distance. He passed an eclectic mix of homes. Old limestone mansions stood next door to bold, sleek slabs with walls of windows overlooking the city below. New construction was everywhere. Once the exclusive domain of Montreal's English elite, Green wondered if most of the homes weren't owned now by Hong Kong millionaires and oil sheiks.

The winter sun reflected off the snow and cast deep shadows that hampered his efforts to read house numbers. Rounding a curve, he was straining to see the next house number when he heard the roar of an engine and a car careened around the corner in the opposite direction. Instinctively Green jerked the wheel and swerved just as the car sped past. Green glanced over just in time to catch a fleeting glimpse of the driver's profile. Head bent, gaze focussed ahead, features in shadow. Green barely had time to register the make of the vehicle and the Avis rent-a-car sticker on the rear bumper before the car disappeared.

Green sideswiped a snowbank as he slithered to a stop. He took a few deep breaths. Up ahead on his left was Cyril's house. Sitting in the car a minute to collect his wits, he replayed the near-accident. Recalled the driver's intensity of focus and complete inattention to his surroundings. A man on a mission, hell-bent on something.

Green had caught only the briefest glimpse of his profile. The sun had glared off the window, casting the figure in light and shadow. Yet the image struck a chord. Was there something familiar about it? Had he seen it before? There was almost no traffic on this exclusive circular street, and the roar of the engine suggested the car had accelerated hard. Where had it come from? Possibly from Cyril's house itself?

Green didn't believe in coincidences. A vaguely familiar face, visiting one of the central architects of this decades-old secret? Green rifled his memory, trying to conjure up the image he'd seen before. It also had been a vague profile, full of shadow and mood. Almost artistic.

217

That was it! Green booted up his laptop and accessed the photos he'd taken at Lise Gravelle's apartment. He scanned through the thumbnails quickly until he came to the framed photos on her wall, among them the Amélie series. He clicked on the first and watched as the image of the little girl filled the screen. She was looking up with outstretched hand, but only the shadow of the adult with her was visible. He clicked on the next photo, and both figures filled the screen. Little Amélie's curly hair, sparkling eyes and round cheeks glowed in the sunlight, but the young man was in shadow as he looked down at her, his fingertips touching hers.

It was the same man! Despite the tricks of light and the decades separating the two, Green was convinced of it. Here was one more person linking the Longstreets to Lise Gravelle, over a span of almost thirty years. Green raised his head to study Cyril Longstreet's house. It looked deceptively calm and unassuming, a solid, two-storey block with leaded windows, an arched oak front door and a grey limestone façade. Freshly painted black shutters framed each window and a sweep of carefully trimmed evergreen shrubs bordered the front walk. All signs of an attentive owner who preferred quality to ostentation.

He was just wondering how he was going to breach Cyril's defences with this latest discovery when his cell phone rang. It was Magloire, triumphantly announcing that the original Longstreet file had been found at last and was on its way to the major crimes offices by cruiser. Green hesitated. Cyril Longstreet was less than a hundred feet away, and he had a dozen questions to ask the man. A return to Sherbrooke Street East in the pre-Christmas Sunday traffic would set him back well over an hour. However, right now he would be going head to head with Cyril lacking the most crucial piece of information in the case to date—the identity of the man in the photo. He doubted Cyril would let it slip by mistake. The old man had not dominated a multi-million dollar empire for half a century by being a poor poker player. He would call Green's bluff and knock down the entire house of cards on which this case was propped.

If the police file contained the identity of the mystery man and even better, his role in the case, the brief diversion would be worth it. Cyril had kept his secrets for thirty years; he could wait another hour.

NINETEEN

At one o'clock on a Sunday afternoon, the Montreal Major Crimes floor was virtually deserted. Dozens of work stations sat idle, but Magloire was at his desk in the corner. A battered legal box sat open on the floor beside him and he was bent intently over a folder, frowning.

"That the file?"

Magloire nodded. "Not going to be much fucking help."

Green wheeled a desk chair over beside him. "Why not?"

"Nothing in it. After all that stonewalling and fuss, it's nothing but a whitewash. Worst example of record keeping I've ever seen. I know this was policing pre-computers, but come on!"

Green reached out a hand for the file, but Magloire was on a roll. He slapped the piece of paper on top. "Autopsy report. Nothing we didn't know. Healthy, well-muscled male died of asphyxiation, ligature bruising to the neck but no other signs of trauma to the body, no defensive wounds, no evidence the body was moved or tampered with after death."

"That's something we didn't know."

Magloire shrugged it off. "Okay, a few things. Tox screen positive for cannabis and alcohol. Tested .15. Our guy was pretty drunk."

Drunk enough to impair his judgment, but not drunk enough to pass out, Green thought. Alcohol was often the drug of choice for depressed men, although it never improved their mood and more often lessened their self-control. Had it been false courage in a bottle to help a suicide attempt? "Is there a doubt about suicide?"

"None mentioned. They found traces of the rope fibre in the ligature marks but no finger marks from clawing at the rope." Magloire tossed the report aside and snatched up the next. "Witness statement from landlord. Gained access to apartment when victim's uncle expressed concern."

"Uncle?"

"Yeah. Cyril Longstreet. Harvey's wife alerted him when he failed to come home."

What is this? Green thought. Nobody in this family says boo without checking with the old man at the top of the mountain? He held out his hand for the report again, but Magloire was holding it close to his eyes, peering at it.

"Wait. It's in French, and the handwriting is impossible. Landlord says the door was locked, and no one else was in the apartment. He found the victim in the closet, hanging out the open door. He was too freaked to notice anything else, but he didn't hear or see anything out of the ordinary in the previous few days."

"Was anyone with him when he discovered the body?"

Magloire glanced at the report. "Doesn't say. Maybe the investigator never asked. Here's another thing. No forensics. No fingerprint report, no analysis of dirty dishes. Just a few dozen crime scene and autopsy photos."

Green snapped his fingers impatiently. "Let me see them. Those I can read."

This time Magloire handed over the thick packet of photos and Green studied the old, slightly discoloured Polaroids. Harvey

Longstreet's body hung from a hook on the closet ceiling, not from the rod as he'd imagined. It seemed a strange place for a hook, as if it had been placed there for a purpose. The body sagged forward. Avoiding the protruding tongue and bulging eyes, Green focussed instead on the ligature marks on the neck. A clear purple line ran below the jaw line and up on an angle behind the ear. Classic example of a hanging death.

Oddly, however, the toes touched the ground, suggesting that had he wanted to save himself, he could simply have regained his footing. The closet was completely bare except for a pair of slippers on the floor and a couple of shirts hanging to one side. All the clothing looked neat and undisturbed. Longstreet had not fought back or thrashed around in his final moments of consciousness, suggesting he hadn't been coerced. Even suicides sometimes panicked at the last minute unless they were extremely drunk. Harvey Longstreet had submitted quietly and willingly to death.

Green flipped through the rest of the photos. Autopsy close-ups of the body showed no other signs of violence, although Green thought he could detect some red marks on the genitals. The apartment was neat, the dishes all washed and the counter clear. There were no ropes, handcuffs, or other paraphernalia of sex play. The queen-sized bed was perfectly made, its pillows plumped and its satin quilt smooth, as if the apartment was there only for show and not for habitation. Amid the perfection, the naked man was an affront.

He looked up. "How often did this guy stay there?"

Magloire leafed through more papers. "The rest of the witness statements are a joke. Neighbours were busy, kept to themselves, didn't notice a thing. Blah, blah, blah. Longstreet's widow said about once a week when he had a late seminar. She also said he sometimes went there during the day between classes, for some peace and quiet." Magloire said these last words with heavy sarcasm.

"Did she say he was a neat freak? That keeping the apartment this neat was usual for him?"

"It's not in the reports. Probably didn't ask that either."

Green was beginning to understand Cam Hatfield's accusation of shoddy police work. It was as if the police had been paid off. Green was betting Longstreet was not alone when he died, but someone had cleaned up the scene after the fact and locked the door, to erase all evidence of another person. The police had failed to ask the crucial question why. Was it just to hide the embarrassment of kinky sex? Or to cover up a murder.

"Let me see the notebooks. Maybe there's more detail in the police notes."

"There are none."

"What!"

"That's what I've been looking for. They're not here. Nada. Almost like the file's been purged."

Green was appalled. "Let me see that!"

Wordlessly, Magloire handed the whole box over and Green pawed through the papers, trying to decipher the French. Formal statements, final reports, photos and an incredibly short witness list, but no officers' notebooks. On the top of the box, however, along with the file summary and table of contents, was the name of the investigating officer.

Agent Adam Jules.

*   *   *

Green slammed out of the police station, fumbling for his cell phone. His heart hammered. Despite his best efforts, Magloire had seen his reaction and watched open-mouthed as he dashed out without a word.

On the trip down in the elevator, Green tried to make sense of this latest shock. He hadn't even known Jules was from Montreal, let alone that he'd begun his police career there. The man had been in Criminal Investigations in Ottawa since Green was a rookie street cop. Thirty-two years ago, Green had barely been in high school. How old could Jules have been?

Yet there was no other officer of record on the file except a note from his supervising sergeant. Had Jules alone been responsible for suppressing the investigation, or had he received orders from above?

Heading over to his car with his fingers freezing and his breath swirling around him, Green phoned both Jules's cell and home number, reaching nothing but voice mail. A cold sense of foreboding gripped him. Where was Jules? What had he been involved in all these years ago, and to what lengths would others go to keep the secret from coming to light?

Now desperate, he thumbed through his contact list and did the unthinkable. He phoned the deputy chief on his Blackberry. On Sunday afternoon, at the height of the holiday season, the man would not be amused.

The phone rang six times and Green was just trying to formulate a suitable message when clipped voice broke in. "Poulin!"

"Deputy Chief, it's Michael Green of Major Case Investigations, sir. I'm sorry to disturb you—"

"What is it, Green?"

Green could hear laughter in the background over the murmur of voices. Terrific, he thought, the man has company. In the chilly confines of his car, he turned the heat on full blast. In his headlong rush, he'd forgotten his coat.

"I've been trying to contact Superintendent Adam Jules for three days without success, sir. There's no answer at either of his phones, no one at his apartment, he's not replying to email or phone messages—"

"What's this about?"

Green took a deep breath, hating to thrust Jules into the middle of a quagmire. But the deputy chief had to take him seriously. "I need to speak to him about a case—"

"What case?"

"Lise Gravelle and Meredith Kennedy."

"What's Jules got to do with it? He's not CID."

"He was involved in a case years ago that's connected—"

"Green, it's Sunday. The superintendent is off somewhere enjoying his well-deserved time off. Take your concern to Superintendent Devine in the morning, and she'll follow up through channels."

Green forced himself to calm down. The deputy chief was an outsider; he couldn't be expected to understand the network of loyalties that knit the old original Ottawa force together. All he knew was the chain of command.

"Sir, I think this is urgent. I'm very worried. Adam Jules is an old friend of mine as well as my boss for years in CID, and it's not like him to disappear without a word. He knows me. He'd never let a dozen messages from me go unanswered."

Silence on the line. Nothing but the trill of distant laughter. Then, "Spit it out, Mike. What are you saying?"

"I'm afraid something bad may have happened to him."

More silence, then a softer tone. "Nothing's happened. He's on two weeks' vacation leave, back home in St. Hyacinth. He came to me last week to request it personally to attend to a family matter. I looked at his record, Mike, and the man hasn't taken a

Christmas vacation in years. He was more than due."

Green felt a rush of conflicting emotions. Relief, but even more so, confusion. Jules had never mentioned any family. "Did he give an address in St. Hyacinth, sir? Or say how he could be reached?"

"He did not, and to be honest, the man is entitled to his privacy. I'm sure when he finds the time, he will return your messages."

The line clicked dead. Green realized he'd been dismissed, without a word of goodbye. Poulin was pissed.

Well, fuck him, that's the least of my worries.

Staring out his car window into the crowded parking lot, Green tried to put together the chronology of Jules's connection to the case. Thirty-two years ago he'd been the young officer of record in the Longstreet case. As part of that, he'd met Elena Longstreet and presumably other witnesses in the Longstreet case, ultimately agreeing to close the investigation and turn a blind eye to any suspicious evidence. Shortly afterwards, he'd not only left the Montreal police to join Ottawa, but he'd never mentioned his Montreal days again, at least to Green.

Flash forward to last week, when Jules had begun to act oddly. First asking Green about a possible missing person hours before anyone was reported missing, then cutting Green off abruptly when he asked for details afterwards. Next he'd begun to avoid Green's calls, failed to attend to his police duties, and finally stopped coming to work altogether, without a word of explanation to his clerk. The crowning touch—his scarf hanging at Elena Longstreet's house on the day he dropped out of sight for good.

Bit by bit, Green was beginning to form the haziest theory of how the pieces of the Longstreet Gravelle puzzle fit together. Suspicious circumstances in Harvey Longstreet's death had been

226

hushed up and witnesses either bribed or threatened to keep quiet. By whom was an open question, although Green suspected Cyril Longstreet was the only person with that kind of power.

Somehow, however, Lise Gravelle had known something and had been trying to keep track of Elena Longstreet ever since, but had lost the trail after Elena's move to Toronto. Perhaps she had only rediscovered her three weeks ago during a lucky internet search, unleashing a tragic cascade of events which began with her contacting Meredith Kennedy and travelling to Ottawa. She'd been murdered en route to Elena's home, presumably to prevent her from bringing the mysterious secret to light. Murdered by whom? Meredith?

Who besides Meredith even knew who Lise was or what she was up to?

A cold sweat formed on Green's brow. Over all these questions loomed the dark, formless shadow of Adam Jules. But Green had known Jules for over twenty years! The man was rigidly moral. Impossibly upright. He might have found himself caught in an ethical trap from his past, he might even have dropped out of sight, at least temporarily, to avoid exposure. His reputation as a police officer was all he had, but it paled against the worth of a human life. Surely, he would never, ever, resort to murder.

Green shook his head and forced himself to confront his worst fear. How often had he told his detectives "Never assume anyone is incapable of murder. Everyone is capable of murder, of the right person in the right circumstances and for the right reason." The right reason. What would make Jules desperate enough, and ruthless enough, to kill? And what from his past, besides the spectre of professional ruin, could have returned to haunt him?

The shadowy images in his head came together with a sudden, startling shock. In his horror, he struggled to breathe.

Reaching under the passenger seat, he retrieved his laptop and booted it up. He watched with fascination as the beautiful, poignant snapshot once again filled the screen. Amélie reaching up, touching fingertips, gazing with awe—and yes, a mixture of fear and adoration—at the dimly-lit man looking down at her. Adam Jules.

*   *   *

Irrational rage billowed through him. Outrage, pain, and fury at being thrust into this position by a man he'd held up as an icon all his years on the police force. He couldn't protect him. Not against a crime this heinous.

What had connected Jules to Lise? Had they been lovers, way back in his Montreal days? And who was Amélie? *Their* child? He studied the strange mixture of emotions on her face, the tentative, almost reverent touch between them. Certainly closer than strangers. But if she was their child, what had become of her?

He forced himself to slow down. He had absolutely zero evidence to support this wild speculation. He needed to put one foot in front of the other, to chip away at the puzzle until one at a time he uncovered the facts to connect the dots.

Heading back upstairs, he found Magloire still at his desk reading a file which he put aside the moment Green appeared. Concern was written all over his face, but Green merely shrugged.

"Ottawa business. Sorry." He sat down. "We need to find out much more deep background on Lise Gravelle. Specifically, did she have any connection to Harvey Longstreet's death? Did she work for the police back then, maybe as a low-level clerk? Was she a neighbour in the apartment building where he died? I want you to phone this..." He paused to read the supervisor's name on the file, "Sergeant Martin, and find out if he remembers her. He's probably retired by now—"

Magloire grimaced. "Retired? Try dead. I attended his funeral myself two years ago."

"What did he die of?"

Magloire shrugged. Sensing hesitation, Green pressed. "This is important. There's something funny going on."

"He was old." More hesitation. "But I don't think his liver looked any too good by the end."

"How many years had he been drinking?"

"Forever. He was one of those old-time cops, always went out with the guys after a shift. Just to unwind, you know? Two hours, three, four..."

"Only after the shift, though? He was good on the job?"

"Maybe at first. But by the time I knew him, he was a..." Magloire searched for words. "Hazard."

Green suppressed his disappointment. He'd been holding out hope that Jules had been a rookie bullied into line by a powerful sergeant who ran the show. It was equally likely, however, that the drink-addled sergeant had not even listened to the briefings nor read the reports he was signing. Seeing conspiracies everywhere, Green wondered whose idea it had been to put the man in charge.

When he handed back the file, Magloire flipped it open. "What about this Agent Jules? Why don't we ask him?"

Green shook his head. "I just tried. He's no longer with the force. But..." He hesitated only briefly, feeling one last twinge of guilt about the investigation he was about to launch against his old idol. "He comes from St. Hyacinth. Where's that?"

"A town about a hundred kilometres east of here."

"Make discreet inquiries to try to locate him, but don't tip him off. Meanwhile I also want you to see if you can find any other police personnel who remember the case. We also need to know if Lise Gravelle ever had a child, or if anyone named Amélie Gravelle even exists."

Magloire was jotting notes. He glanced up in surprise. "We found no record of children."

"Broaden the search beyond Montreal. I'll get my officers to check Ottawa, you check the neighbouring areas and villages around here, including St. Hyacinth. And try searching under the name Amélie Jules as well."

Magloire's eyebrows shot up. "Wow! Boss, what are you digging up here?"

"I don't know. I'm casting a net, trying to see what connects Lise Gravelle to the Longstreets. That connection may start with Adam Jules."

Looking perplexed, Magloire waved his hand across his jotted notes. "Most of this will have to wait until tomorrow. Checking old birth registries in little parishes, that would be a nightmare today. If there was a witness I could ask..."

Green caught his breath. There was one. Two, in fact. He'd been so shaken by the revelation about Jules that he'd forgotten all about them. Grabbing his jacket, he stood up. "Get your notebook, Jean Pierre. I'm going to pay a visit to Cyril Longstreet, and I need you along to make it official."

*   *   *

Magloire steered the staff car down Sherbrooke Street, ignoring all yellow lights and dodging in and out of traffic with an aplomb Green had to admire. He never swore at the winter cyclist who cut him off, nor honked his horn at the puttering old jalopy searching for a parking space in front of him. He never lost his dazzling grin.

Clinging to the ceiling strap, Green thumbed through his cell phone contacts until he found Cam Hatfield. When the reporter answered, Green could hear Springsteen blasting over the rumble of traffic in the background. Was Hatfield in his car?

"You got something for me, Inspector?" he shouted.

Green smiled to himself. "Getting there. Do you remember any mention of Lise Gravelle in the Longstreet case? Police secretary, neighbour, witness, background source?"

"Born in the U.S.A." screamed through the silence. An engine roared by. "No," Hatfield said finally.

"Even the smallest mention? Name ring any kind of bell from back then?"

More silence. "What have you got, Green?"

"More and more evidence that there's a crucial connection in the past."

"Any idea what it is?"

"No, but Lise has a history of low-paying jobs over the years. I think she knew something about the Harvey Longstreet case. Something that was hushed up, possibly something that got her killed."

"Can I use that?"

"All in good time, Cam. I have to figure out what's going on first, without tipping the guilty parties off."

"I guess... I may be able to save you some time."

Magloire veered abruptly right onto Guy Street, causing Green to slew across the seat. His grin broadened as Green hung on.

"What?"

Another engine roared by. The sound of a fast-moving transport truck blocked out Hatfield's reply.

"Where the hell are you?" Green yelled. "The Indy 500?"

Hatfield laughed. "On my way out of town. Wait," he shouted, and Springsteen fell silent in mid-note. "That's better. Here's my tip for you. I called in some of my old sources. Lise Gravelle may have been a low-level clerk in later life, but in 1978 she was a second-year law student at McGill. Here's the interesting part. She never returned for her third year after Longstreet's death."

Green nearly shouted aloud as he made the same deduction Hatfield obviously had. "Our mystery co-ed?"

"My source couldn't say, but they did say she was as pretty and innocent as a lamb straight off the farm."

Green's imagination raced even further ahead. "Where did you say she was from?"

"I didn't. But that's tip number two. I tracked that down too, and she's from a two-bit village called St. Dominique, east of Montreal."

Green thanked him, disconnected, and immediately turned to Magloire. "You got a Quebec map in here?"

Magloire was navigating the winding road up the mountain-side in a suicidal tsunami of cars. He nodded at the cell phone in Green's hand. "Don't you have a GPS on that?"

"I do, but I hate it. Fiddling with buttons, peering at a tiny screen and listening to that infuriating voice. I'm a techie dinosaur."

Magloire chuckled and yanked a very crumpled map from his side pocket. "Welcome to the 1980s."

"That doesn't sound so long ago," Green muttered as he unfolded the map in his lap. He found St. Hyacinth quite quickly, but it was the network of small roads running through the sparsely populated countryside around it that drew his interest. Finally he felt a surge of satisfaction. St. Dominique was a tiny dot on a minor back road, barely ten kilometres from St. Hyacinth. Home of Adam Jules.

Green's hand trembled slightly as he refolded the map. With each successive revelation, Adam Jules was being sucked deeper and deeper into the vortex of this case. Fortunately Magloire was too busy fighting across several lanes of traffic to notice, and by the time they were climbing past the breath-taking mansions towards the top of the mountain, Green had wrestled his apprehension under control. The interview with Cyril Longstreet lay ahead, and Green had even more ammunition now with which to challenge him.

The crescent was quiet, and when they pulled into the double drive, Magloire sat in the car a few seconds staring at the house. "A cool three million," he murmured.

"Or more."

"When I first came from Haiti as a small child, my mother took me on the bus along The Boulevard. She looked at the old stone houses and said, 'Someday we're going to live here.'" He laughed, but without regret. "We live in Saint Leonard."

Green turned his attention to the house. Its façade was still, the curtains drawn and the door to the double detached garage closed tight. He climbed out and walked up the shovelled flagstone walk. Even the door chimes sounded expensive, a few orchestral bars of a classical piece even Green had heard before. Beethoven was his best guess, although most of his musical knowledge ran to Seventies and Eighties rock.

Green rang again. "He has a butler. Someone should answer."

Two minutes later, both detectives were trudging around the house through the snow, peering in the heavily curtained windows in a futile attempt to spot activity inside. Nothing. They stood on tiptoe to look through the tiny side window of the garage. Inside, the vast space was empty.

Magloire chuckled. "By now I bet a dozen neighbours have

called to report intruders, and we've been caught on half a dozen security cameras."

Green laughed. "How long till you guys respond?"

"Up here? Five, ten minutes. We'll wait out front and give them a nice welcome."

Magloire was still laughing, but Green had other things on his mind. Cyril Longstreet had disappeared. The eighty-five-year-old man, who was by all accounts too frail to leave the house, was gone.

And Cam Hatfield, the crafty bugger, was "on his way out of town."

TWENTY

Both detectives were on their cell phones, while in front of them their platters of smoked meat and homemade French fries sat untouched. Magloire talked in rapid, animated French, but Green was listening with growing frustration to the endless sound of unanswered rings. When the voice mail clicked on, he hung up in disgust. He drummed his fingers on the table and popped a small morsel of smoked meat into his mouth. Two smoked meat sandwiches in two days! He should be in heaven, especially since this was the first time he'd ever been to Lester's on Fairmont Avenue, the legendary home of the only smoked meat his father deigned to eat. Shipped up to Ottawa in briskets, it was delicious, but here, freshly sliced and piping hot, it was incomparable.

But Green's mind was elsewhere. The damn reporter was not answering his cell, but Green was absolutely positive he was chasing down a lead in the case and wanted to keep it all to himself. Green suspected he'd been doing it all along, feeding Green only what he felt like, starting with the mysterious flowers on Longstreet's grave. That second set of prints Green had detected at the graveside had probably been made by Hatfield, checking out the story Brandon Longstreet had told him and noticing the extra detail the surprised young man had missed—the small satin heart pinned to the bouquet. Like Green, Cam had realized the significance of the heart and, armed now with the name Lise

Gravelle, had set out to uncover who that faithful lover was.

What else was the bugger keeping from him? "On my way out of town," he'd said. Where? East to St. Dominique to see if Lise's family knew anything about the affair or the circumstances of her death? Or west to Ottawa to confront Elena Longstreet in the hope that a surprise attack would pry crucial secrets out of her.

Fuck, Green thought with alarm. Cam mustn't get to her first. Green had been saving that interview until he returned from Montreal with all the ammunition he could muster. If Cam Hatfield tipped her off, he might ruin it all.

With Magloire still on the phone, apparently climbing the chain of command in the Sûreté du Québec, Green turned on his phone again to call the Major Crimes Unit in Ottawa. In the middle of Sunday afternoon, not surprisingly, voice mail picked up. The skeleton staff would be out in the field. Green hung up and dialled Marie Claire Levesque's cell phone. He knew he shouldn't bother her during her family time, but this could not wait until tomorrow. When her phone also went directly to voice mail, he suppressed the urge to hang up in frustration. Goddamn voice mail was a scourge! After suffering through her bilingual announcement, he left a terse message.

"Marie Claire, an urgent situation has arisen regarding Elena Longstreet. Call me ASAP."

After hanging up, he dialled Bob Gibbs. Ever faithful, Gibbs answered right away. Green winced when he heard soft, romantic music in the background. "Sorry to disturb you, Bob."

A second's hesitation. The music clicked off. "It- it's all right, sir. We're not busy."

"Hey!" Green heard Sue's shout in the background.

"I wouldn't call if it weren't important. I need two things done. First, I need an alert on the vehicle owned by Cameron Hatfield of Greene Avenue in Montreal. I don't know the plate or make, but look it up. Don't intercept, just record the whereabouts—unless he shows up at Elena Longstreet's premises, in which case detain him and call me."

"Yes, sir? Do you think he... I mean, is he armed and dangerous?"

Green chuckled at the picture of the grizzled old reporter wielding an assault rife. "Not unless you count loose cannons. He's a freelance reporter horning in on the investigation."

"What should I do with him once I detain him?"

"Call me. Secondly I want someone to keep a discreet watch on the Longstreet house."

"You-you want me to do this personally, sir?"

Green could hear the dismay in Gibbs's voice. "No, pass the word on to patrol. Frequent drive-bys will do, but nothing that would arouse her suspicions. Make sure I'm called the minute anyone spots Hatfield, especially if he goes near the Longstreet house."

"Are you still in Montreal?"

"Yes, but not for long. I may be..." He glanced at Magloire questioningly. The big detective gave him the thumbs-up signal. "Making a quick trip to St. Dominique."

"Oh."

"What's in St. Dominique?" Sue burst in, presumably on the other line.

"Lise Gravelle's family, I hope. Whatever there is of it."

"We could only find a cousin," Sue said. "And there's no point going to St. Dominique. He's on his way here to Ottawa to claim her body."

"Then I'm on my way too." That solves my dilemma, Green thought after he hung up. Even if Cam Hatfield did go to St. Dominique, he was not likely to find anyone useful to interview.

Back in Ottawa, the list of interview subjects was growing every minute.

Magloire was digging into his smoked meat with alacrity. He looked up between mouthfuls and patted his stomach, which was as firm and flat as a pro athlete's. "If you stay longer, I'll be in trouble even before my wife's Christmas baking."

Green grinned as he picked up his own sandwich. "You're safe. I'm leaving as soon as I finish this. Lise Gravelle's next of kin is on his way to Ottawa."

"The sister?"

"We haven't been able to track her down. This is a cousin. I didn't get his name."

Magloire nodded. "Must be Denis. The SQ detachment that covers that area says the Gravelle farm is abandoned now, and Denis is the only family still in the vicinity. Sister left Quebec when she got married, and Lise hasn't returned for years either."

"Did they say how long?"

"Well, they finally connected me to an old SQ sergeant who used to run that detachment, and he said she'd been estranged from them for years. Didn't want the farm life, wanted the big city and the fancy college degree—the family's words, not the sergeant's. The father used to complain to anyone who'd listen. The final straw was going to McGill instead of the Université de Montréal. A complete *vendue*. Sell-out. Later, the father seemed happy she fell on her face. What did she expect? The old man sounds like a piece of work. High walls, narrow mind."

No wonder the young woman left, Green thought with a twinge of sympathy. With any luck the cousin would be able to shed more light on what exactly had happened at McGill two years later.

"Had anyone seen or heard from Lise recently? Anyone come

looking for her or asking questions about her?"

"I asked them to conduct some inquiries, talk to old school friends and neighbours. It's a very small place, and now the news of her murder is spreading through the community. Everyone will talk about her, and if someone has a piece of gossip, they'll share it. Or they'll make it up."

Green nodded. In his experience, people in small communities lived in each other's pockets. If there was anything to know about Lise Gravelle in the past half century, it should come out.

* * *

When Brandon walked in, the house echoed like an empty tomb. He shook his head to get rid of the spooky image. The air smelled stale and dusty as if nothing had stirred in days. He knew instinctively that his mother wasn't home, especially since her BMW was missing from the garage, but nonetheless he went from room to room checking. Everything was neat and orderly. No sign of haste or panic, until he came to her home office on the second floor. Her filing cabinet was wide open and file folders were scattered on the floor as if someone had been searching in a desperate hurry.

Had his mother discovered that her file on his father was missing? Had she realized that he'd taken it? Is that what had precipitated her departure?

She could simply be out for Sunday lunch with friends or at her office downtown, or even out in the Gatineau for her first cross-country ski outing of the season. She loved the crisp exhilaration of the trails and looked forward to the first good snowfall of the winter. After the record storm of last week, the trails would be fabulous.

But even as he considered the possibilities, he knew they were wrong. The house had been empty far longer than a few hours. Perhaps ever since Friday, when he himself had left.

What the hell was she up to? He had a dozen questions to ask her, yet once again she had outmanoeuvred him. Frustrated, he splashed a little medicinal Scotch over ice and went to sit at his computer, hopeful against all odds that there would be a message from Meredith. Nothing. Not on Facebook nor on his private email account. A faint flicker of anger stirred. Behind the worry and the grief, outrage was gathering. She was alive; she'd been running around Montreal meeting strangers and tracking down some secret from the past, all without trusting him enough to confide. Then, without giving a damn about the anguish she was causing, she'd taken off.

On her Facebook page, he stared at her last cheerful posting of a week ago. "Shots for Ethiopia all done. Ugh. What we do for love ever after!"

His fingers shook over the keyboard. He wanted to type "Bitch! Whatever happened to love ever after?" He wanted to type "Where the fuck are you? Answer me!" He wanted to type "You can go to hell!" He sat back instead and took a slow sip of Scotch. Swirling the ice in the glass, he gazed down into the fractured amber light. After a few deep breaths, he wrote,

"Meredith, I don't care what's happened or even what our future might be. I just want to know you're okay."

He exited Facebook and sent the identical message to her email account. He'd already sent dozens over the past week, as had her friends and family, and all had been met with silence. Why should this one be any different? What could he say that would change her mind? He took another sip of Scotch and typed a new message.

"I know about Montreal. I know about the past. I'd understand if you can't come home, but just tell me you're safe. One little word. Safe."

After pressing send, he picked up his empty Scotch glass and headed downstairs to the kitchen. He wasn't hungry, but he knew he had to eat if he wanted to preserve his strength. He'd had nothing since he'd forced down half a croissant and coffee with the reporter.

He still bristled when he thought how little information he'd managed to pry out of the cunning old bastard. He'd told Hatfield everything—about Lise Gravelle being run over by a snowplow near his house, about the flowers on his father's grave, even about the fairytale his mother had invented about his father all these years. Hatfield had listened without taking a note and pretended to confide important details that were in fact just a rehash of old newspaper reports. He'd pretended to be as baffled as Brandon about the mysterious graveside visitor and agreed that it could well have been Meredith, but Brandon had seen the crafty gleam in his eyes. What did he know, and what was he planning next?

He had the guy's card with his cell phone number, which he'd given to encourage Brandon to keep him informed, but that cut both ways. Brandon intended to keep close tabs on what the man was up to, and what he found out. Everyone was keeping secrets from him—Cam Hatfield, his Aunt Bea, Uncle Cyril, and most of all his mother. How did all the secrets connect to Lise Gravelle, who had ended up dead just blocks from their home? And to Meredith, who had disappeared on the very same night. His breath quickened with fear.

He poured a second Scotch. As he stood at the kitchen counter with his runaway thoughts, he heard a rumbling sound.

He glanced out the window just as his mother's BMW slipped past him into the garage behind the house. He watched as she climbed out and stood studying his car. She walked around the front of it, wiped some salt stains off the front bumper, then strode purposefully towards the house. He steeled himself. That second Scotch had been a mistake.

He stayed where he was and listened as she opened the door, unzipped her boots and hung her coat on the hall rack. He heard a faint gasp and a whispered "Damn!" He wondered what had rattled her, but when she appeared in the kitchen archway, she had a smile pasted on her face.

"Darling! I'm so glad you're home."

He remained rigid in her embrace. She drew back, her eyes searching his, and for the first time he saw her as a stranger, tired, bruised and middle-aged. Her eyes, already haggard, darkened further at the accusation she must have seen in his. She pulled away and turned to the Scotch bottle still open on the counter.

"Right. I'll have some of that."

Once she'd poured herself a shot far healthier than his, she waved the glass towards the living room. As always it was a command, not a request, but nonetheless he followed. No point in escalating the battle before it had even begun. She sat down in the wing chair by the window that had always been hers, but now had the added benefit of casting her in shadow while his every expression would be bathed in light. He dragged the second wing chair over to the window opposite hers. A minor victory, but he needed all the advantage he could muster.

She crossed her legs and gripped her glass in her lap. "I did it for you, darling. And for your father's memory."

"Sure."

She paused. "All right, yes, I did it for me too. Because it was humiliating enough that the whole of Montreal knew how your father died. At first it seemed like the best foot to put forward, and then the story—"

"The lie."

"It wasn't strictly speaking a lie."

"Spare me the legal hair-splitting, Mom. People were paid off, who knows, maybe even threatened, to kill the story and promote this fiction. That this wonderful man, this brilliant, dedicated, overwhelmed professor had succumbed to the pressures of life."

"He was all those things. His...his weakness didn't negate all that. But in the public's eye, in the police eye, it would have. Great men can have—"

He held up a sharp hand. He was surprised by the energy he felt. "Don't! *I'm* a man. That 'great men's weakness' is bullshit. I don't care what the public thinks or remembers him for, I care that the father I treasured and admired for three decades was a lie. I care that for reasons I haven't fully uncovered, it may have cost me the woman that I love!"

She took a deep breath and sipped her Scotch with a rock-steady hand. Before she could regroup, he leaned forward.

"Mom, what the hell is going on! Did Meredith learn something, see something that caused her to disappear?"

"I honestly don't know, Brandon. Everything I know is thirty years old. I can't imagine why it would matter to her."

"I went to Montreal—"

"I know you did. Cyril told me."

A chill ran through him. "You were in Montreal too?"

She nodded. "Your Aunt Bea called me to tell me you'd arrived and she was going to tell you the truth about your father."

"What the hell were you doing? Sneaking around trying to shut everybody up?"

"No, Brandon." She sounded calm. Patient, reassuring Mother talking to him as if he were five years old again. He felt his gut clench. "I only wanted to know what you'd been told, and to talk to Cyril before you did. But you beat me to it."

"Why did you want to talk to Cyril?"

"Because..." She paused, studying him. He had the strangest feeling that she was re-evaluating what he knew and what lie she could safely tell him next. "Cyril was my rock when your father died. I was devastated. I know that's hard for you to believe, but I was fresh out of law school, barely twenty-five years old, a bewildered, hurt young mother with a two-month old baby."

Brandon remembered both Cyril's and Cam Hatfield's opinion that his mother had come off far better with his father dead than alive. He hardened himself against his mother's poignant portrait. "Come off it, Mother. Cyril hasn't a tender bone in his body."

Her eyes narrowed. "That's not true. Your father's death—and the manner of it—affected him very profoundly. He's a deeply wounded man, Brandon. He's always kept those wounds private, but in the aftermath of your father's death, he was the one family member I could count on."

"To pay people off, to threaten the newspapers..."

"To shield me. To shield you, and yes, to shield your father's memory. I know Cyril comes across as austere and calculating, but he's an old man who's lived alone too long—"

"Jesus. Please give me some credit. He's a vindictive, controlling old bastard, and if he was nice to you when my father died, it was for his own reasons. Maybe just keeping the Longstreet name out of the shit, maybe something else."

She drew in a quick breath. "Like what?"

He reined in his anger. Once again he sensed she was holding out and wondering what he knew. He tried a bluff. "You know perfectly well. It's what you've been trying to keep from me all along."

"I haven't been keeping anything from you!"

"Okay, let me ask you this. Did you go to Dad's grave when you were in Montreal?"

She looked blindsided. "Of course not. Why?"

"Did you know Lise Gravelle, the woman who was killed—"

"I know who you mean. I didn't know her."

"Was she coming to see you?"

Her brow furrowed. "I have no idea, Brandon. I'd never met her, never heard of her."

His mother was the consummate actor, used to playing with truth and obfuscation on the courtroom stage. She had mastered every emotion—disbelief, outrage, bewilderment and hurt. Her denial rang with such authenticity that he had to remind himself not to believe a word.

"Why would she come to see you?"

"I don't know that she was! I don't know the woman from Eve."

"Who else did you see in Montreal besides Cyril?"

"A couple of old friends and cousins." She supplied names, all relations who had had no useful information to offer Brandon during his trip.

"Did you warn them not to talk to me?"

Her lips twitched. "You missed your calling going into medicine. You should become a lawyer."

"Did you warn them?"

"Darling, I'm not the enemy! I knew the cat was out of the bag. I told them you were all grown up now and could handle whatever they wanted to tell you."

He didn't believe her for a minute. "And did you say the same thing to Cameron Hatfield?"

"Who?"

"The newspaper reporter who covered Dad's story."

She blinked, and her playful smile grew rigid. The spasm lasted only a second, but it told him all he needed to know. She hadn't spoken to Hatfield, but there was indeed more to the story that she didn't want him to know.

TWENTY-ONE

It was five thirty in the evening. Green had spent the first hour of his westward drive squinting into the setting sun. In the cloudless winter sky, its white rays had shattered prism-like over the horizon before mercifully slipping out of sight. By the time Green finally neared Ottawa, the evening sky had deepened to velvet blue over the countryside, but his eyes ached.

He'd phoned ahead when he was about an hour out to ask Gibbs to pick up Lise Gravelle's cousin and bring him to the station. It wasn't the most compassionate way to handle a next-of-kin interview, but he doubted this cousin, after thirty years of estrangement, would be too grief-stricken.

Gibbs had phoned back half an hour later to warn Green that Denis Gravelle spoke virtually no English, although he'd managed to convey his displeasure at the request. He was hungry, tired and in no mood for English cops. Gibbs awaited instructions.

"Tell him to get some food, and I'll meet him in the restaurant with a translator."

Through some unknown combination of gestures, guesswork and fractured French, Gibbs and Gravelle had settled on the Ethiopian restaurant just up the street from the cheap Rideau Street hotel Gravelle had booked. Green had mulled over the wisdom of attempting the interview on his own, but decided that Marie Claire Levesque might get far more cooperation out of him. Besides being Francophone, she was a lot easier to look at than Green.

Levesque was already waiting for him when he walked into the restaurant, almost deserted on a Sunday night. The pungent smell of spices filled the room with promise and the modest decor was soft and discreet. Far from looking annoyed at the interruption of her Sunday, she was lounging back in her chair chatting with a rugged bull of a man who was grinning from ear to ear. Small wonder. Wearing only jeans and an oversized grey turtleneck, she was stunning even without make-up. As Green approached, she glanced up with a lazy smile. She gestured casually.

"Denis, this is my boss, Inspector Green." Her tone said "boss, but don't bother about him."

"*Bienvenue à Ottawa,*" Green said, extending his hand before continuing with the French speech he had rehearsed, all the more important now after Levesque's subversive start. "Thank you for meeting me at this difficult time. French is not always my strength, so I have asked Sergeant Levesque to join us to help if it's necessary."

The waiter brought two bottles of beer, an Ethiopian brand for Levesque and a Molson Export for Gravelle. The waiter glanced inquiringly at Green, who pointed to Levesque's. While he shed his coat and settled in, Green surreptitiously sized up the cousin. Thickly muscled and tanned, he looked like a man who spent his days at heavy labour in the sun and his nights at the local tavern. Bristly grey hair sprouted in odd patches on his head and his face had clearly encountered too many fists. Or hockey pucks. Missing teeth, flattened nose, torn ear and a network of lumpy scars that suggested old acne. All in all, an ugly, hard-headed son of a bitch, with the expression to match. He took a deep slug of beer before scowling at Green.

"I don't know what I'm supposed to do with her," he said, speaking so fast through his missing teeth that Green had to scramble to understand. "Hardly remember her, with her fancy clothes and her snob ways. Broke her mother's heart, never even came back for her funeral, and you want me to pay for hers?"

Green was still deciphering when the man continued. "But I'm here and I don't want to waste more goddamn time in this city that I have to. So get on with your questions."

Green had been planning a more subtle approach, but decided to match straight talk with his own. "Why did she break with her family?"

"Her and her sister thought they were too good for us. Didn't like putting their hands in cow shit at four o'clock in the morning."

"Just the two of them? Two sisters?"

"Yeah. There was a brother who died as a child, and her mother wasn't right in the head ever since. But don't get me wrong. My uncle adored those girls, his little princesses, and he's the one insisted they get an education. He just didn't expect them to turn their backs on him when they did."

"Where is the sister?"

"Lilianne? Who knows?" He waved a dismissive hand into the distance. "I heard she and Lise had a falling out and she took off to Ontario with some guy. There was always some guy." For the first time his ugly features softened at the memory. "Pretty girl. They were both pretty."

Green leaned forward to draw him out further, only to have the waiter arrive with a huge platter of hot, spicy foods. Denis recoiled in dismay at the display, barely recognizable beyond some hard boiled eggs and chicken legs covered in yellow sauce. He groped around for a non-existent fork.

Laughing with amusement, Levesque explained that one ate

with one's fingers and demonstrated by tearing off a scrap of flat bread and digging in. Denis's face collapsed in a grimace, and he pushed his chair back, signalling for another Molson's.

Green tried to recapture the mood. "It must have been hard on Lise to lose touch with her sister like that."

Denis took another swig and eyed the food out of the corner of his eye. "Harder on her poor *maman*. After losing her son too. She had no friends. You had to drag her to family evenings, she never went out of the house. I don't know, some kind of phobia? Used to run inside the minute a car turned up the lane. When the girls left, well..." He shrugged to express his defeat. "My uncle wasn't much for words either, but I know he never forgave them."

Not a happy home for a child, Green thought. He felt the same twinge of sorrow he'd felt looking at the photos of loneliness and yearning that filled Lise's apartment. Yet maybe the father too had felt the same loneliness on his isolated, loveless farm. Maybe the departure of his daughters was more than he could bear.

"Did you ever hear from Lise? Know what she'd been doing?"

With two stubby, calloused fingers, he picked at the corner of the bread. "If you're asking if I know who killed her, no. But one hears things—people come back from Montreal for the holidays with stories. I know she had a hard life. Dropped out of school, couldn't keep a job. Someone heard she was in a mental hospital." He dipped a piece of bread into the nearby pile of spicy lentils, as if edging into the meal. Levesque cheered him on with extravagant raves about the food. Green's stomach contracted.

As Denis chewed, he sneaked her a grin and tore off a larger piece. His expression softened. "It wasn't much of a life. My wife says the whole family is tragic, and poor Lise never found the dream she was searching for either. No husband, no children, no home or big city success to show for all the years she searched."

Levesque burst in. "No romantic alliances at all, man or woman?"

Gravelle turned red, whether from embarrassment or the spicy chicken leg, Green wasn't sure. "*Eh bien,* she was not a lesbian! Back in St. Dominique, she had lots of boyfriends. Her father was very strict, and it was difficult for her to go out with them, but no, no, she found a way."

"You're saying she played around?"

Denis struggled not to cough. "She was young. She was pretty. It gave her some attention, that's all. I'm not saying she was a slut or something like that. Not like Lilianne. When Lise went to the city, it was for studies. She had big dreams. Pity that it ended like this."

While Levesque was following up, Green had set his laptop on the table and opened it. Now he leaned forward to interrupt. "Were there any rumours of her having an affair with a professor?"

Denis had picked up a second chicken leg and was laying into it with gusto. His eyes widened, and he started to shake his head. Then he stopped, mouth half open, and squinted as if trying to peer into the distant murk of memory. "The lady at the church, who made friends with my aunt, said the parents were very upset about something. Lise had got herself in trouble..."

"Trouble?" Green raised a questioning palm.

Denis shrugged. "I was young. I didn't listen to that stuff much, but my mother was mad about it. It was like Lise shamed the family. She never came home after that."

Green opened up his photo file on his laptop and pulled up Harvey Longstreet's photo on the screen. "Have you ever seen this man? Look carefully."

Denis sucked noisily on his sticky fingers before leaning forward to look. He didn't look for long before he shook his head. "Never seen him."

"Did you know Lise was a photographer?"

"What? As a job?"

"No, as an artist." Green showed him some of the photos on Lise's wall.

Denis reacted to the photos of the dogs. "She always loved dogs. Was good to train them too, even as a little girl. Dogs listened to her." He pointed to the melancholy border collie resting its head on its paws. "That one looks like TinTin, they had on the farm. She took him everywhere. After school he'd wait for her just like that at the end of the lane."

Green called up the first of the Amélie series on the screen. "*Bon Dieu*," Denis muttered. "She had some talent!"

"Do you recognize the little girl?"

His eyes narrowed. "Pretty girl."

"Her name is Amélie."

He was still staring at her. "She looks...there's something about her."

Green clicked on the next photo, of Amélie smiling shyly as she reached up to an unseen adult. Denis sucked in his breath. "What do you see?" Green asked.

"She reminds me of Lise at that age. I was young myself, so my memory is not..." He gave a gesture of uncertainty. "But the curly hair, that little nose. Like it could be..."

"Her own child?" Green asked softly.

Denis gave a sharp shake of his head before pulling back. "But I never heard— No, I would have heard, if there was a child..."

Green's thoughts were doing cartwheels, but he forced himself to keep his movements slow and his voice calm. Beside him, to his relief, Levesque had the sense to remain silent. Green pulled up the next photo showing the profile of the man Amélie was smiling at.

"Do you recognize this man?"

Denis stared for a long time, probably trying to make out the details of the shadowy face. "Is that the father?"

"I don't know. Have you ever seen him before?"

"No. If that's her lover, she met him in Montreal."

"His name is Jules. Adam Jules."

Beside him Levesque gasped. He shot her a warning glance. Her mouth was agape and her eyes were wide with shock, but fortunately she said nothing.

"I went to high school with some Jules, but I don't recognize that name."

"But you knew some other Jules?"

"Yeah, yeah, Lilianne went out with one. They hung around, you know. Not neighbours, but there was a Jules family that owned a farm over the next valley. Bunch of drunks and crooks, ran a still in the woods back of their farm. I remember the kids ran wild. You stayed away from them in school."

"Did Lise ever go out with one?"

"I don't think so. Normally she was looking up, you know? Not down at that gang." His brow creased as he stared at the photo. "*Sacrifice*, I hope she didn't get knocked up by one of them."

*   *   *

Dinner was a tense, silent affair. Brandon and his mother always ate in the kitchen when it was just the two of them, preferring it to the formal dining room with its crystal chandelier and its mahogany table for ten. But even the small kitchen felt empty and the intimacy forced. As soon as he could, Brandon excused himself and went into the den to watch TV. Anything. An inane comedy, a hockey game, even *Canadian Idol*. He was on his third Scotch and was well aware that he should stop.

His mother appeared a few minutes later lugging a large, rectangular box which she emptied into the middle of the floor. A silver artificial Christmas tree slid out. She eyed it glumly.

"I decided it was time we trimmed the tree."

"Why?"

"Because it's almost Christmas, Brandon, and we can't pretend time has stopped. These traditions can help keep us going in difficult times." She paused then resumed more softly. "Believe me, I know."

She stood the tree in the corner, adjusted its placement with a critical eye then left the room again. He glared at the tree, irrationally angry. How did she expect him to care about Christmas, to care about anything, when his whole future had been shot to hell? Then he thought of her last words, about all that she had gone through. Was she a monster, a conniver, or simply a mother whose only crime was to love him? He felt a wash of bewildered shame.

Setting aside his Scotch, he hauled himself out of his chair. He was just straightening the tree when she reappeared with two boxes of tree decorations stacked on top of each other. He caught her fleeting smile of delight.

"Let's put on some music," she said, switching off the TV. "The *Messiah*, or Christmas Carols."

"The *Messiah* would be nice," he said, thinking he wouldn't be able to bear a whole CD of saccharine songs. He found he couldn't even look at her, so he reached for the first box, determined to get busy. Together they trimmed the tree as they always had, in a yearly ritual of just the two of them. It had never felt so empty. He was grateful for the triumphant voices of Handel's *Messiah*, which blocked out all possibility of conversation.

His mother always approached tree trimming as a task of

perfect balance. All the lights were white and blue to complement the silver tree, and they had to be distributed exactly equally. The ornaments were delicate glass, some decades old. No plastic Santas or homemade reindeer. He found himself wondering what Meredith would have thought of it and felt almost grateful that she wasn't here. She wouldn't have argued, but she would have thought it dry as dust.

The thought shamed him again, and he walked over to pick up his Scotch glass. As a soft alto aria began, his mother selected a clear glass angel. With great care, she reached to hang it.

"Brandon." Her voice in the quiet made him jump. "We need to do something about the wedding."

"Why?"

"You know why."

"There's still plenty of time. Anything could happen."

She moved the angel to another branch and studied the effect. "Darling, she's not coming back."

"We don't know that." He paced over to the window, feeling precarious. "We don't know where she is. Maybe—"

She turned from the tree to face him. "I don't know how else to say this. I've been trying to let you have hope—"

"Then let me, damn it. How can I tell her, when she walks through that door in a week, a month, or a year from now, that I gave up on her less than a week after she went missing!"

He realized he was shouting when she held up her hand. Her cheeks were red and her eyes were sad. "Brandon, in this cold, I think she's—"

"Don't! This is *my* girlfriend. *My* wedding. Don't you dare cancel a thing! If I have to on the day of the wedding, I'll call every single guest—"

The phone rang. They both froze, staring at it as they had

every single time in the past week. His mother reacted first, snatching it up from its cradle in the hall. He heard the quick disappointment in her voice.

"Oh! Hello." Her tone dropped as she turned her back. By the time he made it to the hall, she was speaking in a low, urgent voice. "No, that's best. Yes... Yes... Don't worry about him."

He stepped closer just as she hung up and turned, startled at the sight of him. She snatched her coat and began to pull on her boots. "That was an old friend. I'm going out for awhile, but I won't be late. I promise."

He should have stopped her. Grabbed her, shaken her and demanded answers. But the distress on her face stopped him in his tracks long enough for her to slip out the door. She left without so much as a glance in the mirror to check her appearance. For his mother, that was unheard of.

He went back into the empty living room. Music filled the room, building towards the triumphant Hallelujah chorus. Nerves jangling, he switched it off. In the unnatural silence, he took a last look at the perfect, symmetrical tree before heading upstairs. As always, he phoned Meredith's cell. Still straight to voicemail. Flipped on his computer to check online. First his Facebook page, depressed to see the stream of mindless trivia posted by people he barely knew. His wall was full of inquiries from concerned friends. Next he checked his email. Spam ads, notices, six real messages containing the same questions from friends. Most were urging him to call them, but one tactlessly asked if the wedding was off.

There was one name he didn't recognize. Yourgirl. He wondered whether it was an online sex invitation until he clicked on it. One word.

"Safe."

TWENTY-TWO

Green had barely left the restaurant when he dialled Magloire. The big detective tried to sound cheerful, but Green could hear his enthusiasm waning. He glanced at his watch. Nearly seven o'clock. He felt a stab of guilt.

"Jean Pierre, sorry to disturb you at home. Tomorrow when you get to work—"

"I'm off tomorrow." He mustered a chuckle. "My reward because I chased you around all weekend."

"Okay, well, whoever is doing the follow up. I have some information that will make the background check on Lise Gravelle easier. Remember you were going to check if she had any children? I've narrowed down the date. See if she had a baby girl named Amélie sometime in 1978 or early 1979. March at the latest."

"The cousin confirmed this?"

"No, but it's the only thing that makes sense. I think Harvey Longstreet is the father." Green thrust the question mark of Adam Jules out of his mind. Adam played some kind of role, and obviously he knew Lise and Amélie, but what reason could there have been for the cover-up if he'd been the father?

"I'll do it first thing!"

"Handle it however you want, *mon ami*, but it really is grunt work. Hours on the phone, most of it on hold."

But Magloire was undeterred, and when Green hung up, he

couldn't help smiling. He could almost picture the man's ebony face lighting up with excitement. He was going to miss Magloire. In a flash of insight, he realized why. Magloire reminded him of his oldest and closest friend, Brian Sullivan. How many cases had they worked together, with Sullivan trailing along patiently while Green pursued his every whim? How many times had Sullivan drawn him back to earth, tactfully or not, when his imagination ran too wild. Sullivan had always been there with the safety net and without complaint, until the dreadful day when his own safety net had failed.

It had been three months since the catastrophe, and Sullivan had not stepped over the threshold of the police station since. When Green visited him, all talk of the accident, the station and the future were off limits. Mindful of Sullivan's fragile recovery, Green had never pressed the issue and had been content to chat about football, the Senators' chances, or the new boat Sullivan was building with his sons in the garage. The visits felt forced, as if Sullivan didn't really want him there.

But the estrangement had left a huge hole in Green's life, and never had he felt it as acutely as now. Adam Jules's shadow and his whereabouts hung over the investigation like a shroud, and there was no one else on the police force he could confide in. Or share his fears with.

Shoving aside his doubts, Green started the car and aimed it towards the Vanier Parkway and Sullivan's Alta Vista home. It was dinner time, family time, and Mary Sullivan was almost certain to slam the door in his face, but he had to try.

As it turned out, Mary was not even home. When Sullivan himself answered the door, Green stepped back in surprise. He hadn't seen his friend in over a month, and the transformation was astonishing. His six-foot-four frame looked twenty pounds lighter, the jowls and the fatigue lines were gone, and his mottled complexion had been transformed to healthy pink.

He smiled, actually smiled, at the sight of Green. "Come on in, stranger! Just me and the kids tonight. Mary's up in Eganville because her mother's ill. She's looking for a home for her, and I'm praying to sweet Jesus she doesn't bring her back here." He led Green into the family room, which was cluttered with videos, newspapers and take-out containers. In the background, a huge HDTV blared out a hockey game. Sullivan grabbed the remote from the jumble on the coffee table and hit the mute button. Somewhere in the recesses of the house, a radio was playing teenage pop.

"Can I get you a drink? Beer? Scotch?"

"If you'll join me," Green said, wary of this unexpected enthusiasm.

Sullivan grinned. "Mary's not here, so maybe a beer. She's got me on a regime to punish a saint!"

"You're looking good, though. Really good."

"Yeah? I feel pretty good." Sullivan had headed into the kitchen and had to shout over his shoulder. "Better than I have in years, to be honest."

"You're not getting bored?"

Sullivan reappeared with two Coors Light and gave Green a wary look. He pointed to his heart. "This has to come first. For years I never had time to think of anything but the job. I wanted a piece of land in the country, never had time to look for it. I wanted to build my own classic boat, never had time. This is an eye opener, Mike. You should try it."

They sat in opposite lazy-boys nursing their beers while Green let him talk. Finally he leaned forward. "Brian, I've got a problem."

Sullivan's eyes narrowed. "You do, Mike. I don't."

"Can I tell you about it?" Green spread out his free hand in a soothing gesture. "That's all. I talk, you listen. There's no one else on the whole goddamn force I can tell."

"Try the departmental shrink, Mike. They're paid to listen."

"It's about Adam Jules."

Sullivan paused, his beer halfway to his lips. He lowered it. Stared at the floor. "Fuck."

So Green told him, from Jules's very first query to the scarf in Elena Longstreet's hall, to the car outside Cyril Longstreet's home, to the photo on Lise's wall. The recitation took more that half an hour, during which neither man touched their beers and Sullivan didn't say a word. At the end of it, Sullivan stared at the floor again. "Fuck."

"My sentiments exactly, Brian. And I don't know what the hell to do, I don't know where Adam is!"

"You're absolutely sure it was Adam you saw in the car and in the photo? You said it was only a glimpse. Maybe you have him on the brain."

"Wait here." Green heaved himself out of the lazy-boy and headed out to the car for his laptop. Inside again, he booted it up and opened the photo of Amélie. "You tell me."

Sullivan chuckled. "Not a very good photo line-up, Mike. You've already biased me."

"Just look at it."

Sullivan peered at the photo. Zoomed in on the shadowy figure's face, then his hands. He sighed. "Certainly could be. But what are you thinking, Mike? If this is Longstreet's kid and not Adam's, where does Adam fit in?"

"I think..." Green groped through his jumbled impressions. "I think Adam knew Lise from when they were kids, or maybe he just felt a bond because they were both from the same area. When he was assigned the case—"

"Longstreet's death?"

"Yes. He investigated and found out Lise was the man's lover. Pregnant with his child, maybe even present at his death. He saw her for what she was—a naïve country girl who'd been used by her prof. So when he was pressured by the Longstreet family to bury the whole investigation, he did so, because he saw it as a way to protect Lise too."

"But this is Adam Jules we're talking about. Mr. Straight-and-narrow!"

"Now. But maybe not then. He was young, probably in over his head and getting no support from his superiors."

Sullivan bent his head, thinking. "Even so, I don't see Adam doing that. Not just to protect reputations or family names, particularly when the reputation getting the most protection is this sleazeball Longstreet himself."

He was right, and that was a sticking point for Green too. "He stayed in touch with Lise. He probably continued to help her."

"And you're absolutely sure it's not his kid?"

"I'm not remotely sure of anything! But it makes sense. He..." Green pointed to the screen, to the fingertips brushing each other. There was something warm and familiar in the gesture. He was transported back to Jules's apartment, to his bedroom and the album of children on the night table. All ages and colours, smiling out at the photographer with affection and thanks. "He's done this other times."

"Done what?"

"Helped children." Green felt his way forward. "Been involved in their lives somehow, like a big brother. No, more like a benefactor."

"What the hell are you talking about?"

Green told him about his search of Jules's apartment. Once

Sullivan had recovered from his shock, his eyes grew dark. "You could put a whole different slant on this interest in children, you know."

Green suppressed a shiver. He'd had the same fleeting fear.

"Adam's a pretty odd guy," Sullivan added. "No women, no family ties..."

"We have no evidence of that." Green knew his voice lacked conviction. "I found no child porn or paraphernalia in his apartment, just pictures of happy children."

"We both know what that's worth. How charming these guys can be. You'll need to track down this Amélie kid. She'd be a young woman by now, I guess. If your theory is correct, thirty-two?"

"I've got a Montreal detective looking for—" Green broke off. A thought came crashing through his consciousness, driving out all else. "My god!"

"What?"

Green rummaged through his folder, which contained bits and pieces about the case that he'd accumulated. At the bottom was the Missing Person poster of Meredith Kennedy. Without a word he held up the picture side by side with the black and white photo of Amélie. A round, cherubic little girl and an impishly beautiful young woman. The hair was straighter and the dimples gone, but the upturned nose was the same.

Furthermore, Meredith Kennedy was thirty-two years old.

* * *

Green's first instinct was to drive straight over to confront Meredith Kennedy's parents. Even if they didn't know Meredith's biological parenthood, why wouldn't they at least have mentioned it if she'd been adopted?

Unless they had something to hide. Unless it wasn't an adoption but something worse.

It seemed an impossible coincidence, but coincidences happen, and Green couldn't believe he'd missed that possibility when it was screaming to be noticed. He'd been so obsessed with the minutia of the case—the role of Adam Jules, the secrecy of Cyril Longstreet, the identity of the lover—that he'd failed to ask the most obvious question of all.

What the hell did Meredith have to do with any of this?

Why had Lise contacted Meredith rather than Elena or the Kennedys? This explained all the niggling pieces that had not fit anywhere in his grand reconstruction of the case. It explained Meredith's complete meltdown upon learning the truth, for she was about to marry her half-brother. It explained Lise's continued obsession with the Longstreets and her expression of triumph upon meeting Meredith. It explained Lise's willingness to brave snowstorms in the middle of the night to contact the families once she'd learned that the two young people were about to wed.

Most importantly, it could also be a powerful motive for murder.

As he drove away from Sullivan's house, Green almost turned west towards the Kennedys' house but restrained himself with an effort. He needed to step back so he could think through all the new implications, and he needed to confirm some facts before he confronted anyone.

For tonight, he would only set a couple of balls in motion. Tony was asleep when he arrived home, but Sharon was waiting to share dinner and a glass of wine. He slipped away only briefly to make two phone calls. The first was to Magloire, whose cell phone was wisely turned off for the night. Green left him a message asking him to check Montreal birth and adoptions records for

Meredith Kennedy during the same time period as Amélie, and to check for cases of child abduction or disappearance.

The second call was to Gibbs, who picked up on the second ring. He rushed into a report before Green could get in a word. "I-I put out the alert, sir, and Patrol's kind of keeping an eye on Elena Longstreet's house. Nothing to report yet. Patrol sergeant was pretty hopping, said the place is already crawling with RCMP and we should let the horsemen do the damn job. S-sorry, sir."

"Thanks, Bob. I've got one more small thing for you and Sue to do in the morning. I know you're checking into school and community connections between Lise Gravelle and the Kennedys. Try to find out if Norah or Reg ever worked for the Longstreets or for the apartment building where Harvey Longstreet died."

"Oh! Well, Norah did work for the police."

"The Montreal police?"

"Yes. Just a secretary or something."

"When?"

In his urgency, he snapped the word out and he sensed Gibbs recoil. "I-I don't know, sir."

"Then that's another job for the morning. Find out the exact dates, location, who she worked with and what her job was. But try to do it without tipping off the Kennedys."

Green's mind was still racing long after he and Sharon had gone to bed. He slipped out and took his laptop downstairs. Sitting in his easy chair, he drafted a list of questions to which he still had no answers. At the top of it were four people, whose current whereabouts and activities were unknown. Meredith Kennedy, Adam Jules, Cameron Hatfield and Cyril Longstreet. Four people on the loose, each with their own agenda. Some were hunters, some the hunted.

Some of them, perhaps, were both.

Brandon sat at his computer, staring at the word. *Safe.* Adrenaline coursed through him, pummelling his body and washing thought from his brain. Tears blurred his eyes.

His first instinct was to run into the streets, screaming "She's alive! She's alive!" But he remained rooted in his chair. Bit by bit he caught his breath and retrieved his scattered thoughts. She's alive, but where is she and why the secrecy? Why the code name and the ridiculous, cryptic message? He checked the email address, a Yahoo account that told him nothing. Anyone, anywhere in the world, could set up a Yahoo account with any user name they chose.

He typed in a reply asking both those questions. "Where are you and why the secrecy?" Once he'd pressed "send", the adrenaline finally drove him from his chair. He paced. Wrung his hands, pulled his hair, returned to check for a reply. None. It had only been two minutes. Maybe she didn't have continuous access to the internet. He paced again, considering his next move.

The police and her parents needed to know. Even as he picked up the phone, however, he stopped himself. Why the secrecy? Was she in hiding? In danger? What was the reason she couldn't let anyone know where she was? Meredith was smart and level-headed. She was no drama queen, and yet that message, sent after a week of silence, suggested she feared for her life. What other reason could there be? If she'd simply wanted to disappear from his life, she wouldn't have answered at all, or replied 'Sorry to hurt you. I'm fine but it's over.' Or even more likely she'd never have run away at all, but just told him to his face.

Unless she had something to do with the murder. The appalling possibility had been dancing around the edges of his mind ever since the body had been discovered, but he'd refused to face it head on. Now dread raced through him. Could the compassionate, peace-loving woman he knew be capable of such a brutal act? Impossible. He knew that, but would anyone else? What if the police suspected her? Was that why she had fled, because she knew they'd be after her and she had no defence?

As he paced, the questions swirled in his head, refusing to settle, refusing to make sense. No, maybe instead she had witnessed something and feared for her life. But from whom? And why wouldn't she simply go to the police?

Unless the danger lay with someone close to him.

His hands trembled at the thought. Equally horrifying, equally impossible. He needed answers. If he simply blundered in to tell the police, they would try to track her down, thereby putting her at risk. How could he find out more while still protecting her? He sat back down at his computer, created a Yahoo account with the user name yourboy, and sent her a simple message.

"Tell me what to do."

Then he paced some more, replaying every minute they'd spent together, every conversation he could remember and every place and friend she'd ever mentioned. He made a list, longer and more thorough than the one he'd given the police. He studied it with only one question in mind. Where would she have gone that no one would think to look for her? Where no one would know her or recognize her picture from the news?

By the middle of the night his brain was exhausted, but he had no answer. A shorter list, but still no way to go forward. He'd heard his mother arrive home but dared not go downstairs to speak to her, in case his suspicion gave him away. Paranoia paralyzed him. Until he knew what the danger was, no one—especially his mother—could know.

He lay down on his bed to try to rest, leaving his computer on to receive the reply which never came. At five o'clock in the morning, he fell asleep.

TWENTY-THREE

G reen had drifted into a fitful sleep just after two a.m. His last conscious thought was that, like it or not, he had to apprise the deputy chief of his suspicions in the morning. To hold back now, in the face of all the evidence implicating Adam Jules in this tangled web, would not only be career suicide but also detrimental to the case. The senior brass needed to know about this threat by one of their own. Briefly he considered bringing his concerns to his direct superior Barbara Devine, but rejected the notion. Surely even "By the Book" Poulin would see the folly in that.

By the time he arrived at the station Monday morning, however, he was having serious second thoughts about his whole cockamamie theory of the case. The coincidence was too impossible. Of all the women Brandon could have fallen in love with, what were the odds of it being his own half-sister? Neither one even lived in the city in which they were born, neither one had retained any ties to the mutual past that might have bound them. He felt a little sheepish that he'd sent Magloire out to comb through adoption registries and missing child reports from three decades ago in search of the proverbial needle in the haystack.

Before he blew Adam Jules's career to smithereens, he needed more confirmation from Magloire and Gibbs. He didn't expect any results from Magloire for hours, possibly days, but he was pleased to see Gibbs already at his desk on the phone, following up on his assignment.

Green spent a restless, impatient morning dealing with the emails and phone messages that had piled up over the weekend, and combing through all the reports on the case, looking for any small detail the detectives might have missed.

Gibbs was the first to report. Norah Kennedy had worked for the Montreal Police only briefly, in the general typing pool in 1980. Before that she'd worked for a temp agency and after that she'd moved to Ottawa. Green's first reaction was disappointment, for the dates didn't fit. But then he remembered that Amélie had not been a baby in the photos on Lise's wall. She might have been adopted as a toddler, in which case 1980 fit very well.

To his surprise, Magloire phoned back in the early afternoon. It had been a slow day in Major Crimes, and he had enlisted most of the staff to help him. At Saint-Camille Church in Montreal North, they'd found a parish record of the baptism in March 1979 of an Amélie Marie Gravelle, born November 4, 1978. Mother Lise Gravelle, father unknown. This birth had been subsequently registered at the St. Hyacinth town hall, but neither the town nor the province had any further record of a girl by that name. No school registration, no health card, no driver's license or social insurance number. Nor was there any record of adoption or death.

The Kennedy question was more straightforward. There was no record of a Meredith Kennedy being adopted anywhere in the Greater Montreal area, but even more telling, Magloire had found no trace of her birth either. No registration or birth announcement. Little Meredith Kennedy had surfaced briefly as a two-year-old when a Quebec health card was issued, before dropping from bureaucratic sight again. That's because she moved to Ontario, Green thought.

"It's possible she was born in another province," Magloire said. "Even another country."

Possible, Green admitted, although the Kennedys had never mentioned it. "What about missing or abducted child reports?"

"So far, nothing in the system. I asked some of our old-timers, and they don't remember a case like that. Normally you don't forget child abductions, especially a beautiful little girl."

So true, Green thought. The cases involving harm to children stayed with you forever. Despite the negative findings, he still felt a nagging unease. People were hiding something. He was about to sign off when Magloire spoke again.

"There is something else interesting, however. The recorded birth dates of the two girls, Meredith and Amélie. They are only a week apart."

*   *   *

It wasn't much, but enough to justify a visit to the Kennedys. Green was tempted to haul them down to the station for the confrontation, but restrained himself. They were frightened, desperate parents; the fact that they had kept a few pieces of crucial information to themselves did not change that. Besides, he'd always found it useful to observe witnesses on their own turf.

He enlisted Levesque to accompany him. It was technically Gibbs's case, but the two cases had blurred into one and he wanted Levesque to observe, and to learn. Nonetheless, he caught the faint look of reproach on Gibbs's face when they left him behind at his desk.

Green was pleased to find both Kennedys at home. Although the police search for their daughter was still active, the ground search had been terminated and most of the search team's hopes now rested on tips. Norah and Reg looked as if they too were losing hope. Green had not yet met the Kennedys, relying instead on Peters' and Gibbs's reports. Reg answered the door, dwarfed inside an old, baggy sweat suit as if his very soul were shrivelling up. Greasy strands of thinning hair stuck to his scalp, and several days' worth of stubble darkened his face, giving him a haunted look.

Norah came up behind to peer over his shoulder. Unlike her husband, she looked determined to keep up appearances. She wore black slacks and a knitted red sweater with reindeer across its front. Santa earrings dangled from her ears. Green suspected it was she who had put the Christmas wreath on the door and the luminescent plastic snowman on the front lawn. To welcome Meredith.

When Green introduced himself, a spasm of fear crossed their faces. He held up a soothing hand. "No news, I'm afraid. But I have a few new questions."

She dragged aside her husband, who seemed frozen in place, and invited them in. The house was immaculate, each table surface covered in knick-knacks and framed photos. A tall, genuine Christmas tree stood in the corner almost drowning in tinsel and ornaments, and a carved wooden nativity scene sat in the bay window ledge.

Norah saw Green looking at it. "We've put that out every year since Meredith was a baby. She'll want to see it when she comes home."

Green settled casually in an easy chair as if for a friendly chat, pleased to see Levesque slip unobtrusively into the opposite corner and take out her notebook. The Kennedys sat together on the sofa, trying in vain to keep both in their sights.

"Do you have pictures of her when she was little?" Green asked.

Norah looked startled. "Little? Why?"

"She was born in Montreal, right?"

"Yes, but we've already told the other officers that we moved here when she was very little."

"But you have pictures of her?"

"I don't see what—"

Reg stirred himself from his semi-stupor. "We lost them all in a basement flood. Sewer back-up. That was the worst of it. Losing the baby pictures."

"Not a single picture?" Green said incredulously. He thought of the dozens of pictures of his children that filled the walls and side tables of not only his own home but his father's tiny senior's apartment.

Norah picked up the tale. "Not of her first two years. That was what finally made up our minds to leave Montreal. Our house was near the lakeshore and was always flooding in the spring."

Green leaned forward. "I'm curious about those first two years. We've been trying to track your daughter as part of our routine inquiries, and we found no registration of her birth."

Norah blanched. She shot a glance in Reg's direction but quickly stopped herself. She pretended to look confused. "What? She was born at Lakeshore General. I'm not likely to forget that day, ever."

Green shook his head dolefully. "No record of a Meredith Kennedy."

"Well...there must be a mix-up. That's Quebec bureaucracy for you."

"There were no birth announcements in the papers either. *Montreal Gazette, Star, La Presse*—"

"Oh, we didn't put one in."

Green feigned surprise. "Why not?"

"I—I don't know. Reg was supposed to do it, but..."

Her husband looked slightly green. "Truth was, I was afraid to jinx it. She was born ten weeks premature and we weren't even sure she'd make it. Poor Norah was beside herself, because we'd tried for so long. So I held off the announcement, and when she was finally out of danger, it seemed too late."

"What about a baptism certificate? If we checked with your church, would they have it?"

Colour flooded back into Norah's face. "Oh yes, but no need. We have it right upstairs. Reggie, would you get it?"

Reg was out the door like a shot. Norah turned to Green, her face collapsing in on itself. Her breath snagged as she tried to speak. "Inspector, why are you asking this? What do you think has happened to my daughter?"

"I don't know."

"But in your experience, when a young woman goes missing in the dead of winter...?"

"Women go missing for many different reasons, Norah. Sometimes for a fresh start, sometimes to escape the law, sometimes to run away from an abusive or dangerous situation."

"But none of that fits! She didn't need a new start. She hadn't fallen in with bad company. Or..." Here Norah stumbled, as if on an unwanted thought. "Or-or broken the law."

"So what do you think happened?"

"I think..." Her voice trembled and she glanced towards the hallway to ensure her husband wasn't returning. "I think she's dead. God help me for saying it, I think he killed her."

"Who?"

"Brandon."

Green leaned towards her and lowered his voice. Could it be that the perfect son-in-law façade was finally crumbling? "Do you have any particular reason to believe that? Any information?"

"No." She shivered. "But it's what they do, isn't it, these boyfriends? When the girl tries to leave."

"Was Meredith trying to leave him? Did she say something to you?"

"I've been thinking about it. She said something a couple of days before she disappeared. She asked me if I thought she and Brandon were too alike. She asked if her dad and me had been soul mates and if it felt spooky. She seemed to be questioning things."

Reg's footsteps thudded on the stairs, weary and sad. He reappeared and handed Green an old, creased copy of a baptismal certificate. It was dated June 10, 1981, at St. Basil Church in Ottawa.

"This is when she was two and a half years old," Green said. "She wasn't baptised in Montreal as a baby?"

Reg looked at his feet. "We didn't have a church in Montreal. Since I wasn't Catholic, no one would marry us. But we were young back then and it didn't matter. But when we moved here, Norah... " He trailed off.

Norah seemed to notice Green's glance as it flitted from the nativity scene to the large wooden cross hanging on the wall. She flushed. "I decided it was important for Meredith's sake. I grew up with mass, Sunday school, all the sacraments, and I wanted that for Meredith. Everyone should have something spiritual in their lives."

Green thought of Hannah, groping her way towards her Jewish roots from the sterile consumer worship of her mother's world. He thought of Tony, who sang the Shabbat blessings with lusty abandon and revelled in the magic delight of the candles and the white linen. All Sharon's doing, just one more debt he could never repay.

He set the paper aside, clasped his hands and leaned forward. "Here's my problem. There is no registration of Meredith's birth, no announcement in the papers, no baby pictures before age two, and no infant baptism certificate. The Quebec health care system has no record of a Meredith Kennedy except briefly in 1981, but the Ontario health system has no record before that."

Both of them stared at him, unmoving.

"It's as if she didn't exist, at least as Meredith Kennedy, before 1981."

Reg said nothing, but Norah erupted. "That's ridiculous! It's just paperwork, and what does it matter anyway!"

"Because it's the reason she disappeared. You lied to the police and let us beat around the bush blindly for a week instead of telling us right away what we should be looking for!"

Norah half stood from the sofa, a red flush spreading up her cheeks. Tears glittered in her eyes. "What are you talking about!"

"Where did Meredith come from, Norah? Did you buy her, or did you kidnap her yourselves?"

Both of them recoiled as if the blow had been physical. Norah's jaw dropped. "Kidnapped! Is that what you think?"

"Lise Gravelle had a daughter whose records stop at the same time a little girl with an almost identical birth date appeared in your life."

Reg had said nothing. He seemed to sag into the sofa, but Norah didn't flinch. "How dare you... How can you even think...!"

"I just follow the facts, Norah, and that's where they point. I've seen parents do far more desperate things in my twenty-five years on the force. I know the power of the maternal drive. I know how desperate the urge can feel. All around you, your friends are having babies, and even women who don't want a baby, don't deserve a baby, can have them. It's not fair. With each passing month, the unfairness and the emptiness eat away at you."

Green could feel Levesque's curious eyes upon him, but he kept his gaze firmly on Norah's. Willing her to relent. "A momentary impulse, an irresistible urge, and suddenly this beautiful little girl is in your arms. Right now, I'm not concerned with what you did thirty years ago. I just need to know whether Meredith had any inkling before she was blindsided by Lise Gravelle."

Reg stirred. A small moan escaped him. "No," he whispered.

"Reggie! Don't!"

Draped in despair, Reg lifted his head to look at her. "Norah, I can't do this any more. He thinks we kidnapped her. Sweet Jesus, do you want him to think that?"

"Then tell me the truth," Green said.

Norah remained rigid, her hands gripping each other as she willed her tears not to fall. Reg took up the tale. "We adopted her, fair and square, but Meredith never knew. We should have told her years ago, but we could never find the right time or the right words. You read about adopted children never being happy, always wanting to find their natural parents, wanting to know why they were given up. Like they weren't lovable or worthy enough."

Norah came alive, trembling with an emotion that had been pushed aside for thirty years. "Meredith *was* loved. We loved her like she was our flesh and blood, and we never wanted her to have that doubt. After awhile, we thought, why does she ever have to know?"

Because back in Montreal she had a mother who loved her and never forgot her, Green thought. And more practically, because nowadays people needed to know their genetic and medical legacy. But he stayed on track. "Who set up the adoption in Montreal?"

"It was done through a priest and a lawyer at the Good Shepherd's Mission. They were good people, there was never any money exchanged, just a small donation to the mission. In exchange they found homes for the babies who were brought there. Mostly abandoned. We were told Meredith was left in the church sanctuary."

Convenient, Green thought. For the moment he forced his cynicism aside. "Were you given her birth certificate?"

Reg shook his head. "Just the record of her birth. A paper that said 'Infant Female', her date of birth and a doctor's name. Not even a hospital. They said she'd been born at home. Back in those days in Quebec, civil registration of births was not mandatory. It was left to the priest or minister to keep a record of the baptism and send a duplicate to the government. Lots of room to fall through the cracks."

Norah had recaptured her spirit. She thrust out her chin. "Priests had been quietly placing unwanted children with good, loving families for decades in Quebec just by a simple private agreement. Much better than when the bureaucrats start messing around."

Reg smiled thinly. "We were getting the run-around at Social Services because Norah was Catholic and I wasn't. Father Fréchette was a godsend."

"But I thought you said neither of you was religious. How did you even hear about him?"

Reg opened his mouth but Norah beat him to it. "Word gets around."

Green took a stab in the dark. "You were working for the Montreal Police in 1980, isn't that right?"

She blinked. "What? I—I...yes, for a few months."

"And you left when you adopted Meredith?"

"Yes, that was part of the agreement with Father Fréchette. I wouldn't work, and I would raise her Catholic."

"Did your work bring you into contact with any police officers?"

She whipped her head back and forth. "I was just in the typing pool."

Green opened his own notebook and pretended to consult his notes. "Mr. and Mrs. Kennedy, I can't help without knowing all the facts, and all the people involved. You weren't religious and you probably didn't know Father Frechette from Frankenstein, but at exactly the time you adopted Meredith, Norah was working at the police station where a young constable worked who was closely connected to her mother. Was that the person who introduced you to the priest? Was it Adam Jules?"

Her quick intake of breath was all the answer he needed.

TWENTY-FOUR

As Levesque drove, Green studied his notes. Bit by bit, he was chipping away at the mystery of the past. After a little more probing, Norah had finally admitted that she'd known Jules back in Montreal. The tall, handsome eligible young constable with the impeccable manners had been the talk of the typing pool, and they all vied for the chance to do his reports. "Not me, of course," Norah had added with a hasty glance at Reg. He was always the perfect gentleman, always said a personal thank-you, and none of the girls received special treatment. But one day she'd just returned from yet another disappointing doctor's appointment, and she was upset when Jules came in. He brought her a cup of tea and listened.

"What a sweetheart! He never talked much, but you knew he listened. Afterwards, he never mentioned it again, but a couple of months later he asked if Reg and I would like to meet a friend of his."

Green was surprised by the story. He'd never known Adam Jules to have a tender side. He'd cared about his officers and done a lot to protect and nurture their careers behind the scenes, but rarely was a word spoken about it. Green remembered the touch of fingertips between Amélie and him. Something had changed in the man over the years.

The Good Shepherd's Mission was in Montreal's northeast

district, not far from the simple bachelor quarters where Adam Jules lived. He told Norah that he'd been volunteering at the mission every Sunday since he'd moved to the city, running the soup kitchen. Occasionally his work brought him in contact with frightened, desperate young women. He never knew where the babies ended up, just that Father Fréchette was very careful with his adoption choices.

Norah didn't know when and why Jules left Montreal, since he'd never been in touch with them since the adoption. Both Kennedys hotly denied having spoken to him in the past week. Curiously they seemed more relaxed and talkative once they'd confessed. Was it the relief of letting go of the secret they'd kept dammed up all these years? Or relief that Green appeared to accept the story? Norah wept unabashedly. Even Reg's eyes brimmed with tears as he talked about how the news would have destroyed Meredith. Terrified that she would somehow find out, they had sworn their family to absolute secrecy. Except for Norah's mom, Reg said. That was the one person they could no longer trust, now that her mind was going. They were so scared she'd blurt it out during one of her rants.

"Touching story," Levesque muttered as she steered the car up towards the Queensway. "We did it all for Meredith."

Green thought of his own colossal mistakes with Hannah. "Even with the best intentions, parents make mistakes and find themselves in corners which they can't get out of."

She shot him a skeptical glance. "You believe them?"

"I'm keeping an open mind. Their emotion seemed pretty real." He didn't mention the role played by Adam Jules. Their story did not exonerate Jules from shady dealings, but it was far easier to think his mentor was facilitating private adoptions than running a baby peddling racket.

"They've had years to rehearse it," was all she said before turning her attention to the road. Green knew she was right. He had not even had to push that hard before their sad, self-serving tale came pouring out.

Elena Longstreet would be a different story. She was next on the interview list, and as Levesque accelerated east towards Rockcliffe, he reviewed the questions he wanted to ask her. He knew he was going up against one of the foremost cross-examination tacticians on the Ottawa Bar, and he had to have every angle covered. Elena was not going to be bullied, outmanoeuvred or driven to tears.

He'd phoned her as they were leaving the Kennedys to let her know he was coming. He considered the advantages of a surprise attack but decided the risk of her wrath outweighed the good. If he wanted any chance of cooperation, an honest, straightforward approach was best. She had been impeccably polite but non-committal on the phone when she informed him she could spare him half an hour. "I'm due in court," she'd said as if to remind him how important she was.

A sleek, champagne-coloured Town Car was parked at the curb in front of Elena's house, the silhouette of its driver visible through the tinted glass. Idling chauffeur-driven luxury cars were such a common sight in Rockcliffe that Green gave it no thought. Elena greeted them at the door dressed in what he assumed was her court attire—a simple black dress to be worn under her gown and a string of white pearls at her neck. She gave Levesque only the faintest nod before turning to lead the way to the living room. She didn't offer to take their coats, as if she didn't intend them to stay long. Ignoring the subtext, Green hung his coat on the coat rack on his way past. Jules's cashmere scarf, he noted, was gone.

To his surprise, the wing chair by the bay window was occupied by an old man who seemed to be all head above a tiny, wraithlike body. He peered at Green through hostile eyes but made no move to greet him.

Green stepped across the room with his hand extended. "Mr. Cyril Longstreet, I assume? I'm Inspector Michael Green of Ottawa CID, and this is my associate Sergeant Levesque."

The man's hand felt like dry twigs in his, but even so he emanated strength. Perhaps it was his unblinking stare or the pugnacious set of his jaw, so different from Green's own father. Despite his frailty, Cyril wanted him to know who was still the boss.

As the two men appraised each other, Green quickly rethought his approach. With Cyril at her side, Elena was twice the adversary. She had not yet invited him to sit down, but before she could choose a place for him, he selected a seat on the sofa with a view of them both. He was again pleased to see Levesque take a chair without prompting on the opposite side of the room. She extracted her notebook.

Green leaned in. "Mrs. Longstreet, since we haven't much time, we'll skip the preliminaries. We all know why we're here; to find out what information you can give us regarding the disappearance of Meredith Kennedy and the death of Lise Gravelle. After a week of intensive investigation, we've uncovered considerable evidence linking Lise to Meredith and to you—both of you, in fact—but to save us some time, perhaps you can tell us what you know."

From the second wing chair, Elena eyed him, deadpan. After a long moment, she shrugged. "Nothing more than I read in the papers, I'm afraid."

"All right, here's what we know." Green held up his hand to begin ticking off points. "For the past thirty years, Lise Gravelle has been keeping tabs on you. She saved clippings of your husband's death, of your departure for Toronto, your court trials, and three weeks ago, an internet story about your son's engagement to Meredith. Two weeks ago, she also began placing calls to Meredith's cell phone, six in all, and last Monday, Meredith paid her a visit in Montreal. Lise caught the bus up here immediately after the visit, placed a call to Meredith during which Meredith became hysterical and accused her of wanting to ruin everything. A few hours later, she was killed, on her way over here to see you."

Elena looked about to object but seemed to think better of it. Green knew the facts alone did not begin to support any wrongdoing on her part, but perhaps she was hoping to give him enough rope to hang himself.

"Since then," he continued, "the Kennedys have admitted that Meredith was in fact adopted and that a young police officer who volunteered at a Catholic mission arranged it with the priest. Until last Monday, Meredith never knew."

Now Elena did react, her lips parting in shock. She breathed a single "no."

Green tried to interpret her shock. Was she reacting to the news that Meredith was adopted or that she'd never been told? He decided to press further.

"So we go back thirty years now, to your husband's death. I've looked at the Montreal police file and crime scene photos, talked to a newspaper reporter, and this much I do know. Lise Gravelle was a second-year law student of your husband's—young, pretty and straight off the farm. Your husband was not alone when he died, but his apartment was cleaned up to erase all trace of his lover. The young police officer who helped the Kennedys adopt Meredith was also the investigating officer who looked the other way." Green paused, debating whether to mention Adam Jules's name. In the end he chose to hold back. For now. "Five months later, Lise Gravelle gave birth to a baby girl who has since vanished into thin air. These are some of the facts. I'm sure you can see how I'm connecting the dots."

Still shaken, Elena had flushed more deeply at the mention of her husband's lover. She sat very still as she considered her next move. Before she could speak, Cyril cut in. "I'm sure you can connect the dots in all kinds of imaginative, entirely unsubstantiated ways, but what is it you actually want from us today?"

Green kept his eyes on Elena. "The answers to some questions that would help me move the investigation forward. Firstly, were you aware that Lise Gravelle was your husband's lover?"

She looked across at him. If looks could kill, he thought. "At what point?" she asked.

"At any point. Either before he died, or in the weeks that followed."

"Not before. But afterwards, yes."

"How did you find out?"

"The police told me."

Adam Jules. Had that been the beginning of their connection? "Did you know she was pregnant?"

She glanced at Cyril, not for guidance it seemed, but in reproach. "Yes, I did. The officer told me that too."

"What arrangement was made?"

"What do you mean?"

Green gave a gesture of incredulity. "A hapless young student was having your husband's baby, and all of a sudden the whole investigation is buried and none of the witnesses remember a damn thing. Was Lise hung out to dry?"

"No," Cyril interrupted, his voice like a shot. "And cut the 'fresh off the farm' crap. She played the oldest trick in the book, and if he hadn't died, she'd have taken him to the cleaners. She was

284

failing law school, not cut out for the rigours of the profession, and she was facing an ignoble retreat back to the farm. As it was, she got an apartment, child support, payment for photography courses and equipment, and all she had to do was keep quiet. She accepted the deal before the ink was dry."

People like her don't have much choice, Green thought. "Who brokered the deal?

Cyril eyed him. "You don't want to know."

Green's heart sank. He took a few seconds before refocusing on Elena, who looked unnaturally pale. "In the past three weeks, did Lise Gravelle try to make contact with you?"

Elena shook her head.

"She managed to locate Meredith's cell phone number and her parents' home line, and she obviously knew where you lived. You're telling me she never phoned you?"

"That's what I'm telling you."

"You're aware I can check phone records."

"I'm well aware of that. With a warrant."

"What were you doing last Monday evening, between six p.m. and midnight?"

"Oh my. I need an alibi." Her lips twitched as she fought a smile. Green found it interesting that the discussion of her husband's lover had distressed her more than suspicion of murder. "I arrived home at about eight o'clock. The storm was dreadful, so I cut short a Christmas dinner with friends and came home to read by the fire. Brandon was on night shift so I had the house to myself. I went to bed around eleven. And no, I did not hear or see anything unusual."

"Was Brandon at the hospital all night?"

"Presumably, but I don't keep tabs on my thirty-two year old son. He's asleep upstairs if you want to ask him."

"Where is Adam Jules?" He dropped the name as quietly and unexpectedly as he could, but she showed no surprise. She's been waiting for this, he thought.

She arched her eyebrows. "He's here in Ottawa. You should know, he's your boss."

"I mean, where is he right now?"

The eyebrows arched further. "I have no idea. His office, I assume."

"Adam Jules hasn't been seen or heard from in four days."

She blinked, and a spasm of bewilderment crossed her face. Green swung on Cyril. "Correction, sir. I saw him myself on Saturday when he almost ran me over up on Summit Circle as he was leaving your place."

Cyril smiled. "If you're looking for a conspiracy, son, you're missing the mark. Neither Elena nor I kept up any contact with Jules, although we watched his career success with some satisfaction. He'd been smart when smart was called for, and he'd always kept his word with us."

"He kept in touch with Lise and the baby."

Cyril nodded. "Well, he would. He was an honourable man. We didn't want to have any further contact with her, but we did ask him to keep an eye on her. For the child's sake."

Green felt the interview slipping from his control. He was venturing into emotional territory that didn't seem to faze the old man one bit. Surreptitiously he tightened his fists to fortify himself. "Why did he visit you on Saturday?"

"It's simple. He wanted to ask me what I knew about Lise Gravelle's death. He knew who she was and he knew she'd died only a couple of blocks—"

"Murdered."

"Murdered. Ah." Here at last Cyril paused and took out a

286

linen handkerchief to wipe some spittle from his mouth. Green thought his hand shook more than earlier. As the silence echoed through the house, Green heard a floorboard creak overhead. Finally Cyril resumed. "I hadn't realized. Elena told me she'd been hit by a snowplow."

"No," Green said, looking from one to the other, noting the hidden tension in their faces. "She was killed by a blow to the back of the head from something blunt and hard."

Cyril recovered first. "Well, then that explains why Jules was so upset when he visited me. He wanted to know whether Lise Gravelle had been in touch with me, whether she'd told me anything about the baby, and whether I'd told—" He broke off as if he'd only just seen the implications of the question. He pressed his handkerchief to his mouth again.

"Whether you'd told Elena?" Green prompted. "What? About Lise's search for her baby?"

"Well, Lise hadn't been in touch with me, so it's all moot. We hadn't heard from her in years, and neither Elena nor I had the least idea she was searching for the child."

"Her name was Amélie. What happened to her?"

"We have no idea. Jules told us later she'd been adopted—"

"Sh-h." Elena held up her hand. She looked alarmed, and Green realized how quiet the house had become.

When she resumed, her tone was hushed. "We knew nothing about the baby by choice. I know that sounds cruel, and in retrospect, it's a decision I've come to regret, but at the time I was a young mother myself, trying to deal with some dreadful blows. I've thought about her often and wondered what became of the baby. Brandon's sister, after all."

"But never enough to contact Lise to find out how she was doing?"

"No." She dropped her gaze. "We left all that to Adam."

Green leaned forward, forcing her to look up at him. "When did you yourself connect the dots and realize that Meredith and Amélie were the same person? That your son was about to marry his half-sister and that Meredith herself had uncovered the truth."

"I didn't. Not until just now, when you told us Meredith was adopted. It had never quite made sense to me before, but there was something about the girl that made me uncomfortable—" Elena's answer was cut off by the rush of footsteps on the stairs. Brandon appeared in the doorway, pale with horror and rage.

Elena leaped to her feet. "Darling!"

"What the hell have you done!" he shouted before whirling around, snatching his jacket, and slamming out the door.

Green was on her heels as she raced to the front door and flung it open just in time to see Brandon disappear into the garage. Pushing past Elena, Green rushed out towards the drive, his stocking feet sinking deep into the snow. Just as he reached the garage, a silver Prius shot past him backwards down the drive and slewed into the street. Seconds later it was out of sight.

TWENTY-FIVE

As he accelerated down Beechwood Avenue towards the Vanier Parkway, Brandon tried not to think. His sister! It was preposterous. Impossible. Of all the women in all the world, what were the odds? What kind of proof did this Gravelle woman have? Did she have papers? DNA results? Or, as Uncle Cyril had hinted, had she seen the chance to cash in on a little blackmail? His mother had always warned him to watch out for gold-diggers more interested in his bank balance than in his humanity. Had she been speaking from bitter personal experience?

From his course work and case studies, he was familiar with the power of genes to influence not only a person's physiology and medical history but also their psychology. Temperament, attitudes, values, habits, interests and even choice of career were affected by one's genetic inheritance. Identical twins who'd never met often had more in common than siblings raised together.

Rationally he knew all this, but his emotional side refused to follow. Meredith didn't feel like a sister. He didn't look into her eyes and see hints of himself. He saw the beautiful, fiery young woman he loved. Unique, compelling and powerfully erotic. Reflecting back on her now, he didn't feel the slightest twinge of shame or aversion at that arousal. Didn't that count for something? Surely if there was a blood tie, no matter how hidden, he would have sensed it.

Yet somewhere, his half-sister existed. Cyril and his mother had admitted as much. How could his mother have kept this from him all his life? How could she have written Dad's flesh and blood out of their lives as if the baby were no more than a pawn? All those years he'd spent growing up in the company of a nanny, alone in the playroom creating imaginary friends from his action figures while he waited for his mother to come home. To think that all along, there had been a sister his own age...

Rage and panic bubbled up in equal measure, squeezing off his breath. He forced his thoughts elsewhere, away from the appalling question that rose unbidden in his mind. What had Cyril and his mother done to Lise? And worse, to Meredith? He didn't believe for a minute that they'd had no knowledge of Lise's impending visit. Despite the Valium and the exhaustion, he'd distinctly heard his mother's words—*"That woman...a hundred thousand dollars"*—hours before Lise Gravelle's body had even been found.

He shook his head sharply as he turned onto the Queensway. He couldn't think about any of that now. He had to find Meredith. Whatever the reason, the woman he loved was running scared and afraid to come home. He glanced at the laptop on the seat beside him. There had been no reply to his second message. If she still had access to the internet, she'd chosen not to answer him. Was she on the run? Or holed up in an isolated hotel somewhere?

The germ of a solution had come to him when he'd awakened earlier that day, re-energized for the search. He had the single email from her. Perhaps a clue to her whereabouts lay deep in the coded circuitry of his email program.

He had a rudimentary knowledge of computer software, but the intricate, arcane codes inside the machine had never interested him as much as animate things, so he always brought his technical problems to an IT specialist. As he drove west in the vague direction of Ottawa's IT sector in Kanata, he ran through the various firms he'd used. Most had been manned by an ever-changing parade of near-adolescents. Some were just voices on the other end of the phone, who'd taken over the inner workings of his computer by remote control and fixed the problem in less than fifteen minutes. He wasn't sure he'd even learned their names.

One computer geek stood out in his memory, however. Dylan, a cultural anthropology student and reformed video game junkie, who was now doing his PhD dissertation on gaming cultures. To finance this obscure academic pursuit, he did websites, trouble-shooting and software set-ups. He lived in a minuscule apartment on the third floor of a dilapidated old house in the Preston Street area, as close as he could afford to the university. Brandon had been there only once and couldn't even remember the guy's last name. Now, as he cut across three lanes of traffic to the Bronson Avenue exit, Brandon prayed he still lived there.

Guided entirely by instinct and sight memory, Brandon drove up and down the jumbled back streets that spread out in the shadow of St. Anthony's Church. Formerly the working class home of Ottawa's Italian community, the area was now an eclectic mix of multi-national new immigrants, university students, the working poor and the criminals who preyed on them. However, the occasional Volvo and Subaru in the laneways suggested that gentrification was sneaking in.

He stopped in front of a narrow white clapboard house that listed slightly to the right. He'd not called ahead since he had no telephone number nor even a full name, but he hoped Dylan was home. The young man hadn't seemed to have much of a life beyond his computers and his books. On the doorframe, there was a column of four rusty buzzers without identifying names or apartment numbers. Brandon took a guess and pressed the top one. There was no sound from within, no distant buzz or footsteps. He tried again, clutching his laptop and peering up at the top window for signs of life. Still nothing. A slight push opened the front door, however, and he found himself in the same cramped hall he remembered. A door off to the right, a radiator shelf piled high with junk mail on the left, and steep stairs straight ahead.

He climbed up two flights and hammered on the plain white door at the top. Rustling within. He hammered again.

"Who is it?" came a squeaky voice.

"Dylan, it's Dr. Longstreet. Brandon. You did some work for me last year. I need your help."

The door cracked open and a young man peered out. Dressed only in boxer shorts, he was even thinner than Brandon remembered. His hair hung about his shoulders in lank strands and his chin bristled with patchy stubble. He blinked at Brandon with uncomprehending eyes.

"Sorry, I pulled an all-nighter. Can you come back?"

Brandon pressed his palm against the door. "Please. I have one simple task. You can either do it, or you can't."

"But I don't—"

"This is important!" Brandon stepped forward then saw the alarm on the young man's face. "Sorry, I know it's an intrusion. If you could just look at this."

The young man managed a crooked smile and moved aside to let him in. "All right, but you enter at your peril."

Once he was inside, Brandon saw what he meant. A cloak of hot, rancid air closed around him. The apartment was even worse than he remembered. Food-crusted dishes, bits of computers, tangled cables and splayed books littered every surface, including the floor. Dylan kicked a path through to what had presumably once been a kitchen, although dismantled computers sat on the counters and stove top and the table was covered with papers. Dylan pushed these aside to clear a space for Brandon's laptop.

"I've been pretty much holed up here for the past month," he chattered, as if to hide his nerves. "My advisor wants the first draft before Christmas! This is my third extension, and I'm not coming this far just to get thrown out on a technicality."

"It shouldn't take long, and I'll make it worth your while."

"Yeah, yeah, it's okay. This way, maybe I'll get to eat tonight." He took Brandon's laptop and with expert fingers booted it up. "So what's the problem?"

"Can you trace the origin of an email?"

"You mean the source computer?"

"No, I mean the physical location of the person."

Dylan looked surprised. "Depends. Sometimes it's tricky, but I can give it a try this evening."

"Could you please do it now?"

Dylan grabbed his hank of hair and pulled it back into an elastic. "No, I've got a couple of things in the pipe already. Just leave it with me and I'll call you. I'll have the source ISP number, owner information, whatever you need."

Brandon glanced at his watch. Three o'clock. He cursed his forced inaction. "How long?"

"Nine o'clock, latest."

He could have taken the laptop elsewhere, but it might take hours to find someone else to do the job faster. In the end, he booted up his email program and opened Meredith's single email reply. Sitting alone on the screen, surrounded by the clutter and decay of the kitchen, it looked both poignant and sinister. Dylan, however, barely gave the email a second glance as he took down Brandon's passwords and contact information.

As Brandon descended the steep, narrow staircase to the street, he turned his restless thoughts to his next move. He was due at work to cover the evening shift, but he couldn't even think about that now. Not when he was so close. He mentally reviewed the list of Meredith's friends and contacts he'd compiled the night before when he was trying to figure out where she was hiding. Last night his mind had gone around and around in futile circles, but now, without the fog of fatigue, alcohol and emotion, one name jumped out. Tanya Neuss, one of her childhood friends, who was away on a six-month overseas posting.

Perhaps that was why he hadn't given her a second thought last week when he was trying to find out where Meredith was.

*   *   *

Tanya Neuss lived in a spacious apartment on the top floor of a chunky brick low-rise in Westboro. Brandon parked on the side street in front of it and studied the façade, trying to pick out the window. For the second time in less than twenty-four hours, his hopes soared. How had he been so stupid as to discount Tanya simply because she was overseas? How could he have forgotten that she had left Meredith her keys so that Meredith could keep an eye on her apartment? What better place to hide out than in an obscure apartment building on a dead-end side street, where it was possible to come and go through a back door that opened onto the parking lot?

Tanya lived modestly. Working for NGOs overseas was never guaranteed to make you rich, but in addition, Brandon knew she funnelled all her savings back into the organization. He was grateful for her frugality as he opened the Sixties-style glass door and entered the tiny vestibule. No lavish lobby here, no fancy security system or coded entry buzzers. Just an old-fashioned intercom and a panel of buzzers labelled with the apartment numbers, which he contemplated with dismay. He and Meredith had visited only once and he could picture Tanya's apartment in his mind. Top floor, but that was all. In any case, if Meredith was in hiding, she would never answer the buzzer.

He began to buzz other apartments and was astonished when one of the tenants came on the intercom. "Apartment 402," he mumbled in falsetto. "Forgot my key."

The door buzzed open and he was in. Too impatient for the balky old elevator, he bounded up the stairs two at a time, huffing by the time he exited the fire door onto the top floor. He padded along the deserted hall and came to a stop partway down, outside #408. There was a peephole but no extra deadbolt on the flimsy wood-panelled door. Meredith had often bugged her about that. This had to be the one.

The hallway was utterly silent. Not even the murmur of TV or tenants emanated from the nearby flats. Holding his breath, he laid his ear to the door. Silence, except for the beat of his racing pulse. Leaning against the wall, he drew deep breaths to slow himself down. Tried again. Still no sound from beyond the door.

On a wild chance, he reached above the door for a spare key. The walls were high and the door tall, discouraging all but the biggest of burglars from reaching it. But there it was, a single brass door key covered with dust. He blew it off, inserted it and heard a satisfying click as the door drifted silently open.

He searched the one-bedroom apartment in less than five seconds. Nothing. He returned to the kitchen for a closer look. The whole place looked tidy and uninhabited. There were no dishes in the sink or on the rack. The garbage pail under the sink was empty and scrubbed clean, the fridge, coffee maker and toaster all unplugged. The cupboards contained only some pasta, spices and a few cans.

No one had used this kitchen in a long time. Disappointed, he moved on to the bathroom. Also clean and dry. The bed had been stripped and a dust cover spread over it. Not a single rumple disturbed its surface. It took him ten minutes to go through the apartment inch by inch, methodically looking for any signs of covert habitation that Meredith might have missed. There was nothing. The phone was disconnected and unplugged. Tanya was nothing if not thorough.

He wanted to scream. He had come so close, yet he was nowhere. She was not here. She had to be somewhere else, but where? This had seemed like such a perfect idea—a friend out of town for months and her apartment lying empty for the taking. As he travelled back down in the elevator, he thought about the last time they'd seen Tanya. It had been her going away bash, held not in her apartment but at her parents' cottage on Loon Lake. It was a ramshackle cottage built with spit and salvaged lumber by her grandfather and his brothers decades ago. The other cousins squabbled over it during the premium weeks of summer, but Tanya loved to party there in the autumn, when the colours were glorious but the bugs and other cottagers were gone. It was on a dead-end dirt road, all alone on its section of the lake, and they could make as much noise as they wanted. Bonfires, guitars, off-key singing, and way too many coolers of beer.

Halfway out the front door, Brandon froze. Tanya had been drunk and maudlin by the end of the party when she'd given Meredith the keys to her apartment. "I'm so sorry I'll miss the wedding. If I could, I'd fly home. But you guys have a great time and if you want to use my apartment or my car for—you know, a getaway—just do it. It's my present to you."

The car! Brandon sprinted around the edge of the apartment building into the parking lot at the back. Meredith had planned to move the car every few weeks to make sure it didn't seize up. It was an ancient, rust-riddled red Honda, and Meredith had joked that she wouldn't let it die on her watch.

The parking lot held about a dozen cars, each parked in their designated numbered spot. Nowhere among them, however, was there an ancient red Honda.

TWENTY-SIX

As soon as they arrived back at the station, Green sent Levesque to begin work on the DNA warrants while he shut himself in his office to redraft his notes on Adam Jules to include the new revelations from Elena and the Kennedys. The deeper Jules's involvement became, the more worrisome his absence. Deputy Chief Poulin had vetoed a missing persons report but had reluctantly agreed to an off-the-record meeting Tuesday morning.

Green was on his third reworking and ready to pack it in for the day when his phone rang. It was the front desk. "There's an individual down here, Dylan Whyte, sir, who says he has information on the Kennedy case."

Glancing through his half-open office door, Green spotted Gibbs bent over his phone, scribbling in his notebook. "I'll send someone down to see him."

"Sir, he insists on speaking to you. Well, to the head honcho that runs the show."

To Green's knowledge, the man's name had not come up in the investigation. Could this be a new angle, new information, he wondered, as he told the officer to bring him up. Or just another glory-seeker.

Likely the latter, Green decided when the young man got off the elevator. The kid was one step away from a cadaver. Even his bulky parka could not disguise the protruding bones and the hollow cheeks. Jesus, Green thought, what's he on? The man's clothes were clearly thrift shop, but he looked too well groomed to be a street person. His face had a few fresh razor nicks and his hair was pulled back into a neat ponytail.

"Bob," Green murmured as he walked by, "get some sandwiches and coffee and meet us down the hall." He extended his hand to the newcomer. "Mr. Whyte? I'm Inspector Green."

Dylan nodded towards Gibbs with a nervous laugh. "I hope that's not Detective Brown."

Oh boy, Green thought as he led the man down the hall. He hoped it was just nerves. In the interview room, the young man shed his parka, unwound his long wool scarf from his neck and placed a laptop case on the table between them. His body trembled with anxiety, but Green was reassured by the clear intelligence in his gaze.

The young man took a deep breath. "This is Brandon Longstreet's computer." He moved to open it.

Alarmed, Green stopped him. "Wait a minute, where did you get it?"

"He brought it to me and asked me to trace the source of an email he'd received. It's all legal."

"For you, but without a search warrant, not for me." Green looked for a way around the procedural snag. Elena Longstreet would have his head. "Why don't you tell me the entire story from the beginning. Who you are, what happened, and why you've come to the police."

Dylan sat for a moment frowning at Green in bewilderment before the light seemed to dawn. With a nod, he embarked on his tale. Gibbs arrived with the food, and Dylan became visibly more enthusiastic as he tucked into a slice of pizza. His story came out in a flood.

"It took me awhile to figure out who he was. I've been barricaded in my own little world for over a month, so I haven't really been following the story. His name was sort of familiar but I'd done some work for him before. But anyway, when I started searching his computer for other emails to and from the same person, I realized what this was—an email from this girl who's been missing all week. When I checked news websites, I saw not only was the whole police force looking for her but it might be connected to another woman's death. So—"

Green's pulse leaped. "Hold it! You're talking about a recent email from Meredith Kennedy?"

"Yes. From last night." Dylan bit off another chunk of pizza. "It didn't say much, just 'safe', but I got to wondering why Brandon didn't bring it to you. You're the guys investigating, and he must know you have the resources to trace this even better than me, so I got worried. I don't want to get involved in anything criminal, or obstruct a police investigation or anything. And what if the girl was running from him, and I hand her over to him? I'm your quintessential peace and love geek, just want to study how people get along and how their play reflects their values. I...I could just have called him up and said I couldn't find anything, but I figured he'd go to someone else, and besides, this is something the police should know, right? That she's alive, but it looks like she's in hiding."

Green's mind was racing ahead, but he said nothing. He knew he needed to let the young man make his statement in his own way, that he mustn't ask specific questions about the contents of the computer. Gibbs too was so excited that he'd stopped taking notes, but at least he also remained quiet. This girl's fate had consumed them for almost a week, they had explored every aspect of her life and felt they knew her very soul. They had tried not to imagine the worst. Now this! Yes, she was alive, but not yet out of danger. Technicalities stood between her and rescue.

"Is there more?" Green finally prompted, as vague as possible.

Dylan hesitated. Fingered the laptop uncertainly. "He's sent her a whole lot of emails over the week, and there's stuff on Facebook as well, but until last night, there was nothing from her. Then this reply from a brand new Yahoo account. Like she was expecting her regular emails to be intercepted or something. The thing is, it's hard to track an email to its exact source. It takes a lot of detective work and cross-checking. Cyberspace doesn't know physical boundaries like we have. It's easy to find the IP address it came from and to track down who owns that IP address, but that might be a company in Windsor or Quebec City that's managing servers in Ottawa, St. Catherine's, Guelph, wherever. See what I mean?"

Green nodded. He had only the vaguest idea, but it didn't matter. He just wanted the young man to keep talking.

"I considered searching that IP address on Google to see what other emails had come from that address. Had she sent out any others? Or had someone else used it and mentioned where they were sending from? But that would take time, and I was still trying to figure out if this guy was a danger to her and if I should bring it to you guys. So I started looking at recent activity on his computer. There were a whole lot of email inquiries and website searches. Nothing rang an alarm bell until I checked his recent documents file."

Green held his breath while Dylan gulped his coffee and once again half-opened the laptop. "I really wish I could show this to you."

"Just keep talking."

"I found a list he wrote last night, after he got this email.

Names of people and places, with pros and cons listed beside them. Questions like 'would she trust them, would anyone else know them?' Places where no one would recognize her or get the Ottawa news. Then below that a list of the most likely places and people. It spooked me out. He's got an idea where she is, and he was using me to narrow down the search. When I found that, I thought, that's it. I'm handing this over to the cops."

Green nodded. "You did the right thing. We don't have any specific suspects in this case, but we do need access to all available information if we're going to have a safe resolution to the case for all involved." He paused, took a sip of coffee and held the young man's gaze. "You do understand I cannot by law examine the contents of that computer without a warrant. I could get a warrant, of course—" Inwardly he winced at the likelihood of that if Elena Longstreet was on the opposing bench. "But it would take time. Do you have any further details to add to your statement?"

Dylan's eyes held his, and Green was grateful for the intelligence reflected in them. "From that list of places and from the IP address I tracked down, I've got some pretty good clues where she might be. That is, where she sent the email from. Am I allowed to tell you?"

Green smiled. "As a private citizen, you're allowed to provide me with any information you have that you consider relevant to the case."

"Then she's probably at someone called Tanya's cottage, somewhere in West Quebec."

"Tanya?"

"That's all there was on the list. Tanya's cottage. But the IP address could be from somewhere in the Buckingham Papineau area. I figured, cottage, Buckingham—probably go together."

Green was already weighing the odds. Buckingham was in

the heart of Quebec cottage country about an hour north east of Ottawa. He pictured rugged lakes and forested slopes settled decades ago by simple working families looking for a slip of lakeside to put out a dock and a row boat. Most of the cottages would be boarded up for the winter, with few neighbours to spy and ask questions. The locals might notice someone living there, but would be unlikely to concern themselves with news of a missing woman out of Ottawa.

If there was plenty of firewood, it was a perfect place to hide.

*   *   *

Dylan Whyte had no sooner left the station than Green was on the phone. First to Brandon, in the hopes that the young man would volunteer Tanya's last name and the cottage address without Green having to betray Dylan's involvement. Dylan had been instructed to claim failure when Brandon showed up to ask what he'd found out. Brandon's cell phone remained unanswered, however. The hospital said he had phoned in sick, but a quick call to Elena revealed that he'd not come back home. Elena was so furious about Brandon overhearing the truth that Green didn't ask her about Tanya. Given that a killer was still roaming free and Elena's behaviour was far from innocent, the fewer people he tipped off to Meredith's location, the better.

Green hung up with a glance at his watch. It was now well past five thirty, and the Major Crimes Unit was nearly deserted. Everyone had wanted to go home early. Families were decorating Christmas trees or braving shopping malls. Levesque had booked off shift on the dot, but Gibbs was still hanging around, waiting for Green's okay. Green felt restless and impatient. He hated to leave a question unanswered.

He reached for his phone again, this time with some reluctance. He had left the Kennedys in an uproar earlier that day, upset that their daughter had found out about her adoption through a phone call from Lise Gravelle. Upset that she hadn't trusted them enough to come to them for confirmation. Upset that she was out there alone somewhere, suffering. Or worse, dead.

When Reg answered the phone, Green hesitated about how much to disclose. He hadn't told them about Meredith's latest email to Brandon, but no matter how badly they had mishandled the story of her adoption, they deserved to know she was alive. But he didn't want yet another potential player running around on the loose, any more than he'd wanted Elena. It was bad enough that Brandon was out there on his own, doing God knows what.

In the end, he elected to say nothing. "Mr. Kennedy, I'm following up on some of Meredith's friends, in whom she might have confided about the whole adoption business. We have a name—Tanya. Do you know her last name?"

"Tanya's out of the country."

"Oh. But with email these days... Were she and Meredith close?"

"Pretty close. Whenever Tanya's in the country, they..." His voice trailed off as if something had just occurred to him.

"What?"

"Oh, nothing. I'm just...you know. It's a lot to take in."

"Tanya's last name?"

"I don't know. They weren't really that close. Tanya's away a lot. I think I met her maybe once, a couple of years ago. My memory... I'm sorry, this has just been so hard."

Tears clogged his voice. It was on the tip of Green's tongue to tell him that Meredith was safe, but he stopped himself at the last moment. Muttering vague platitudes that he shouldn't give up, he hung up. Now what?

He called Gibbs over and together they looked over the list of Meredith's friends. Green settled on Jessica, Meredith's maid of honour and presumably her closest friend. If anyone knew, it should be her.

"Tanya Neuss," Jessica replied instantly. "But she's out of the country. She's always out of the country. I don't know why she doesn't sublet her place—omigod, you think Meredith might be there?"

Green thought of the latest email, sent from an IP address in West Quebec. "We're checking all her friends' places again. I understand there's also a cottage?"

"Oh, it's a dump! A beautiful piece of property, gorgeous lake, loons, ducks, perfect canoeing. But in winter? A wasteland. No electricity, no water."

"Where is it?"

"Up north of Buckingham somewhere. I've only been there once and I'd get lost if I was driving myself. Talk about boonies."

Green jotted notes. "Thank you, that's most helpful. Meredith's father couldn't remember her last name."

"What?" Jessica snorted. "That's ridiculous. Tanya and Meredith went to primary school together."

Green paused. Had the man been that rattled? Or drunk? He ignored a niggle of concern as he doublechecked the spelling of Tanya's name, thanked Jessica, and disconnected. Without missing a beat, he turned to Gibbs.

"I want you to find out the exact location of the Neuss cottage on a lake somewhere near Buckingham."

Gibbs couldn't mask his dismay. "There are dozens of lakes near Buckingham."

Green glanced at his watch and cursed. Outside, the winter night had descended. It was too late to contact land registry offices and too dark to try searching the vast Quebec back country. He was dog-tired, and despite his impatience, he had nothing to justify an emergency response.

Sensing his concern, Gibbs's gaze drifted to his computer. "I could start calling all the people called Neuss in the phone book."

Green brightened. "Good idea, but be vague. I don't want anyone tipped off. Call me the instant you learn anything."

*   *   *

Green arrived at the office at the crack of dawn the next morning, feeling refreshed and anxious to get on with the search. He had celebrated the fourth night of Hanukkah with Sharon, Tony and his father the night before and for a few brief hours had managed to forget the case. They had indulged in a spectacular feast of Lester's smoked meat, latkes smothered in un-Kosher but delicious sour cream, and a salad on the side, Sharon's rueful nod to healthy eating. He had phoned Hannah, managed a civil conversation with Ashley, and listened to his daughter grumble good-naturedly about the Vancouver rain, traffic and crowds. The only worrisome note in the whole exchange was Hannah's rave reaction to the University of British Columbia, whose spectacular seaside setting and hot guys had her excited to learn more.

It made him think of Norah and Reg Kennedy, whose loss eclipsed his own. Not only had their daughter disappeared, but quite possibly in her outrage she had written them out of her life. He was still thinking of that when he sat down at his desk in the morning to check his messages. Reg might have been confused and drunk last evening when Green had called, but Jessica was certain he knew full well who Tanya was. Was Reg's impairment sufficient explanation for his lapse, or had he been lying?

Green was listening to his voice mail with only half an ear until the hesitant, squeaky voice of Dylan Whyte came on. "Um, it's late, but I guess you'll get this in the morning. I thought you should know Brandon never came back for the information last night. Never picked up his computer either."

According to the time log, the call had been placed at 2:48 a.m., typical hours for a graduate student in that last desperate push to a deadline. Green felt a flicker of concern. Now, not only were the Kennedys possibly up to something, but so was Brandon. Did they both have a theory about where Meredith was? If so, why were they keeping it secret from the police?

We're the ones in charge of the fucking investigation, he wanted to shout. But even as he cursed, he knew the reason. This case was not just about a missing person, it was about murder, and the lines between the two had become very blurred. Even for Meredith herself.

He spotted Gibbs rising from his desk and summoned him hastily. "Any luck locating that cottage?"

Gibbs nodded. "Yes, s-sir. No luck with the phone book, but I just got through to the land registry office. It's on Loon Lake, off county road 315." He flourished a printout and laid it on Green's desk. "I just tried a Google map search to find out the exact location and how to get there, but I could only get the general vicinity."

"Jessica said it's at the end of a road."

"But the addresses are not all in the system. I tried to get a satellite view so we can see what's around it and maybe spot the cottage, but the satellite's not detailed enough up there. All you can see is trees, lakes and streams."

Green bent over the map to trace the roads. The main road showed as a narrow ribbon twisting and weaving through the forests and lakes in the general direction of north. Away from civilization. There were several dead-end spurs, but only one ended up at the edge of a good-sized lake. Loon Lake. On the one hand, anyone hiding there would have no escape. On the other hand, the lack of alternative access routes should make it easy to control the entry and exit points.

A sharp knock at his door startled him. He looked up to see Marie Claire Levesque leaning against the doorframe, her eyes travelling from Gibbs to the map. "Any new developments?" she asked.

He gestured her inside and filled her in on Dylan Whyte's tip. "We have a pretty good lead on Meredith's whereabouts," he said, showing her the map. "But we have to move quickly because Brandon and her parents may be on to her as well."

Levesque's eyes lit with excitement. "Do we need a full tactical response, sir?"

Green shook his head. "It's the Sûreté's jurisdiction, so we need to get them on board—"

"Should I call them, sir? I have a cousin who works that district."

Green smiled to himself. He had not relished the idea of negotiating interprovincial cooperation through official channels using his rusty French. Personal connection was always better, family best of all. "Yes, get on it. Arrange for a unit to meet us at..." He studied the map. Given the windy, narrow road, most of it likely gravel or ice, it would be at least an hour's drive from here to the cottage, even if they pushed it. The SQ would have a considerable head start and could get there well ahead of them. Was it necessary? He tried to pinpoint his sense of unease. Both Brandon and the Kennedys were off pursuing their own agendas, perhaps even now converging on Meredith's hiding place. Nothing he'd uncovered in the past week suggested that Brandon was a threat to her, except Norah's suspicion. The Kennedys, for all their flaws, were her parents. Throughout the week-long search, all three of them had seemed desperate for one thing. To find her safe and sound.

But even as he puzzled over his unease, he knew the reason. This was not just about missing persons, it was about murder. And a big unknown hung over the whole case. Who had murdered Lise Gravelle and why?

His finger hovered over the map as he debated his options. In the end, his own need for control won out. This was far too delicate a situation to send an uninformed SQ patrol unit in blind. He found a small dot at the intersection of two country roads, halfway to the cottage.

"Mayo. We'll go from there together."

Levesque paused on her way out the door and glanced at Gibbs, who was watching Green like an eager puppy. She arched her brow. "We?"

"The three of us. Marie Claire, I'll drive with you. Bob, you can take..." He peered out his door at the small collection of officers in the unit room. With this skeleton holiday staff, he really couldn't afford another detective.

"Sue Peters, sir?"

Green shook his head. This time he really had to draw the line. Even though Peters had put her heart into this case and many of the breakthroughs had been hers, she wasn't cleared for full duty. Regulations aside, she wasn't nearly ready to handle a crisis or a physical response should something unexpected happen. They were going into an unknown, potentially dangerous situation with a killer on the loose. The risk to all of them was just too great.

"Not this time, Bob. Take Zdanno from General Assignment. And get radios, vests and the full range of use of force, just as a precaution."

Even Gibbs knew better than to argue the point. Bobbing his head, he followed Levesque to the unit room to make the preparations.

Green grabbed his coat and boots and took his Glock from his drawer. As an afterthought, he stuffed some latex gloves and evidence bags into his pockets. He needed to cancel his meeting with the deputy chief and bring both him and Superintendent Devine into the picture, but all that could wait until they were en route. He felt the familiar rush of adrenaline that accompanied the unknown. The hint of danger, the thrill of the hunt. He locked his door and was heading across the room just as the elevator door slid open. A uniform constable from the front desk emerged, followed by a plump, middle-aged woman with a pile of sun-bleached hair and the leathery brown complexion of the Florida beach. The tip of her nose was bright red from the cold.

"This is Inspector Green," said the constable.

The woman's gaze met his, level and frank. "Hello," she said in a rich, smoke-laden voice. "I am Lilianne Gravelle."

TWENTY-SEVEN

Green could have demanded proof, he could have dismissed it as a hoax. Whenever a dramatic, high profile case captured the public's heart, the glory seekers surfaced to claim their moment in the spotlight. The fact that almost no one knew about Lilianne did not negate that possibility; Lise herself could have talked about her sister. But Green only needed one look to see the resemblance. The woman had shoehorned her middle-aged body into a fake leopard fur jacket and slathered on black eye liner, but the upturned nose and sharp blue eyes were unmistakable.

"Adam—Adam Jules—told me to come," she said. "You're the cop in charge of my sister's death?"

Green shook off his astonishment. "Yes. Come this way, Ms Gravelle." Signalling Gibbs to follow, he led her into their most comfortable interview room, still little more than a sterile cubicle with a coffee table and four fake leather chairs. "When did you see Superintendent Jules?"

She flounced down in a chair, perspiration beading her cheeks, and began to pry herself out of her jacket. Large rings adorned all her fingers and bracelets jangled on her wrists. "He came to see me Saturday. First time I seen him in—oh, thirty years—and we didn't exactly part as friends back then. When I saw him standing on my doorstep, you could have knocked me over with a feather. He'd done well for himself, not that I ever doubted that, he was the smart one—"

"Why did he come to see you?"

She tugged at her blouse to rearrange her ample flesh. "To tell me about Lise's death. Not that it was a surprise. I thought she'd killed herself years ago. Like our mother that way. Life just kept knocking her down more times than she could get up." Lilianne paused to wipe the sweat from her face, which had turned bright red in the heat of the room. "I don't suppose I could have a cold drink?"

"Coffee?"

She pulled a face. "Diet Coke would be better. Menopause is a curse."

Green dispatched Gibbs to get the drink then steered the woman back on track. "Where did this visit from Jules take place?"

"I have a place in Belleville. Not much more than a shoebox, really, but it's mine and it's more than my last husband got out of the divorce, so I can't complain. I got a job at Swiss Chalet where the tips are good if you're nice to people. I meet lots of people, so it suits me fine. I was never ambitious like Lise. All I wanted was a nice little home with a husband and children." She paused for breath and chuckled wryly. "Well, I got four of the first but none of the second. That's why I had such hard feelings towards Lise and Adam."

Green tried to hide his confusion. "Because she had a child and you didn't?"

"No. Because she wouldn't give Amélie to me when she had her breakdown. They decided I wasn't good enough to provide for her, and Adam persuaded Lise to give her up to strangers instead." Lilianne's cheeks flushed red again and her nostrils flared. "I should have been the one to raise her, then we could have all been happy. I'd have let Lise be involved as much as she wanted. Instead it damn near killed her the day Adam marched her into that Catholic do-gooder's office and handed her flesh and blood over without so much as a proper goodbye. Father Fréchette wouldn't let Lise give her anything. Not a letter, not even her favourite blanket. Said she had to make a clean break from the past. I don't have much use for the church, as you can tell—"

Gibbs arrived with a tall glass of Coke. Lilianne downed half of it greedily then pressed the cold glass to her flaming cheeks. "Holee-e, I needed that."

"What was the relationship between Adam Jules and your sister?"

She cast him a sidelong glance. "Not what you're thinking. I always thought if it was up to him, there would have been much more, but Lise was a broken soul. Harvey Longstreet did that to her. With his curls and those dimples, he could charm the pants off a nun. And he was so full of life, he lifted everyone along with him. She fell for him hard, and when he died—in her arms, actually, but that's all I'm going to say—she was a basket case. Amélie was all she had left of him and she became Lise's whole world. No room in it for shy, stuffy Adam Jules."

"And yet he persuaded her to give Amélie up."

"Well, Lise wasn't much of a mother. She tried, but some days she couldn't even get out of bed. Our mother was like that, and I can tell you it's not much fun for a kid. It's cold, lonely and confusing. You're always wondering what you did wrong, what you can do to make it better, how you can make her happy. In her good times, even Lise could see it wasn't good for Amélie. She knew she'd made Amélie too much her whole world and she was always scared she was going to lose her. She'd freak out every time Amélie got sick, she'd sit by her crib staring at her while she was sleeping, like she was afraid Amélie was going to stop breathing. Like Harvey, I guess."

She paused as if caught up in the past, and Green let her collect her thoughts. When she resumed, her voice was softer. "Now I know it was the hardest thing Adam ever did. But back then I only thought about me, and about the kid I could never have, or Lise either. She haemorrhaged after the birth and had to have a hysterectomy. Still, he was probably right about me. I've not made such a success of things since then either." A look of sorrow crept over her flushed face. "Ain't life a bitch."

Regret hung heavy in the silence of the interview room. Even Gibbs had stopped taking notes and sadly looked across at her. Green was the first to pull his thoughts back to the present.

"Do you know where Adam Jules is now?"

She shrugged. "Going home, I think. Don't we all go home sooner or later, if we have any home left to go to?"

"St. Hyacinth?"

"He wanted you to know the whole story. He said if he didn't call back by Sunday night, I should come here myself. I'm sorry..." She ducked her head and played with the bangles on her wrist. "It took me a couple of days to decide if..."

"Decide what?"

She stopped twirling and looked up abruptly. "There's more." She took a deep breath and reached into her purse to extract an envelope. "He gave me this. He wanted me to give it to Amélie. I mean Meredith. It's the letter Lise wrote to her that the priest wouldn't let her have. Damn near broke my heart."

Green reached out, but she made no move to give it to him. "It's taken many years and miles to put this all behind me, and now... It's like opening it all up again, you know? "

Green gently extracted it from her fingers. It was a short, simple note written in a beautiful French script. *'Darling Amélie, I'm doing this for you. You deserve more than I can give you, and because I love you more than myself, I must put your need above mine. But always know that you were conceived in love and will be forever loved.'* Green felt his scalp prickle. The message spoke across the decades, across the divide of death.

"It's beautiful, isn't it?" Lilianne said.

He nodded. But he also understood why the priest had not let Lise give it to Amélie. It was a burden beyond a young child's years.

"I think Lise would have been all right, you know? If Harvey hadn't died. She said he loved her."

Green had his doubts but didn't voice them. What mattered was not what might have been, but the present. "Why could Jules not give her this himself? Why didn't he come himself?"

"I don't know." She spoke slowly, frowning as if trying to bring a vague impression into focus. "Maybe it would bring back too much. I think he had a lot on his mind. He said he'd made a mess of things, and he couldn't fix it."

Green felt a twinge of alarm. Belleville was a town on the St. Lawrence River between Montreal and Toronto. It was a good four-hour drive, yet Jules had visited Lilianne in Belleville the same day after his visit to Cyril in Montreal. He'd been so upset after seeing Cyril that he'd nearly run Green off the road. What had sent him on such a frantic drive?

"Did he say what the mess was? Or why he couldn't fix it?"

"Because it was too late. Lise was dead." She paused and drained her Coke. She looked calmer now, but troubled. "I tried to get more details, but he didn't say much. Somehow he saw her death as his fault. He'd made one too many mistakes, and because of that, someone had panicked."

"And killed Lise."

"Yes. And killed Lise."

315

"Who?"

"He didn't say. Just that he shouldn't have tried to play God, and now a whole lot of innocent lives were ruined." Lilianne leaned forward, her face still moist but drained of colour. The brash, blowsy façade had gone. "I had a bad feeling when he said goodbye that night, Inspector Green. It felt...so final."

* * *

Levesque squealed the tires as she accelerated out of the police parking garage. Behind them Gibbs was struggling to keep pace. Once she'd wrestled the car onto Elgin Street, she glanced over at Green, who was already dialling Magloire.

"Do you really believe Meredith is in danger? From Brandon? From her own parents?"

Green listened to the ringing. "Adam Jules is a very astute man. If he said someone was panicking, he must know something." Relief surged through him when Magloire picked up. "Jean Pierre, I want you to contact your SQ friend out at Ste. Hyacinth again. Not about Lise Gravelle, but about Adam Jules. He's still missing but he may have gone home. I'm concerned for his safety."

"Why?"

"Lise Gravelle's sister has shown up." He filled Magloire in as fast as he could. Precious seconds were ticking by. "I believe Jules may have guessed the killer but more importantly, the killer may know that. We need to find him first." He left Magloire to draw his own conclusions, likely erroneous. Shielding Jules's reputation was only one reason. The SQ would search far more vigorously for a fellow officer under threat than they would for one about to kill himself.

Moreover, Green had a nagging fear that Jules was trying to play God one last time, by drawing the killer after him and away from the innocent players in the drama. A redemption of sorts.

Magloire needed no further urging. He recorded the sketchy details Green knew of Jules's rental car and signed off abruptly, a man on a mission. Levesque was in the fast lane now, streaking across the Macdonald-Cartier Bridge to Quebec. The car was rock steady beneath her capable hands. Glancing at his watch, Green saw that he'd already missed his meeting with Poulin. He thumbed through his contacts and dialled the deputy chief's cell phone. This time he was prepared to go to battle for Adam Jules's life.

The man picked up with his characteristic "Poulin!"

"Sorry about our meeting, but I have new information," Green said before Poulin could cut him off. "I believe Adam Jules is in danger. He's been conducting his own investigation—"

"Green, what the man does on his own time is his prerogative."

"But he may have spooked the killer. I'm not sure he's aware he's in danger." I'm also not sure he cares, Green thought but kept the doubt to himself.

"Have you solved the case, Green?"

"I'm coordinating things with the SQ. We're on our way—"

"What the hell is going on!"

For the first time, Poulin's voice roared through the line, full of urgency and indignation. Is that what it takes to get your attention? Green thought. Not concern for a missing officer, not the possibility of threats to his life, but the spectre of an inter-jurisdictional turf war? And the failure to follow the proper chain of command?

Taking a deep breath, he filled Poulin in with all the patience and calm he could muster. To his credit, the man stopped interrupting and actually heard him out.

"All right, what do you need me to do at this end?"

"We have the cooperation of the Papineau district in the area and we're planning a joint response—"

"Tactical?"

"No, sir. The SQ will handle the operation." Anticipating another protest, he said, "But I'd appreciate your involvement to coordinate operations at the higher level. Time may be critical, that's why we're moving ahead."

"Done. What else?"

"And we have to examine Adam's telephone records to see who he's been talking to and where he's made any financial transactions."

"You think he's involved in this current incident?"

Green considered the idea. He didn't see how Jules could know about the cottage unless Brandon or the Kennedys told him. But Jules had been full of surprises. "All the more reason to know what he's been up to," he replied.

There was a longer pause. Levesque was now playing slalom with the transport trucks on the four-lane highway that ran east along the Ottawa River. Green glanced back. In the cruiser behind them, he could see that Gibbs had a terrified look on his face.

"Done," Poulin said finally. "But I'm getting our Tac unit commander on board at this end, Green. Stay in touch."

Green hung up and stared grimly ahead. The unknown hung over him like a cloud. Was Poulin overreacting and would he authorize a joint tactical raid on a flimsy little cottage in the back woods? Where for all Green knew, a fragile, devastated family was just trying to put the pieces back together.

But that was the problem. He didn't know.

Levesque shot him a quick, questioning glance. "There may be no cell phone reception out there, but we should at least try phoning Longstreet. Pretend it's a routine follow-up. It might help us evaluate his state of mind."

Green toyed briefly with the idea before rejecting it. He had no idea why Brandon had set out on his own to find Meredith, if indeed he had, nor why he'd chosen to circumvent the police. The young man was a loose cannon, overwhelmed with horror and despair.

"As long as we don't actually know the situation, it's too risky. Without being right there to contain their reaction, we could spook someone or scare them away."

Or worse, he added privately.

TWENTY-EIGHT

Snow began to fall as they turned left off the four-lane Highway 50 onto the twisting country road that ran north into the rolling foothills of the Laurentians. The road ran like a bobsled run between two ridges of snow left by the plow, and the car bucked on the cracked, pothole-riddled surface. The wind picked up, and Green watched the blowing snow with alarm. Not only would it threaten driving, but it would also obliterate any tire tracks or footprints left around the cabin.

When they reached the village of Mayo, which proved to be little more than a crossroads, a country store and a church, there was no sign of the Sûreté du Québec cruiser which was to meet them. Levesque phoned her cousin, who apologized and said the unit was delayed because procedure dictated that it be sent from Papineauville detachment headquarters further east, at least an hour away. They were on their way, but still fifteen kilometres out.

Green grumbled in disgust. The SQ's jurisdictional red tape was as strangling as any on the Ontario side. "I don't want to wait. Tell them we're going ahead and to meet us out at the cabin as fast as they can."

Levesque passed on the message, but he could hear the doubt in her tone. Afterwards, she lifted her foot off the brake and eased the car back onto the road. They drove in silence through rocky, wooded terrain dotted sporadically with farms, then along a small lake bordered by cottages. Many were closed for the winter, but huge Christmas displays of Santa and mangers adorned the front lawns of the others.

The road grew narrow, hilly and slick with snow as they followed the map towards the tiny red dot Gibbs had marked at the end of the road. Gravel replaced pavement, forcing Levesque to ease off the accelerator. To make up time, she gunned it again as she rounded a corner onto a straight stretch. Careening towards them, full tilt down the centre of the road, was a dirty pick-up which showed no sign of slowing. Levesque jerked the wheel hard to the right and brought the Impala onto the shoulder just as the pick-up shot past. Green caught a glimpse of a woman at the wheel, open-mouthed in terror.

"Jesus H! That was Norah Kennedy!" He swung around to see her barely miss Gibbs's car before slewing around the corner out of sight. He grabbed Levesque's cell phone and pressed redial, grateful there was still a signal this far out. When her SQ cousin answered, he described the situation.

"She's heading south on 315, about 10 k north of Mayo. Send someone to intercept her, and call me the moment you have her!"

After he'd hung up, he sat in silence, wrestling his apprehension under control. What had freaked Norah out? Was she fleeing for her life? Going for help? Was it possible that Meredith—or Brandon—had turned on her parents?

"What next?" Levesque finally said.

"We continue. It's more important than ever that we find out what's going on. But we'll scout it out carefully before we make any move."

"Out there, there's going to be nothing but bush and silence. No way we'll come up on it unnoticed."

He mentally reviewed their equipment. Radios, Glocks and vests, but nothing but city boots and light winter jackets against the building storm. But how much danger could one frightened young woman present, even if she was the killer? A big if.

Levesque shook her head in disapproval as she pulled back onto the road. As they drew closer and turned down the final spur, Green had to admit she was right about being noticed. There was no sign of a cabin visible through the thick trees, but the lane was rutted with tire tracks and a hint of wood smoke drifted on the damp wind. They crept forward, peering through the blowing snow. Gradually contours took shape, filmy silhouettes that filled with detail as they came near. A silver car was parked in the lane up ahead, and further up was the angular roof line of a cabin. Green told Levesque to back up out of sight. Then all four detectives climbed out of their cars, left the car doors ajar, and stood in the falling snow, deciphering the silence. Green thought he heard a distant cry, but as he strained to listen, the snow swallowed it up. Maybe it was just an animal call or the wind in the trees.

"Someone is definitely here," Levesque murmured. "There's a fire."

Green sent Gibbs forward to check the vehicle. "A silver Prius, Ontario plate," he reported upon his return, and without being asked, he slipped into his car to run the plate. Meanwhile Green studied the ground for tracks. Snow blanketed the boughs of the trees and lay in a soft, pillowy quilt on the forest floor, crisscrossed with animal tracks. He could see no boot prints, but at least two distinct sets of tire tracks overlapped in the ruts.

Gibbs returned. "Brandon Longstreet, sir."

Green wasn't surprised. "There is only one road exit out of here, but we'll spread out through the woods and approach the cabin as quietly as we can. Bob, you go left side, Marie Claire right side. Zdanno, you stay with the vehicles in case he makes a run for it."

He looked down at their city rubbers. It couldn't be helped. They fanned out and moved forward, Green staying to the edge of the road and trying to keep the Prius between him and the cabin windows. The tire tracks leading up to the Prius were partially filled in with snow, but another fresher set overlapped for part of the way before coming to a halt behind the Prius. A faint drop of oil stained the snow. The Kennedys' aging pick-up truck?

They reached the clearing, which was heavily trampled with footprints. The cabin sat in the middle, a squat, rectangular bungalow made of wooden planks aged almost black. Its back door faced the lane and a boarded up screen porch stretched the length of the opposite side. Down the slope beyond, the flat expanse of a lake glistened in the muted light. A ramshackle shed and outhouse sat at the far edge of the clearing, and firewood was stacked high under a lean-to behind the house. An axe was propped against the lean-to, and splinters of wood littered the snow nearby. Levesque had taken cover behind the outhouse, Gibbs the woodpile. The cabin looked peaceful. No murmur of voices, no shuffling of movement. From their positions, the other two squinted through the snow at him questioningly. Green almost laughed. The three of them made a great take-down team.

He undid the holster of his Glock as he made a run for the back stoop. Nothing. He peered through the small window into the gloom of the cabin. There was a single light illuminating the kitchen, but the rest of the space was in shadow. The boarded up screens prevented all but a few shafts of pale daylight from penetrating the interior. However, it looked like one large room with a kitchen at one end and a chair and sofa in front of a woodstove at the other end.

The whole place looked deserted. Green tried the door, which creaked open easily beneath his touch. He signalled to the others and slipped inside. The smell of wood smoke and damp wool was strong, and his footsteps clomped on the plank floors as he checked out the rooms. In addition to the main room, there were two minuscule bedrooms along the back. One bedroom contained bunk beds that were stripped bare. He paused in the doorway to the second bedroom. The double bed was rumpled and unmade, the one pillow bunched in a ball and the heavy duvet tossed half on the floor. A heater glowed orange in the corner.

He heard footsteps and returned to find Gibbs and Levesque examining the kitchen. "No one here," he said.

"The fridge is stocked and one stove burner is still warm," Levesque replied. "Someone's been here recently."

Green took in the living room. There was an old Fifties-style sofa against one wall which had a pillow and blanket bunched up on it. Two logs were burning down in the wood stove, but the room was still toasty. On the pine table at the edge of the kitchen sat an open carton of milk, two empty coffee cups and two plates with traces of egg yolk. The sink was piled with more dirty dishes, including two dinner plates.

He inspected the contents of the fridge and cupboards before peering out the window to consider the tire tracks in the laneway. "Two people were here since last night. Norah Kennedy arrived this morning after breakfast was over. She doesn't appear to have even shared a cup of coffee, so we can assume she didn't stay long. She left in a hell of a hurry. But there's no sign of disturbance in this room. Nothing knocked over or broken." He paused to look out the side window down the slope to the lake. "Brandon appears to have come last night in time to have some dinner, and he slept on the sofa. Meredith, I would say, had a restless night on the double bed."

Levesque had been watching him and now she broke into a smile. Respect or disbelief, he wondered. He hoped she'd taken note.

"The question is," he continued, "how did Meredith get here? You can hardly grab a cab or a bus."

"Oh!" Gibbs flushed. "Th-there's an old car parked behind the woodshed. It looks abandoned."

Green looked out the side window again. From this angle he could just see the hood of a red car hidden behind the shed. The hood was clear of snow, not what one would expect from a car left there for the winter.

They went outside to check out the car and the surroundings. Snowshoe and cross-country ski tracks radiated out from the clearing in several directions. One trampled path led down to the lake, another into the pine woods. Several of the trails were partially filled by the falling snow but some, including a trail of boot prints, looked fresh.

He was about to radio SQ to request a full search and rescue team when a blur of movement in the woods caught his eye. Another. Someone wearing a brown jacket and snow shoes. The figure was approaching fast, thrashing and slipping as he tried to run. Ragged breathing filled the still air. A few minutes later the figure burst into the clearing and looked around, red-faced and gasping. It was Brandon..

"Oh, thank God!" he said, doubling over to catch his breath. "I thought I heard cars."

"What's going on?"

"Meredith's out there! She's run away, and she doesn't have a jacket or proper gear. Not even a map or compass. The lake isn't frozen yet, and I'm afraid she might fall through. She's not thinking straight."

"How long has she been out and what is she wearing?"

"She's been gone about two hours. She left when her parents arrived. But it's cold, and she's only got a sweater and woollen slippers."

"Hat and mitts?"

Brandon shook his head. "I know it's a short time, but in this weather, hypothermia—"

"She's not going to freeze in two hours," Green said. "Let's go inside and get a Sûreté du Québec search team out here. When we find her, we're going to need a good fire and hot water ready."

Inside, Green sent Gibbs to brew a fresh pot of coffee and Levesque to radio SQ to include cold water rescue equipment. Drawn by the excited voices, Zdanno radioed from his post by the cars. "Any sign of that SQ back-up?" Green asked him.

"No sign of anything but two deer, looking spooked," Zdanno replied.

Green had no time to dwell on where the back-up was. He turned to Brandon. "Tell me what happened this morning."

The young man was red and perspiring, but still shivering. "She was calm this morning. We talked half the night. She wasn't freaked out. She said she couldn't tell me why she left, could never tell me, but I just had to trust her. She had to think some things out, she said, and get some results back—"

"Results?"

"She sent some samples for DNA testing to this private lab in Winnipeg. Just double-checking. She seemed fine. Resigned, but fine."

"Happy to see you?"

"Not at first. She seemed shocked that I'd tracked her down, but when I told her I hadn't told anybody where she was and I knew all about the adoption, she seemed okay with it. Until her parents showed up this morning. That's when she took off."

"Wait a minute. Both parents?"

He nodded. "She didn't even want to talk to them. She saw them through the window and she said to me, 'Get rid of them. Don't even tell them I'm here', and she grabbed her sweater and went out the opposite door. She didn't even put snowshoes on."

Green's mind raced. "Then what?"

"They knew she was here. They saw the dishes and her jacket on the peg. I tried to say she'd gone to town, but they started to argue. They hadn't passed anyone on the road. Then they wanted to know what she'd told me and why would she be avoiding them. I said I didn't know, but I don't think they believed me. Especially Reg. By this time, quite a bit of time had passed and I kept thinking about her out there in the cold. Reg and I wanted to go after her, but Norah was trying to persuade him not to. With his weight and drinking, he's a heart attack waiting to happen. When I left, they were still arguing, but their truck's gone, so I guess they finally left."

Green felt himself grow cold. "We met the truck. Only Norah was in it."

Brandon frowned in surprise, but before he could voice the thought on all their minds, Levesque reappeared from the bedroom. "SQ was delayed because this crazy woman had crashed her truck into the ditch and she flagged them down in hysterics. Her husband had killed a woman, she said, and now he's so upset she doesn't know what he'll do."

*   *   *

Norah was able to tell Green very little over the radio about the risk Reg presented. She was barely coherent. "No, he doesn't have

327

a firearm," she said, "but then he didn't have one the night he went out after Lise Gravelle either, and that didn't stop him. He's a strong man when he's in a state. Reg loves Meredith with all his heart, but he's afraid she'll never forgive him for killing her real mother. I just…don't know."

"We can't wait for the SQ," Green said when he signed off. Out the window, the snow was falling more thickly now. He knew it would be obliterating the tracks and wiping out all chance of picking up Meredith's trail. Yet how far could they get in city boots that had neither the traction nor the protection for deep snow hiking?

"Brandon, how far did you track her trail?"

Joining him at the window, Brandon gestured to the right alongside the lake. "Maybe a kilometre along the edge of the lake. It's rough going through the bush and there's nothing else out there. I remember Tanya saying there were no cottages on the other side of the lake. It's part of the Papineau reserve over there. Acres and acres of bush. If she was trying to run away…"

"Are you sure you were on the right trail?"

"I'm not sure of anything. I was trying to follow the prints. It was hard to tell which were hers, but they seemed to go out on the lake."

Green had started to pull on his winter coat again. "How deep is the snow?"

He gestured to the city boots Green was wearing. "Too deep for those. But there are spare boots in the closet."

At that moment Levesque came back in juggling skis and poles. "These were in the shed."

Green eyed them dubiously. Being an inner-city working class boy, he had mastered skating, but Sharon had never managed to get him on skis.

"You can wear my snowshoes. I'll use the skis." Brandon said, already unlacing his boots. As if he sensed Green's hesitation, he gave him a sharp look. "I'm going with you. You may need a doctor out there."

Green weighed the alternatives unhappily. With a panicked, potentially dangerous man on the loose, the search party was no place for a civilian. Yet the man knew what trail he'd taken and his medical training could be an asset. In the end, Brandon made his mind up for him by hefting a knapsack onto his back.

"Emergency medical supplies, the best I could throw together. Hypothermia is the biggest danger, especially if she's fallen in the lake. I've got hot tea, a tuque, dry clothes and a waterproof jacket, plus packing and bandages if she's hurt."

Green nodded, grateful for the man's forethought but hoping medical intervention wouldn't be necessary. After much cursing and sweating, he managed to strap the snowshoes on and waddled out the front door, leaving Gibbs and Zdanno behind to guard the cabin.

Levesque and Brandon glided ahead, silent and effortless while he floundered about in the soft snow. They moved through the tall, swaying trees without talking, their ears attuned to every sound and their eyes straining to track the trail. The snow lashed through the branches in stinging pellets that swallowed up sound and reduced the footprints to vague outlines. All around, whiteness blurred the contours of space. Sky blended with snow and with the very air they breathed. Brandon and Levesque would ski ahead then stop to listen and scan the woods until Green caught up.

He was puffing and drenched with sweat by the time they reached a point of land that jutted out into the lake. The tracks ended here at the edge of the white expanse that marked the lake.

"This is as far as I'd got when I thought I heard your cars," Brandon said. "I wasn't sure if she'd gone out there..."

Green followed his gesture out onto the open expanse, where the wind swirled the snow into thick drifts. Further out from shore, patches of open water glistened black through gaping holes. Despite himself, Green shivered at the appalling thought. They squinted at the surface of the snow, looking for tracks leading out onto the lake. His mind played tricks as he studied the small hollows carved by the wind. It was Levesque who headed the other way, inland. A moment later, she called out. She'd found a faint trail heading up the slope toward a dense stand of spruce. Brandon dug in his poles and raced off to join her. Green was grateful to turn his back on the black open water for the protection of the trees. His eyes were attuned to the ground by now, and he could distinguish not just a vast blanket of white but the small tracks of squirrels and rabbits, the deep, delicate cloven hoofs of deer, and even the maze of bird tracks etched around the base of a tree covered with pine cones.

He pressed on doggedly, trusting the two younger people to track the trail while he concentrated on keeping up. One foot in front of the other, swinging his snowshoes in huge, awkward steps to avoid tripping on the tips. Damn, he was out of shape! After what seemed an eternity, he came upon Brandon and Levesque waiting for him again under cover of a huge, spreading pine. Levesque pointed to the bits of broken bark littering the snow below.

"Porcupine," she murmured, peering overhead. "He lives way up there somewhere, but he's hidden by the pine needles. Nature is perfect, isn't it?"

Green leaned against the tree trunk, trying not to appear too winded. Porcupines and perfection were the last thing on his mind. "Look, why don't you two go on ahead. You can get to her faster than me."

Brandon wasn't listening. He'd skied impatiently a short distance up the trail and was tilting his head intently. Then he raised his hand to silence them. As quietly as possible, they moved to join him.

"Hear anything?" he whispered.

Green stood stock still, holding his breath and straining to hear past the pounding of his heart. In the utter silence, even the falling snow seemed to whisper. Far off, some bird tapped a rhythm on a tree and a squirrel chattered a warning. Nothing else.

"There!" Brandon's whisper was hoarse with excitement. Green listened again, and faint snatches of sound drifted on the breeze. A sound that didn't belong in the forest. A human weeping.

"Oh my God!" Brandon plunged in his poles and struck out ahead. Forgetting his fatigue, Green struggled to catch him, swallowing up the distance with huge, clumsy steps. The sound softened, then stopped. Green forced himself forward, chasing only the memory now. With every step his fear grew.

A fresh wail broke the silence, much closer now. Green's scalp prickled. It was a deep, guttural sob torn from the throat of a man. Green was almost upon them before he saw Brandon bent over two figures huddled in the snow under the shelter of a pine. Reg was on his knees, rocking back and forth as he cradled his daughter in his arms.

"I'm sorry. I'm so sorry," he wept. Dread raced down Green's spine. Please God, don't let us be too late. But then he saw Meredith move and extend her own arms around her father's shaking form to hug him back.

TWENTY-NINE

A re you arresting me?" Reg asked as Green handed him a cup of coffee. Gibbs had brewed it, and it smelled as if it could strip paint. They were the first words Reg had uttered since Green and Levesque had pried him and Meredith apart. He'd hung his head in defeat and allowed himself to be guided back to the cabin without protest or explanation. From time to time during the long trek, Meredith had cast him a worried glance but like the others, she'd said little, as if preserving her strength.

Darkness had begun to shroud the forest by the time they reached the cabin. Green had dispatched Levesque to handle the SQ, who had arrived en masse for the search, and asked Gibbs to make coffee and food while he brought Devine and the deputy chief up to date. Brandon was tending to Reg, who had collapsed into an easy chair by the wood stove and sat staring through the glass at the glowing flame. His face was still alarmingly grey, but his breathing had slowed.

Green hesitated. Poulin had asked him the same question, and he gave the same answer. "I want both you and Meredith checked out at the hospital just as a precaution, and then I'll take both your statements. There's no rush."

"I killed her mother," Reg said. "There's no getting around that."

"Reg, don't talk now. Drink some coffee and get your strength back."

"I don't know what came over me. Yes, I do. Panic. I've lived in fear of this happening for years. Ever since all those organizations and websites started cropping up allowing parents and children to reunite. Meredith was so different from us, and I heard those horror stories of children who met their natural parents and felt this instant connection to them, like some kind of telepathy, and the parents who'd loved them since they were little are shoved aside to make room for some stranger who dumped them outside a church when they were babies."

"Reg, before you make any statement, I need to warn you—"

Reg waved him aside. "I don't give a fuck about Miranda or whatever you call it. I'm not going to fight this. I'm not going to put Meredith through any more. She's lost her mother, she's lost the man she was going to marry—"

"Meredith is fine." Green thought fast. Reg's statement should be done by the book, complete with the Charter warning, properly prepared questions and a video record. Green had been burned too many times by suspects eager to confess in the heat of the moment, only to recant when their lawyers got hold of them. He made a quick decision.

"For the record," he said, signalling Gibbs to take notes, "I'm going to give you the Charter warning and then we can talk. Detective Gibbs will document it."

Reg listened with disinterest while Green recited the warning. At the invitation to consult a lawyer, he scowled. "Bunch of bottom feeders. I always said crooks shouldn't be able to weasel around the law, and now it's my turn to stand up and take it like a man. I'm sorry for what I did to that woman. I haven't had a moment's peace since it happened. But she wouldn't listen to me. Wouldn't take no for an answer."

"You spoke to her?"

333

Reg shrugged. "Well, you know that, don't you? At least he does." He jerked his thumb at Gibbs. "I could tell him and his partner didn't believe that story about the phone call. Norah knew I'd answered a call that night too, but she had nothing to do with any of this. I told her it was my buddy's car stuck in the snow and I had to go out and help dig him out. I threw a bag of salt and a shovel in the back of the truck to prove the point, and that's all she figured it was."

Shovel. Green thought about the blunt force wound on Gravelle's head. A strong swing, the momentum of the blade through the air...

"It was your partner tipped her off." Reg thrust his chin at Gibbs. "When she asked us about those phone records. Lise had called before, about two weeks back, at my work. She wanted to know about the adoption, where we'd gotten Meredith from and all. I told her she was nuts, Meredith wasn't adopted, and if she called again, I'd call the cops. I thought that would scare her off. I didn't know..." He faltered and the coffee cup shook in his hand. Green rescued it. "I didn't know she'd go straight to Meredith."

He shook his head bitterly. "I was ripping mad when I found out she had. When she called that night, she said she was in town and she was going straight to the Longstreets to tell them the truth. The rich bitch owed her, she said. I don't know what I thought. That I could stop her, I guess, and make her see sense. I didn't believe that Brandon was Meredith's brother. I mean, what are the fucking chances! I figured she was lying just to tap into all that Longstreet money, but she was going to ruin my daughter's life and blow our whole family sky high, and for what? For what!" Reg had grown red and spittle had collected at the edges of his mouth. He swiped at it savagely.

"It was snowing a bitch and you couldn't hardly see a thing

334

in front of you, and I had a couple of beers inside me that didn't help. So I spot this woman walking down the middle of the road and I think how easy it would be to run her down, but I stop. Ask if she's Lise. She won't get in the truck, so I get out. She looked super pissed off at me, says she's got nothing to say to me, that this is between her and her daughter and the Longstreets now. And the next thing I know, I whack her."

He stopped. He shook, and tears seeped into his eyes. "I whacked her. Fuck. She went down and I thought... Well, it wasn't that hard a hit, eh? Maybe I knocked her out, but someone will come along and find her. So I grabbed her wallet and phone—I don't know, hoping maybe nobody would connect her to us. Then I got back in the truck and gunned it out of there. When no one was reported dead, I figured I was safe. That she'd recovered or someone must have found her on time."

"*I* found her."

They all turned to see Meredith standing in the doorway. Brandon stood behind her, his hand on her shoulder. "You don't have to do this, Mer," he said.

She shrugged him off and came into the room. "No more secrets. We are all responsible. I was walking up the street myself, hoping to get to Brandon before she did. It was so much to absorb. I needed to check out her story and if it was true, he needed to hear it from me, not from some stranger showing up on his doorstep."

Green found he was holding his breath, praying she wasn't about to confess to another crime herself. "Meredith, I think all this should wait till a doctor—"

"It's waited long enough. A woman is dead because of a dream she'd held on to for nearly thirty years. From up the street I saw Dad arguing with her, I saw her shove him away and him

335

grab the shovel from the back and hit her. He crouched at her side for a moment and then took off."

Reg grabbed her arm in panic. "No, Meredith! Don't! I would have seen you."

"I ducked out of sight when you drove past. You weren't seeing anything, Dad. You were staring straight ahead like a wild man. I ran up to her. She was lying face down in the snow, eyes open, blood all over the place, and I knew she was dead. I should have called 911, but all I could think of was how much trouble you were in, and how it was all my fault. I'd been so angry at her. I'd told her I didn't believe her, so she got in touch with you instead."

Reg had grown deathly pale. She reached out to take his hands in hers and fixed her eyes on his. "We're both to blame for what happened, Dad. We both ran, and we both left her alone in the street. I was completely freaked out. My life was shot. The man I was going to marry had turned out to be my half-brother, and the woman who claimed to be my mother was lying dead at my feet. Because of me, my father had panicked and killed her. If anyone found out who she was, the clues would point straight to him."

Reg clutched her hands as if they were a lifeline to hope. "I was so scared. I was so afraid you knew, because I didn't know where you'd gone!"

"I didn't know what to do. I couldn't go home and face you and pretend nothing had happened. I couldn't go to Brandon and snuggle up in his arms the way I wanted to. Even though he was my brother, I still wanted to. But I couldn't, maybe ever again. So I checked into a hotel, and all night I thought about what to do. At first, I thought of dropping out of sight altogether. I could just start a new life. But I knew the police would be checking my bank accounts and credit cards, even my passport if I left the country. So I holed up here, buying myself time to think of the best way out. It was only going to be for a couple of days, but as I thought about it, I realized I had to find out the truth above all else. Was I adopted, and was Brandon my brother? Once I had those answers, I might know what to do next."

She sat down on the sofa, her head bowed, and continued so quietly that Green had to strain to hear. Everyone sat transfixed. "There's no phone or internet access out here, so I didn't know exactly what was going on in Ottawa. I figured people would be worried, especially Brandon, but when I checked the *Ottawa Citizen* at the village store on Wednesday, I found no mention of either me or a dead woman. So I hoped you'd figured I just had cold feet about the wedding because we'd had that huge fight about it on Sunday night. After a few days I went back to the village. I had to know if they'd identified Lise and traced her to us. That's when I saw there was a massive search on and everyone was frantic. The village store had an internet connection, so I sent an email to Brandon hoping at least to reassure him while I waited for my DNA results." She raised her head finally and her gaze met Brandon's. She smiled at him sadly.

"But I think it's a formality. I look at you and I love you, but in my gut I know the truth. Holed up in this place, I had a chance to look over the proof she gave me—the newspapers that had no announcement of my birth, the birth registrations for November 1978 that had no record of me. And I've been doing some research on the web about family members raised apart. There is a powerful attraction based on similarities in temperament, values, interests, even habits and tastes. It's as if our DNA bonds us even if we're unaware. I thought about how we laugh at the same jokes, share the same dreams and even finish each others' sentences."

Brandon was watching her, anguish and resignation reflected in his eyes. Yet he didn't argue with her.

"If you aren't raised together, a powerful, physical attraction is normal. Oedipus and Electra weren't far off the mark. We can't be together, but I don't feel guilty that I love you. I wish..." Her eyes brimmed with sudden tears. "I wish things were different, but at least in all this, I haven't lost everything. I have a very cool, very kindred brother."

*   *   *

"Talk about bizarre," Sharon exclaimed. "To discover that the man of your dreams is your brother. To think you slept with him and planned a life with him. I can't imagine feeling that way about Jake! I don't think we're the least bit alike."

She and Green were sprawled out side by side on the sofa, sharing a late night bottle of wine. For the first time in days, Green felt peaceful. Every muscle in his body ached and he knew he would pay for his snowshoeing expedition the next day, but for now the universe was the best it could be, considering a woman had died and Jules was still missing.

Reg was in custody but his confession, and the end to all the secrets, seemed to have buoyed his spirits. He knew he'd have to do time but some of his more dubious bar patrons had already slipped him the name of a good defence lawyer who could wring a tear from the most jaded judge.

After consultation with the Crown, Green had elected not to charge Meredith in connection with Lise's death. She and Brandon were last seen heading out for a showdown in Rockcliffe, no longer hand in hand but united in purpose. Elena Longstreet had a lot to answer for.

It was six o'clock by the time Green escaped the station. He had just put the finishing touches on his report to Barbara

Devine when he heard a great cheer outside his door. He peered out in time to see Brian Sullivan walk into the squad room with a silly red Santa tuque on his head, a sack of gifts in his hand, and a broad grin on his freckled face. He strode from desk to desk as if he owned the place, handing out gifts and accepting bear hugs. When he reached Bob Gibbs's desk, he pulled out a box wrapped with silver bells.

"I heard some fool is brave enough to take on our Sue."

Gibbs flushed purple. "H-how..? Who...?"

"I know everything that's going on around here, and don't any of you young lads forget it."

Green had brought his own blue-wrapped Hanukkah gift home. A bottle of vintage Merlot. Does he think I earned it, or need it, he wondered as he closed his eyes and took another sip. He thought about Sharon's last words, about blood ties and love and that sense of connection that defied all geography.

"You and Jake were raised together," he said. "Your relationship was molded by the rough and tumble of childhood, the sibling jealousies and competition, and the intimacy of shared experience. There's no magic of discovery, no sense of a mysterious destiny at work. But I feel it with Hannah all the time."

"But at least you knew what your relationship was. Brandon and Meredith were lovers. How are they going to get past that?"

"Time and distance for starters," he said. "He's going on to Ethiopia as planned, she's going back to Haiti. And she's taken on the name Amélie. Part of redefining herself, distancing herself from the Meredith who'd planned a life with him."

"It's not going to be as easy as that," Sharon said. "She can't erase who she's been for thirty years. She can't erase the Kennedys."

"I don't think she wants to. She says the name change is unofficial, at least for now, while she gets her head around this new identity. After reading the letter that her mother wrote to her, it just felt right. The little girl who was Amélie should never have been lost."

"Uncanny, the power of that mother-child bond." She snuggled up beside him. "Makes me wish..."

He looked into her eyes. Deep, luminous, and full of hope. He looked at the fire she had lit, and the dog asleep at her feet. It was on the tip of his tongue to answer her when the doorbell rang.

Sharon held his arm. "Don't answer that. It's ten o'clock!"

No sooner had he settled back down when it rang again. Two soft, short rings. He hauled himself to his feet.

Standing on the doorstep, his tall, stooped frame bathed in yellow porch light, was Adam Jules. With a rush of joy, Green yanked the door wide.

"Michael, sorry to disturb you at this hour, but a phone call would be insufficient. I wanted to explain, before tomorrow's news came out."

Green invited him in and offered him a glass of wine, which he politely declined. He perched on the edge of Green's old lazyboy and crossed his hands in his lap. He was controlled and still, but Green could see the haggard circles beneath his eyes. The week had aged him.

Sensing the pain in Jules's stillness, Sharon excused herself and withdrew. Jules pursed his lips. "I have just been to see the deputy chief. I handed in my resignation."

Green stifled his dismay.

"It seemed the wisest choice, given the circumstances, which you know."

"I know some, Adam. Not all."

"There's no need to know more. You have the facts you need. Lise Gravelle is dead, Meredith Kennedy knows the truth, Reg

Kennedy is in custody. A tragic, tragic story, Michael. No need to compound the tragedy."

Green exploded. "I spent a week searching for you, worrying about you, wondering if you were impeding my investigation. Wondering if the man who taught me ethics had himself been as dirty as they come. Afraid in the end that you might have taken your own life! I think I deserve more than a fucking 'no need to know more'!" He broke off, shocked. In all the years he'd lost his temper with Jules over the frustrations and restrictions of the job, he had never sworn at him. Never made it personal. Jules didn't flinch, but a tightness around his eyes betrayed him.

"I'm sorry I caused you distress, Michael."

"Did you accept a payoff from Cyril Longstreet?"

Jules didn't answer right away. He steepled his fingers and pressed the tips to his lips while he considered. "Perhaps I'll have some wine after all."

Green remembered the array of fine brandies and whiskies in Jules's apartment. "How about a Scotch instead. It's Glenlivet."

Jules arched an eyebrow. "Neat, please." He swirled the amber liquid around and took an appreciative sip before resuming as if there had been no interruption. "Not a payoff, no. But I made a deal. Not one I regret. One that spared several innocent lives, including two babies, from humiliation and possible destitution." A faint smile played across his weary face. "That much you will learn when tomorrow's edition of the *Montreal Gazette* hits the stands. That clever reporter tracked me down in St. Hyacinth, where I admit I thought I had reached the end of the road. He said he had a deal with you to expose the old cover-up."

"He was stretching the truth a bit."

Jules savoured another sip. "I had no doubt. I remember him well. But secrecy had gotten us all to this appalling juncture—

Lise dead, Meredith missing, Brandon betrayed, Reg and Norah Kennedy sucked into the maelstrom. While the two people who'd orchestrated the cover-up and profited the most from it—Elena and Cyril Longstreet, who got to keep their dignity and family honour—were still unscathed by it all."

"So you told Cam Hatfield what? That Lise had been at Harvey Longstreet's apartment when he died, and that you'd helped cover it up?"

"Not directly. Lise was at the apartment. They were in bed when they...miscalculated. She called Elena in a panic to ask what to do. Rather than telling her to phone the police, Elena told her to get out of the apartment and never say a word. Then she phoned Cyril and together they unhooked Harvey from the bedpost, hung him in the closet, cleaned the whole place up, and locked the door on their way out. Then they left him for two days before Elena phoned in a missing persons report."

Green shuddered. What ice ran in the woman's veins?

Jules's mouth twitched in disgust. "I knew someone had tampered with the apartment, but I hadn't proceeded very far in my investigation before Lise contacted me with the truth. She recognized my name from home, St. Hyacinth, and she hoped I would tell her what to do. She was pregnant but when she'd phoned Elena to ask for her help, Elena denied all knowledge of her and insisted it was all a lie to extort money. Lise was a babe among wolves. She was convinced Harvey Longstreet loved her, but Elena laughed in her face. I could have pursued the case and charged Elena and Cyril with some offence, but that wouldn't have benefited Lise."

It was the longest speech Green had ever heard Jules make. The most passion he had ever displayed. In the silence, he looked spent.

"So you made a deal with the devil."

He nodded. "To get her some child support. But in the end, it wasn't enough. Lise never recovered from the trauma of Harvey dying in her arms. And poor little Amélie..."

"Did you keep in touch with either of them after the adoption?"

"No. In Amélie's case, it was not allowed, of course, and Lise blamed me for pressuring her into giving Amélie up. I'd thought it was best for all, but... We don't cut those ties so easily, do we. So I left Montreal and joined up here. I thought about her often, but I knew her recovery was too fragile." He took a deep breath as if to say more but stopped himself, tightened his lips and sipped his Scotch.

"So what happened? How did you get involved in this present case? You said it was your fault."

"I got a call. Voice message, at the station. From Lise."

"When?"

Jules squinted. "About three weeks ago. In her message, she asked two things. Was I the Adam Jules from the Montreal Police, and was Meredith Kennedy her daughter?"

"What did you tell her?"

"I didn't call her back right away, because I wasn't sure. I'd helped the Kennedys connect with Father Fréchette, but the actual adoption details were kept secret. There were many babies. So I started checking. Father Fréchette was dead, as was the lawyer, and the old mission was torn down. The church records had been travelling around in church vaults for years. I was able to confirm that Reginald and Norah Kennedy had indeed adopted a girl in the right time frame. I called Lise back a week later. I told her the adoption records were lost, but it was possible. My worst mistake. My absolute worst mistake." He sipped on his Scotch with a trembling hand. "Before I knew it, Elena Longstreet phoned me."

Green leaned in, holding his breath. "This was...?"

"Last Tuesday morning. The day after Lise's death. Elena was upset with me. She said some woman claiming to be Lise Gravelle had phoned her the night before to tell her she was on her way to the house with important information about Harvey's daughter. Elena thought there was a threat in her words. A hint of blackmail."

"Was that likely?"

Jules shrugged. "Not the Lise I knew. Stopping the marriage and getting Amélie back, that's all Lise would want. But in her line of work, Elena has been a fighter for so long that she sees adversaries and dishonourable motives where there are none. She even thought I'd put Lise up to it and told her where Elena lived."

"Had you stayed in touch with Elena?"

Jules grimaced. "As little as possible. Our paths crossed from time to time at charitable or legal functions. I admire her skill, and she claims to feel bad about her treatment of Lise. That's possible. She was young, and the shock must have been considerable. But she was suspicious when Lise renewed contact out of the blue, and when Lise failed to show up, she wondered whether I knew anything."

Which is when you asked me about missing persons and accidents, Green thought. So Elena had been lying. What a surprise. She had known Lise Gravelle was coming to her home that night, and possibly had some idea why. He felt a hard knot of anger for the woman.

Jules had drained his glass and gave no hint of protest when Green topped it up. He heaved a deep sigh. "Once I learned Lise was dead, I did wonder whether Elena might have had a hand in it. But she is a woman of some stature and integrity in her own right, and to risk it over old news seemed unlike her."

"Not if that news might cost her the love of her only son," Green said.

Jules didn't seem to hear. His own thoughts swept him on. "My worst mistake… When she disappeared, I thought Meredith herself had done it. Cyril Longstreet told me she was beside herself with shock and anger when she visited him in Montreal." He cast Green a silent glance, as if acknowledging it was indeed his car that Green had encountered up on Summit Circle that day. "Poor, innocent Amélie. What we put that young woman through—the shock, the loss of her dreams—it was my fault. I had set it in motion, thirty years ago and once again three weeks ago. How could I betray her now? How could I turn her in?"

Jules's eyelids were drooping now, betraying the exhaustion the week had wrought. "Instead," he said, draining his second glass, "it was that poor bugger Reg Kennedy who got caught in the trap." He set his glass down abruptly and hauled himself to his feet, swaying slightly.

"How did you get here, Adam?"

"Cab."

"Let me drive you."

Jules shook his head. "I'll walk a bit. Hail a cab on Carling. I've imposed enough." He made his way to the hall, where he pulled on his coat and wrapped a brand new cashmere scarf around his neck. "The silver lining in this? I found Amélie again. In looks, she's like her mother, but her brains and her willpower, that's all her father. Ironically, both of them are like their father. On balance, that's a good thing."

Green stood at the open door watching him walk down the driveway into the night. He seemed to be enjoying the soft magic of the Christmas lights on the fresh snow.

Green heard Sharon come up behind him, felt her arms slide around his waist. "Such a lonely man. Do you think he's loved her all these years?"

Green thought of the photos of the children in Jules's apartment. Of the tender fingertip touch between him and Amélie. Of the resolutely solitary life he'd led.

"Possibly," he said slowly. "I think he loved Amélie, would have loved to be a father to her, but I don't think loving a woman came easily to him. He put the welfare of her child before his love of Lise. He's been paying ever since."

"Such a waste, for all of them."

He smiled faintly. He felt equal parts of sorrow and hope. "But at least he has reconnected with Amélie."

"A daughter of sorts." She paused and tipped her head to look up into his eyes.

"Yes," he said in answer to the question he saw in them. God help me.

Acknowledgements

Behind every good writer there is a critiquing group, and in my case, I am indebted to the continued patience and perceptive advice of fellow writers Joan Boswell, Mary Jane Maffini, Sue Pike and Linda Wiken. Another friend and fellow writer, Robin Harlick, provided advice and information about setting, and my nephew Paul Cullum helped decipher the mysteries of ISPs. I'm grateful to Emma Dolan for her wonderful cover design and to my editor Allister Thompson and my publisher Sylvia McConnell for their ongoing support and belief in me.

For his humour and insight, which persists even after eight novels, I'd like to thank Mark Cartwright of the Ottawa Police for his technical information and advice. Since part of the action in *Beautiful Lie the Dead* takes place in Montreal, I'd also like to thank the Service de Police de la Ville de Montréal for their assistance with Montreal police procedure, in particular Detective-Lieutenant Denis Bonneau of the Major Crimes Section, and Agent Jean Pierre Leblanc of PDQ26. Any errors in police procedure, whether accidental or intentional, are mine alone.

Most importantly, I'd like to thank Napoleon & Company for continuing to champion the cause of excellence in Canadian crime writing despite all the challenges posed by the modern book industry.

Barbara Fradkin was born in Montreal and obtained her PhD in psychology at the University of Ottawa. Her work as a child psychologist provides ample inspiration and insight for plotting murders.

The novels in the Inspector Green series are *Do or Die, Once Upon a Time, Mist Walker, Fifth Son, Honour among Men, Dream Chasers, This Thing of Darkness* and *Beautiful Lie the Dead*, the fourth and fifth having won the Arthur Ellis Award for Best Novel in 2005 and 2007.

An active member of Canada's crime writing community, Barbara resides in Ottawa with assorted pets and children.

More info can be found at www.barbarafradkin.com